THE *Malibu* ARRANGEMENT

BELLA CHRISTINA

VINCI
BOOKS

Vinci Books

vinci-books.com

Published by Vinci Books Ltd in 2026

1

The publisher and the author have made every effort to obtain permissions for any third party material used in this book and to comply with copyright law. Any queries in this respect should be brought to the attention of the publisher and any omissions will be corrected in future editions.
A CIP catalogue record for this book is available from the British Library.
Paperback ISBN: 9781036703455
The EU GPSR authorised representative is Logos Europe, 9 rue Nicolas Poussion, 17000 La Rochelle, France contact@logoseurope.eu

Printed and bound in Great Britain by Clays Ltd, Elcograf S.p.A.

Dark Temptations

Wicked Temptations

Bella Christina as Rachel Sinclair

Kansas City Legal Thrillers

Bad Faith

Justice Denied

Hidden Defendant

Injustice For All

L.A. Defense

The Associate

The Alibi

REASONABLE DOUBT

The Accused

The Hate Crime

Secrets and Lies

Until Proven Guilty

Southern California Legal Thrillers

Presumed Guilty

Justice Delayed

Insanity Defense

Wrongful Conviction

The Trial

Chapter One

CELESTE

I'm running late for my meeting with Max Kensington, and he can just deal with it. He gave me exactly zero notice about this meeting, and with every minute I spend thinking about this meeting, my blood pressure climbs another notch. Who does he think I am—some medieval peasant who drops everything when the lord of the manor summons her? Not happening. I have self-respect, and the moment I start jumping when he says jump, he'll be impossible to work with after his mega movie studio, Kensington Pictures, devours our little boutique studio, Dreamscape Pictures.

So Kensington Pictures is about to gobble up my studio like we're nothing but a light snack. Fine. Corporate mergers happen. But that's not why His Royal Highness (Max is the CEO of Kensington Pictures, natch) demanded my presence today. No, I'm being hauled in because I screwed up on something, and now he wants to flex his authority.

As a Development Executive at Dreamscape, I hunt for diamonds in the rough—manuscripts and screenplays with that special something. Our studio sits in Claremont, this postcard-perfect town that feels worlds away from LA despite being just twenty minutes down the freeway. I'm the one who polishes scripts until they shine, matches directors with perfect-fit actors, and—this is the part that's currently biting me in the ass—convinces the studio execs to open their wallets.

That's exactly where everything went sideways. I championed Nora Davis's memoir about living with Dissociative Identity Disorder (used to be called Multiple Personalities). The book was flying off shelves, and I pitched it to the Dreamscape Execs as "*Girl, Interrupted* for the TikTok generation." Then the bombshell dropped: every tear-jerking moment was fabricated. Complete fiction. By then, we'd already sunk two million into directors, talent, and distribution rights. The whole house of cards collapsed, and now Max Kensington wants my head on a platter. He could've excoriated me via email or torn me apart over the phone, but no—he's summoned me to some overpriced Beverly Hills restaurant to publicly execute my dignity.

Fine. Let him sit there with his sparkling water getting warm. I'm taking the scenic route from Claremont today. Petty? Absolutely. But it's the only power move I've got left.

I mentally tally what this little cross-town errand for Max is costing me. I had to late-cancel my Pilates class - $30 fee. More importantly, I'm missing my check-in with Mom. The chemo's been rough this week. My sister Lexi's technically there, but between her film classes at UCLA, her hosting gig at Mastro's in Malibu, and whatever project or friend has captured her attention this week, she's basically a ghost in her own home. Mom tries not to let on, but I can hear it in her voice when too many days pass between visits.

So tonight, I'll be crawling through traffic toward Beverly Hills instead of being where I should be.

I leave the office at 4:30 and saunter over to my Pilates studio to make sure Gretchen, my evening instructor, is okay with a last-minute cancellation. If she isn't, I'll blow off Max and go to class—I refuse to pay a late fee just because Mr. Thing decides he needs me on a whim. I explain everything to Gretchen; she says it's fine—there's a wait list and someone's dying for my spot—but warns me not to do it again. I promise I won't.

Then I crawl through rush-hour traffic to Beverly Hills, cursing Max's name with every breath—inhale "fuck," exhale "you"; inhale "fuck," exhale "you."

I finally arrive at the fancy country club, The Patrician - my meeting with Max will take place in the club's Michelin-starred restaurant, The Centurion- in my ten-year-old Prius, sticking out like a sore thumb among the Bentleys, Rolls-Royces, Bugattis, Lamborghinis, Aston Martins, and Paganis. Every car here is worth at least a half-million, some much more, and honestly—could there be a more useless vehicle than a Lamborghini? Eight miles per gallon, and you can't actually floor it to 200 MPH in L.A. Oh, but the owner is rich, so rules don't apply. He (and it's always a he) probably floors it anyway, endangering everyone, then sweet-talks the cop who pulls him over.

The valet tells me it's fifty bucks to park. Nope—not paying that. Even if I were a zillionaire like the Patrician Club members, I wouldn't shell out that much on principle. I smile, turn around, and plan to find street parking. Good luck with that—the club sits on a cliff overlooking the Pacific, and the winding access road has zero parking.

Obviously that plan fails. I drive back to Los Angeles proper, pay twenty dollars to park in a public lot, and call an

Uber. I'm spending more than fifty dollars between parking and ride fare, but I'd rather burn money than hand anything to that valet.

I'm thirty minutes late when I finally push through the heavy doors of the club, and the concierge's gaze slides over me like I'm something the cat dragged in. Fair enough—my secondhand sweater has a coffee stain I tried to hide with a brooch, my rainbow Doc Martens squeak against the marble floor, and the ocean wind has turned my hair into something birds could nest in. Work was chaos, no chance to change, and Fridays are my "whatever's clean" fashion day anyway - it's "Casual Fridays" at the office, as long as there are no meetings scheduled, which there weren't.

But in this temple of designer labels, I might as well be wearing a neon sign that says "Doesn't Belong," but Max can just deal with it.

I tell the concierge I'm seeing Max Kensington. She checks the list, gives me the Little Orphan Annie look, then directs me to the restaurant.

Everyone here drips wealth like it's their sweat. A woman in a cream Dior suit casually adjusts her diamond-encrusted watch while chatting on her phone, not even glancing at the waiter refilling her champagne. Three men in Brioni and Tom Ford suits with fabric so fine it catches the light like water laugh too loudly near the bar, their custom Italian loafers probably worth more than my monthly rent. Even the tennis players walking through the lobby flaunt money—a blonde in a pristine white Lacoste dress that's never seen actual sweat, her tennis bracelet flashing with actual diamonds as she tosses her hair.

The club dazzles with old-money opulence: thirty-foot ceilings adorned with Venetian crystal chandeliers that catch the sunset through floor-to-ceiling windows, marble floors so polished they mirror the designer heels clicking across them, and dominating the grand foyer, a colossal M-shaped light fixture made of what must be thousands of hand-cut crystals, each refracting golden light that makes even my shabby outfit momentarily shimmer with borrowed wealth.

The maître d' seats me at a table draped in crisp white linen, and there he is—Max Kensington, exactly how I imagined yet somehow worse. He can't be more than thirty, with that trust-fund glow that screams nepo-baby. How else is he CEO of a major studio while I'm still eating ramen three nights a week? But damn, he's unfairly good-looking —the kind of man whose face makes your train of thought derail and crash into a ravine. His hair is obsidian dark, swept back just enough to look careless while clearly taking an hour to style. Green eyes like expensive jade, framed by lashes so long they cast shadows on his cheekbones when he blinks. His jawline could cut glass. The charcoal Tom Ford suit hugs his broad shoulders like it was tailored by angels, and that Patek Philippe gleaming on his wrist? I could sell it and pay off my student loans, and probably have enough left for a down payment on a studio apartment in the Palisades.

His glare alone raises my heart rate, sending a flush up my neck that I'm praying doesn't reach my cheeks. Those green eyes narrow beneath thick brows, his jaw clenching so tight I can see the muscle twitch beneath his five o'clock shadow. The temperature between us heats up ten degrees, and my palms are suddenly damp. Is it because he's magnetic—this ridiculous Adonis in his custom suit with shoulders that fill the frame of his chair—or because I'm pissed he's giving me these imperious death glares when he should be on his knees grateful I showed up at all?

Then I notice the woman at the table and my inner fangirl squees. Elody Martin is right there—my favorite actress. Her Oscar-winning turn in that Joan Baez biopic was astounding, and the box-office numbers prove it. She's equally brilliant in rom-coms, action flicks, sci-fi, and period dramas. Now she's also a top model, being chosen to be the new face of Chanel N° 5, so her flawless face is seen everywhere around the city. I dig in my purse for something to sign and find only a tattered, ketchup-stained Bubba Gump napkin. Why do I keep this thing? It's from the night I dined with my mother when she told me her diagnosis—a good-luck charm, a promise of more dinners to come at her favorite seafood joint.

Now the napkin will be even more special. Elody smiles and signs it, then departs, leaving me disappointed. I'd rather she stay and chat than sit across from this striking man shooting daggers with his eyes.

I sink into the plush velvet chair, smoothing Elody's autographed napkin across my lap like it's priceless silk. Max's eyes narrow to emerald slits beneath those perfect brows, his full lips pressed into a bloodless line. The air between us crackles with tension as thick as the fog rolling in off the Pacific outside. I extend my hand across the pristine white tablecloth, my chipped nail polish suddenly glaring under the warm glow of the crystal sconces. His gaze drops to my fingers, then back to my face, leaving my hand suspended in humiliating limbo while he continues to glare with such intensity that the fine hairs on my arms stand at attention. The heat crawling up my neck threatens to consume me whole, and I wonder if spontaneous combustion from a man's stare is scientifically possible.

I clear my throat. "Hello," I say, my voice shaky. Why is my voice shaking like this? I was so angry coming here that

I planned on giving him what-for once I arrived. I practically had my Norma Rae speech rehearsed in my head, complete with indignant finger-pointing and a righteous quiver in my voice that comes from standing up to power. I was going to tell him that he can't treat his underlings like this, that we're human beings with rent payments and sick mothers and dreams beyond the glass-walled offices. I was going to dramatically give him a piece of my mind and then storm out of the restaurant, just like in the movies. Yet, here I am, timid as a damn mouse and feeling like maybe I've done something wrong. There's something about this man's aura that's really throwing me.

The script has veered off-course without my consent, and I can't seem to find my rhythm again. I press my lips together, then release a breath. *Speak up, Celeste. The words are in there somewhere.*

He doesn't say hello back, just coolly raises an eyebrow and then puts his glass of wine up to his beautiful and full lips. "Ms. Jenkins," he says and, just like that, I remember my earlier anger coming over here. Ms. Jenkins? Who addresses people like that? "Let's dispense of pleasantries, shall we? You know why I'm meeting with you and I'd like to get your side of the story."

He hasn't yet offered me a glass of wine even though there's another Baccarat crystal wine glass on the table, just beckoning me. And I really need a drink of that wine. I'm about to melt down like the candle on our table.

"Yes," I say, eyeing the empty glass meaningfully. He still doesn't offer me a glass of wine. "You wanted to talk to me about the the Nora Davis...incident."

"Right," he says, and I look around the dining room. So many luminaries have dined here and a very talented artist, I'm not sure who, immortalized just a few of them in charcoal and watercolor portraits. Cary Grant, Marilyn Monroe, Charlie Chaplin, James Dean and Humphrey Bogart represent Old Hollywood on the walls. Julia Roberts, Emma Stone, Daniel Day Lewis, Jack Nicholson and Meryl Streep represent New Hollywood. Directors are immortalized too - Martin Scorsese and Steven Spielberg have their portraits proudly displayed. There are also portraits of people who aren't in the movie business. Every American president of the past century, prominent CEOs such as Jeff Bezos and Elon Musk and....there's also a portrait of Max.

Max is apparently important enough to be immortalized alongside the household names that everybody knows, which is hella intimidating. My heart hammers against my ribs, but I force my expression to remain neutral. One trembling hand or wavering glance, and Max will pounce on my vulnerability like it's wounded gazelle day at the corporate watering hole.

He's obviously trying to psyche me out because he's not saying a word. He's just studying me. Taking in my windswept hair, my chipped nails, my Plato's closet get-up and now he's staring at my boots.

I'm tempted to give him a word-vomit excuse for the Nora Davis debacle, but keep my mouth shut. That's probably the wisest thing to do right now because I'm trying to figure him out and talking right now would be counterproductive.

"Ms. Jenkins," he finally says after what seems an interminable amount of time. His voice is clipped, measured, yet still drips out like warm honey. He has the voice of a billionaire CEO, despite his obviously tender age - baritone, smooth, magnetic. I could just imagine him leading board meetings, spell-binding everyone around the conference table. If his intimidating looks don't enthrall them, his commanding voice certainly would. "You did know what kind of club this is? And that this restaurant has three Michelin stars?"

Three Michelin stars? I wasn't even aware that three Michelin stars was possible. I know that one Michelin star means excellent, but I thought the Michelin designations stopped with that.

And anyhow, I should be indignant that he's clearly judging me for my clothes. If he wanted me to roll up head-to-toe in Chanel or Prada like the rest of these ladies, then he needs to personally buy me a new wardrobe.

"What do you mean, three Michelin stars?" I ask.

"There are millions of restaurants in the world," he says. "Approximately 20 million or more. And there are just over 150 restaurants with three Michelin stars. In the world. You are about to dine at one of them." Then he looks down at my boots again. "So it's inappropriate and disrespectful to show up in Rainbow Doc Martens."

I take a deep breath and feel my defensive hackles rise. Finally, my inner Norma Rae is about to make an appearance. Like the iconic union organizer who used her voice to lift up other downtrodden workers who were being steamrolled by corrupt and wealthy bosses, I'll use my voice to tell Max that he can't treat girls like me disrespectfully without being called out on it.

"Max," I say.

"Mr. Kensington," he says. "Address me formally."

Address me formally? Oh, no he didn't. Now he really is acting like a king about to throw a lowly peasant into a dark dungeon for no good reason at all.

"Max," I say again, narrowing my eyes. He narrows his eyes right back, takes another sip of his wine and I feel like I'm about to burst into flames right in front of him. "You gave me zero notice about this meeting." He still hasn't offered me a glass of wine, so I take the bottle of wine and pour it into the empty glass and take a sip. "I didn't exactly have time to shop on Rodeo Drive, and even if I did, I couldn't afford anything in any of those stores. This one Baccarat crystal wine glass probably costs more than what I take home in a month. I can't help but wonder if you chose this place knowing I wouldn't fit in." I smooth my napkin across my lap, meeting his eyes directly. "If the goal was to make me feel like shit, I should tell you—it didn't work. I couldn't care less about what these people think about me, and as for your opinion of me..." I pause, a small smile playing on my lips. "My ability to care is subterranean."

I close my eyes, expecting him to whip out his phone right at that moment and call Iris and demand my firing. Instead, when I open my eyes, he has a casual smile on his beautiful face. I'm not at all sure what that smile means - it could be that he's trying hard to tamp down rage and doesn't like to lose control, so he smiles to cover up. That happens a lot. Or it could mean he's amused by me. Which means he's not taking me seriously. Which option is worse? Hard to tell.

"Well," he finally says. "At least you used the phrase 'couldn't care less' properly. Most people say 'could care less,' which means the opposite of what they're trying to say."

"Well done me," I say, forcing my lips into a tight smile while my fingers curl into my palm, nails digging half-moons into my skin. The urge to call out his patronizing tone burns in my throat like acid reflux.

"So, the topic at hand," he says. "Nora Davis." Then the waiter comes around to take our order and I realize I haven't even looked at a menu. Saved by the bell, though. I'm putting off my execution for a few more minutes.

"I'm sorry," I say to the waiter. "I haven't had a chance to look at the menu."

The waiter glides away and returns with a prix fixe menu bound in soft leather. I scan the offerings: butter-poached lobster with black truffle emulsion, A5 Wagyu beef carpaccio with shaved white alba truffles, caviar service with mother-of-pearl spoons, and a champagne-infused risotto with gold leaf. Nothing appeals. The foie gras torchon with Sauternes gelée? Absolutely not. I've seen the videos of force-fed geese and can't stomach the cruelty. The seafood tower looks good with its promise of Alaskan king crab and oysters, but there, nestled between them: abalone, the endangered shellfish, harvested to near extinction, their numbers dwindling in the Pacific. I consider the lobster, but those poor creatures are boiled alive, so I can't possibly order that, either.

Max is waiting for me to decide what to order, his mani-cured fingers drumming against the white tablecloth, each tap sending tiny ripples through my water glass. His sharp green eyes keep darting between me and his Patek Philippe, and I'm quite sure he wants me to hurry the hell up so he can commence yelling at me about the Nora Davis thing. So I'm somewhat deliberately taking my time with the menu, pretending to be fascinated by the difference between the pan-seared and herb-crusted salmon, because I really don't want to get to the main course just yet - the main course being his dressing me down.

I flip the page hopefully and spot a few vegetarian options tucked at the bottom: a roasted heirloom carrot tartare with black truffle and smoked almond cream, followed by wild mushroom risotto with aged balsamic and microgreens. Even the dessert—a coconut panna cotta with passion fruit coulis—seems crafted for someone like me.

"I'm ready," I say, handing Max back the menu. Max signals the waiter again, who appears and takes our orders. Max orders the seafood tower and chocolate soufflé with Grand Marnier and hand-churned vanilla bean ice cream for dessert and I order my carrot tartare and risotto with the coconut panna cotta coulis for dessert.

"And the abalone medallions for our first course," Max says and I cringe. I'd rather have the garden heirloom tomato salad, and, anyhow, he'll be eating abalone with his main course. Why would he want that for our first course too?

"Very good, Mr. Kensington," the waiter says with a bow.

"Uh, wait," I say to the waiter and then I glance at Max. ""I'd like the heirloom tomatoes as my first course," I say to the waiter, pointing to the vibrant display of misshapen fruits—some striped purple and green, others sunset orange—arranged artfully on crisp white plates at a nearby table. "Thank you."

The waiter takes my order and then disappears. Max is now looking at me with an indiscernible expression."You're making a mistake in not ordering the abalone," he says, leaning forward slightly, his platinum cufflinks catching the amber light from the restaurant's crystal chandeliers. "It's delicious—tender as butter. Very prized and rare. The chef simmers it in a reduction of Sauternes and black truffle. You won't find abalone on most menus, especially not prepared like this."

"Exactly," I say. "Abalone's rare on menus these days, and for good reason. They've been fished almost to extinction. Conservation efforts have only just started to make a dent after decades of damage. Putting them on a menu now? It's like advertising you don't give a damn about the ocean's future. I can't support that—not with my name, not with my business, not with my conscience."

His mouth quirks up at one corner—a movement so slight I almost miss it—and the skin beside his eye creases just enough to notice. When he tilts his head, light catches those green eyes, turning them amber-gold like whiskey in crystal. Is that amusement? I can't be sure.

"Have you ever used the phrase 'a woman needs a man like a fish needs a bicycle' by any chance?" he asks.

"No, but that Gloria Steinem quote is a good one. Why do you ask?"

"I'm trying to figure you out," Max says, his green eyes narrowing as they studied my face. His voice dropped to a quieter register, almost contemplative. "You're not afraid of me. Everyone else is."

"Should I be?"

Max's shoulders snap back, the movement rippling through his tailored jacket like a predator flexing before the kill. "When I walk into conference rooms, executives who make ten times your salary practically piss themselves trying to escape." His mouth curls into something too sharp to be a smile. "Yet here you are, staring me down like you've got nothing to lose. Most people in your position wouldn't be."

I take another sip of my wine, letting the liquid linger on my tongue while I process his words - *people in your position*. The phrase hangs between us. Is he actually impressed by my resilience, or is this just another way to remind me I'm beneath him? I swallow hard. Must be nice becoming a billionaire CEO before thirty—all it takes is having your last name already emblazoned across half the theaters in America and a corner office waiting for you since birth.

"People in my position," I say. "Go on."

Max shrugs, obviously wanting to change the subject. "Now. Nora Davis. What were you thinking?"

"Are you thinking that I deliberately championed a false memoir because, what, I wanted to cost my studio $2 million? Her memoir was the hottest thing published last year, if you can remember, and Nora Davis made the rounds with all the usual suspects from Kimmel to the ladies of *The View.*" I shrug. "I read the memoir, saw the potential for it to be a *Girl, Interrupted* for Generation Z and championed it to our studio. I had to clear it through layers of senior executives and producers, and they approved it."

"They rubber-stamped it, you mean."

"No, they approved it. I passionately pitched it to senior leadership and the project was approved." I take a sip of the water. "So, why am I on the hot-seat here? I didn't make the final approval. Lots of people were involved in developing it."

He closes his eyes and then, when he opens them again, they're almost a different color. The green has turned almost amber and I see fury behind them. I'm automatically chilled to the bone.

"Ms. Jenkins," he begins in an even voice. "Development executives are the gatekeepers. A development executive at Kensington Pictures can't afford to hemorrhage millions on every unvetted memoir that lands in their inbox. I need someone who can recognize garbage before it costs us. And frankly, after this disaster, I'm not merely questioning your instincts—I'm having nightmares about what you might do to my bottom line if I let you anywhere near acquisition decisions."

I blink fast, trying not to cry. His words hurt more than just criticism—they tear open old wounds I've covered up with excuses. All those rejection letters for my screenplays are saved in a folder on my laptop, like a cemetery filled with "sorry" and "not for us." I've told myself it's okay because I'm good at finding other people's talent, even if no one sees mine. But now Max makes me doubt the one thing I thought I was good at. If I can't write and I can't do my job, what's left? My whole career feels like it's built on sand, sinking under me.

"So, you're concerned about my judgment. Couldn't this have been an email?" I bite my tongue because I really want to ask him if it could've been a *fucking* email. But Elaine would absolutely murder me if I tanked this meeting. Like, literal murder. Body in the Pacific Ocean, sharks having Celeste tartare for dinner.

"I just got off the phone with Iris about that memoir debacle. Two million dollars down the drain." His jaw tightened. "We need to address this now, and I want you to deliver a message back to your studio: pull something like this again, and heads will roll."

"Heads will roll? Everyone at Dreamscape is flesh and blood, just like the people who work for you. We slip up sometimes. I regret how the Nora Davis situation unraveled, but that's the nature of this business. You start axing staff over one error, and by Christmas, you'll be running the studio without any help."

He leans forward, his green eyes flashing like polished stone. "In the future, people will lose their jobs over mistakes like this," he says, voice dropping to a dangerous whisper. "That's the only reason you're sitting here. Not for the wine list or the view—just so I can make something perfectly clear. When $2 million disappears because someone wasn't paying attention, I don't just shrug it off. You might not be scared now, but wait until the papers are signed and your entire studio answers to me. I want you to spread the word. Make sure everyone understands exactly what's coming."

"Oh, I see," I say. "I'm the sole survivor." That makes sense, actually.

"Excuse me?"

"The sole survivor. The one gangster they leave breathing after the bloodbath, just so he can stagger back to the neighborhood and spread the word." I puff out my cheeks, drop my voice to a gravelly whisper, and stroke my jawline with my knuckles. "Joey got what was coming to him. Nobody betrays the family and lives to tell about it," I rasp in my best Marlon Brando as Don Corleone, though I'm pretty sure I sound more like someone choking on a fishbone. "That's your play here—send me crawling back to Dreamscape with your boot print still visible on my ass."

"You get it then," Max says.

I take a deep breath. "I get it then? I get it then?" I bite my lower lip as realization washes over me. This meeting wasn't just a power play—it was a calculated humiliation. An hour in bumper-to-bumper traffic, my canceled Pilates class, fifty dollars wasted on parking and Uber, the stares when I clomped into Patrician, a five-star fine-dining restaurant, in my rainbow boots. All of it orchestrated by him. And Mom... her voice on the phone last night had that papery quality it gets before a bad spell. I should be at her apartment right now with soup from that deli she likes, not sitting here while this asshat makes his point.

I push back from the table, my chair legs scraping against the floor. The urge to stand and storm out burns in my chest, but I remain seated, watching him through narrowed eyes. He's picked me to humiliate, turning me into his cautionary tale. Each word he speaks, each gesture he makes, screams control. The message is clear: he commands, we obey. Just pieces on his board, to be sacrificed when convenient.

My fingers dig into the chair's armrests until my knuckles bleach bone-white. I've endured enough. He wants me to break, to send me crawling back to Dreamscape as his cautionary tale—the development exec who faced the wrath of our new corporate master. Not today. Let him find someone else to terrorize.

"You know what?" My chair scrapes against marble as I stand. "I'm done. Take my carrots home in a brown paper bag—oh wait, The Centurion doesn't do takeout for the ruling class, does it? What a waste." I grab my purse, knuckles white around the strap. "I won't be your verbal punching bag another minute. I'm a person, not some pawn you can push around your little corporate chessboard. Game over."

I slam my napkin onto the table, nearly knocking over my water glass, and wrench myself out of the chair. The legs screech against the floor as I storm out, my heels stabbing the polished wood with each step. Every instinct screams to look back—is he already calling Iris? Is he watching me leave with that cold, calculating stare? My heart hammers against my ribs like it's trying to escape.

Jesus Christ, what have I done? Three years at Dreamscape—three years of late nights and weekends sacrificed—all of it incinerated in ten seconds of stupidity. My throat tightens as I push through the door. By tomorrow morning, my keycard probably won't even work.

I stumble out of the club, vision blurred from crying, and fumble with my phone to summon an Uber. Tomorrow's first task: dusting off that resumé.

Chapter Two

MAX

After Celeste stormed out of the restaurant, I stared at the empty chair across from me, my knuckles white around my phone. My thumb hovered over Iris's contact. One call and Celeste would be packing her desk by morning. The waiter approaches with a hesitant smile, refilling my water glass that I hadn't touched. I straighten my tie and force my shoulders back. Employees don't walk away from Max Kensington. Not if they want to keep their jobs. Not if they want to stay in this industry at all.

I can't decide if I'm more pissed at Celeste or at Elody Martin's surprise appearance. The woman has an Oscar now, for Christ's sake—Hollywood's golden girl opening hundred-million-dollar weekends like it's nothing and staring down from every Chanel billboard in existence. And she's also my clingy ex.

Six months we lasted. The tabloids branded us "Max-ody"—I swear these name mashups are worse than dental surgery—while she whispered marriage plans to anyone with a microphone. Perez Hilton, Harvey Levin from *TMZ*

Ian Mohr from *Page Six*, plus every vulture from *The Star* to *In Touch* to *The National Enquirer*.

Marriage? Hell no. Not to her, not to anyone. Period. But Elody never got the memo. She's been following me like a shadow ever since, including tonight. That's why she was sitting at my table when Celeste finally showed up, waving that Bubba Gump napkin for an autograph. Between Elody's presence and Celeste's lateness—which I absolutely cannot stand—I was both thrown off-balance and furious.

I change after dinner and go to the Patrician gym. I check my phone. 7:58 PM. Two minutes until Gianni shows up. My hands already itch for the cold metal of the barbell. I picture myself under the bench press, Gianni's steady hands hovering just inches above the bar as I push through that final rep, his voice counting down—"three, two, one"—until I can finally exhale. My jaw unclenches just thinking about it. The vein that's been throbbing at my temple since Celeste stormed off might finally stop pulsing.

Gianni and I have been inseparable since Malibu Montessori at five—navy uniforms with dolphin logos—through Harvard-Westlake prep's calculus hell. We split for college; I chose USC for film while he went to Harvard. But he's always been there when it mattered. Like when I was seven, hiding in the garage that rainy February afternoon my father loaded his Porsche and drove away forever, leaving only the echo of a slammed door and my grandparents sobbing on the porch. Gianni found me there, my world shattered.

While I wait for him in the gym, I slam my fist into the speed bag until the chain rattles. Then I destroy Steve, my sparring mannequin. I lunge, vision narrowing as I drive my knee into his gut. My split knuckles leave blood on the vinyl. I can't stop. Something feral claws inside me. Is it because

Celeste walked away like I was nothing? Or because she made me feel alive? Those emerald eyes cutting through my bullshit. Her copper hair falling across ivory skin. The freckles I wanted to trace. My chest seized when she spoke, and I hated it. Hated how much I needed her next words.

Gianni materializes beside me, palms raised in mock surrender. "Hey now, let's not traumatize Steve for life." His smile crinkles the corners of his eyes as his arm settles across my shoulders. "I haven't seen those worry lines since the Paramount pitch. What's up?"

I shrug. As much as I want to spill my guts to my best friend, the guy who's seen me through some of the worst times of my life, I can't quite articulate exactly why I'm feeling so pissed. "Nothing, man. Let's go."

For the next hour, we pump iron. I grunt through squats until my quads scream, metal bar digging into my trapezius. I load another plate onto the leg press, determined to crush my fury beneath 300 pounds of steel. My goal: exhaust myself enough to finish work tonight with a clear head. But even after this punishment—shirt soaked, hair plastered to my forehead, salt on my lip—the tightness in my jaw remains. My gaze finds Steve, the sparring mannequin in the corner, his blank face begging for the beat-down I still crave.

Gianni just shakes his head as he sees me eyeing Steve. "Max, you pounded Steve enough. I know you have a lot of merger reports you need to get to at home but maybe it all can wait. Let's get a drink. You look like you need it."

I nod, remembering the Cabernet with dinner. No more drinks tonight. Still, the thought of Neon and Noir beckons —that speakeasy tucked behind the Orpheum where Gianni and I have spent countless nights. Those reports can wait. Tomorrow I'll power through them twice as fast, but tonight I need to untangle the Celeste situation before it consumes me entirely.

"See you there," I tell him, ducking into the locker room. After a quick shower, I swap the suit for dark Ferragamos, Seven jeans, and a gray cashmere V-neck. The valet brings my Bugatti around, its engine purring like a predator. Sliding behind the wheel, I force myself to ease onto Mulholland rather than tearing down toward the Arts District at 120, though God knows the car could handle it.

I duck through the unmarked door behind the Orpheum, past the hostess who recognizes me with a discreet nod, and into the amber-lit sanctuary where crystal decanters catch the light from Edison bulbs. Gianni is already perched at the copper bar, one Italian leather loafer hooked on the brass rail, swirling what is presumably a thirty-year-old Macallan in a hand-cut crystal tumbler, his go-to drink.

I join him at the oak-stained bar, with the mirror behind it and crystal glasses lined up overhead, sinking into the red leather bar stool and order a tonic water over ice. I'm sticking to my no-drinking pledge, only because the wine from earlier makes alcohol here seem redundant, and face Gianni, his dark eyes looking at me with worry. Of course Gianni would know when there's something wrong with me. He's known me my entire life. Literally.

He puts one tan hand on my shoulder and squeezes. "Out with it," he says, raising one dark eyebrow.

I shake my head. "You know about the meeting I scheduled tonight with Celeste Jenkins." I shake my head. "Didn't go well."

"Ah, Celeste Jenkins," Gianni says, his lips curving into a knowing smile. "Your randomly selected sacrificial lamb from Dreamscape. The one you planned to humiliate as a warning to the others." He tilts his head, studying Max's expression. "But she didn't play along with your little power game, did she?" One eyebrow arches perfectly. "Am I getting warm?"

"Goddamn you," I say. "How can you see through me like I'm made of glass?"

Gianni just grins and shakes his head. "I knew when you told me about your little plan that it would backfire, my friend. And I told you that, too. So not surprised it didn't go well. But what happened?"

I tell him the story and Gianni just nods along. He takes a sip of his scotch, the ice clinking against the crystal, before he lays into me. "Max," he says, leaning forward with his elbows on his knees. "Look, I get it. The Nora Davis memoir was a shit show that needed handling. And yeah, Celeste fucked up by not vetting it properly before sending it upstairs. But Christ, man—you could've shot her an email instead of summoning her like some medieval king. I know you're trying to establish dominance with the Dreamscape people, but this alpha male bullshit? Sometimes it just makes you look like a dick."

I say nothing and he stares at me. "There's something more, isn't there?"

I shrug, but my jaw clenches until I taste blood. Celeste. Her name burns like acid. Gianni's seen everything—the nightmares at seven, the bloody knuckles at twelve, me staring at my father's empty chair until Granddad had to shake me back. When I learned how my mother died, I understood why I felt like an outcast. Everybody knows that I'm responsible for her death. I've kept women at arm's length since, letting them touch my body but never what's broken inside. But Celeste? One look and something cracked open in me, something I've spent twenty-two years sealing shut. That terrifies me more than anything my father did.

"I'm talking to Iris tomorrow about letting her go," I mutter. I pretend it's about her mistake, but the truth is simpler. I can't bear to see her again. Something in those flashing blue eyes and that wild red hair makes my chest tighten. She looked at me like she could see straight through me, and I felt naked. Exposed. If she peered any deeper into the cracks, she might actually make me believe she'd stay. And then she'd walk away, just like my father did.

"You're firing her? Over one mistake?" Gianni's eyes narrow as he leans forward. "Must be nice being infallible. The rest of us mere mortals have to live with our flaws." He drums his fingers on the desk. "Look, she pushed for that script, sure. But she didn't sign the check. That disaster had signatures all over it—development, legal, finance. If you're hunting for sacrificial lambs, why stop with her? Hell, might as well clean house entirely. A train wreck that spectacular requires multiple conductors."

I just shake my head. Celeste needs to go. My decision is final. Gianni called her a sacrificial lamb—he doesn't know the half of it. She has to go because her being in my company would be too much for me. Despite my CEO role keeping me away from development, I'd eventually manu-facture reasons to see her. I'd feign interest in projects just to be near her. That's exactly why she has to leave. She'll make me forget quarterly projections in board meetings. Pure kryptonite.

"So, what's going on with you these days?" I ask him, changing the subject. "It's been awhile since we've hung out like this." And that's true - we meet at the gym four evenings a week, as our schedules allow, but we don't usually hang afterwards and catch up like we're doing now.

His eyes flick down to his beer when I glare at him. The name "Celeste" hangs in the air between us for a moment, then dissolves. He clears his throat. "Lakers looked good last night." I nod, grateful that he can always pick up what I'm putting down - I don't feel like talking about Celeste anymore. We drift through the safety of box scores and quarterly projections until, inevitably, we're laughing about Master Dawkins' econ final from senior year. The bartender rings the bell for last call. I check my watch: 1:15 AM. The Kensington merger folder sits unopened in my briefcase, sticky tabs marking twenty pages I need to memorize before 7 AM. My temples throb at the thought of it.

But thank God I have work to drown in when I get home. I need something—anything—to obliterate the memory of Celeste's hair, that untamed flame that haunts me even with my eyes closed, and those blue eyes that cut through my defenses like they were nothing, leaving me exposed, vulnerable, terrified of what she might have seen inside me.

Chapter Three

MAX

I push through the heavy mahogany front door of my Malibu estate at 3 AM to find my housekeeper Rosa still awake, the woman who bandaged my skinned knees and packed my school lunches after my father vanished and my grandparents retreated into their social obligations. The warm yellow light from the Tiffany lamp casts a halo around her as she sits in the breakfast nook, her weathered hands cupping a steaming mug of Jamaican Blue Mountain coffee—the only brand she'll drink. The scent of it mingles with the faint coconut oil she's used in her hair since I was seven.

"It's 3 in the morning," I say, loosening my Italian silk tie. "What's going on?" The worry lines etched around her mouth tell me something's wrong before she speaks. I slide into the hand-carved chair across from her, the cool marble tabletop against my forearms as I pour myself coffee from the silver carafe.

She shakes her head, the gold hoops in her ears catching the light. "My father's not well. I just got a call from my sister in Kingston." Tears glisten in her eyes, turning them obsidian in the dim light.

I reach across, covering her cocoa-butter-soft hand with mine. "How not well?"

"She doesn't think he'll make it." Her voice cracks like thin ice.

"I'll send you down there on my jet." I raise my palms when her expressive eyes widen in protest. "No argument. You need to get down there as soon as you can, and you don't need the added stress of navigating TSA and cramped economy seats."

"Max, that's too much." Her Jamaican accent thickens with emotion.

"Well, I don't need the Gulfstream right now and I won't for the next few months as I'm chained to my desk here in LA, so go. I'll call Thomas tomorrow and arrange it and I'll get Ross to bring the Bentley around first thing."

Rosa shakes her head, the silver strands in her dark hair catching the light. "You are too good to me, Max," she says, my name rolling off her tongue with the familiarity of thirty years—not "Mr. Kensington," never that.

"Rosa, it's nothing, really." I drain the last of my coffee, the bitter dregs coating my tongue, and circle behind her chair. I bend to hug her shoulders, breathing in the familiar scent of her jasmine perfume. "Godspeed to your father. Let me know how he is when you get there."

She nods. "I promise, Max." Her eyes crinkle at the corners as she adds, "Beneath all that CEO armor beats a good heart. You show that every day."

"My reputation would be ruined, so don't let that get around" I say, pulling her in for one more embrace. Then I retreat to my study, where stacks of quarterly projections and merger proposals for tomorrow's - actually today's -

board meeting awaits, illuminated by the amber glow of my desk lamp, demanding attention I can barely give them now.

I feel for Rosa. Though at 101, after a lifetime of daily cigars since boyhood, her father had a good run. Last week he was still charming the ladies on the beach, Rosa told me. Still, watching a parent slip away cuts deep, regardless of when it happens—something I understand all too well.

I just hope she makes it in time for a final goodbye.

Chapter Four

MAX

I drag my ass into the 7 AM board meeting after no sleep and a million cups of coffee. I was stupid to meet Gianni last night after our workout. A more responsible me would've begged off. But I needed a sounding board for my Celeste encounter and he brought it like he always does. He never minces words, nor would I want him to. But even though he told me how ridiculous I'm being in getting Celeste fired, I'm more determined than ever to do it. So, the plan is to call Iris after this meeting and tell her that Celeste has to go. We're already working together on who'll make the cut after the merger, so I know Iris will do as I say.

I rap my knuckles on the mahogany table, bringing the meeting to order. Gerard Oslo, the chairman of the board, rises from his seat at the far end, tugging at his silk tie. His gaze darts around the room, landing everywhere but on me, and the slight tremor in his hand betrays him as he adjusts his glasses. In fifteen years as chairman, I've never seen the old bulldog's confidence waver like this.

"Max," he says. "Before you get started, there's a matter we need to discuss."

"Go ahead," I say, knitting my brows. I'm already not in the mood for this, whatever this is. I wouldn't be in the mood for bad news even on a full night of sleep, but, considering my lack of sleep last night, I could be ready to cut a bitch by the time this meeting's over, judging by Gerard's serious expression and obvious fear of addressing me.

"There's no easy to way to say this," he says. "Except just to say it. The largest group of investors, the McLaughlin group led by Clarence McLaughlin, are... uneasy about your continuing on as CEO after the merger." I put my fingers on the table and just stare. I'm not hearing this. "They're suggesting Iris become the CEO of the new company."

I close my eyes and count to 10, feeling the tension in my jaw like a vise grip. I learned that little trick when I was seven, sitting cross-legged on Dr. Lowenstein's leather couch that squeaked whenever I shifted my weight. The child psychologist with her silver-rimmed glasses and perpetual smell of peppermint had called it "emotional regulation." It doesn't always work, and right now, with my temples throbbing from twenty hours without sleep, the numbers blur together as I mutter them through clenched teeth.

"Gerard," I finally say, my voice tightening. "That's complete bullshit and you know it. What did McLaughlin say exactly?" I grip the edge of my desk. McLaughlin controls twenty percent of our shares and whispers in the ears of everyone who matters. If they're gunning for me, the vultures will circle within days. The thought makes my stomach clench. We've delivered three consecutive billion-dollar box office years. Our streaming shows dominate the cultural conversation. Just last month, I closed deals with Nolan and Scorsese that had my competitors seething. Spielberg calls me directly now, for Christ's sake.

And they want Iris Dimas in charge? She's built Dreamscape into a respected boutique studio, but they handle just a fraction of Kensington's annual business. It's like comparing a critically-acclaimed indie press to Random House. Dreamscape excels at creating those thoughtful films that light up Cannes and Sundance—artistic triumphs that earn critical praise rather than blockbuster numbers. They've carved out their niche beautifully. But Kensington consistently delivers both commercial success and awards season dominance. Our films win Oscars while breaking box office records. Handing the reins to Iris after the merger simply doesn't make business sense—it would upend everything we've built. And would be a slap in the fucking face.

Gerard is intently studying a paper on the conference table, obviously wanting to be anywhere but in this conference room. I'm still staring at him, willing him to tell me what the hell is going on.

"McLaughlin expressed reservations about your... personal situation. The lack of stability in your home life, combined with your extreme youth—well, there are concerns about your ability to handle the increased pressures once the merger goes through."

"The lack of stability in my home life?" I blink twice, heat rising to my face. My fingers curl into my palms, nails digging half-moons into skin. "Since when," I say, each word measured despite the tremor in my voice, "is my personal situation either unstable or relevant to this conversation?"

Gerard clears his throat. "You've had a lot of girlfriends

in the past few years. McLaughlin has concerns about that, along with your age and rapid rise at Kensington Pictures." He raises his palms defensively. "Clarence is old-fashioned. Views your romantic history as a sign of instability." My jaw clenches. The rational part of my brain understands that Gerard is just the messenger and strangling him wouldn't change Clarence McLaughlin's Victorian opinions about my love life. But McLaughlin isn't sitting across from me right now. Gerard is. The conference table between us is the only thing stopping me from wrapping my hands around his throat.

I know Clarence McLaughlin—he's one of Granddad Joe's oldest confidants since the early Kensington days. This realization hits me and I shake my head. Of course. The puppet master behind this little ambush is none other than the patriarch himself. This is his not-so-subtle nudge toward matrimony. Clarence would never dare cross me without the old man's blessing. He's too loyal to go rogue.

The bad part is, I can't really defend myself against the charge Clarence is making against me. I *have* had a revolving door in my bedroom. I've lost count of how many women I've dated. It's a pattern I can't seem to break. They all start to blur together after a while—the same conversations, the same disinterested nods from me, the same inevitable ending. Right now it's Rayna Hayes, a super-model with a huge billboard on Sunset, before that it was Elody and—hell, I'd need both hands to count just the actresses and models from the past year. I never overlap them; that's one line I won't cross. But when you're burning through relationships every few months, people talk. The tabloids love it. "Max Kensington's Revolving Bedroom Door" was actually a headline last month. No lie detected.

I start pacing around the room. "So what am I supposed

to do about this? I'm 29. Can't change that. And I have a colorful love life, which is nobody's goddamn business, by the way. What the fuck does Clarence want from me?" Or Granddad, I think. The puppeteer, the Geppetto to Clarence's apparent Pinocchio role. I'm going to have a word with Granddad, the sooner the better.

I'm looking at Gerard, whose face is now getting very pale. He's trembling and I feel half-sorry for him. He has the shittiest job in the world right now, bringing me this bad news. So I take a deep breath and try not to treat Gerard like I was treating Steve the sparring mannequin last night.

"Your grandfather has a solution that will calm Clarence. If Clarence is smoothed, then…"

"Bullshit," I say. "I doubt Clarence could care less about my romantic situation. Granddad is behind this mutiny and you can't tell me differently. He just doesn't want his finger-prints on the knife in my back." I glare at Gerard and one look at his reddened cheeks and his downcast eyes and I know - my instinct about who's responsible for shivving me is right. "You might as well just admit it."

Gerard takes a deep breath and proceeds to lie for Granddad. Of course he would. He's fiercely loyal to my grandfather. "No," he says, his voice faint and his eyes still staring at the conference table. "That's not true." His fingers are shaking as they graze the top of the oak wood table and, once again, I'm feeling a great deal of sympathy for him. Man, it must suck to be him right now. Talk about being caught between Scylla and Charybdis - the poor guy is caught between my grandfather's bullshit demands and my temper, which is about to blow. I must calm down. He's not the one I'm mad at, nor should he be.

"I know differently," I say. "Call him right now. I want

him at this meeting. I want him to look me in the eye and tell me that Clarence has a problem with me and not him." I look at the conference room phone meaningfully then look at Gerard. "Call him now."

Gerard's hands tremble violently as he snatches the phone, punching in my grandfather's number like he's stabbing at a lifeline. The old man materializes in the doorway barely four minutes later, his presence hitting the room like a thunderclap. No coincidence. The crafty bastard was lurking somewhere in the building, waiting for this exact moment. At 84, with arthritic knees and a pacemaker, Granddad should be nursing a scotch at the Cabrillo Beach Yacht Club, or teeing up at the Riviera Country Club, not prowling the Kensington Pictures headquarters like some corporate vulture circling fresh carrion. This was a goddamn ambush, and I walked right into it.

"Granddad Joe," I say, narrowing my eyes. "Have a seat."

He smiles that goddamn smile—the one that means he's already won. I've known that smile since childhood. My jaw clenches so hard my teeth might crack. Every executive in this boardroom thinks I'm in charge, but it's all theater. One word from Granddad and the investors scatter like roaches. One nod and the shareholders fall to their knees. CEO of Kensington Pictures? Might as well be "Granddad's Puppet" on my office door. The old bastard's eyes are gleaming now, his liver-spotted hand tapping the table. My stomach churns acid. Whatever bomb he's about to drop will obliterate everything I've built. I can taste the humiliation already.

"Max," he says gleefully. "I guess you heard about Clarence's concerns."

I'm so pissed that there's no way I can regulate the

words coming out of my mouth. I don't even try. "Cut the goddamn crap," I say to Granddad. The cunning smile that's still plastered on the wily old man's face is making me want to cut a bitch. "Clarence has no such concerns. You have the concerns. So why don't you tell me exactly what your problem is. I need this on the record."

The board members squirm in their ergonomic chairs, ties loosened and knuckles white around their Mont Blanc pens. Gazes dart between laptops and watches—anywhere but at the Kensington bloodbath unfolding before them. Thompson's face has gone the color of printer paper; Martinez's jaw clenches so hard I can practically hear enamel cracking. Johnson is sweating through his Armani. It's a Thanksgiving dinner from hell, complete with verbal carving knives and emotional hand grenades. I see Patel eyeing the emergency exit like it's salvation itself. Fuck their discomfort. As I growled at Granddad when he stormed in, this carnage needs witnesses.

"Max," Granddad says. "You've done splendid work with Kensington Pictures. I couldn't be happier with your performance. Nailing down the latest Nolan project was chef's kiss." He kisses his fingers for emphasis. "Billions in profit, every quarter dwarfing the quarter that came before it. Everybody's buzzing about our streaming projects, our theatrical releases have been tearing up the box office and awards seasons. You've been a steady and innovative hand on the till."

I raise an eyebrow. Another Granddad move, and I know them all. He's buttering me up before going in for the kill. He knows how to soften the shiv going straight into my back. Not falling for it, even if every fucking word he just said is absolutely true. I resist the temptation to just tell him to get on with it. I don't have all day and I feel a migraine forming behind my eyes. I haven't had one of those for years, yet today will be the day that my non-migraine streak comes to an end. I can feel it.

I motion with my hands that I want him to get the point and he nods.

"Max, listen to me. You have a revolving door of women and you can't keep living like this. How many times have we had this conversation? With the Dreamscape merger, Kensington Pictures won't just be your responsibility anymore—it'll be twice the empire, twice the pressure. You need someone in your corner. Someone who sees you when the cameras aren't rolling. I've watched enough successful men in this industry to know—the ones who last aren't standing alone."

I narrow my eyes. "My personal life is nobody's business. What you said earlier is exactly the truth. Kensington Pictures is one of the most successful film studios in the world right now. I've been CEO for five years, since I was 24 years old. And since I've taken over, profits have exploded and our movies and streaming projects have done platinum numbers. That's all been me. My leadership. My hard work. So I don't need to be lectured about how I somehow need a stable love life and how that's even relevant to my performance."

Granddad pushes himself up from his leather armchair, his arthritic knuckles whitening as he grips the mahogany armrests. His eyes, still sharp despite the wrinkles framing them, lock onto mine with the same determination that built the Kensington empire. "Max," he announces, his voice carrying the weight of decades of getting exactly what he wants, "I've made up my mind. You need to be married." He pauses, the hint of a satisfied smile playing at the corners of his mouth. "And I already have the woman for you all lined up."

"MARRIED?" The word explodes from my mouth like a gunshot. "What the actual FUCK?" My head whips around, scanning the room where every single pair of eyes now bores into me. Seconds ago they were all staring at the floor, walls, ceiling—anywhere to escape the bloodbath between Granddad and me. Now? They're practically salivating, relief washing over their faces like I've been sentenced to community service instead of execution. As if marrying a complete stranger is somehow the merciful alternative to whatever horror show they'd been imagining Granddad would demand.

Granddad puts his hands up and shakes his head. "You won't get me off this. I found the perfect-"

"No." My voice cuts through the room. "Absolutely not. I won't be manipulated into this arrangement." I scan the boardroom, making eye contact with each member seated around the polished table. "Everyone here has witnessed my objection. Should I lose my position as CEO following the Dreamscape merger, you'll all be receiving subpoenas." I turn to Granddad and point at him, my finger steady despite my racing pulse. "This won't stand."

"Max," Granddad says, his voice deceptively gentle. "Take a breath. I've found her—the perfect match. Something in her eyes... there's a kindness there. A goodness." He leans forward, the leather of his chair creaking. "And you will marry her." The temperature in the room seems to drop. "Unless you want the board to reconsider your position." His pupils contract to pinpoints, the same look he wore when negotiating the Turner acquisition. Gone is the doting grandfather who sneaks candies to children at family gatherings. In his place sits the man who once bankrupted three competing companies in a single quarter just to prove he could. I feel my throat go dry as those bright green eyes —the same color as mine—fix on me with predatory focus.

I stare at him and he stares back, his eyes scorching me with the same merciless fire that incinerated every competitor in Kensington Pictures' path. My jaw locks like a vise—I taste blood where I've bitten my cheek. This ends one way: Granddad will use the morality clause in my contract to tear me up like a great white through a hemorrhaging seal, then unleash Clarence McLaughlin on the remains. One goddamn phone call and the shareholders will be circling, howling for my execution by market close.

I could detonate back and sue the living fuck out of him —Jesus Christ, every cell in my body screams to—but that means total annihilation of the man who hoisted me onto shoulders that felt like mountains when I cracked that first home run. The man who kept vigil through seventy-two hellish hours after Dad abandoned us, who guided my trembling fingers through fishing knots with hands granite-steady when I couldn't even hold a spoon. The man who appeared like clockwork at every baseball diamond, hockey rink, auditorium and concert hall for eight devastated boys with eight shattered hearts. His gnarled hands strangle the armrests, and I see the same calluses that once collected my blood and tears from playground concrete. No. I will not crucify us both, will not rip this family into bloody pieces. Not even for this.

I slam my fist on the table and hang my head. Goddamn it to hell. Marry some random woman I've never met or watch my CEO position burn to ashes. Is Granddad bluffing? My gut says yes, but my brain screams no. When that old bastard latches onto an idea—no matter how deranged or batshit insane—he'll ride it straight into the ground like a kamikaze pilot. If he's decided I'm marrying this woman, then I'm fucking marrying her, period. Testing his resolve would be like pulling the pin on a grenade to see if it's real. The second I refuse, he'll torch everything I've built just to watch me scramble through the flames. That's who he is. That's who he's always been.

The conference room freezes into a goddamn cemetery. Not a breath, not a shuffle. Every suit around this table knows what I know - when Granddad gets that look in his eye, that fucking gleam, we're all about to get dragged into his madness. But Jesus Christ, the man's insanity has built empires. While Harvard MBAs were calculating risk assessments, Granddad was setting fire to the rulebook and pissing on the ashes. His instincts weren't just good - they were supernatural. A fucking Scottish orphan kid tossed onto American shores at SEVEN, sleeping on his distant cousin's floor in Chicago's armpit, and by age 23 he's running a factory! He did that with brass balls, and that terrifying Kensington conviction. The board members sitting here? They'd follow him off a cliff. Hell, I would too. Because when Granddad leaps, he doesn't fall - he fucking flies.

"Who is this woman?" I finally ask, my jaw clenched so tight I can feel a vein throbbing in my temple. My fists ball at my sides. Some random nobody is going to hijack my life? Fuck that. I'll play the part in public—the Instagram announcement dripping with fake adoration, the engagement party where I'll smile until my face cracks, the wedding where I'll say vows that mean absolutely nothing—but behind closed doors? Ice. Cold. Silence. She'll be sleeping in another wing of the house. I'll make sure she feels like the intruder she is. And the second—the very second—that merger paperwork hits my desk and I still have "CEO" on my business cards, I'm cutting her loose with whatever cash it takes to make her disappear.

Granddad thinks he's got me cornered? Watch me. I'll have every major shareholder eating from my hand before the ink on our marriage license dries. I'll find their weaknesses, their vices, their secrets—I don't care if I have to spend nights digging through their trash. When I'm done, I'll have so much blackmail material that they'll all vote me in as CEO and Granddad won't be able to touch me when I divorce this woman. I love the old man, but I'll burn this whole company to the ground before I let him or anyone puppet-master my life. When this is over, he'll never try to fuck with me again.

Granddad's smug smile makes my blood boil. The old man has no fucking clue what hurricane I'm about to unleash. God help this woman—whoever the hell she is—because I'm going to make every single day of her existence a waking nightmare. A year from now, that self-satisfied grin will be wiped clean off his face. He'll be drowning in guilt for dragging some innocent woman into the toxic wasteland of our family drama. And I'll make damn sure of it.

"She's a lovely girl I met a few months ago when I was visiting the UCLA hospital." Granddad's voice trembles with conviction. His name is etched in gold on half the wings at UCLA—the place where his first wife, Gracie, fought and lost to cancer at just twenty-one. The memory still burns in him like a live coal. They treated her like royalty in those final days, and he's bled money into their coffers ever since, a debt he can never fully repay. When he walks those sterile corridors now, doctors practically genuflect. "She was visiting her mother—cancer too—and the moment our eyes met, something seized me. She's ancient inside, Max. Pure. I haven't slept right thinking about her, and three nights ago, I woke up drenched in sweat with absolute certainty. She belongs with you. I'd stake my life on it."

Well, this just keeps getting batshittier by the moment. She's a complete rando. To both of us, apparently. "Granddad," I say, my voice steadier than I expected. The fury that had been boiling inside me has burned itself out, leaving nothing but exhaustion in its wake. "Most grandparents slip a number into their grandson's pocket at Thanksgiving. They don't arrange marriages like we're living in some medieval kingdom. Couldn't you arrange a coffee date like a normal grandparent?"

He shakes his head. "No. You've never given women like her a chance, Max. Your dating history speaks for itself—actresses with magazine covers, models with billboards on Sunset. You see a woman without a glam squad and your eyes slide right past her." He leans forward, his weathered hands clasped together. "This time, you can't walk away after one dinner. My gut says you need to be forced to see beyond the surface, and that's exactly what this marriage will do. Sometimes the right path isn't the one we'd choose for ourselves."

I scan the boardroom and catch the knowing glances. They've seen the Instagram posts—me with Alessandra at Cannes, Vivienne at the Met Gala, Sophia on that yacht in Santorini, with Elody at various parties around LA. Perfect bodies, perfect smiles, perfect bank accounts. And me, perfect at walking away when they inevitably start planning our futures. The tabloids have branded me "Hollywood's Most Eligible Commitment-Phobe" for a reason. These board members have deleted more of my PR disasters than I can count, so watching Granddad manipulate me into matrimony like some sixteenth-century royal merger hardly shocks them. If anything, the old man's heavy-handed tactics make him the villain in this particular boardroom drama, not me.

I finally sigh. "Okay. What is this mystery woman's name?"

"Celeste Jenkins."

Oh. fuck.

Chapter Five

MAX

No. No fucking way. Nope. Not doing it. It'll be a cold day in the ninth circle of hell before I ever, and I mean, ever, marry Celeste fucking Jenkins. Granddad can pound sand. Anybody but her.

I sit down and calmly steeple my hands. I do something I probably should've done before, except I was too apoplectic to see straight. "This board meeting is tabled," I say to everyone. "Until tomorrow morning at 7. Thanks."

Everyone files out of the conference room, disappointment in their faces. They wanted to keep watching the fireworks. Probably was the highlight of their day. Not that I care. We're all practically family, my board members and I, and they've been privy to many a food fight before. This meeting will prove no different in the end and everybody will settle down soon. Besides that, they're all under an NDA, lock and key. So, much like Vegas, whatever happens here stays here.

"Granddad," I say, my voice hardening as I grip the

edge of the table. "You know I love you, and I've followed your guidance my entire life. But this—" I shake my head, jaw clenched. "I know Celeste. I've seen what she's capable of. She is not the woman for me. She will never be the woman for me."

I can't forget those goddamn blue eyes challenging me, her spine ramrod straight, strutting into that five-star restaurant like she owned the place while wearing what had to be consignment store rags. Christ. I called her to meet with me because I intended to humiliate her and now I can't get her out of my mind.

Granddad smiles. "I've made up my mind," he says. "There's no getting me off of it, so don't even try. You must marry Celeste Jenkins, assuming she's willing…"

I shake my head. "Oh my God. You haven't even asked her yet?" Is he senile? I never thought he was, but, good lord, doing this without even knowing if Celeste is on board…not a good sign.

He shakes his head. "I still need to contact her team at Dreamscape. No direct line to her—no cell number, no email—so I've got to wade through the corporate gate-keepers first. But once I do…" He smiles, tapping his fingers against the table. "Let's just say the financial incentive I'm offering should make her decision quite simple."

I narrow my eyes to slits. "How much of a financial incentive?" My pulse hammers in my throat as the solution crystallizes. Find out granddad's price and double it—pay her off. I need numbers. Leverage. I need granddad to tell me exactly what he's offering her so I can destroy this arrangement before it destroys me.

"$250,000 and she has to stay married to you for at least one year." His eyes gleam like a shark that's scented blood.

"One year to chisel through that fortress you call a heart. One goddamn year, Max. And don't think I haven't calculated every angle. The moment she says 'I do,' that poor girl will be counting the seconds until she can escape you. I've watched you destroy every relationship you've ever touched. But mark my words—if she breaks after a month, if she flees screaming into the night—and Christ knows I wouldn't blame her—she gets nothing. Not. One. Cent."

I steeple my hands, wheels turning. I must call Celeste and head this mess off at the pass. "Okay, Granddad," I say. "Talk to her and see if she's on board with this and let's get this show on the road."

Granddad's eyes narrow to slits. "Max, do I look senile to you?" He shakes his head, the gesture slow and deliberate. "Twenty-nine years I've watched you grow, and you still think you can pull one over on me? I see right through you. The minute that door closes behind you, you'll have Celeste on the phone, dangling a million-dollar bribe to turn me down. Try it, and I'll know. Then you'll be sitting pretty without your CEO title and with your bank account a million lighter."

Damn! I walked right into his trap. The old man's been outmaneuvering sharks his whole career. Nobody builds a fortune like his by missing what's coming—especially when it's this obvious.

Okay, so bribing her to walk away is out of the question. Granddad would find out—he always does. He'd probably sic John Englund on her financials the second he suspected something. I was ready to transfer a cool million into whatever offshore account she named, but John would find it. The man's a digital bloodhound.

Plan B. I need to make her see reason. I'll work with

what I have. I close impossible deals with charm every day. This time I'll flip the script—deploy calculated repulsion to show her exactly what she's signing up for.

His weathered hand settles on my shoulder, light as a bird. "Max," he whispers, voice cracking with age. "You see me as the villain in this story. I understand. But I've watched you hollow yourself out for twenty-two years since that day —since your father disappeared and you learned the truth about your mother's death." His fingers tremble against my collar bone. "The emptiness in you, Max... I recognize it. I've tried everything. The therapists couldn't reach it. Becoming the youngest billionaire CEO in America couldn't fill it. The multiple *Forbes* covers haven't made a dent. None of it touched that void." He leans closer, eyes suddenly clear and certain. "She'll accept my offer, and when she does—" his mouth curves into a fragile smile, "— you'll finally remember how to live again." I bite down hard on my bottom lip, tasting blood.

"Okay, Granddad," I say. "Game on."

And, at that, I leave the conference room, and Grand-dad, behind. I call Celeste the second I leave the conference room. "Celeste Jenkins," I say. "This is Max Kensington."

"Oh," she says, her voice as flat as a frozen lake. "Let me guess. You're calling to fire me." I can hear her drumming her fingers on her desk. "Fine. I've got a cardboard box under my desk and enough packing paper to wrap every coffee mug and sad little succulent in my office. You think this breaks me?" Her laugh is short, sharp. "I'll walk out that door and straight into something better. I know what I'm worth, even if you don't. So go ahead. Call Iris. I'll be gone before the elevator - ."

"Would you fucking shut up?" I snap into the phone,

cutting her off mid-sentence. "I need to see you. Right now. Drop whatever you're doing and meet me in an hour."

"Oh, no. You won't do that to me two days in a row. Nope. Not doing it. Call Iris, have me fired, whatever you need to fucking do. I'm not playing your game. Bye, Max." The call cuts off with a sharp click that feels like a slap. I slam my fist against the desk, then grab a fistful of my hair and yank until my scalp burns. The earlier threatened migraine explodes behind my eyes—white-hot daggers of light stabbing through my vision. My stomach lurches. The room tilts. I grip the edge of my chair, knuckles white, sweat beading on my forehead. Doesn't matter. I'll crawl there if I have to. I have to reach her before she talks to Granddad and takes that goddamn offer.

I fumble for my phone and call my driver. The thought of driving to Claremont with my vision blurring at the edges makes my stomach turn. I'd wrap my Aston around a telephone pole before I made it halfway there. But I need to reach her office, corner her if I have to. Every minute counts. If Granddad gets to her first with his ridiculous proposal, I'm screwed. The quarterly reports can gather dust. The market analyses can wait. The merger papers— worth billions—suddenly mean nothing. My entire focus narrows to this: find Celeste, make her understand why she absolutely cannot marry me.

Oscar pulls up outside the building in record time. "Dreamscape headquarters. Claremont. Now," I manage through clenched teeth. The car lurches forward. Oscar knows the drill—he's seen that look in my eyes before. The Rolls Royce limo weaves through traffic like a needle through fabric, each swerve amplifying the jackhammer behind my eyes. My migraine has colonized my entire skull, radiating from my jaw upward. I grip the leather seat, focusing on the cool material under my fingertips instead of the pain threatening to black me out. Celeste first, darkness later. I'll have my sanctuary waiting—office sofa, blackout curtains, silence—but only after I see her. Everything hinges on this moment. The pain isn't real, I lie to myself. Nothing exists except getting to her.

Chapter Six

IRIS

"Celeste," Elaine's voice slices through the air like a chainsaw as I sit at my desk, staring into the abyss of my shattered career. My throat burns from swallowing back sobs all morning until my chest feels like it might explode. This job was EVERYTHING to me. The cruel irony crushes me - you never truly appreciate something until it's being ripped away, and now I'm free-falling into a pit so dark I can't even see the bottom. My desk has become a goddamn funeral parlor, with co-workers filing past like mourners, offering pastries and awkward embraces, their eyes screaming what their mouths won't say: "Poor Celeste is finished." The restaurant disaster spread through this office like wildfire before I even made it back to my desk.

Just yesterday I thought I'd move up at Dreamscape. Maybe get my name on movie posters, fix broken scripts, or run things myself one day. My scripts just sit on my laptop where no one important will ever see them—each "no" chipping away at my dream bit by bit. But I had choices yesterday. Today? Dreamscape will fire me, and people will talk. "That's her—the one Kensington ruined." I could run to New York, try to work in TV, but who am I fooling? When Max Kensington says you're done, you're done everywhere.

"Yes?" I ask Elaine, my fingers freezing over my keyboard. My stomach drops as she hovers in my doorway.

"Iris needs to see you right now."

Six words from Elaine, and my mouth dries up. My heart races as I walk behind her down the hall, getting closer to what feels like the end of my job. Iris shuts the office door, and the small click sounds as loud as a gun. I try to calm down, but I can't. I might faint.

Everybody knows that when your superior shuts the door, nothing good will come of your meeting.

Iris smiles, obviously seeing my distress. Then she says something that I cling to like a lifeline. "Relax, Celeste. This meeting isn't what you're thinking."

Whoosh. My breath, which I was holding, came out in one long tendril and I start to cry.

"I'm sorry," I say to her. "I've been on pins and needles ever since last night. I shouldn't have been so disrespectful towards Mr. Kensington. It's just that I feel he disrespected me. But I'll be more circumspect in the future, I promise."

Iris wraps me in a hug, her perfume a cloud of vanilla and something floral. "Oh, Celeste," she whispers against my hair, "he had it coming. Everyone knows what Max Kensington is like. He's a monster in Armani." She pulls back, her hands still on my shoulders, and gives a little dismissive shrug. "But I shouldn't speak ill of him." Her eyes dart away, then back to mine as she inhales sharply. "Although..."

"Although?"

She sighs and rustles some papers on her desk. Her eyes

aren't meeting mine and the mood of the room is some-thing different than it was earlier. She shakes her head. "Celeste, I received an interesting phone call. From Joseph Kensington."

"Joseph Kensington? The billionaire who owns most of Los Angeles?"

"Yes, Joseph Kensington. When exactly did the two of you cross paths? He just called with the strangest proposi-tion, and I'd like to understand what prompted it. I told him I'd speak with you, but frankly, I'm at a loss."

Wait....Damn. "Can I see a picture of him?"

She shows me his picture and I feel embarrassed. Of course! That man I met at UCLA hospital seemed familiar to me, but I couldn't place his face. Now, as I stare at the picture, it becomes a bit more clear on who that angel was who visited me the night I was sure I'd lose my mother.

So, I tell Iris the story....

Three Months Earlier

Mom is hospitalized with an infection, and I'm terrified about her, but I don't want to scare Lexi. So, I didn't call her to let her know what's going on. She's staying on campus with a friend tonight because they're working on a short film together, so she doesn't need to know our mother is so sick.

I wish Olivia were here with me, but she's staying the night with her on-again, off-again boyfriend. So, I feel alone.

I reach for my phone, fingers already tapping toward the comfort of Taylor's voice—the *Life of a Showgirl* album has been my emotional crutch lately—when an older gentleman approaches. My reflection in the window shows everything: dark circles under bloodshot eyes, lips pressed thin, shoul-ders hunched forward like I'm bracing for impact. The thought of Mom's empty chair at Thanksgiving, of Lexi's graduation with no one to cheer from the other side, of evenings without her laughter—it's all there, written across my face for anyone to read.

"Hello," he says. "My name is Joe. You look like you need a shoulder to cry on."

My eyes burn with the effort of containing tears, but the gentle creases around his eyes invite rather than judge. Something loosens in my chest—a knot I didn't realize I'd been carrying—and I let a single tear fall, no longer afraid of what might follow.

He hands me a handkerchief from his coat pocket. I assume it's a new one, so I take it gratefully. "Thank you," I say and then dab my eyes.

He looks at me, his green eyes shining. He's probably in his 80s, but he looks attractive for his age. "Can I help you with anything?" he asks.

I let out a deep breath. "Thank you so much, but I don't know what I need right now. Except for my mother to get out of the hospital and beat her cancer. That's what I need," I say, hanging my head. "But unfortunately, you can't give me that."

His Adam's Apple bobs up and down, as if he's holding back tears himself. "Cancer," he says, shaking his head. "It took my Gracie all those years ago. I was 20, she was 19. We just got married when she was diagnosed." He smiles. "Gracie and I didn't have much, but our love got us through those tough days and nights when there wasn't food on the table or heat running through our tiny place in Skid Row."

Skid Row is an actual area of Los Angeles. It's known, then as now, as a place where alcoholics and people on the margins of society live.

I put my hand on Joe's hand as he gets out his own

handkerchief and dabs his eyes with it. "I'm so sorry," I say softly. "You never got over that, did you?"

He shakes his head. "No. Never did. But I remarried and we lived happily. I'm still with her today, Ruth. But I never forgot my Gracie."

I wonder if he managed to get off Skid Row, but I don't want to pry. It's none of my business, but I'm curious.

"Well, that's a good thing, huh? You found a new love."

"Yes," he says. "But you can't find a new mother. I'll pray for you tonight, if that's okay with you."

I nod, my vision blurring as tears well up without permission. It's always the kindness that breaks me—never the tragedies, just the unexpected moments of grace. My throat tightens around the words. "Thank you," I whisper, the sound barely making it past the knot of emotion.

For the next hour or so, Joseph and I sit and talk. I tell him about my job, about my sister Lexi and how proud I am of her for excelling in the UCLA film program, and, of course, about my mother. I tell him about how Mom worked 12-hour days between her three jobs when Lexi and I were younger. How Mom sacrificed her whole life to make sure Lexi and I could eat and have shelter. How I feel guilty because Mom only had to work that hard because she had us kids at home, and if we were never around, she could've had more of a life. And maybe she wouldn't be sick today if she could've taken life easier.

There's something about this kind-hearted man that makes me feel comfortable opening up about my deepest fears and insecurities. In return, I gain a wealth of information about him. He shares stories about Ruth and their grandchildren, but he deliberately avoids revealing his profession. I suspect he's retired, but I have no idea what he did during his working life. He seems to be deliberately withholding that information.

Despite this, I found it acceptable.

At some point, I feel the need to stretch my legs, so I descend to the coffee shop to grab a cup. I return with a cup of coffee for me and one for him even though he didn't request one, and he smiles, placing his hand on my shoulder.

"You're a lovely young woman," he says. "You'll find a suitable husband someday."

I shrug. I've dated here and there, but, aside from one jerk I dated for a year, nothing ever stuck past the third dinner or the awkward morning-after coffee. When they ghosted or I let the texts fade away, I never found myself crying into ice cream, driving past their home or drunk-dialing at 2 AM. They were all wrong anyway—too loud, too quiet, too ambitious, not ambitious enough.

Finally, the doctor arrives and informs me that Mom is awake. I can see her and talk to her.

I extend a grateful handshake to the kindly older gentle-man. "Thank you so much, Joe," I say. "You truly made a difference today, more than you'll ever know."

As I leave that day, I anticipate never seeing Joe again. He undoubtedly served as one of those angels sent to provide comfort during my time of need.

He did offer me comfort, more than he could ever know.

———————————

Iris's eyes glisten as I finish telling her about my mother. "Oh, Celeste," she whispers, reaching across the desk to squeeze my hand. "I had no idea about your mother. Would it be alright if I sent her some flowers?" I watch as she jots a quick note on her planner, drawing a little star beside it for importance. A smile tugs at my lips. In a world of Maxes, it's the Irises who make the unbearable somehow bearable.

Now, I'm crying, but I nod. "My mother loves flowers. She likes orchids the best. Also sunflowers. Reminds her of our life in Kansas."

"The state flower of Kansas," Iris says with a nod. "Okay, then, done. Orchids and sunflowers." She inhales sharply, her fingers twisting the silver ring on her right hand. Her eyes dart to the window, then back to me, then down to the floor. The smile she attempts doesn't reach her eyes. My stomach tightens—something isn't right.

"Celeste," she gently says. "I feel weird even asking you for this, but, again, Joseph Kensington called and was adamant that I bring this...offer...to you." Then she shakes her head and mutters under her breath. "What am I doing here?"

"Iris, what is it?"

"Well, here's the thing. I don't know what your financial situation is, but I know you have a sister in film school at UCLA and a mother who's not working. I have an offer to make things more comfortable for you."

"What kind of an offer?"

She glances at me, then back at her desk, which she's now sitting on. Then looks out the window and back at me. "Joseph Kensington wants you to marry his son, Max. If you stay married to him for one year, you'll receive $250,000. He says he wants a year commitment because he's afraid that you'll turn around and run from Max if there's not a pot of gold at the end of the rainbow, as it were. And he feels that a commitment on your part for a year would be enough for you to see what a great guy his grandson is. And, I'd like this conversation to stay between us, if that's okay with you."

I'm just staring at her. What. the. hell? Me, marrying that beast of a man I met last night? The one who made me feel three inches tall? Who cut me down where I stood, telling me how incompetent I was? She's staring at me like she's dead serious. As if the words that just came out of her mouth were not the batshittiest words in the history of the English language.

The "proposition" hits me, and suddenly I'm bent double, a burst of laughter exploding from somewhere I'd forgotten existed. My stomach muscles clench as tears stream down my face. I gasp for breath, manage to compose myself for half a second, then collapse into fresh peals that echo across the room. The release floods through me like a dam breaking—when was the last time I'd actually laughed? Not since before Mom's diagnosis, before "Stage 3" became the center of our vocabulary. My body remembers what it's like to feel something besides dread. I wipe my eyes, thinking of Joe Kensington with something close to gratitude. First, he came through for me when my mother was in the hospital and I thought I might lose my mother. Now, he's inadvertently come through for me in introducing this ridiculous proposal that's given me the first real laughter in what seems like eons.

Iris nods. "Yes, I think your reaction is realistic to say the least. But I want you to know that this is not some interoffice prank. I wouldn't put one over on you or anybody else in this office like that. Nobody would respect me if I did that. So. I know you're literally laughing this proposal out of this office and I don't blame you. But if you change your mind, you only need to tell me and I'll get word to Joseph."

I shake my head. "Max is on board with this?" I think

about last night. About how he scowled at what I was wearing, then berated me about the Nora Davis thing. About the mere fact that he summoned me out of the blue, giving me no choice but to grovel to him on his turf, on the pain of losing my job if I dared beg off. I somehow think that he doesn't want this anymore than I do.

"I don't know," Iris admits. "I'm sorry, I probably shouldn't have brought this to you, except that Joseph Kensington was adamant that I do and he was adamant that I do it this morning. And, since he's scheduled to be one of our overlords in the near future, although Max Kensington will be more of our overlord than him....I don't want to get on his bad side."

"Tell Joseph I said absolutely not. There's no scenario where I'd ever agree to marry Max Kensington. I'd rather —" I stop myself, my fingers pressed against my temples. "Look, I can barely stand being in the same room with him. Marriage? That's beyond absurd." I cross my arms, then uncross them. "And what's Joseph's angle anyway? Why is he so desperate to marry off his grandson to a complete stranger?"

"Joseph's worried sick about Max. On paper, the guy's got everything—billions in the bank, *Forbes* covers, that whole *People's* 'Most Beautiful People' nonsense. You've seen how people jump when he walks in a room. The press eats up his quotes, women throw themselves at him, men want to be him—the whole cliché. But Joseph sees what the cameras miss. There's something... hollow behind those magazine smiles. Joseph's tried everything to reach whatever's buried under all that success. Nothing's worked. So now he's grasping at straws. Hence this whole arrangement. I'm sorry you got caught in the crossfire."

So, Prince Charming has demons lurking beneath that

flawless facade. Welcome to humanity. I've been wrestling my own monsters since breakfast; except I do it from a tiny condo with a roommate, not a beachfront mansion. If his soul is as twisted as Joseph suggests, signing those marriage papers would be like locking myself in a gilded cage with a wounded animal. Hard pass.

"Please give Joseph my condolences, but my answer is a definitive no. I'm content with my life as it is, and I have no interest in marrying someone I don't know, let alone someone like Max Kensington. I understand an arranged marriage worked out for Robert and Cora on *Downton Abbey*, but they're fictional characters who had the luxury of a scriptwriter guiding their lives. I prefer to take my chances in the real world, thank you very much. So, please tell Joseph I appreciate the offer, but it's a hard no from me."

Iris nods. "I don't blame you. I'll call him. Now get back to work." She smiles and makes a shooing motion with her arms and I leave and go back to the office.

When I push open my office door, the lights are off and I find Max sprawled across the love seat, a damp towel draped over his face, his chest rising and falling with each rumbling snore.

What.the.hell.

Chapter Seven

CELESTE

I flip on the light and Max bolts upright. "Turn those fucking lights off!" he screams.

I shake my head. The audacity of this man. Max struts into my office—his office now, technically, after the merger —and has the nerve to dictate my lighting preferences? I find myself wishing for a stadium floodlight concealed in my desk. I'd love nothing more than to blind that chiseled jawline with 10,000 watts of pure spite. And while we're indulging fantasies, why not add the air horn I should stock in my desk for just such a billionaire ambush?

"Max," I say. "What are you doing here, why are the lights off and why did you just scream at me to turn the lights off in my own office?"

He lunges for his suit jacket crumpled on the floor, slams it over his face and lets out a guttural moan that sounds like it's being torn from his chest. "Kill those fucking lights right now," he hisses through clenched teeth, "or I swear to God I'll drag myself down to Iris' office this second and watch your career die before lunch. One word from me is all it takes."

I go over to my desk, not making a move to turn off the lights and proceed to pore over some overdue projects. The Richards screenplay, set for a theatrical release in January, is demanding my attention. Several emails from some high-powered agents, the same agents I've submitted to several times and have rejected me, are in my inbox waiting to be answered.

"If you don't turn out that light…" Max gets off the sofa and hunts around for the light switch. His eyes are closed, so his hands are searching blindly. "Where the fuck is the switch."

"Don't you dare touch my light switch. I can't read in the dark, unlike you, since you're apparently a vampire. An emotional vampire, that is." I jab my finger toward the door, my hand trembling slightly. "Go haunt some Michelin-starred restaurant or whatever corner of the universe you usually terrorize. This office—my office—is off-limits to you. Get out."

He somehow finds the light switch and turns off the lights. I go over to the light switch and turn it right back on. "I said leave."

"Would you shut the fuck up," he says, turning off the light again. "I need to talk to you and I need it dark."

I cross my arms in front of me and tap my foot. So now he's bossing me in my own office. It apparently wasn't enough to humiliate me in the at The Centurion, an event that still has the office tongues wagging even if it didn't - yet- result in my unceremonious departure from Dream-scape. But now he has to drive across town to invade my space. I'm now thisclose to calling security. And I would, except there's a tiny voice that's telling me that I need to hear him out. If I want to keep my job, I need to calm down.

We battle over the light switch for what feels like an eternity until Max's hand clamps down on mine with crushing force, pinning it against the wall. That contact - Max's hand gripping my wrist - suddenly makes my entire body jolt like I'd been struck by lightning. Every nerve ending is suddenly, violently alive. I hate this. I hate how my pulse hammers in my throat, how I can't draw a full breath with him this close. His face hovers inches from mine, jaw clenched, those impossibly long eyelashes still pressed tightly together. The heat radiating between us is unbearable. My knees nearly buckle as a white-hot ache spreads through my core, my body betraying me completely as desire floods every inch of me.

My throat closes. I can't breathe, let alone speak. His peppermint breath hits my face in hot waves, and I'm seized with a violent urge to sink my teeth into his lower lip, to invade his mouth with my tongue, to consume that goddamn mint taste straight from the source. His eyes remain squeezed shut, like he's bracing for impact, and the space between us crackles with something dangerous— primal attraction or pure hatred, I can't tell which. The distinction blurs as electricity shoots through me. My body betrays me, molten heat flooding my core, while my mind screams in protest. I want to hate this. I need to hate this.

"Leave the fucking light off," he spits, teeth grinding like tectonic plates. The words hit me with physical force—a slap across my face. My stomach plummets as if I've missed a step in the dark. This magnetic attraction I'd been feeling —this electric current I thought was crackling between us— evaporates into nothing. Just my pathetic imagination. Again. Heat floods my cheeks as humiliation burns through me, acid-sharp, dissolving whatever gossamer thread had momentarily connected us.

"I won't," I say. "The light stays on and you'll leave before I call security."

"The light goes OFF!" He slams his palm against the switch with such violence that the wall shudders. The room plunges into darkness, but not before I catch a glimpse of his face—eyes clenched so tightly that the skin around them has gone white, jaw locked, a vein pulsing at his temple. My stomach drops as realization hits me like a physical blow. Those aren't the eyes of someone annoyed or angry. Those are the eyes of someone trying desperately not to scream.

"Okay, okay," I finally say. "I'll leave the light off."

"Thank you," he mumbles, then collapses onto the couch. The cold rag trembles against his face as he presses it there. My stomach knots. What an idiot I've been. All this time, I thought his insistence on darkness was just another power play—the spoiled heir making demands because he could. But seeing him now, curled like something hunted, I recognize it. Mom after her third round of chemo, her fingers clawing at bedsheets, voice breaking as she begged me to "kill that light, please Celeste, it's like knives." And I've been doing this to him. Deliberately flooding his space with brightness. Using against him the very thing that once tortured someone I love.

I sit down in one of my chairs. "Is there anything I can bring you?" I ask softly.

He shakes his head, then winces at the movement. "I called my doctor," he says through gritted teeth. "He wants to send a nurse over with the Triptan, but it's like throwing a water balloon at a forest fire. When the pain gets this bad —" his voice catches as he presses his palms against his temples "—I always end up in the ER with an IV drip, begging them to knock me unconscious."

"Oh. Do you get migraines a lot?" The words escape before I can stop them, my voice betraying me with its softness. A violent wave of guilt crashes over me for being such a bitch about the light—damn it—though not enough to make me forget he invaded my space without permission. Why the hell is he even here? My eyes burn into his face, desperately hunting for answers while my heart hammers against my ribs with pathetic, humiliating hope: maybe he came for me, maybe he's finally going to apologize for his cruelty. I swallow so hard it hurts. Right. And maybe unicorns will burst through the fucking ceiling and shower us with glitter.

He shakes his head, the motion causing him to grip the edge of the table until his knuckles blanch white. "No. Haven't had one in years. And have never had one this..." His face contorts as a fresh wave hits him, eyes squeezing shut, jaw clenched so tight a muscle jumps in his cheek. "Christ. Just put a bullet in my skull and be done with it."

I pace the length of my office, heels clicking against hardwood. The Ayana Chawinga meeting looms in my calendar—a showrunner every studio in L.A. is courting, yet somehow is interested in us. Jayden Harris's new screenplay sits half-read on my desk, already promising enough that I've dog-eared several pages. My phone blinks with unanswered calls; my inbox counter shows double digits. Yet here's Max, sprawled across my love seat with a damp washcloth over his eyes, his migraine pills nowhere in sight, making no move to leave. His cologne still hangs in the air between us. I watch the slow rise and fall of his chest and bite my lip, caught between wanting to smooth his furrowed brow and needing to shove him out the door.

I finally clear my throat. "Um, when will your nurse be here with your meds?"

"She's not fucking coming, I'm going straight to the hospital," he says. "Listen, I need to tell you why I'm here. I need to get this out before I mercifully pass out from the pain. Because when it gets this bad, I usually do pass out, but I need to get to the hospital before that happens. Let me get this out and then I'll call my chopper to take me over to UCLA."

"A chopper? Where will a chopper land?"

"On the roof of your building. My pilot's standing by for clearance. The pain—Christ, it's like someone's drilling through my skull with a jackhammer. I need UCLA's migraine unit now. Every second we waste, I can feel another piece of my brain being shredded. I can barely see straight anymore."

"Fine," I say, crossing my arms. "Just tell me why you're here, and I'll point you to your helicopter." My pulse throbs in my throat. Something in his words—something I don't want to acknowledge—makes me brace myself for impact. The realization that his words could hurt me comes as an unwelcome surprise. When did I start caring what this arrogant man thinks? One minute I want to slap him, the next I'm fighting the urge to remember how his cologne smelled last night at dinner. I need space to untangle whatever *this* is.

His words hit me like a physical blow. "Don't take my granddad's offer. Please." He runs a hand through his thick dark hair, not meeting my eyes. "I came here thinking we could talk this through, but I just—I can't right now." His voice drops. "I needed to make sure you understood. Under no circumstances should you accept what he's proposing." Then he delivers the final cut, each word measured and cool. "I think we both know that we're like two cats in a bag and should avoid each other from now on." The air between us seems to solidify, pressing down on my lungs until I can barely breathe.

I lift my chin, the sting of rejection catching me off guard. Hours ago, I would have laughed at the mere suggestion of seeing Max again. Then his fingers circled my wrist as I reached for the light switch, and something shifted. A current ran from that point of contact straight to my chest, leaving a trail of warmth I can still feel. Now his insistence that we never cross paths again feels like a slap—unexpected and far more painful than it should be.

"Don't worry," I say, steadying my voice. "That offer was so absurd I nearly choked laughing when Iris mentioned it." The space between us feels like winter. I force myself to ask, "Is that why you're here?" I swallow the hope rising in my throat—the childish wish that he came to apologize, to make things right. But I see the truth in his eyes. Max Kensington dragged himself here in agony when he should be in a hospital bed, just to ensure I wouldn't accept his grandfather's proposal. As if I would marry him for any amount. Still, something in my chest tightens at how desperately he wants to avoid me.

"Yes," he says. "What other reason would I have for being here?" The words hit me like a physical blow. He's struggling to breathe, each exhale a pained hiss between clenched teeth, his features twisted into something I barely recognize. "I need to get to your roof. My helicopter's coming to take me to the hospital. I appreciate you crushing my grandfather's hopes, by the way."

He struggles out of the office and I flick the light back on. I should be relieved. This morning I'd been mentally rehearsing my exit speech, imagining my career obituary spreading across Hollywood in hushed whispers. Now I've dodged that particular bullet.

Yet as I trace my finger over the spot on my arm where Max touched me, the victory feels strangely empty. My pulse quickens at the memory. I shake my head. I'll return to my routine, my sensible life. Marry Max? Ridiculous. Not for all the beachfront property in Malibu. Still, as I sit down to catch up on my projects, I find myself wondering what his kitchen looks like in the morning light, how his voice might sound in the morning, sleepy and unguarded. The man's impossible—arrogant, demanding, cold. Yet something about him lingers on my skin like expensive cologne.

I wish I could wash it away.

I can't.

Chapter Eight

CELESTE

Joseph got the message that I would not be marrying his grandson Max, not for $250,000, not for a million, not for all the tea in China.

But things change when I see my mother. She resides in a modest two-bedroom apartment in Palm, a working-class area of Los Angeles, with my sister, Lexi, a sophomore at UCLA. Lex has just been accepted into the Film and Television BA program at UCLA, with the ambitious goal of pursuing a master's degree. Her ultimate aspiration is to become the fourth woman to win an Oscar for directing, following in the footsteps of her idols, Kathryn Bigelow, Chloé Zhao, and Jane Campion. Throughout the history of the Academy Awards, it was striking that only three women had ever won the prestigious directing award.

And I'm certain that Lex would one day join that elite group.

"Hey, Mom," I say as I enter the dingy apartment with the worn carpeting and moldy ceilings, which is all she can afford, especially right now. She's sitting in her easy chair in the living room, sleeping in front of the TV. I join her, placing my hand on hers. Her skin feels cold to the touch, as if her circulation isn't working properly. She's lost a significant amount of weight, possibly around 20 pounds or more, weight she can't afford to lose. Her scalp is now completely bald, and she wears a scarf to cover it up.

My beautiful mother has transformed into a shadow of her former self. Seeing her shatters my heart. However, I remain steadfast in my belief that she will overcome this challenge. Her cancer was diagnosed in Stage 3, which is not the most best stage, but it's not the worst either. She has a good chance of survival, with a 80% chance of recovery. I was determined that my mother wouldn't be one of the 20% who don't make it through at this stage of cancer.

She smiles weakly. "Celeste," she says. "I'm so glad to see you." Then, she closes her eyes, wraps her blanket tighter around her, and drifts back to sleep.

Lexi emerges from her room. "Hey, Celeste," she says to me. Then, she gestures towards Mom. "She can't go back to work," she explains. "She wants to, but she can't. Her doctors have advised her to rest as much as possible to allow her body to heal."

"I understand," I reply. "I'll just keep giving you money every month like I've been doing and you and Mom will be fine." Since Mom fell ill and lost her job, things have been really tight. She lacked savings, and the rent for this apartment is $2,500 per month. Although it's an extremely modest two-bedroom apartment that has lots of issues, this is Los Angeles, and $2,500 per month doesn't go far. I've been struggling to help them cover rent, utilities and food, in addition to my own mortgage and expenses. However, if I have to do it, I will.

Lexi shakes her head. "Sis, we genuinely appreciate your

help. Believe me, we do. But I need to drop out of UCLA." She lowers her head. "My job has offered me a position in their restaurant management program. I can go into management training, earning $25 per hour while in training instead of my current $18 per hour. And I'll be working full-time instead of part-time. Then I can jump into management, starting out at $70,000 a year. I need to take this opportunity, Celeste." She motions to Mom. "We can't afford for me not to."

Lexi currently works as a hostess at the Mastro's Ocean Club, a renowned fine-dining restaurant located on the beach in Malibu. While she's in school, she works part-time. This job enables her to contribute to the cost of rent, food, and utilities, but it barely makes a dent in her tuition, which stands at $13,000 annually. While it may not be astronomical, it certainly isn't affordable. Fortunately, Lex has always been a driven student and has qualified for numerous scholarships.

I blink in disbelief. I can't believe what I'm hearing. "Lex, you can't do that," I say. "You have big dreams and goals. You've wanted to be a movie director since you were five years old."

I recall the days when she was a young child, directing our parents and me in her own self-written plays. Even then, she displayed exceptional talent. Being a movie director was her sole aspiration from the time she was a kid, and now she's telling me she wants to abandon film school for a restaurant management program?

"I understand, Celeste, but UCLA is a luxury we can't afford. I need a full-time income, not a part-time one, and we simply can't afford my school expenses anymore. I know I'm on scholarship, but-"

"But what? You know how competitive film school is.

You'll want to get back in, and they won't save a place for you," I shake my head. "I can't let you do this, Lex. You'll regret it for the rest of your life. Every time the Oscars comes on in the future, your heart will break because you're not up there yourself accepting that statuette."

"Celeste, we have to be realistic," she says. "There's nothing wrong with restaurant management, especially for a place like Mastro's. It's a beautiful place, and when I become a manager, I can make six figures."

I sigh. "Lexi, there's nothing wrong with managing a restaurant. I mean, I hear it's a beyond-stressful job with long hours, lots of people complaining, and you have to know numbers and be able to be firm but fair with all your staff. Running a restaurant doesn't look like fun when I watch *Kitchen Nightmares*. It looks like a nightmare just like the title says. But none of that is the point. The point is, you're turning your back on your dream."

I know about dreams dying. God, do I know. But I can't think about that now. This isn't about me. It's about Lexi and Mom. Lexi still has a chance. Me? Every rejection letter is another shovelful of dirt on the grave of my screenwriting career. But Lexi is ALIVE with possibility. She HAS to make it. If I have to bleed myself dry, if I have to marry the devil himself, if I have to sacrifice every last thing I am—she will get what I couldn't. She has to. She HAS to.

Lexi takes a deep breath. "Celeste, I didn't want to tell you this. I didn't want to worry you, but-"

I brace myself. Lexi is serious now, something she rarely is.

"Go on," I say.

Lexi's hand trembles as she pulls the envelope from the stack of mail. The red stamp across the front screams before I even open it. Eviction. The paper burns in my fingers, each typed word a hammer blow. Thirty days. My throat closes. I've been draining my account every month, eating ramen for dinner, canceling my phone insurance—and for what? The landlord might as well have signed it in our blood.

Of course this happened. Mom hasn't earned a dime since her diagnosis in January. The emergency fund vanished by March. Now she's juggling rent on her two-bedroom in Palm while Lexi's textbooks pile up on the counter next to unpaid electric bills. Even before cancer, they were just one missed paycheck away from homelessness.

I can't afford to do more than I've been doing. I've been giving every extra penny to Mom and Lex, but it's not enough.

It's not right. Not after everything. Mom's hands used to bleed from cleaning rich people's bathrooms all day before heading to the Wal-Mart store for the night shift. I still remember her soaking those raw fingers in ice water at 2 AM, whispering "it's worth it" when she caught me watching from the hallway. She later worked three jobs at the same time - as a Denny's waitress, a Wal-Mart checker and a medical transcriptionist. She worked her fingers to the bone to make sure Lexi and I had everything we needed. Dad's been gone since the skiing accident, and she never complained once. Now I can't keep her afloat when she needs me?

And if I fail them, the consequences will ripple beyond just Mom. Lexi's future hangs in the balance too.

"No," I say. "You're not quitting school. I'll figure it out."

"Celeste, you can't. You've been giving us all you can give for the past nine months. You can't give anymore unless you want to move in here. And, no offense, I love ya, sis, but there's no room for you here."

And there's not room in my condo either. I'm buying a two-bedroom in Claremont, and I'm only making my mortgage with the help of my best friend, Olivia.

I suddenly realize I might not have a choice. I think about the offer to marry Max Kensington in exchange for $250,000. I'd only have to stay married for a year to get that money.

Why I was the one chosen for this, I don't know.

What I do know is I need to take that offer.

I hope and pray it's still on the table.

"Lex, don't worry," I say. "Don't do anything until I talk to you next. Don't tell the Mastro people you'll be a part of their restaurant management training program and certainly don't inform UCLA you're dropping out. Okay? Promise me you'll do those things. Promise me, Lexi."

She nods. "Okay. I'll promise you. But what are you going to do, Celeste?"

I take a deep breath. "Something I might regret." Then I shake my head. "No. I won't regret anything that'll keep you guys in this apartment and you in school." I kiss her on the cheek and hug her. "It's going to be okay."

I pray I'm telling the truth.

Chapter Nine

MAX

"What the fuck?" The words escape my lips as my phone screen illuminates with a most unwelcome email from my granddad, arriving like an unwanted visitor the day after my hospital discharge. I was only at UCLA Medical for twenty-four miserable hours—just long enough for the nurses to thread an IV into my arm and push that familiar cocktail of Toradol that makes the jackhammer behind my eyes finally stop. When the neurologist suggested additional tests, I waved him off with my discharge papers already in hand. The Kensington-Dreamscape acquisition documents sit in a leather portfolio on my desk, each page requiring my signature in blue ink—the kind of work that defines a movie studio CEO's existence and doesn't pause for something as inconvenient as a debilitating migraine.

But there it is in my inbox, my grandfather's message demanding I meet with him and Celeste to "hammer out the terms of our impending nuptial agreement." Fuck. I slam my fist against the desk, making my coffee slosh over the rim. The words blur as I squint at the screen, that familiar vice-grip tightening around my skull, those goddamn sparkles creeping in at the corners. So much for thinking the migraine is gone for good. But no. Not today. Not right now. Mind over matter, forget about the pain.

Finalize marriage details with Celeste? What the hell? When I walked out of Dreamscape yesterday, we had an understanding. Zero marriage. Zero announcements. Zero social media. And definitely no exclusive with *Vanity Fair* magazine, which apparently Granddad is pushing for in this email—"someone's going to get the story, might as well be *Vanity Fair*." He's acting like I never spoke to Celeste at all, like she didn't literally laugh in Iris's face when this ridiculous idea came up. As she damn well should have.

Fuck! My chest constricts like I'm being crushed by a boa constrictor. This marriage can't happen. It just can't. Every morning I'd wake up, see that copper hair spread across the pillow next to mine, and feel another hairline fracture in the walls I've spent twenty-two years building. I've never let anyone see what's behind those walls. Not once. And now I'm supposed to let this woman—this stranger—live inside my house? Inside my head? My fist clenches. The nearest drywall suddenly looks inviting.

No. I flex my fist, then release it. Another trip to UCLA with a fractured hand isn't what I need right now. The X-ray techs know me by name. Christ, I'm already drowning after one day out of commission. My inbox has exploded, the Chen Chinese distribution deal is hanging by a thread, and Spielberg's people keep calling about tomorrow's dinner. Three of my execs are circling like sharks with their pet projects, all needing eight-figure greenlight decisions. The marketing team's blowing up my phone about budget approvals for the Scorsese picture—the one everyone's already whispering "Best Picture" about. And somewhere in this mess, there's a quarterly report that the board expects on their desks by Friday.

And now Granddad's goddamn summoned me tonight for his half-baked matchmaking scheme with Celeste Jenkins. Fucking perfect. Because running a studio doesn't already devour every second of my existence like some ravenous beast. I had to reschedule lunch with Selena Farley —the Selena Farley—who's sitting on scripts that would make Scorsese weep. All so I can spend an hour pummeling Steve, my six-foot canvas punching bag, until my knuckles bleed through the wraps. If I don't beat something lifeless into shreds first, I swear to God I'll launch that dinner table through Granddad's bay window the moment he utters the word "marriage."

I storm through the Patrician Club's glass doors. The doorman's greeting dies in his throat. Familiar faces—trainers, members, even the smoothie bar girl who usually waves —avert their eyes as I pass. My reflection in the weight room mirrors shows why: jaw clenched, nostrils flared, eyes narrowed to slits. The crowd around the boxing ring parts without a word. They've seen this look before. They know what it means. And right now, it means Steve is about to get exactly what's coming to him.

I spend an hour destroying Steve with every punch and kick I can muster. My screams echo off the walls of the private room the club reserved for me and Steve, and I'm grateful no one else can hear my unhinged howling. By the time I'm done, it's a miracle the training dummy hasn't collapsed into a heap. Sweat pours down my face, my knuckles throb, my throat burns raw, but the rage has subsided enough that I probably won't make a scene at Granddad's tonight—which was the whole point of this session. Still, this helplessness, this lack of control... I never deal with these feelings in my normal life. That's what really fuels this rage. No one asked what I wanted. No one cared. Now this woman—this gorgeous, infuriating woman I wish I'd never met—is about to completely derail my life, and I have absolutely no say in the matter.

After showering, I pull on my Armani suit, yanking the sleeves straight before hammering through the buttons. The Stefano Ricci wing-tips wait by the door—expensive as hell but worth every cent. Back at the office, my heart rate's finally normal after granddad's bombshell email. Five o'clock deadline. Shit. Usually I'm here until ten, minimum. The pressure starts drilling behind my eyes. Goddamn it, not now. I grab the beta-blocker the hospital forced on me after last night's episode, dry-swallowing it. No time for this migraine crap. I crack my neck, square my shoulders at the screen. Work will fix this. Work.

There's no getting out of this, not if I want to avoid the whole "sue granddad for turning my shareholders against me for no reason" scenario. So, at 5 o'clock sharp, I power down my laptop and head for Granddad's Malibu estate. The document in my briefcase contains my non-negotiables for this sham marriage with Celeste.

I tap my fingers against the steering wheel, reminding myself that in any business deal, leverage matters. Mine has evaporated like morning fog. Granddad wants this wedding, and what Granddad wants, Granddad gets. I curse under my breath. Four years as CEO, and I never bothered to secure my position with the major shareholder groups or gather the kind of information that I could use to blackmail those SOBs into not ousting me whenever Granddad gets a fucking wild hair. Now I'm cornered, with only a flimsy list of demands as my shield.

I get to his house and there she is—Celeste—and something in me ignites. Her copper hair is twisted up, exposing the elegant curve of her neck. The black dress she's wearing might be modest for dinner with the grandparents, but against her skin it transforms into something else entirely. The subtle makeup around her eyes makes the blue more intense, like warning signals I'm choosing to ignore. My fingers twitch at my sides. I clench my jaw against unwelcome thoughts, against the urge to pull her aside and taste those lips until neither of us can think straight. No rainbow boots tonight. I miss them—miss how she wore them into Centurion with quiet defiance, past every A-lister and power player in Hollywood, not giving a good goddamn what anyone thought.

Her eyes lock with mine, tight-lipped and impatient. The message couldn't be clearer if she'd written it on her forehead: mutual misery, mutual desire to escape. I give a slight nod in silent agreement. Yes, let's power through this nightmare and be done.

"Max," she says, her voice as cold as the marble beneath our feet. "Your grandparents are waiting on the back porch. I only arrived moments ago." She gestures toward the uniformed woman hovering nearby, granddad's longtime maid, Ingrid. "Ingrid let me in." Her voice drops to a whisper. "This feels surreal. Are you sure your grandfather isn't filming an episode of *Punk'd?*"

Her confusion cuts through my annoyance. I catch myself almost smiling. "That show's been dead for twenty years. We're both screwed." I roll my shoulders back. "Welcome to hell, roomie." I track her eyes as she takes in the Italian Bianco marble terrace beyond the French doors. The space could fit a hundred people for dinner, easy. The infinity pool drops off into the Pacific like a knife edge. *Back porch indeed.* Jesus.

The two of us walk out on the terrace where Granddad and Nana are waiting for us. Granddad already has his go-to drink - an Old Fashioned, a drink that makes me want to hurl because it's too damned sweet. Thank God he also has *my* go-to drink at the ready - a 60-year-old Macallan scotch, double-casked and smoother than silk. Granddad always brings out the good scotch only on special occasions and when he wants to impress and it occurs to me that Granddad must really want to impress Celeste because he couldn't care less about impressing me.

Celeste wraps her arms around Granddad like she belongs to us, then does the same with Nana. What the actual hell? This is my grandfather—the man who fired Thompson for a congratulatory back-pat after we landed the Westridge account—letting some stranger hug him. And Nana? Christ. The woman stands like she's balancing a dictionary on her head, keeps her hair yanked back so tight it could double as a facelift, and has a stare that's made VPs forget their own names. Now she's grinning at Celeste like she's the golden child. These people drilled into me that a firm handshake was the pinnacle of human contact, and here they are, practically adopting this woman.

I shake my head, watching Granddad laugh at something Celeste says. The man who once lectured me for an hour about wasting five dollars on lottery tickets is now throwing a fortune at a woman he barely knows. If somebody told me that aliens abducted my actual grandfather and left this imposter in his place, I wouldn't be surprised. The man who taught me about sound investments and rational decision-making is suddenly throwing a quarter-million dollars at a stranger to solve a problem that doesn't even exist.

"Max," Granddad booms. "Have a seat. Ruthie and I

are just kicking back, enjoying some Old-Fashioneds and we have your favorite Scotch, neat like you like it. Celeste, what would you like to drink?"

"Um, a Perrier if you have it," she says, and my stomach plummets. Jesus Christ. No alcohol? Is she kidding me? Every Kensington since the dawn of time has practically bathed in scotch. She'll stick out like a teetotaling thumb at our holiday gatherings where champagne flows before noon.

I need Granddad Joe to see this girl is wrong—dead wrong—for the family. I scan his face for a flicker of disapproval, a twitch, anything. Nothing. He's beaming at her like she's the second coming. My hands clench. I need an escape hatch from this nightmare, and I need it now.

I'll have to destroy her credibility myself. Make her slip up. Maybe she'll use the wrong fork, or say something ridiculous about the Monet in the hallway. Maybe she's a Democrat and that'll come out in the inevitable political discussion that always erupts after the first course. My mind races through possibilities, each more desperate than the last. The problem is, I know nothing about this woman except that I want her gone. Tonight.

Jack returns to the terrace with drinks—sparkling water for Celeste, my usual scotch neat for me. The amber liquid catches the light as I take a sip, the sixty-year-old double casked perfection warming my throat. I scan Granddad and Nana's faces for any hint of disapproval toward my forced fiancée. A grimace? A subtle eye-roll? Nope. Instead, they're practically glowing at her, hanging on her every word. Maybe it shouldn't be such a surprise that they're acting like this with her. After all, Granddad's the mastermind who decided I should marry this woman after he talked to her for one hour in the hospital. And now he's looking at her like she's the granddaughter he always wanted.

An hour later and it's time for dinner. Granddad's personal chef Jacques—poached from a three-star Michelin in Paris for a seven-figure package—has outdone himself tonight. The spread is worth every penny: A-5 Wagyu that runs $400 a pound, swimming in Bernaise; black truffles flown in from Alba this morning; firm asparagus grown in Granddad's garden, topped with hollandaise; saffron risotto; and Maine lobster tails that my distributor usually reserves for the Four Seasons. The '08 Dom is chilling.

I check my Patek—right on schedule. I can already picture Celeste's performative disgust when the carpaccio arrives. At the Centurion, she practically delivered a TED talk on sustainable seafood when the abalone appeared. If she's one of those non-drinking, vegetarian types, that's two strikes against this arrangement. One more dealbreaker and I'm off the fucking hook.

I watch as Celeste takes a bite of the Wagyu beef, then practically swoons over the risotto. The lobster, though, she pushes around her plate without touching. Interesting. Not the full-on vegetarian I pegged her for, then. Damn. I was counting on her being one of those crystal-clutching, Mercury-retrograde-fearing types who'd clash spectacularly with Granddad. Downward dog at dawn, meditation apps, vegan diet, MAHA, the works. If she starts spouting off about solstice dancing or her chakras being blocked, Granddad would implode.

The light catches on her wrist as she reaches for her water glass—several crystal bracelets slide down her arm. I lean forward slightly. Are those just fashion accessories, or does she actually believe they channel energy? If I could just get her talking about alternative medicine or sustainable farming or trans rights or whatever, Granddad would lose it. The old man still thinks climate change is a hoax and gay marriage will bring about the apocalypse. His religion? The almighty dollar. One conversation about her rising sign, and he'd show her the door before the chocolate soufflé arrives.

I need to figure her out. Those crystal bracelets jangling on her wrist tell a story. So does the way her nose wrinkles when the lobster arrives, and how she picks at the Wagyu beef without enthusiasm. Her Prius in the driveway screams recycling bins and canvas grocery bags. If I can get her talking about billionaires paying their "fair share," Granddad might just have an aneurysm right here at the dinner table. The old man guards his portfolio like a dragon with gold.

Still, I could be reading this all wrong. Maybe those crystals are just pretty accessories, not some healing chakra bullshit. Maybe she hates lobster because she once had food poisoning. Maybe she drives a Prius because it was a good deal and she doesn't like to pay for gas. Hell, for all I know, she could be a closet libertarian who thinks our tax shelters are genius. Only one way to find out—I'll drop some bait and see if she bites. One hint of socialism and I've got my exit strategy.

I clear my throat. "So, Celeste," I say. "Ever seen *Poldark* on Netflix?"

"Oh, I love that show!" Her eyes light up instantly. "All those love triangles and period drama scandals. It's addictive."

I swirl my drink, watching the ice cubes clink against the glass. "I'm more drawn to the class commentary, actually. The way the Cornwall aristocrats crush the miners while dining on pheasant."

"God, yes," Celeste nods enthusiastically. "George

Warleggan is such a—" Her gaze darts to Granddad, and she catches herself. "Well, he'd do anything to destroy Ross. Just another greedy little... person."

I glance sideways at Granddad, suppressing a smile. She's carefully tiptoeing around calling the wealthy villain what he really is. I can see the restraint in her eyes—the unspoken critique of privilege hanging in the air between us. She spears a piece of risotto without eating it, then takes a long sip of water. I wonder what it would take to make her say what she's really thinking.

I lean forward, not letting her off the hook. "What's your take on those plotlines where the aristocratic bankers crush the working class? You know—shuttering the mines, foreclosing on owners who treat workers decently, shipping grain overseas during famines..."

Celeste's knuckles whiten around her glass. "And what happens to those who speak out? The gallows." She draws a sharp breath. "Two hundred years later and it's the same damn story, just with different costumes." Her eyes narrow as she stares into her drink. "Every Sunday night I watch those Poldark aristocrats in their stone fortresses, scheming how to squeeze another penny from people who can barely feed their children. The miners' faces covered in grime while the lords and ladies sip tea from fine china." She gives a bitter laugh. "Only Ross and Sir Francis seem to have a conscience. The rest? They're no different from today's billionaires—different century, same playbook."

Bingo! Bing-fucking-o! I catch Granddad's eye and smile. Perfect timing. He'll throw her out the door in a heartbeat after that little screed.

But he leans forward, patting Celeste's hand.

"Tell me, dear," he says, "how would you feel about a winter wedding at our place in Scotland? The castle looks

magical with snow on the turrets. The village below cele-
brates Christmas with these charming little markets—all
very Dickensian."

Damn. He must not have heard our conversation. If
he'd heard her passionate speech about aristocratic exploita-
tion in *Poldark*—her apparent favorite show—he wouldn't be
casually offering up his literal castle as a wedding venue,
he'd be putting his boot in her rear as he gives her the bum's
rush out the door. Strike one.

I stare at my grandfather. "You want us to get married at
your drafty old castle? In the dead of winter? In Scotland?"
I shake my head. "The bridesmaids will be wearing parkas
instead of dresses, and we'll have to hire polar bears as
groomsmen."

"We'll discuss it later," he says.

About fifteen minutes later, my fingers tap a restless
rhythm against the mahogany as I nurse my port. Across
the table, Celeste raises her glass of sparkling water to her
lips—again with the abstinence. Didn't she have a cabernet
that first night? The memory slips away like smoke.

Too bad Granddad wasn't paying attention to our
earlier *Poldark* conversation, but I have to keep trying, but
subtly. If Granddad catches even a whiff of sabotage, he'll
cling to her out of pure stubbornness. The old man's
contrarian streak runs deeper than the family fortune.

Over coffee, I decide to try again with Halloween,
which is less than a couple of months away. Part of me
hopes she'll interrupt with a correction—"Actually, it's
Samhain"—followed by some lecture about bonfires and
spirit communication through the thinning veil between
worlds. That'll do the trick. If she's a Wiccan, Granddad
would send her out of here on a broom. Not that I need a
lesson about Samhain. We produced a middling horror flick

about Celtic harvest rituals last year. Box office was decent, not spectacular, but enough that I can spot a potential witch from fifty paces.

"So, Celeste," I say. "Halloween." I raise my eyebrows and smile. "Do you like that holiday? Do you do costume parties or do you get a lot of trick or treaters? Do you decorate your yard with 12-foot skeletons and scarecrows?" *Do you dance naked around a bonfire while jangling a tambourine and chanting with your Wiccan friends, right after you enthusiastically took part in a drum circle?*

She sips her mug. "Actually, Halloween was one of my father's favorite holidays. He used to dress up as different movie characters every year - one year he was Freddy; the next, Jason. He's the one in the hockey mask, right?" Yes, he was, but she doesn't wait for the answer. "He was Michael Myers one year and Johnny from *The Shining* another. He was Chucky a time or two and Jigsaw a few times."

I raise an eyebrow. "Halloween *was* your father's favorite holiday?" Part of me had been hoping she'd reveal some crystal-gazing ritual or mention how Mercury retrograde affects her mood. Even a discussion of one of those barefoot meditation equinox/solstice mazes where people shuffle around looking dazed while claiming they're "grounding their energy" would have been perfect. Granddad would have written her off immediately. Instead, she's mentioned something normal—though I can't help noticing she spoke about her father as if he's gone.

She nods. "My father died in a skiing accident when I was 15." The coffee mug trembles between her fingers as her gaze drops to the table. Something in my chest tightens, but I force it away. *Remember who she is.* "My mother tried to keep our Halloween tradition going," she continues, "but the female horror villain options are pretty limited. After the third year as Carrie's mom with that awful frizzy wig, she had to admit defeat."

I chuckle softly, picturing a whole family of redheads like her. Celeste's mom must be a carbon copy. But watching her with my grandparents deflates me. She's playing it safe. At dinner, she mentions her favorite movie is *Love Actually*, gushing over Bill Nighy's aging rockstar, and suddenly Nana lights up like a Christmas tree. The two of them spend thirty minutes dissecting every Richard Curtis rom-com ever made - *Notting Hill*, *Bridget Jones Diary*, *About Time*, *Four Weddings and a Funeral*.

Then comes the inevitable *Downton Abbey* conversation. Nana practically vibrates with excitement as they debate Lady Mary's character flaws and mourn Sybil's tragic death. I stab at my potatoes, wanting to stab at my eyeballs, while they analyze the "epic love story" of Anna and Bates. When my eighty-year-old grandmother uses the word "hotter" comparing Matthew to Henry, I nearly choke on my wine.

Then the even more inevitable Travis and Taylor wedding discussion nearly drives me to self-harm with my dessert fork, but there's Nana, equally invested in what they call the "royal nuptials" of pop music and football. Even Granddad isn't immune when she rattles off Los Angeles Kings stats like a seasoned sportscaster, naming every player on that team and reciting Stanley Cup victories by year. She's good—too good. They're completely under her spell.

She steers clear of politics throughout the rest of the dinner, and Granddad surprisingly follows suit. I'm keeping that grenade pin in my pocket, though. The moment this evening becomes tiresome, I'll casually mention the latest tax proposal and watch her eyes light up with that righteous fervor I already saw a hint of at our first dinner when she lectured me about the abalone, not to mention our *Poldark* conversation. One passionate word about "equitable distrib-ution" and Granddad will practically teleport her back to that eco-friendly sardine can she drove here in. For now, I'll let the pleasant conversation continue—it's been unexpect-edly tolerable so far.

Still, I can't help myself—I need to stir things up a bit. The rainbow of stones circling her wrists catches my eye, and I lean forward. "Those crystals you're wearing, Celeste," I say, nodding toward her bracelets. "Tourmaline, citrine, amethyst, lapis... let me guess—protection, health, wisdom, and creativity? I've got a friend who swears by her chakra alignment sessions." The lie rolls off my tongue easily. No such friend exists, but if Celeste believes I'm not judgmental about people who believe in crystals, maybe she'll open up about whatever healing powers she thinks those pretty rocks possess. A little bait to draw her out.

She nods. "Yes!" And then she beams. "So you know about crystals? I never would've thought."

I smile and nod, guilt pricking at me. Her eyes light up like she's found a fellow believer in this crystal bullshit. She leans forward, her bracelets jangling against the table. The citrine, she explains, was some kind of investment in her screenwriting career. "It's for abundance," she whispers, stroking the yellow rocks like they're lottery tickets. "It hasn't paid off yet, but..." She shrugs with that blind optimism that makes me want to check my watch. Then comes the lecture: raw amethyst—"never polished, that's crucial"—for sleep. Lapis lazuli for emotions. Tourmaline as some magical disease barrier. She delivers this whole crystal manifesto with the dead seriousness of a kid showing off their science fair volcano, and I'm trapped here nodding like I give a damn.

Jackpot. The crystal conversation is gold, but something

in my gut sours. Part of me wants to mentally high-five myself
—perfect ammunition—while I watch her eyes light up. Her
hands keep moving as she rattles off which rocks supposedly
block bad vibes, boost health, spark creativity. She's leaning in
now, a curl falling over her eye, no clue she's loading my gun
for me. I open my mouth to go for the kill with questions
about tarot readings and astrological birth charts—because
of course she's had her whole astrological blueprint mapped
out by some bullshit psychic named Lady Starlight or something like that—but the words die somewhere in my throat.
What the fuck? I need this. I need her to look like an idiot.
But I just can't do it. I can't plunge that knife in and twist it,
even though it'll give me my freedom. Why?

I catch Nana and Granddad trading looks. So, they're
listening this time. And there it is—exactly what I've been
waiting for. Nana's eyebrow shoots up, her mouth pinched
tight like when she caught me sneaking out at sixteen.
Granddad's giving Celeste that empty stare, the one that
makes you feel about two inches tall. I could end this whole
mess with just a few more lines of questions. Ask her about
more New Age beliefs, then ask her about what she thinks
about taxing the wealthy and that would be all she wrote.
She'd be gone. I'd be free. Back to normal. So why the hell
am I racking my brain for something—anything—to make
her stay?

"So, you mentioned you're a screenwriter," I say,
needing her off the woo woo topics and back onto something my Granddad can relate to. "What kinds of movies
have you written?"

She lifts one shoulder. "Did I say that?" She shakes her
head. "No. I just have these screenplay ideas floating around
in my head. Nothing serious—just a silly dream I've never

actually done anything about." Her eyes flick toward my grandparents, and something crosses her face—there and gone in an instant—that makes Granddad's expression gentle. He catches my eye. We're thinking the same thing: the industry's ruthless numbers game. Thousands of hopeful scripts piling up on desks, most tossed aside after a single page. No agent, no shot.

Granddad's weathered hand covers hers, and just like that, he's in her corner again. I suspect—and I bet he does too—that Celeste has already written screenplays, already faced rejection, and can't bring herself to say it aloud. As though admitting the attempt would somehow be worse than never trying. Something tightens in my chest— sympathy mingled with guilt.

I could have sunk her with the crystal thing. Could have pulled that thread until it unraveled into her spouting about tarot cards, chakra alignment, astrological birth charts and mercury retrograde until Granddad made excuses about the late hour. By tomorrow, I'd have had an email explaining why this marriage scheme was being abandoned. Instead, I just threw her a life preserver.

The question hammers in my chest: why?

My shoulders drop before I can stop them. Damn it. She's biting her lip, and those terrace lights are making her eyes shine. I didn't sign up to marry this woman, but after what she just said about her dad and giving up on her dreams—I'm not that much of an asshole. I don't know about professional failure, but knowing what it's like to lose a parent? Oh, yeah. Can relate to that all day long. My leg bounces under the table while I think. I could easily bring up tax policy—watch her go off about billionaires paying their fair share, and this whole arrangement would implode in five minutes flat. Instead, I grab my water and take a long drink. Not tonight.

Granddad gives me that look—the one that says he's made up his mind about Celeste. Time to negotiate terms. The grandfather clock in the hallway chimes midnight. My eyes burn from staring at spreadsheets all day, and my inbox still has forty unread emails waiting for me. Unlike him, I don't have the luxury of afternoon naps and gardening breaks, so I need to go to bed soon.

I check my watch. *Let's get this over with.* I know when I've lost. At dinner, when she went on about her healing crystals, and I saw my opening—one well-placed comment would've ended this whole charade. But the words stuck in my throat. And now here we sit.

"Okay," Celeste says when Granddad prompts her to start the negotiation. The old man's eyes light up like he's spotted a weakness in a competitor's defense. This is the same shark who made Goldman Sachs' CEO cry like a little girl over fine print. He leans forward, fingers steepled, ready to go for the kill.

Meanwhile, I'm staring at Celeste's profile like an idiot instead of watching my own back. Something's changed since yesterday. That knot in my chest is gone, but now there's this other thing happening whenever she does that thing with her hair. If she looked like my last three assistants, this would be manageable. Roommates, basically. "Morning." "Coffee's ready." Done. But Christ, every time she talks I can't stop looking at her mouth. Fuck that. I need a game plan: separate wings, minimal interaction, bury myself at the office. Keep it professional enough that she sticks out the year, then we end this bullshit contract and I can breathe again.

"Celeste," Granddad says. "Go on."

"The thing is, waiting a year for the money won't work for me. I need it now." Celeste twists her watch band around her wrist. "My mom's medical bills are piling up, and my sister Lexi's talking about dropping out of UCLA to work full-time. I can't let her sacrifice her education." She swallowed hard. "That's my only motivation here. The money isn't for me—it's for them."

Granddad nods. "Okay, we can work around that. What do you need?"

"Look, I don't need that much money. Just cover my family's rent for a year—$2500 a month. That's all I'm asking. Two hundred fifty thousand is... I mean, it's way more than necessary. I couldn't possibly—"

"Oh, now," Granddad says, his eyes crinkling at the corners. He taps his cane once against the marble floor. "A young woman like you should know what she's worth. Don't sell yourself short! That quarter million? Consider it hazard pay for dealing with my grandson." He chuckles, then his expression softens. "But I hear you about your mother's condition, and your sister at UCLA. I'll cover their housing for the next two years—separate from our original agreement, of course. The quarter million stands."

"No, that's too much, that's-"

"Don't overthink this, Celeste," I say, watching her hesitate. "Two-fifty's nothing to Granddad. You deserve every penny." I can't help but shake my head at the old man's eagerness. No negotiation, no pushback—just handing over more than she even requested. Whatever his reasons for wanting this marriage, they must run deep. If she were smarter about this, she'd ask for double. Hell, the way he's acting, he'd probably toss in his vintage Rolex collection if she so much as glanced at it.

Celeste just nods. "Well. That was easy enough. I was

really nervous asking about my mother and sister being taken care of. But thank you, Joseph. I mean, you really don't have to pay me anything at all, I-"

I shoot her a look. Her eyes dart away, fingers fidgeting with the edge of her sleeve. Granddad's net worth hits $50 billion. This quarter-million? It's a rounding error. But across the table sits someone who calculates whether she can afford both gas and groceries in the same week. And now an old man she barely knows is promising her a check that could buy a house. Well, a small condo at any rate, in Nebraska somewhere. Maybe.

Granddad slides the contract across the table to her—he's already added that bit about covering her family's rent for the next two years. When she picks up the pen, I notice her fingers trembling. The scratch of ink on paper sounds like a death sentence. Christ. This is real now. I'm actually going to marry this woman I barely know, this stranger who's about to become my wife. My collar tightens around my throat, and the room shrinks around me.

The walls are closing in and there's nothing I can do.

Chapter Ten

CELESTE

I stare at my signature on Joseph's contract, the ink still glistening. My hand trembles. Marrying his grandson Max? For money? This wasn't how my life was supposed to go. But what choice did I have? The alternative was watching Lexi abandon her UCLA dreams, seeing Mom forced from her home while battling cancer. They could find somewhere cheaper, sure—if landlords would overlook an eviction record, if Mom could survive the stress of moving while on chemo. The eviction notice sitting on their kitchen counter told me everything Lexi had been hiding. Months behind on rent. Utility shutoff warnings. Why hadn't she called me sooner?

So this is my life now—becoming Mrs. Kensington for a quarter million dollars. My knees don't just wobble—they threaten to buckle entirely as I stand on the terrace, Joseph, Ruth and Max's eyes burning into me like laser sights. The man I'm about to call husband might as well be from another planet. Every glimpse of him sends electric shocks through my body: that vicious curl of his lip when he's displeased, the arctic calculation in his eyes during our ambush at the Centurion, the way his tailored shirts strain against shoulders that make my mouth go desert-dry, and that jawline—Christ—sharp enough to draw blood. I'm utterly screwed. This devastating attraction will torture me daily when we're trapped together, sharing walls, sharing air. I'll suffocate slowly. We exist in different universes—him soaring in private jets and savoring thousand-dollar wines, while I drown in student loan statements and calculate which happy hour offers the most calories per dollar.

I nod and hand the contract back to Joseph. Max narrows his beautiful green eyes, regarding me coolly, one hand resting on his chin. Of course he doesn't have to sign anything—I'm the only one being paid. Paid! The distinction matters; this isn't sex work because I don't plan on sleeping with Max. Ever. Though I'll probably fantasize about it while exiled to some forgotten wing of his mansion. Not that he'd want me anyway. I've studied his type through late-night Google searches: A-list actresses whose faces grace magazine covers, supermodels who glide down red carpets while flashbulbs pop. Women whose names everyone knows. Meanwhile, I'm lucky if I accidentally photobomb someone else's picture. No wealth, no class, no fame—nothing that would catch the eye of a man who dates exclusively from *People's* "Most Beautiful" list.

"Uh," I say, my voice shaking. "So, what happens now?"

Joseph rubs his hands together, grinning like he's just solved world hunger. Meanwhile, my stomach plummets through the floor. Olivia's face flashes in my mind—how is she supposed to manage the condo? I can't dump my mortgage on her, which means I'll be keep paying it. And Mom and Lexi? God. Lexi will want to sign me up for electroshock therapy and I can already see Mom's expression, that mix of concern and disappointment she perfected when I was twelve. "Marrying a stranger? Celeste, honey, are you having some kind of breakdown?" Maybe I am. Maybe Lexi's eviction notice short-circuited my brain. And then there's Tally, my other best friend that I met through Soul Cycle several years ago. I now have to tell her I'm selling myself like some modern-day courtesan. They're all going to want me involuntarily committed.

What have I done?

"Well," Joseph says, leaning forward with a glint in his eye. "Three months. That's all I need. My castle in Scotland is just sitting there waiting for an occasion like this. I've got people—the best people—on speed dial. One call to my wedding planner, and we'll have the works: Wolfgang Puck catering, Alicia Crawford with a camera, the whole nine yards. Everyone who matters will clear their schedules for this. Spielberg's tied up shooting, but Marty and Christopher will be there. And you know Leo and Oprah—they never miss these things." He taps the table decisively. "Trust me, when the trades get wind of this guest list, they'll be falling over themselves for an invitation."

I gasp like a goldfish flopping on carpet. Black spots dance at the edges of my vision as the chandelier above starts to swirl. A panic attack. I'll need a paper bag soon to blow into to calm me down. I mean, Martin Scorsese? Christopher Nolan? Oprah Winfrey herself? Alicia Crawford, photographer to the stars, aiming her camera at my panic-stricken face? Wolfgang Puck? All within two months? At some drafty castle in Scotland? Just hours ago I was scraping congealed Spaghetti-Os from the can with a plastic fork, and now I'm supposed to walk down the aisle with Leonardo DiCaprio in the front row?

"Media strategy is critical," Joseph continues, completely

missing my hyperventilation. "We'll offer *Vogue* or *Vanity Fair* exclusivity—keeps the gutter press like *Star* and *In Touch* from fabricating nonsense. Though expect helicopters regardless. I'll have *TMZ* and *Page Six* outbidding each other for digital rights. As for the musical guest—" The room tilts sideways. *Please don't say Taylor Swift.* They'll need to shock my heart back to life right here on his imported marble. "— I'm thinking Olivia Rodrigo, Chappell Roan or Ed Sheeran if those other two aren't available. I'll secure one of them."

I nod while Max stares at the ceiling, his jaw twitching with impatience. "Three months? That's it? Don't these Hollywood weddings usually require, like, a year of planning?" My stomach knots as I try to process the timeline. Seven days ago, Max Kensington was just a name in *Variety* headlines and industry gossip—the CEO with the golden touch, beautiful face and glacial personality. I'd heard the whispers about his revolving door of model girlfriends and impossible standards. The assistants who quit in tears. The directors who wouldn't work with him twice. Now I'm initialing a marriage contract with the man. If someone had predicted this a week ago, I would have snorted coffee through my nose.

"Planning for a year would be a luxury we can't afford right now."

Max rolls his eyes. "In this town, Granddad's word is law. Anyone not filming on location that day will show up, guaranteed. Hell, some will fly in from active sets just to be there." He lifts his hands, fingers curling into air quotes. "To witness Hollywood's most eligible and ungettable bachelor finally captured."

The moment his grandparents look away, he jams his finger down his throat in an exaggerated gag. Something about this powerful CEO—this billionaire who graces countless magazine covers—making such a childish gesture breaks through my anxiety, and I laugh despite myself. It's exactly what I need amid the chaos swirling around me. "God, those tabloid stories," he mutters. "As if these journalists have any clue why I'm single. They don't know me, don't care to. Just chasing easy headlines."

Joseph puts his arm around me. "You probably feel shell-shocked right now. You'll be fine."

It hits me like a freight train why Joseph's check has so many zeros. This isn't just twelve months of tolerating Max's cold shoulder. I'm expected to transform into some poised socialite who can chat up Spielberg over canapés without hyperventilating into a paper bag between courses. That awkward feeling at the Centurion? Just the appetizer. The main course of humiliation is still being plated.

I stare at my signature on the contract, the ink a permanent reminder of my impulsivity. No attorney reviewed it. No one advised me. Just Celeste, diving headfirst into the deep end as usual.

My *Google* search on Joseph Kensington revealed the truth behind that gentle smile and those kind eyes—the man's left a trail of crushed opponents in his wake. If I tried to back out now, he'd unleash legal hell. I vaguely remember something from Business Law 101 about contracts against public policy being void, but that's a flimsy defense against Kensington's army of attorneys billing $1500 an hour. I'd drain every penny fighting him, leaving nothing for Mom's medical bills or Lexi's tuition. My only option would be Tony Callahan, Esq., whose face I know not from *Harvard Law Review* but from bus stop benches across Los Angeles.

Max is studying me and narrowing his eyes, his beautiful

and elegant manicured hand on his chin. He finally shakes his head.

"Granddad," he says with a sigh, running a hand through his hair. "Let's dial this back. I'm not looking for some royal spectacle here. Fine—Crawford can shoot it, and *Variety* can have their exclusive. But Thornewood? In Scotland? We're talking late November at the earliest. We'll be getting married in the freezing rain. St. John's Cathedral for the ceremony, my house for the reception. Small gathering, just the people who matter. We keep it quiet—Wolfgang caters, everyone signs NDAs, and the press finds out when we decide they should. JFK Jr. managed to pull off a secret wedding, and so can we."

With Max's words, the boa constrictor that was squeezing my mid-section loosens and I can breathe again. Maybe I wouldn't be rushed to the ER with a panic attack after all.

I decide to go to the restroom to freshen up my makeup and make sure nothing is smudged, because I swear to God, I was ready to cry when Joseph started talking about the gigantic celebrity wedding he had planned for us. Maybe tears didn't actually fall, but they were ready to, so I hope my mascara stayed in place. "Would you excuse me," I say. "I need to…"

"First door to your left," Max says, his voice softening slightly. I nod and follow his directions, pushing open a heavy mahogany door to discover a bathroom bigger than my entire apartment. Gleaming marble countertops stretch beneath a mirror framed in gold, while a freestanding tub that could fit four people dominates the center of the room. Even the toilet looks expensive, with some kind of electronic panel I'm afraid to touch. Everything is pristine white with gold accents—like something out of a magazine spread rather than a space where actual humans are supposed to perform bodily functions.

The mirror shows a passable reflection. Not stunning—my foundation has settled into the creases beside my nose, mascara flecks dust my under-eyes, and my lipstick has retreated to a thin line around the edges of my mouth. But what do I expect? It's now 2 AM and I need to feel my mattress beneath my body soon.

I walk back out and hear Max and Joseph arguing.

"Granddad," he says, his voice tight with frustration. "She's not some debutante you can parade around. The woman makes sixty grand a year developing other people's stories. She shops at Target. She probably thinks Givenchy is a type of cheese." He rakes his fingers through his hair. "You can't just throw her to the wolves and expect her to know which fork to use when Spielberg shows up."

"Steven probably can't make it. He's on location."

"You know what I'm trying to say. She's drowning. I watched her while you were talking about the guest list and Ed Sheeran performing—her fingers kept twisting that little silver ring she wears, and I could see the panic in her eyes. The girl was practically hyperventilating. She's got two options right now: walk away from this whole arrangement or have a complete breakdown. Neither scenario works for anyone. You'd drag her through legal hell if she bailed. But mark my words, she's right on that edge."

Joseph murmurs something I can't quite catch, and I clear my throat to let them know I'm here. Earlier, when Joseph started rattling off his guest list—Scorsese, DiCaprio, even suggesting Ed Sheeran or Olivia Rodrigo as wedding performers—my eyes must have widened to the size of dinner plates.

Max noticed. He jumped in, told his grandfather we

wanted something smaller, more intimate. I'd call it sweet if this weren't all pretend. My hands still tremble at the thought of Olivia Rodrigo singing while I walk down an aisle toward a man who I'm being paid to marry. Joseph missed my panic entirely, but Max caught it. Though I doubt it's about me—he's probably using my discomfort as cover for his own reluctance. What guy wants his grandfather planning his wedding, even a fake one?

Joseph smiles when I return to the terrace. Max doesn't meet my eyes, but that's fine. I'm feeling calmer now. Still, it's overwhelming—marrying a man I barely know. Even if the wedding won't be the circus Joseph envisions, I'm definitely in over my head. This marriage to Max will likely become a spectacle: my privacy invaded, paparazzi cameras thrust in my face, my name dragged through social media mud. It's inevitable when you're marrying Max Kensington —three-time *People* magazine "Most Beautiful" honoree, a man whose wealth and power have people either kissing his ass or scurrying away in fear. Last night's *Google* search confirmed he's considered the most eligible bachelor in town. I won't measure up, and the trolls will tear me apart. Yet another detail I failed to consider.

Joseph hands me and Max a glass of champagne and he raises his glass in a toast. "To my grandson Max and the beautiful Celeste. May the two of you be as happy for 60 years as Ruth and me." Then he winks as I raise my glass with a shaking hand. I glance at Max, who's looking uncomfortable. He's not into this. Neither am I.

But yet, here we are.

Stuck with each other.

And now I have to break the news to the people I love.

Before social media does it for me.

Chapter Eleven

CELESTE

I text Olivia, Tally, and Lexi: "911 EMERGENCY MEETING TONIGHT. WINE REQUIRED." I need to tell them face-to-face about Max before *TMZ* breaks the story. We're aiming for a JFK Jr. level of secrecy for the wedding, though that comparison makes me shudder. Besides, he had it easy—no TikTok, no Instagram, no rabid comment sections dissecting his every move. Max doesn't have that luxury. Just this morning, instead of reviewing scripts, I fell down another Max Kensington hashtag rabbit hole. The fan accounts are terrifying—some women analyzing the way he dots his i's in autographs, other women creating elaborate conspiracy theories about which coffee order might indicate his relationship status. One post had 50,000 likes just because he wore navy instead of black. It's only a matter of time before some eagle-eyed superfan spots us together and the headlines start. I need my people to hear this from me, not from their phones.

The rooftop bar perches right over the Pacific, catching the last golden light of a cool September evening. My friends arrive in sequence as the clock hits six, each wrapped in those barely-there cardigans that pass for winter wear in Los Angeles. We claim a table outside—the air carries just enough bite to make the first sip of wine feel warming. Perfect backdrop for what I'm about to tell them: I'm marrying Max Kensington. The sun will sink into the ocean, and my bombshell will explode across our table.

"So," Tally says, leading the way. "Where's the fire?" Tally—short for Tallulah—carries a name inspired by Demi Moore's daughter, not Tallulah Bankhead as older people often assume. Her mother had been obsessed with the Demi Moore back in the day. Tally embodies the free spirit Bankhead was known for, minus the legendary actress's "sleep with anyone that moves" reputation. With her jet-black natural hair now streaked in vibrant colors, bright blue eyes rimmed in charcoal, and signature red lips, Tally turns heads even on her bare-faced days. A tattoo artist of remarkable talent, her beauty could easily outshine the supermodels Max typically favors.

Lexi tucks a strand of blonde hair behind her ear. "I've got a short film due tomorrow that's barely half-edited, so this better be good." Her look says it all—same face as mine, different destiny. She's a film school prodigy, while I'm nothing but a corporate shill. I'll tell her about marrying Max for money, but as a sacrifice for Mom's medical bills, not the truth: I'm doing it so Lexi won't quit UCLA to manage some restaurant. Once Mom recovers enough to work, Medi-Cal disappears, and the insurance vultures circle. By then, I'll have my quarter-million.

Olivia bursts in, tossing her knockoff Louis Vuitton onto the table like it's authentic. Only I know she haggled for it from a guy in a van in Cozumel last summer. Neither of us would drop three grand on the real thing—especially not

Olivia, who just invested her entire savings in her catering business. She moves with kitchen-bred grace, a woman who's been perfecting Italian recipes since kindergarten.

"What's going on?" Olivia asks, leaning across our high-top. I take a long sip of my vodka soda, stalling. How do I tell her she'll be roommate-less? Not that I'd leave her with the full mortgage, but our Wednesday wine nights with kung pao chicken and Netflix screaming sessions are over. No more coming home to her eye-rolls when producers trash my pitches. Just Max's cold shoulder in a Malibu mansion. The ice in my glass clinks as my hand trembles.

"Well..." Three pairs of eyes lock onto me—Lexi's sapphire, Tally's electric blue, Olivia's warm chocolate. "Christ, there's no cute way to package this." I inhale sharply. "I'm marrying Max Kensington in two months." I scan their stunned faces as moonlight dances on waves calmer than the storm I just unleashed.

At first, nobody speaks. They're all just staring at me. And then Tally bursts out laughing and Olivia and Lexi follow suit. "Oh, God," Tally says. "Is this payback for when I convinced you that Chris Pine was staying at the chalet and you spent three hours in the lobby with that ridiculous autograph book? Your timing is off, girl, but I guess you just really wanted us to get together. I mean, if you're going to play a prank on us, you can think of something more realistic than telling us you're marrying the hottest man on the planet."

Tally's specialty is off-season April Fool's pranks. Like at Mammoth in February, when she convinced me Chris Pine was staying at our Groupon chalet. I spent twenty minutes stalking the lobby with my autograph book before trudging back to find them doubled over laughing.

"Is this about Chris Pine?" Olivia asks. "Or your

birthday last year?" I groan, remembering the six-foot singing chicken that burst into my pitch meeting, hip-thrusting to "My Ding-A-Ling" while my potential client watched in horror. I nearly strangled Olivia that night—would have if I hadn't somehow still signed the writer.

This makes telling them harder. They think I'm pranking them back, and I desperately wish I was. I want to yell "PSYCHE!" and laugh it off, but I can't. I have to convince them I'm serious, then weather their reactions. They'll want me committed—hell, I want me committed. A padded cell sounds better than what's coming.

I clear my throat, stare at the my wine glass and open my mouth. But Tally jumps in before I can say anything. "Oh my fucking God. You're serious. What the hell?"

Tally's known me for years and she's been my most loyal friend, aside from Liv. The skeptical arch of her eyebrow softens as she realizes I'm not joking. There it is—that flicker of recognition. She believes me now.

Olivia's eyebrows are still raised in skepticism, and Lexi's lips have pressed into that thin line she gets whenever she's torn between calling me out and feeling guilty. I've seen that exact expression since we were kids—it's the same face she made when she accidentally broke my science project in fifth grade and tried to convince me I'd built it wrong.

"Oh, God," I say. "I'm so sorry, guys. You all will think I'm nuts and if you don't, you should. But I'm marrying Max Kensington-"

Lexi's eyes narrow to slits. "Wait a minute. You and Max Kensington? No way. I've shown you, what, fifty magazine spreads of him? All those yacht photos? And you never once mentioned knowing him." She taps her fingernails against the table. "So either you just met him, or you're lying. And now you're marrying him?" Her face hardens as she leans forward. "This is a money thing, isn't it? He's paying you. You're selling yourself for me and Mom." Her voice breaks on the last word, tears spilling over. I watch recognition dawn across her features—that same look she gets when she figures out a film's twist twenty minutes before everyone else, the way she called every turn in that Nolan thriller. Those filmmaker instincts I've always admired are now dismantling my charade in real time. Even as my stomach drops, I feel an unexpected flicker of pride.

She's right about her Max obsession, too. Her bedroom wall is practically wallpapered with *Variety* covers featuring his face. She's spent countless dinners describing how Kensington Pictures will someday bid on her first film. But Lexi's just one devotee in a global phenomenon. From New York happy hours to European cafés, women analyze the angles of his jawline, scroll through stolen beach photos during their commutes, and debate the authenticity of each rare smile he gives photographers. The billionaire has cultivated an unwitting fan club spanning continents, and my sister's just another card-carrying member.

"Lexi," I say, trying to lighten the mood, which is turning very dark, as dark as the sky is right now. All three ladies are now staring at me with a mixture of confusion, sadness, more confusion, and even a hint of anger. Of course they'll be mad at me, the same way I'd be mad at them if I thought they were making a really, really, really batshitty mistake that they'll regret for the rest of their lives. I'd want to shake some fucking sense into any friend telling me news like mine, so I don't blame them if they're feeling hostile. "You really hit the nail on the head. I'm impressed."

"This isn't funny," Lexi says, her voice tight. She crosses her arms over her chest. "This whole thing is bullshit, Celeste. You promised you'd handle our money problems, and this is your solution? Selling yourself like some—" She stops, shaking her head. "If I'd known this was your plan all along—keeping Mom in the condo, keeping me in school— I would've shut it down immediately. I told you I was ready to quit UCLA and manage the restaurant. That was a real plan. Not this." Her eyes flash. "I never asked you to sacrifice yourself for us."

My vision blurs with unshed tears as Olivia recovers from her initial shock. She leans forward, her brow furrowed with the practical concerns I can see mirrored on Lexi and Tally's faces. "Hold up," she says, hands raised. "You're telling me Max Kensington—THE Max Kensington—is paying you to be his wife? That's... I mean... The man has women throwing themselves at him daily. He could snap his fingers and have a supermodel bride by sunset." She presses a hand to her chest dramatically. "Hell, I'd volunteer as tribute and he wouldn't even have to pay me. Where do I sign up for that?"

"Yeah, Celeste, what the actual hell?" Tally slams her palm on the table, making the glasses jump. "Why on God's green earth does Max Kensington—billionaire, most eligible bachelor, and *People's* Sexiest Man runner-up—have to PAY someone to marry him? And why YOU? A complete stranger to him?" She leans forward, eyes burning into mine. "What aren't you telling us? Because this makes zero sense." Lexi and Olivia exchange a look before fixing me with identical stares that pin me to my chair, their silence more demanding than any question.

I sigh and spill everything. The chance encounter with Joe Kensington at UCLA Hospital when I had no clue who he was. The way we connected over lukewarm coffee at 2 AM while the fluorescent lights buzzed overhead. Then the batshit crazy marriage proposal—not for himself, but for his grandson—followed by last night's awkward meeting where Max glared daggers at me and tried to trip me up while his grandfather outlined terms like we were negotiating a corporate merger. "I still can't figure out why Joe's so determined to see Max married," I tell them, shrugging. "But sometimes I wonder if Max's perfect life is just gift wrap around an empty box. Behind those magazine covers and billion-dollar deals... maybe there's just a guy who's completely alone. You know what they always say - if you think someone has it all, look closer."

When I finish my story, the girls sit in stunned silence. Their wide eyes and frozen postures remind me of people staring at a Dali painting for the first time, trying to make sense of clocks melting over barren landscapes. Lexi finally breaks the silence, her head shaking so hard her earrings sway. "I can't let you do this," she says, her voice cracking. "You won't marry a perfect stranger just because—"

I press my trembling hand over hers. "It's done. I signed a contract." The words hang between us as I search her face. Her expression shifts like quicksilver—first shock, then anger, a flash of something like envy, then settling into shame. Of course she's conflicted. Max Kensington has been her celebrity crush for years, the untouchable, unbelievably handsome and sexy billionaire she's followed in magazines. Now her sister is marrying him. For her. For Mom. I swallow hard as a realization forms: the shame in her eyes isn't about my sacrifice—it's about knowing she wouldn't do the same for me. That knowledge cuts deeper than I expected.

"Just tear up the contract, sis," Lexi says, tapping her fingernail against the table. "I didn't sit through Business Law 101 for nothing. Contracts against public policy don't hold up in court. This is textbook void—literally textbook.

You can't legally bind someone to marry another person, especially not with money changing hands. That's, like, nineteenth-century stuff."

"Lexi, you think I didn't consider that?" I snapped. "The second I signed that contract, I panicked. Spent half the night researching legal loopholes." I tap my wine glass against the table. "Is it void because it's against public policy? Maybe, but unlikely. It's not like Joe's paying me to divorce his grandson, which would be an illegal contract, all day long. And this arrangement is like a dowry, which is perfectly legal. The only restriction on dowries is you can't force payment." I sigh, rubbing my temples. "Even if I wanted out, Joe would unleash lawyers who bill more per hour than I make in a week. We can't afford to fight that."

Last night's desperate research session had cost me sleep and money. The Westlaw trial subscription alone had eaten half a day's pay. I scrolled through case law until my vision blurred, finding only the faintest possibility a judge might void the contract. But realistically? Joe's legal team would crush that argument. Just imagining myself stammering before a judge while surrounded by a team of Harvard-educated attorneys in tailored suits had sent me hyperventilating into a paper bag at 3 AM.

Lexi's arms fold tight across her chest, her chin trembling. "Goddamn it, Celeste. I never should've opened my stupid mouth about UCLA. You've sold yourself off because of me." She blinks rapidly, fighting tears. "If I'd known you'd do something this crazy, I would've just quit school and never said a word."

Olivia squeezes Lexi's shoulder. "Be grateful you told us. We'd never have forgiven you for throwing away everything without a word. What your sister did took guts." She glances at me, eyes soft. "When you're up on that stage accepting your Oscar someday—and you will be—you better thank her first. She's the reason your dream stays alive."

Lexi falls silent, but I see through her anger. My little sister isn't mad at me—she's ashamed. The guilt is written all over her face: that our family's situation has come to this, that the only solutions we could find were her abandoning film school or me signing marriage papers with a stranger for cash.

"Man," Tally says with that smile that always breaks tension, "a whole year with this guy? What if he's secretly filming you? Or worse—what if he's the next *Dateline* special waiting to happen?"

"Is *Dateline* even still on?" I ask.

She nods, eyes wide. "Oh, it'll never die. Not as long as there are creepers in the world." She leans forward. "And trust me, that supply chain isn't breaking down anytime soon. Even Jerry Springer eventually ran out of people willing to throw chairs, but *Dateline*? They've got material for centuries."

I sigh, my shoulders dropping. "I doubt he's hiding bodies in his basement." But my voice lacks conviction. The truth is, I know as much about Max Kensington as I do about quantum physics. I've spent all of about a total of 5 hours with the guy, all of which was spent with him glaring at me and trying to trip me up in front of the grandparents. "It doesn't matter anyway. This is the only option I have left."

Olivia's face crumples, and I slide my arm around her shoulders. "I know," I whisper. "Wednesday nights won't be the same." For three years, we've guarded those evenings like sacred territory—no dates, no work events, nothing could intrude on our Netflix ritual. "Remember how we've gotten each other through everything since you moved in? And now Malibu might as well be another planet."

"Like when Mark dumped me for Lisa?" Olivia's voice cracks. "You crawled into bed with me for a week straight while I was a complete disaster."

God, what a week that was. I'd unlock the door after work to find her in her bed with a nest of empty Ben & Jerry's containers, scattered paperbacks with tear-stained pages, and that remote she clutched like a lifeline, frantically channel-surfing through her pain. Each night, I'd slide under the covers beside her with fresh popcorn and tissues, gently prying the remote from her fingers to find something —anything—that might anchor her attention away from the heartbreak for even an hour. I'd drift off right there beside her, our breathing eventually syncing in the blue glow of the screen. Seven nights we repeated this ritual until finally, she found the strength to plant her feet on the floor again.

Tally's eyes narrow, her lips curling into that shark-like smile that always precedes a verbal massacre. She lets the silence hang for exactly three beats before launching her attack. "For God's sake, this table looks like someone just announced the apocalypse! Celeste, snap out of it. We're talking twelve months of your life. Then? Freedom, baby. Or who knows—maybe you'll end up actually wanting the guy, which, hello, have you seen those abs? Win-win either way. Look, I know sharing oxygen with someone you can't stand makes every minute feel eternal, but this is temporary. So enough with the tragic heroine routine. You're literally living in oceanfront real estate with a walking Calvin Klein billboard while collecting a paycheck for it, not serving hard time in some gulag. Get a grip." She punctuates this by slamming her martini down, glass meeting table with a crack. Behind the brutality, though, her eyes hold that fierce protectiveness only true friendship can explain—Tally's unique brand of tough love that never lets you wallow for long.

I giggle, setting off Olivia and Lexi too. We do sound ridiculous, like we're auditioning for a telenovela instead of discussing my life. Tally makes a fair point—twelve months will vanish in a blink, and then I'll be initialing divorce documents.

But wait—Mom. Her face materializes in my mind, disappointment etched in every line. A one-year marriage? The woman taught me that wedding vows were sacred promises, not temporary contracts. Her heart will shatter. I press my lips together, resolving: she cannot know about the arrangement with Max. Lexi knowing is already one person too many. Mom will never comprehend why I'm marrying him or why I'll leave him just as quickly. I've tangled myself in a web I can't possibly explain away.

Lexi's eyes soften as she reaches across the table, her fingers cool against my knuckles. "Ces," she whispers, her voice catching. "I was awful before. About all of this. But I can see it now—you're terrified for Mom. What are you going to tell her?"

I inhale slowly, counting to three. "I'll figure it out. But you can't breathe a word, Lex. Not one. Swear to me. She's counting her sunrises these days, wondering how many she has left. The last thing she needs is to carry this burden too."

Mom....what will I tell her?

Chapter Twelve

CELESTE

I visit my mother and find her sitting up in bed when I arrive, her eyes bright and focused. Even now, with her hair growing back in wisps after chemo, she's striking—the kind of woman who turns heads at the grocery store. Before cancer, her blonde waves and unlined face made her look a decade younger than her fifty-four years. People always said she could be Patricia Clarkson's twin, especially when she laughed, her voice carrying that same husky warmth that could fill a room.

I ache thinking about Mom's lost decades. She used to pack our lunches with little notes inside, volunteer for every field trip, be waiting at the door when we got home. Then Dad was killed in a freak accident on the ski slopes. After that, I'd find her asleep at the kitchen table at 3 a.m., doing medical coding on her laptop, still in her Walmart vest, her Denny's tip money scattered across the bills she couldn't quite cover. All those doubles at Denny's, all those medical transcription deadlines, all those Wal-Mart shifts, all those wealthy people toilets cleaned, just to keep our heads above water in a city that seemed determined to drown us.

She smiles when I come through the door. "Celeste," she says softly. "So happy to see you."

Her eyes sparkle today in a way I haven't seen since before the diagnosis. She's reading a book, her rainbow framed reading glasses perched on her nose. I can't remember the last time she's read a book. I want to believe it's all a sign she's getting better, but I've learned not to trust these glimpses of the old her. This moment—her sitting up with a light in her eyes that I haven't seen in way too long and reading a book—might vanish by my next visit, replaced by the hollow-eyed woman I found last Tuesday, slumped in her recliner, barely able to acknowledge I'd entered the room.

I sit down and take her hand in mine. As before, she feels cool to the touch, too cool. I try hard not to cry before I drop the bomb on her head.

"Mom," I begin. "I have some news."

She nods. "Okay," she says. "What's your news?"

I take a deep breath. "I'm getting married. In two months."

She looks at me, and then drops her hand from mine. "What do you mean? Celeste, you haven't dated anyone for several years."

Heat crawls up my neck and into my cheeks. I press my palms against them, as if I could push the blush back down. How do I explain this? The last guy I dated was that assistant director who kept calling me "babe" in meetings. That was—what—three years ago? Four? I've been too busy paying Mom's medical bills and keeping Lexi in school to swipe right or make small talk with strangers in dimly lit lounges.

My hand trembles violently as I try to muster the courage to tell my beautiful mother an absolute lie. *Sell it, Celeste.* "Mom," I whisper, my voice breaking. "There's someone who's completely shattered everything I thought I knew about love. I know it sounds insane—God, I can barely believe it myself—but the second our eyes met, it was like lightning struck my soul. We're moving at warp speed, but Mom, I swear on everything I am, this is it for me. This is the one."

Was my voice breaking? Was I meeting her eyes? Will she buy this from me? This is my mother. I feel like she can see through me like I'm made of glass. But maybe, in her illness, her senses and intuition might be dulled just enough that I can pull this one over her. *Please let that be true. Please let her believe me.*

She adjusts her reading glasses, her expression concerned but measured. "Celeste, this isn't like you. You've always been the one who makes spreadsheets before buying a coffee maker. The one who researches every decision. This sudden marriage seems... uncharacteristic for you."

I take a deep breath. "Maybe you have a point, but being careful hasn't exactly worked out for me. Twenty-five years old and what do I have to show for it? A string of three-month disasters with guys who looked good on paper but turned out to be walking red flags. All that analyzing and second-guessing just to end up alone anyway." I shake my head. "I'm tired of overthinking everything. Maybe it's time I trusted my instincts for once."

She shakes her head. "There's something you're not telling me," she says. "I can see it in your eyes."

I push back my chair. "We're basically Tony and Maria with a beach house," I say, knowing Mom would catch the *West Side Story* nod, considering that's her all-time favorite movie. "Love at first sight, whirlwind romance, marriage pact—just with fewer switchblades and more prenups."

"Yes, and look how well that turned out," she says, arching an eyebrow. "One dead boyfriend and one traumatized girlfriend. You do realize *West Side Story* is just *Romeo and Juliet* with better choreography, right? Teenagers with raging hormones mistaking infatuation for true love. Trust me, modeling your relationships after Shakespeare's tragedies is a terrible idea. There's a reason those plays end with funeral processions instead of wedding receptions."

"Well," I say. "I'm getting married and that's that. I want you at the wedding, of course. It'll be happen at St. John's on Adams." Mom's right - how can I emulate play and movie characters who end up dead? I'm sure there are other examples in literature or film where two people meet, fall in love, and get married in a matter of months. But I can't think right now of better examples to give my perceptive mother. Maybe that old sitcom *Dharma and Greg?* I seem to remember they married the same day they met.

"Celeste, please think about what you're doing," she says, her voice softening. "Marriage isn't just a piece of paper. This man—whoever he is—you've known him what, a few weeks? That's not love, honey. That's a chemical reaction." She leans forward, eyes searching my face. "Real love builds slowly. It's in the small moments—noticing how he stirs his coffee, how he apologizes after an argument, what makes him laugh on his worst days. And frankly," she hesitates, "what kind of man rushes into a lifetime commitment with someone he barely knows? That should tell you something. It doesn't speak well of his character."

Of course, Mom isn't telling me that it doesn't speak well of my character, either, that I'm rushing into a lifetime commitment with somebody I don't know. She's too kind to come right out and tell me I'm a fool. But she's thinking it. I can see it in the way her fingers twist around each other in her lap, in how she keeps opening her mouth and then closing it again without a sound.

I clear my throat. "Mom, I know what you're saying. But I'm doing this."

"Have you told Alexandra?" The way she says my sister's full name sounds so formal, like she's announcing royalty at a ball. Mom's the only person who calls my sister Alexandra—she's Lexi to everyone else in the universe. I've always figured Mom clings to "Alexandra" because she spent weeks agonizing over baby name books before my sister was born.

"Yes. And Olivia and Tally, too."

"That's right, Olivia. She lives with you. What will happen to her? Will she have to find a new place to live?"

"Olivia can stay at my place," I say. "The condo's a solid investment I'd rather hang onto." What I don't mention to Mom is that in twelve months, when this charade with Max ends, those laminate floors and that tiny balcony overlooking the park will be waiting for me again.

"She can't keep up your mortgage payments and you shouldn't ask her to," Mom says.

"No, Mom, I'll just ask her to keep paying her half."

"So, you'll be paying two mortgages, then," she says. "Your mortgage on your condo and I'm sure you and your new husband will be buying a house on mortgage, too. You'll be stretched too thin, Celeste."

I start to speak, then catch myself. Of course Max doesn't have a mortgage, but the idea of someone without a mortgage would be alien to Mom—in her world, everyone struggles with thirty-year loans and fixed interest rates. A man who buys a Malibu beach house outright, with cash, marrying her daughter, who clips coupons and drives a ten-year-old Prius? She'd smell something rotten before I finished the sentence.

"Mom," I say. "Please don't worry. I've figured it all out, I promise you."

She narrows her eyes, shakes her head, but then finally shrugs. "It's your life, Celeste," she says. "I'm just worried, that's all."

"Of course you are," I say. "That's what mothers do. But I'm going to be fine. Really. I'm not making a mistake."

"I guess," she says. "I'll be at the wedding, of course. This cancer won't keep me from seeing my daughter make a lifetime commitment."

She says the words "lifetime commitment," and I cringe. I imagine myself, a little over a year from now, telling my mom that she was right and I was wrong. I would have to break her heart with a quickie divorce just one year after breaking her heart with a quickie marriage.

But I'm doing this for her. She'll never know that, though. I'll never tell her the real reason I'm marrying Max Kensington.

I'll take that secret to my grave - that I'm doing this to make sure she and Lexi are okay.

Chapter Thirteen

CELESTE

The woman in the mirror has hands that won't stop shaking, her French manicure catching the harsh bathroom light with each tremor. Her eyes are wide, pupils dilated with fear, rimmed with smudged mascara from the night before.

In four hours, I'll be Mrs. Max Kensington. The ivory Vera Wang hanging on the door—a $150,000 dress I never would have chosen—looks more like a shroud than a wedding gown. Each tick of the grandfather clock pushes me closer to the inevitable. Mom needs that experimental treatment. Lexi needs UCLA. I need Dreamscape. So I'll walk down that marble aisle like the condemned, one Louboutin in front of the other, my pulse drowning out everything but the knowledge that there's no turning back.

Olivia and Tally keep shoving flutes of Veuve Clicquot into my hands, but my stomach lurches at the mere sight of the bubbles. "Just one sip," Olivia insists, but I shake my head. God, I wish I could down the entire bottle and float through this nightmare in a champagne haze. *TMZ* would have a field day: "Dreamscape Exec Weds Kensington CEO, Can't Stand Without Swaying." But my rebellious stomach won't even allow me that small mercy. Each time I bring the glass to my lips, bile rises in my throat.

Lexi perches on the chair beside me, shadows beneath her blue eyes. We've been over this already—first at our emergency summit on the rooftop bar, then daily in her desperate phone calls. "I could juggle full-time work with classes," she insisted yesterday, her voice cracking. I had to remind her that humans need sleep. Besides, if she goes through the restaurant management program, her restaurant would, you know, expect her to manage the restaurant. Duh. When she texted about a cheaper apartment listing, I shut that down too. "Mom can barely make it to chemo appointments. A move would destroy her." Lexi's shoulders finally slumped this morning. We're cornered, both of us. This arrangement is the only way forward.

Olivia's eyes flick over my wrinkled sundress. "You look pretty," she lies. She and Tally perch on a leather love seat in this ridiculous penthouse suite Max and his Granddad rented for me. Soon, celebrity makeup artist Lita Wilson will arrive with her entourage to transform me—chapped lips, day-old mascara and all—into someone Instagram-worthy enough to marry a Kensington.

I give Olivia a look that could wither a cactus. *Goddamn it, Olivia, stop lying to me.* I know how I look. I have eyes and what I see is skin the color of day-old oatmeal, raccoon-dark circles under bloodshot eyes that haven't closed for more than three hours at a stretch in nine days, lips cracked like the Mojave Desert floor, and last night's mascara smudged in sooty half-moons beneath my lower lashes because I've been too numb to even splash water on my face. I see hair that looks like I stuck my finger in an electrical socket—a rat's nest of tangles that snaps every tooth off my comb because it's as dry as straw and twice as brittle.

No matter about the hair, though—part of Lita's team consists of hairdressers to the stars, who'll arrive like a SWAT team armed with that legendary Moroccan deep hair conditioner that costs more than my mortgage payment, smells like an expensive bakery, and transforms even the most damaged strands into silk ribbons. They'll bring professional scissors that could probably cut through metal and those magical industrial-strength bobby pins that hopefully will defy gravity and hold up the Golden Gate Bridge of hair disasters.

Max assigned me a personal assistant, Aimée, who has been my saving grace—or my emotional support human, as I'd taken to calling her. Without her, I'd have drowned in Wedding Wonderland's parade of absurdities: food tastings where Wolfgang Puck (yes, THAT Wolfgang Puck) watched me like I was judging the Olympics of Canapés; cake designers who stroked fondant samples and whispered "feel the texture" while maintaining uncomfortable eye contact; and florists who'd gasp "but the SYMBOLISM" when I suggested substituting peonies with something—anything—more original. During dress fittings, I'd hum the Imperial March while perfect strangers circled my butt with pins. Then there was Alicia-Fucking-Crawford, photographer to the stars, who kept demanding I practice my "candid laugh" until I started snorting like a congested hippo. The makeup squad insisted I pick a "face aesthetic" from their sacred scroll of options: Natural? Matte? Dewy? Smokey? Glam? Bridal? I deadpanned "Option G—Goth bride. Think Morticia Addams meets Edward Scissorhands." Their collective gasps could've inflated a hot air balloon. Worth it. I was feeling spicy that day.

So, yeah. That was my past 59 days of wedding-prep hell squeezed between my regular 60-hour workweek like stuffing an elephant into spanx. My Netflix queue has gone from "Recently Watched" to "Are You Still Alive?" My yoga mat has developed its own ecosystem. My running shoes actually hissed at me yesterday.

Meanwhile, Max has ghosted me so thoroughly I'm considering hiring an exorcist. I've sent him a ton of texts about the wedding prep, only to get the dreaded monosyllables in return—"yes," "no," and the ever-eloquent "k"—to digital tumbleweeds. Part of me keeps hoping he'll text "JK LOL WEDDING'S OFF" with a confetti emoji, but nope. This matrimonial train keeps chugging along, and I'm tied to the tracks in a white dress. Now I'm sitting here with bags under my eyes so large they require their own zip code, developing what feels like the plague. If I sneeze on some billionaire and get sued, I'm adding it to the wedding registry.

I arch an eyebrow at Olivia. "Pretty?" My voice cracks. "Stop lying." I glance at Tally, who stares back with unblinking eyes, red lips pressed thin. Tally—silent. Verbose, never-stops-talking Tally. I see their pact hanging between them—don't upset the bride. But Olivia's gaze keeps darting to my puffy eyes, while Tally fixates on my $150,000 gown's bodice. I need them to be the friends who told me my bangs looked like they'd been cut by a lawnmower, who warned me my ex was cheating.

"Okay, okay," Olivia says. "You look kinda tired."

Tally rolls her eyes dramatically. "Celeste, honey, you look like a nuclear disaster. Those aren't bags—they're luggage sets. Thank God for Lita Wilson, or you'd terrify the children at the reception." She gestures at my head. "And that situation needs industrial equipment. You're the 'before' photo where the model lives in a wind tunnel. Even Anne Hathaway's *Princess Diaries* makeover started with better raw material. You need José Eber himself to style your hair." Then she laughs. "Wouldn't that be fabulous?"

I snort despite myself. "For your information, it's Keeley Sanchez doing my hair, not José Eber. Though I wouldn't mind if José showed up. I've always wanted to meet a man whose hair is more fabulous than ninety percent of his clients." Keeley Sanchez, with her signature silver-streaked bob and collection of vintage Cartier bangles that clink as she works, reigns as Hollywood's most sought-after hair-stylist. Her nimble fingers have crafted the Kardashians' sleek updos for Met Gala appearances and transformed the Hadid sisters' tresses into windswept perfection for *Vogue* covers shot on Mediterranean cliffs.

Then I smile at Tally. "Thank God. For a minute there I thought you'd lost your mind or joined some kind of cult where they remove your personality and replace it with a greeting card." Then I look at Olivia. "You're up."

Olivia winces. "Uh, you've looked better." I sigh. Classic Olivia—she'll never give me the brutal assessment Tally would deliver without hesitation. But that's why I need them both. Last month when I came home from Mom's chemo appointment, Olivia showed up with tissues and homemade soup, while Tally texted me memes about cancer wigs until I laughed so hard I forgot to cry. They balance me out and I need them both like air. And soon I'll have neither of them. Malibu might as well be Mars compared to downtown LA or Claremont—especially with that PCH traffic. Max's beachfront paradise might as well be solitary confinement.

I give her a thumbs-up. "Good enough." Then I catch my own reflection in the mirror. "Think they can work their magic on me?" I tilt my head, examining the dark circles under my eyes. "I look like I've been awake since Tuesday." I lean closer to the mirror, pressing a finger to the crease between my brows. " The tabloids will have a field day with this—' Max Kensington Spotted with Exhausted Mortal Woman.' I mean, how does anyone look human standing next to that family?" I smooth my hair back, attempting to tame a stubborn cowlick. "Maybe I should start a support group for normal people who somehow ended up with the genetically blessed." I offer a small, self-deprecating smile.

Lexi's voice cuts through Celeste's spiral. "Would you listen to yourself? You're beautiful. Sure, maybe the Diet Coke IV drip and three-hour sleep schedule have you looking a little rough around the edges, but that's temporary. What isn't temporary is that Max hit the jackpot with you, not the other way around. So enough."

I nod. My friends know their roles. Tally calls me "Skeletor" and I call her "Thunder Thighs," though we both know she's a knockout and I clean up pretty well when I try. Olivia's the one who reminds me I'm worth something when I forget. And Lexi? She's the reality check—the one who grabs my shoulders and tells me to get it together. She's right this time. A few months ago, I was Celeste 1.0—five-mile runs, downward dog at dawn, perfect sleep schedule, and a fridge full of kale. Now I'm running on four hours of sleep, Diet Coke, takeout containers, and whatever wine is on sale. Between my insane work hours and the low-grade panic of marrying a man who despises me—a man whose cologne makes my pulse quicken despite everything—I've become someone I barely recognize.

I force a smile. "Thanks, everyone." My stomach churns as I glance at the clock. "Is it too late to request general anesthesia? Or maybe there's some memory-wiping service I could hire afterward—like that Jim Carrey-Kate Winslet movie where they zap away all the bad stuff?" I tug at my sleeve, unable to meet anyone's eyes. "Because the way I'm feeling right now, this whole thing is going to be a train wreck. There's just no way this ends with me keeping my dignity intact."

Five minutes later, my suite becomes beauty central. The hairdresser attacks with products, applying some ridiculously expensive masque that smells like bottled luxury. The makeup artist examines my face with bomb-squad focus—fair enough, given my raccoon eyes and blotchy skin. My bridesmaids - Tally, Liv and Lexi - circle in burgundy off-shoulder gowns, offering champagne and chatter to distract me. I focus on my breathing—four counts in, seven hold, eight out—and hope I make it to "I do" without passing out.

"So, tell me about Max's house," Olivia asks. "After all, this is where the shindig will take place. What's it like?"

I shake my head. "No clue. I've never set foot in the place. You'd think with all his money, his mansion would be plastered across every tabloid spread from here to TMZ, but I haven't seen it anywhere. Probably too high-brow for the gossip rags—more like *Architectural Digest* territory. Not that I've had time to flip through those either."

Tally's eyes brighten. "Oh, I've seen his house in Architectural Digest." She leans forward slightly. "Twenty-thousand square feet of Mediterranean design perched on a cliff. Stone walls, those beautiful arched windows that frame the ocean view." She taps the table once. "There's this courtyard with a fountain surrounded by lemon trees. Portuguese tiles everywhere. And the master bath—" she pauses, collecting herself "—makes my entire apartment look like a storage closet. The tub is carved from a single marble slab." She lowers her voice. "And the infinity pool seems to just disappear into the Pacific."

I let out a nervous "Oh," followed by uncontrollable giggles. "When Max suggested having the reception at his house, I pictured string lights and intimate gatherings, not some Malibu fortress with infinity pools and disappearing glass walls." I twist my engagement ring. "I should've known better. A Kensington wouldn't live in a normal home where neighbors can actually see your yard." My smile fades. "I just wanted that ordinary life—patchy lawns, barking dogs, and Sunday neighbors dropping by with beer."

Tally rolls her eyes. "Honey, please. His 'house'?" She makes air quotes. "It's practically the Getty Museum. We're talking marble columns, infinity pools, and a cobble-stone driveway that could double as a Formula One track. There will be Lamborghinis, Bentleys, Aston Martins in that driveway today and those will be the cheaper cars pulling up. The fountain in front spouts champagne on weekends—I'm barely exaggerating."

Olivia shoots Tally a look as I gasp for air. The room tilts, my vision tunnels. She grabs the paper bag from my purse—the one I packed just in case. Four hundred guests wait at the church. So much for Max's "small, intimate gathering." I count breaths against the crinkling paper. One-two-three in. One-two-three out. Five minutes later, the pressure eases. Crisis averted—for now.

Several hours later, I stare at my reflection. Smoky shadow widens my eyes, and my skin glows from the esthetician's magic. Gone are the shadows beneath my eyes and my chapped lips. Even my sparse eyelashes now fan out thick and dark—extensions I'm definitely keeping. The hair team created an elegant half-updo secured with diamond pins worth more than my mortgage, while the rest of my usually unruly curls cascade down my back in gentle waves. I touch it, surprised by its kitten-soft texture. This polished stranger in the mirror bears no resemblance to the exhausted development exec who walked in earlier.

When I stand, the wedding dress transforms. Pale ivory silk cascades from the structured bodice, cool against my skin where the back dips low. It hugs my waist before releasing into a skirt that whispers with each step, gathering in folds that catch the light like moon on water. At my collar, Belgian lace forms a delicate edge so fine it seems to float. Nothing fussy—just understated elegance that costs more than five years of my mortgage. For once, I don't look like I'm drowning in someone else's clothes. "Not bad," I whisper to my reflection. "Not bad at all."

The three girls—Lexi with her champagne flute frozen halfway to her lips, Tally clutching the doorframe as if she might faint, and Olivia whose mascara-rimmed eyes have gone so wide they might pop from her skull—are looking at me like I'm the Venus coming out of the half shell in that famous Botticelli painting. They're speechless, mouths hanging open in perfect O's, as if the oxygen has been sucked from the room and replaced with pure, unfiltered astonishment.

Tally's eyes shimmer with unshed tears as she takes in the transformation. "Oh, Celeste," she whispers, her voice catching. "That champagne silk drapes like it was made for you. The way it catches the light when you move..." She circles me slowly, fingertips hovering just above the delicate beadwork at the neckline. "Stunning! For once, you won't look like the hired help at one of their Malibu galas."

I laugh at Tally's transformation from fashion critic to stammering fangirl. Olivia blinks back mascara-smudged tears while Lexi's freckled cheeks flush pink, all of us tangled in a cloud of designer perfume and hairspray. Their approval echoes off the mirrored walls as I bite my trembling lip. The stranger in the reflection—hair swept up, silk hugging my curves—finally looks like she belongs beside Max. For once, I won't be Instagram's punching bag.

And now, it's time. The sleek black limousine idles at the curb, waiting to ferry us to St. John's Episcopal on Adams. Ironic choice—I abandoned Catholicism after Dad died, and Max is agnostic according to my late-night Googling. Not like we've discussed religion, or much of anything. I doubt any Kensington has darkened a church door in years, except with checkbook in hand. Joseph must have made quite the donation to secure a bishop in full regalia for our little charade. The ceremony, like the marriage itself, is just window-dressing. Fitting, really.

As we head to the limo, I smooth my hands over the silk of my Vera Wang dress, its champagne color catching the late afternoon light.

The stylist's magic has transformed me into a socialite bride, but dread still twists in my stomach like ice. My reflection shows a stranger—perfect makeup, elaborate updo—yet my eyes betray the truth. I can wear this costume for now, but becoming Mrs. Max Kensington demands more than designer labels and borrowed diamonds. My manicured hands tremble against the beaded clutch, terrified of being exposed as the fraud I am.

As I step from the limo, a tsunami of flashbulbs crashes over me, burning my retinas even through closed eyelids. Jesus Christ. The crowd roars—hundreds of bodies pressing against security barricades, their faces contorted with a hunger that makes my skin crawl. Security guards in full riot gear form a human wall between me and them, as if I'm the President, not some development exec in a dress worth more than five years of my annual salary.

"CELESTE! CELESTE!" They're screaming my name like I'm supposed to know them. "HOW DOES IT FEEL MARRYING MAX?" one shrieks. What am I supposed to say? That my stomach is a concrete mixer? That I'm selling myself like medieval chattel? That I'd rather walk naked through Times Square than down this aisle?

"ARE YOU MARRYING FOR MONEY?" The question slices through me. Yes, you vulture. Yes. I'm whoring myself for cash because my mother is dying and my sister deserves a future. But the truth sticks in my throat like a fishbone.

"WAS IT LOVE AT FIRST SIGHT?" someone howls, and I almost laugh. Love? It was pure, visceral loathing. Still is. I'd sooner fall for a rattlesnake.

"WHO ARE YOU WEARING?" A fashion blogger thrusts her microphone at my face. I jab my finger at her, mouthing "Vera Wang," and she practically orgasms on the spot.

I finally breach the church doors, gasping like I've been underwater. The paparazzi fade to white noise. And there he is. Max. Waiting. My chest constricts so violently I might pass out.

I am so monumentally, catastrophically fucked.

Chapter Fourteen

MAX

So here I stand at the altar, trapped in my own private Francis Bacon canvas. The bishop looms before me in his white robes and pointed mitre, and I can't help but see him as Pope Innocent X from Bacon's famous portrait—mouth stretched in a silent scream, face twisted into something barely human. A small, bitter smile tugs at my lips. All these guests, dressed in their Sunday best, waiting for Celeste to appear—they think they're witnessing a celebration. They have no idea they're actually extras in a horror show.

Anybody who's anybody in LA is here. The person not here, though? Elody Martin. Whoo, boy, when she found out I was to be married... My iPhone nearly melted from the heat of her rage coming through the speaker. I didn't—don't—want to marry Celeste, yet here we are, being forced into it, but I have to admit that Elody's reaction makes this sham wedding almost worth it. Her normally sultry voice transformed into a banshee wail that had me holding the phone six inches from my ear. Mascara-stained tears probably streaming down her porcelain cheeks as she called me every profanity in her extensive vocabulary. She even hissed that she'd sleep with Gianni just to twist the knife. I had to laugh at that one—Gianni, with his meticulously tailored Armani suits and perfectly coiffed hair, doesn't have that bad of taste to take my sloppy seconds, and Elody, with her tendency to throw champagne flutes at hotel walls, is probably the sloppiest seconds I could give.

As for my other ex-girlfriends—a veritable catalog of Victoria's Secret runway walkers and *Vogue* cover models and a *Who's Who* of Hollywood? Various reactions, most of them meltdowns, though none as technicolor as Elody's. My model girlfriends probably just did a line of coke off their vanities and moved on to the next billionaire, while my actress girlfriends, with their Oscar-worthy performances, threatened to trash my name across their millions of Instagram followers. I simply reminded them with a cold smile that I could ensure their next role would be in a deodorant commercial in Kazakhstan. They all kept quiet, though their perfectly plumped lips quivered with rage.

Yes, I've left a trail of broken hearts in Malibu beach houses and Beverly Hills mansions, but I'm strangely numb to that fact. No wonder the press has dubbed me "The Ice King."

I look around. Four hundred people. So much for small and intimate. The church swims before my eyes—a sea of faces worth billions. I scan the pews, my stomach twisting into a noose. Eight Fortune 500 execs with their shark smiles. Fifteen Hollywood A-Listers with eyes that strip you bare. The collective net worth in this room could buy a small country, and they're all here—watching, judging—front-row tickets to witness my complete and utter humiliation.

But the luminaries here are all witnesses to this charade,

thanks to Granddad's meddling. I catch his eye across the aisle, his satisfied smile only fueling my irritation. He thinks he's clever, surrounding us with the most influential people in the country, as if social pressure will keep me from showing Celeste the door the moment this farce concludes. As if I care what these people think when they inevitably receive news of our separation. I can already picture the pitying looks, the complaints that they wasted a perfectly beautiful Saturday for this. Granddad thinks he's built a fortress around this sham marriage, but he's about to learn—

I snap back to reality just as Lexi takes her place at the altar as maid of honor. The other bridesmaids sit in the front row rather than stand—a concession to balance since I've only got Gianni as my best man. No way I would invite one or two of my brothers to stand up for me and start WWIII with the others, so I just didn't include any of them, even Ansel, who is by far my closest brother, both in age and emotionally.

Then Celeste appears at the end of the aisle, and everything else fades away.

I've been dodging her since she put her signature on that damn contract. Radio silence, basically. Yeah, I handed off all the wedding details to her. Dick move? Probably. But if I started picking out floral arrangements and cake flavors, she might get the wrong idea—that I'm invested in this charade.

Marriage. Just the word makes my palms sweat. When I was seven, Dad's closet emptied overnight. No goodbye, just gone. Taught me something I never forgot: loving someone doesn't mean they'll stick around. The pieces of me that scattered when he left? Took years to find them all. Not looking for a repeat performance.

And this woman... there's something in her eyes when

she looks at me. Something that could slip past my defenses if I'm not careful. She gets her pay day and I get what? A cracked-open chest? Hard pass. This stays strictly business. So I keep my distance, let her think I'm just another entitled rich guy with an ego problem. Better that way.

She clutches her mother's arm—a petite woman in burgundy with a vibrant headscarf who shares Celeste's unmistakable eyes. But it's Celeste who steals my breath. Her Caribbean-blue gaze, enhanced by smoky shadow, darts nervously across the crowd. That white gown hugs every curve, revealing just enough to make my collar feel two sizes too small. With her hair swept up, the elegant line of her neck draws my eyes downward to—

I force myself to look away, silently cursing Granddad for this circus that's clearly overwhelming her. When the bishop eventually asks me to kiss my bride, I'll be in trouble. One taste and I might forget we're standing before God and four hundred of California's elite. The way she looks right now, I'm fighting the urge to whisk her away somewhere private and forget this ceremony entirely. She takes her place next to me, and I look away - from her, from these uncomfortable feelings that this "marriage" might become real for me, but probably not for her. Which would be the worse-case scenario for me, of course.

Both of us in place, it's now time for the "sermon," and the bishop is droning on and on about love and commitment or whatever these bishops prattle on about at ceremonies like this. I stare at the ceiling, willing my hand not to make the universal "wrap it up" gesture.

Christ, did Granddad arrange this torture on purpose? The bishop adjusts his ridiculous hat—seriously, who decided mitres were a good look?—while rambling about a divine union. Divine my ass. Unless "divine" is code for an octogenarian who measures exactly seventy-two inches in socks and owns seventeen identical cardigans, each with elbow patches shaped like Rhode Island. I should've vetoed this whole cathedral setup when I had the chance. If this turns into one of those marathon ceremonies with communion wafers and hymn books, just wheel me straight to the cemetery.

But I keep my eyes locked on the bishop for self-preservation. One glance at Celeste is dangerous. Not the calculated danger of a business deal, but the kind that makes my chest tight. Unlike Elody Martin, the A-List actress who's obsessed with me and blows up my phone weekly—Celeste has no clue how she affects a room. How she affects me. That unconscious grace only amplifies everything about her. Two seconds of eye contact and I'm already imagining whisking her away somewhere private where I could... Jesus. Where I could make her call out my name until her voice gives out. No. That's exactly what can't happen. Not today, not ever. Because Celeste is the one woman I wouldn't want to be in a hurry to leave my bed in the morning, and that makes her absolutely lethal.

I'm fixated on the ceiling cherubs—seventeen pudgy babies with middle-aged faces—rather than acknowledging the crowd witnessing this charade. A cough punctuates the silence. Someone's phone vibrates. Then another phone blares the opening notes of "Creep" before a symphony of shushes drowns out the Radiohead classic. The poor soul who forgot to silence their phone is getting murdered with glares. Been there. The unexpected soundtrack nearly cracks my composure so I have to keep myself from laughing out loud, especially because the bishop is droning on with funeral-director solemnity. The contrast makes everything feel even more surreal. And Celeste? I'm deliberately avoiding her gaze. One look and I'd grab her hand and drag her out of here, consequences be damned.

When the bishop finally - finally! - asks if I take Celeste as my lawfully wedded wife, I catch at least three executives checking their watches. The collective sigh of relief is practically audible. These Hollywood types aren't exactly Sunday regulars—unless there's a photographer from *Variety* outside the church. Half the guests are probably nursing hangovers from last night's afterparty at Soho House, scrolling through Instagram under their programs. My grandfather sits in the front row, nodding along to every word like it's gospel, but I doubt the bishop's sermon on holy matrimony is landing with the rest of this crowd.

My "I do" rips from my throat like a confession under torture. Holy shit—did those words actually leave my mouth? My heart slams against my ribcage like it's trying to escape, and lightning bolts of pain shoot behind my eyes. I'll need those beta blockers the second this ceremony ends or I'll be convulsing on a gurney while everyone else is downing top-shelf liquor and devouring Wolfgang Puck's culinary masterpieces. No fucking way am I missing that reception. I've sold my soul in this sham marriage—I'm damn well collecting my thirty pieces of silver in champagne and lobster puffs. Missing this reception would be like choking down poison without getting the antidote.

Her "I do" sounds like she's being waterboarded. Christ, did she actually say it? Her face is sheet-white, jaw clenched so tight I can see the muscle twitching. She keeps blinking rapidly, like she's also fighting off a migraine. I should also get her those beta blockers the second we're done here or she'll collapse while everyone's getting wasted on Macallan 25 and inhaling Wolfgang's overpriced appetizers. I'm sure she'll be eyeing the reception bar like it's salvation. Can't blame her—she's just legally shackled herself to me for a quarter million. Might as well enjoy the champagne and lobster puffs she's earned. Poor thing looks like she'd rather swallow cyanide than my last name, but at least there's an open bar waiting.

The bishop declares us husband and wife, his voice echoing through the vaulted ceiling. I lean in and brush my lips against Celeste's cheek, feeling the warmth of her skin, the subtle scent of jasmine in her hair. My body tenses with restraint. What I truly want—what I need—is to taste those full, rose-petal lips, to feel her sharp intake of breath as my mouth claims hers. In my mind, I'm already tracing the delicate curve of her bottom lip with my tongue, gently catching her top lip between my teeth, our tongues meeting in a dance that promises so much more. Her champagne-colored dress rustles as she shifts slightly, and I force myself to pull away. The innocent kiss on her soft cheek is my only defense against the tide of desire threatening to drown us both - or probably just me - in front of God and everyone.

The crowd erupts in applause as I paste on a smile, walking beside Celeste down the aisle. I keep my hands to myself. One brush of her fingers against mine in this moment—with her looking like that—and I'd be dragging her into the nearest confessional, turning sacred space profane in seconds flat.

We step out into the blinding California sun, the heat already making my collar stick to my neck as we slide into the waiting Rolls Royce Phantom limo. The butter-soft leather seats creak beneath us. I fix my gaze out the window, watching palm trees blur past, counting each one to keep my mind occupied. My jaw clenches so tight I feel I might crack some teeth. Celeste shifts beside me, the silk of her dress whispering against the seat, and I catch a hint of her perfume—something floral and expensive. Am I being an asshole again? Absolutely. But it's either this silence or my reaching for that privacy partition switch, pressing her against these pristine cream seats, and making her forget her own name.

I make the fatal mistake of looking down. Her white satin Louboutins might as well be weapons—$3,000 stilettos slicing through my resolve. Her toes, painted the exact shade of sin, peek out like a promise. The slit in her dress isn't just revealing a leg; it's an invitation I can't accept, the lace garter a boundary I'm forbidden to cross. When my gaze betrays me, traveling to where silk meets skin, my throat closes. I slam my attention back to the window, jaw clenched so hard my teeth might crack. The migraine I'd feared hasn't arrived—this is infinitely worse. Twenty-seven miles. Sixty minutes of exquisite torture. I don't count the minutes to scotch anymore; I count heartbeats, each one hammering with the knowledge that I can memorize but never map the geography of her body. Never trace the curve of her calf with my fingertips, never follow the arch of her foot with my tongue, never explore the shadows between her breasts. Never know how her skin would taste beneath my teeth.

All those things can never, ever happen, because if they ever did, I'd be obliterated. Annihilated. She'd consume me whole, leaving nothing but ashes where a man once stood. I'd crawl across broken glass just to watch her sleep. I'd forget my own name, my empire, my goddamn reason for existing. One taste and I'd become her slave, her addict, her willing sacrifice.

She has no idea she's a loaded gun pressed against my temple, and I'm keeping it that way.

Chapter Fifteen

CELESTE

The leather seat of the limo sticks to my dress as I shift away from Max—my husband as of twenty minutes ago. God, that word feels wrong in my mouth. He's staring out his window, jaw clenched, a good foot of empty seat between us despite the champagne flutes knocking together with every turn. During the ceremony, his eyes fixed somewhere above my left shoulder, as if meeting my gaze might turn him to stone. I even ran my tongue over my teeth twice, checking for lipstick smears or bits of food. Nothing there. Just me, apparently, that he can't stomach looking at.

I white-knuckled through the ceremony, sweat trickling down my spine as my mind screamed for escape. The bishop's voice droned on like a death knell while my pulse hammered in my ears. Every fiber of my being vibrated with the urge to bolt—to rip off this suffocating veil and sprint down the aisle, kicking off these torture-device heels as I went. But the headlines flashed before my eyes like neon warnings: "KENSINGTON BRIDE FLEES ALTAR!" I could already see the vultures circling—*TMZ*, *Page Six*, every bottom-feeding tabloid salivating over my public execution.

These weeks have been hell on wheels—I'm drowning in wedding details while Max has conveniently vanished into thin air. Real classy move when I'm already having panic attacks about marrying a stranger for cash. Last week, I spent my lunch break sobbing in a bathroom stall between cake tastings. The week before, I nearly stabbed a florist with his own scissors when he suggested peonies for the fifth time. Even Vera Wang—yes, THE Vera Wang—looked concerned during my last fitting when I showed up with mascara streaks and yesterday's clothes. Meanwhile, my actual job keeps piling up, and I haven't slept more than four hours a night in weeks.

All of this special kind of hell has been endured for Mom and Lexi. If I ran, all that would've been all for naught and I wouldn't just be unemployed—I'd be unemployable. Max Kensington would crush me like an insect, and his Granddad would sue me into oblivion. Lexi would be forced out of UCLA, and Mom—God, Mom would have to watch her daughter become a national joke while battling cancer. Her voice echoes in my head: "Celeste, we always finish what we start." So I stood there, a prisoner at my own wedding, and smiled through clenched teeth because the alternative wasn't just humiliation—it was annihilation.

Max stares out the window, jaw clenched, teeth grinding. At the altar, he'd looked everywhere but at me. Now, trapped in this limo for an hour, he's pressed against the door like I'm diseased. He disappeared for five weeks while I planned this wedding alone. Walking down the aisle past Hollywood royalty, his hand hung limp, broadcasting his disgust to everyone. The hatred coming off him tastes metallic. I want to find a lawyer tomorrow and end this sham. If Mom and Lexi weren't depending on this arrangement, I'd throw this ring out the window and watch my future go up in flames.

After about an hour—was it really only an hour, not an entire geological epoch as our limo inched through LA's gridlock, the leather seats squeaking with every shift of my weight, Max's jaw clenched so tight I could trace the outline of every muscle while he stared out the tinted window like a man contemplating which freeway overpass would provide the cleanest exit strategy (join the club)—we arrive at his compound.

Holy shit. This isn't a house—it's a compound. The kind of house that I'd look at and always assume to be a condo complex or some luxury resort, not a home. Three stories of white stucco and terra cotta tile cascade down the cliff like a wedding cake for giants. Floor-to-ceiling windows reflect the sunset in blinding gold sheets. A circular drive surrounds a limestone fountain with mermaids. Mediterranean palace? Try billionaire fever dream: infinity pool suspended over the Pacific, private beach access carved into the cliff, even a helipad on the far wing—the whole thing perched above the ocean like an architect with a God complex went wild.

The Malibu property sprawls across what must be six acres—worth more than my lifetime earnings multiplied tenfold. My new home? The electric meter probably spins like a carnival ride just to cool this glass-and-concrete monument. That infinity pool alone could power my entire apartment building. Classic Max—taking without considering consequences. While wildfire ash still hung in the air, he built this: the mansion, the cars, the jet always captured in those glossy magazines. One man's carbon footprint, crushing everything beneath it.

"Come on, time for pictures," Max says, motioning to an enormous three-tiered fountain where water cascades over hand-carved marble dolphins. It stands majestically in the center of a garden bursting with star-shaped jasmine blossoms, their heady perfume hanging in the crisp November air. The impossible flowers glow alabaster white against glossy dark leaves, as if winter doesn't apply to Max Kensington's world. I want to meet the gardener that makes sorcery like late-fall/early-winter jasmine blooms possible.

Pictures. Right. Forgot about that. Annie Leibowitz herself was approached for this job, but apparently even a Kensington wedding couldn't tempt her from her no-weddings policy. So we "settled" for Alicia Crawford, the razor-thin, silver-haired photograph editor-in-chief for *Vogue*, who will be documenting our charade for the *Vanity Fair* exclusive that will run in next month's glossy issue. The Condé Nast empire, which owns both magazines and many others, ensures such convenient arrangements.

Alicia's portfolio reads like a Hollywood A-list roster. Her signature black and white and full color portraits— Ryan Reynolds' half-smirk captured in dramatic shadow; Cillian Murphy's ice-blue eyes piercing through the frame; Benedict Cumberbatch's angular face transformed into living sculpture; Zendaya's elegant silhouette backlit to perfection—hang in galleries worldwide. And now she circles us like a meticulous hawk, her Hasselblad camera clicking rhythmically.

For a torturous hour, we pose like mannequins beneath Alicia's exacting direction. "Chin down," she commands. "Hand on his chest." "Look at each other, not the camera." I force my lips into a crescent moon smile while

Max's arm circles my waist, his cologne—something expensive with notes of cedar and bergamot—making my head swim. We twirl on cue, laugh on command, press foreheads together while gazing into each other's eyes. Every artificial moment captured in perfect resolution for a wedding album I'll stuff into the darkest corner of some forgotten closet.

After the torture of picture-taking with a man who clearly despises me is over, I follow Max through mahogany double doors inlaid with gold filigree that could swallow my entire condo building - not my condo, but the building itself - whole. My four-inch Louboutins, bought as part of my unlimited wedding wardrobe budget, click-clack against Italian Carrara marble floors that stretch so far I feel like I'm crossing state lines into another tax bracket.

"The ballroom," Max announces with casual indifference. I stare at the Corinthian columns, the crystal chandeliers dripping from painted ceilings, the spiral staircase leading to a velvet-roped catwalk. Through the windows, white-gloved waiters move between tables on a terrace that costs more than my life. Beyond them, the Pacific gleams like something the wealthy have purchased along with everything else. My wedding reception. Fucking right.

"What do you think?" Max asks as I peer through the French doors. Guests file in across the marble terrace— women in Louboutins, men in Tom Ford, all with the bored expressions of people who've seen it all before. Then there's my crew: Mom in her JCPenney dress, Olivia with her knockoff handbag, Lexi wearing Claire's Boutique jewelry, Tally wearing a necklace she bought on sale at Marshall's. They'll stare at the chandeliers, the gold moldings, the ice sculpture dripping onto seafood worth more than my Prius. Mom will touch the silk wallpaper, wondering how a man who drinks from Baccarat could want someone who considers Lucky Charms a splurge.

I blurt out, "So do you actually pay taxes, or do you have some fancy accountant hiding your money in the Caymans while your yacht guzzles fuel that costs more than my mortgage payment?" The words tumble out before I can stop them. My eyes dart around the marble countertops. Great. I'm legally bound to one of those billionaires I've spent years ranting about on Twitter, and now everyone will think I've sold out too.

He smiles, and something shifts in that face of his—like watching a marble statue suddenly come alive. Those teeth could be in a Colgate commercial. I wonder if he went through that awkward metal-mouth phase like the rest of us mortals, or if the Kensington fortune just bought him a shortcut to dental perfection. Probably the latter. It's like those before-and-after Hollywood transformations—one minute they're in some indie film with crooked teeth, next thing you know they're flashing million-dollar smiles on red carpets. Money doesn't just talk; it gleams.

His eyes light up. "There she is. The real Celeste, the one who gave me that lecture about abalone that first night. I've missed her." He cocks an eyebrow. "And for the record, I pay what I owe in taxes. No creative accounting, no loopholes, no paying a lower rate than the people who clean my office. This country runs on revenue, and I'm not about to make everyone else cover what should be my share." He holds my gaze. "Ask my accountant if you don't believe me —though I'm guessing you won't."

I narrow my eyes but decide to trust him, though every instinct warns me not to. Men with private jets and multiple luxury cars don't exactly have stellar track records for keeping their word, or paying taxes for that matter. And regardless of how his smile makes my stomach flip or how that jawline could cut glass, his carbon footprint alone is probably visible from space, which automatically makes him a jerk in my book.

He cocks his head towards me, suddenly deciding to become human. "Well," he says. "Everybody seems to be in their places. Guess they're expecting us to have our first dance."

I frown at Max. "Wait, shouldn't we be standing somewhere, shaking hands with people? You know, like a receiving line?" I glance around at the glittering crowd, suddenly unsure of myself. Maybe that's just something normal people do at normal weddings, not at whatever *this* is. For all I know, reception lines went out with disposable cameras on tables, the Electric Slide and the Macarena.

He laughs, and I realize I've never heard that sound from him before—it's even more startling than that unexpected smile earlier. "Receiving lines went out with dial-up internet, Celeste." He gestures toward the ballroom where an L.A. DJ - probably somebody famous, not that I would know, as I don't know which DJs are famous and which ones aren't - is getting ready to spin some tunes. "God knows what song Granddad picked for our first dance."

So his grandfather selected our first dance song? Figures. Max's entire contribution to our wedding was showing up. I handled everything else while he just materialized in that perfectly tailored Tom Ford tuxedo, black tie knotted with mathematical precision. Now he's scanning the reception with those infuriating eyes—green with that ring of deep blue around the pupil—barely acknowledging the event I spent weeks orchestrating. Just more proof I'm nothing but an inconvenience, a blip in his schedule between business calls and weekend jaunts to

Catalina on whatever absurdly named yacht he probably owns.

He shrugs. "I'm not good at..." His eyes dart away from mine, then back, his usual confidence wavering. Wait—is Max Kensington actually being shy? Impossible. "Well, I just didn't want you reading into whatever song I picked. Like it meant something. I'm not good at…"

He trails off again, leaving that sentence fragment hanging between us. The unspoken part is clear enough: he's terrible at vulnerability. Choosing our first dance would mean admitting he has feelings about this marriage, about me. For a second I wonder if letting his grandfather handle it might be his way of still making it special without exposing himself. Then reality crashes back. Occam's Razor - the simplest explanation fits best: he couldn't be bothered to spend ten minutes picking a song because that would suggest he cared about our wedding. And clearly, he doesn't.

I wave my hand dismissively. "You should've let me pick the first dance song. I'm thinking Taylor Swift's 'I Knew You Were Trouble.'"

"What about 'We Are Never Ever Getting Back Together'?" Max's eyes crinkle at the corners.

I tilt my head. "That doesn't quite work, does it? We'd need to actually be together before we could get back together."

He nods and smiles. "True enough. Let's head inside." His fingers close around mine, and a jolt races up my arm. I inhale sharply, fighting against the heat blooming in my stomach and spreading outward like wildfire. My pulse quickens traitorously. Every casual brush of his skin shouldn't leave me this undone, yet here I am. Living under the same roof with this constant awareness of him will be torture—though I suspect I'll barely see him in a house this size. He'll probably stash me in some distant corner of his mansion, like Mary Queen of Scots locked away in a tower before being executed for treason.

We walk into the ballroom and the room erupts in applause as everyone rises to their feet. Their eyes shine with what looks like genuine belief in our whirlwind romance—as if Max and I simply collided one day and couldn't help but marry months later. I scan the faces of the Hollywood and Fortune 500 elite and wonder: are they truly this romantic at heart, or have years in this town perfected their performance of sincerity? I suspect it's the latter, though something warms inside me at the thought of the former—that beneath the designer suits and power plays, these titans of industry might just be hopeless romantics who believe in love stories like the fiction Max and I are selling.

Cameras flash around us as we step onto the dance floor. My heart hammers against my ribs, my fingers trembling as the first notes of "Baby, I'm Yours" drift through the room—the Arctic Monkeys cover, not the original. I glance at Max, suddenly suspicious. His grandfather chose this? An 84-year-old man selecting a track from a British indie post-punk rock band? The song itself is beautiful, a faithful rendition of the classic '60s era Barbara Lewis song that stands apart from their usual sound, but Joseph Kensington knowing about them seems... unlikely. Which means Max probably selected it himself. I'm not sure what to make of that—this unexpected gesture from a man who's barely acknowledged me for weeks.

Max's hand presses firmly against the small of my back, his other hand gripping mine as we sway. I rest my head against his chest—partly for show, of course. Can't have the gossip sites buzzing tomorrow. But then something shifts.

Heat spreads through me, electricity running up my spine like lightning finding ground after a storm. My knees nearly buckle. His fingers thread gently through my hair as I lean against him, and a sigh escapes before I can catch it. Damn. Why does this charade feel so real? As we turn slowly across the floor, my eyes drift closed, his steady heartbeat against my ear. For a moment, I let myself wonder if this thing between us might be... No. I shut that thought down immediately. That path only leads to madness.

The singer's voice wraps around us, promising devotion until stars plummet and mountains dissolve into the sea. My heart skips. If Max selected this, what does it mean? I press my cheek against his starched shirt, inhaling his cologne, a warm blend of sandalwood and citrus that seems to wrap around me like an invisible embrace, both comforting and dangerously intoxicating. No—this is just theater for our audience. Perfect theater.

Around us, Hollywood's elite exchange knowing glances. The studio head to my left leans toward her husband, nodding approvingly. The Netflix VP smiles. They're all buying it. My fingers curl slightly against Max's shoulder as I savor these final measures. I'm willing this song to never end. When the music stops, he'll remember I'm just a contract, just a favor to his grandfather. His hand rests warm against my lower back now, but soon he'll drift away, finding someone more important to speak with. I hate how much I want him to stay. I hate how my body betrays me, leaning into his. Enough. I straighten my spine slightly. This isn't real. I'm just another acquisition.

The song ends. Max's smile doesn't reach his eyes as he nods, squeezes my shoulders like I'm his basketball buddy, and says, "Okay, that's out of the way. If you'll excuse me, I need to make the rounds." Then he's gone, swallowed by the crowd while Dua Lipa's bass thumps through the speakers. No one even glances my way. I stand frozen on the dance floor, watching diamond bracelets catch the light as women throw back champagne, men in bespoke suits laugh too loudly at each other's jokes. This is his tribe—sleek, moneyed, connected—and I'm the anthropologist who accidentally went native by marrying into it. These people wouldn't remember my face if I weren't wearing Max's last name like a VIP pass. I scan the room for familiar faces—Olivia, Tally, Lexi, Mom—my real people.

I spot them at the bar, Mom throwing her head back with that throaty laugh I haven't heard in months. Tally leans in, whispering something that sends Mom into another fit of giggles. This is the woman I remember—the one who'd swagger into a Vegas poker room at midnight and leave with everyone's chips and phone numbers. The woman who orders whiskey neat without blinking and curses so creatively that sailors take notes. When I think about Thanksgiving without that laugh, or no more "surprise" roses appearing on Valentine's Day (her annual reminder that I don't need a man to feel special, though she'd never say it that way), something cold settles in my chest. But tonight, watching her eyes crinkle at the corners, I can breathe again.

Max and his cold shoulder suddenly seem very small.

Chapter Sixteen

MAX

Goddamn. That dance destroyed me. Her head nestled against my chest, my fingers lost in her hair, the rhythm of her heart matching mine—I've never felt so undone. For three minutes, the world disappeared. Just her. Just us. Then the music stopped, and reality crashed back. I did the only thing I know how to do with her: I bolted. Now I'm working the room solo, making small talk with familiar faces. Let them whisper about why the groom's abandoned his bride at their own reception. I don't care. I need air. I need distance. I need to remember who I am without her clouding my judgment.

The song choice was mine, though I lied to Celeste about that. Couldn't risk her deciphering what those lyrics meant—how perfectly they captured everything I wasn't ready to admit. I hadn't heard that song since college, but one morning, it just popped into my head. Strange how it ambushed me after all these years, surfacing in my mind unprompted and refusing to leave. Like it had been waiting for this exact moment. For us. What else could explain a forgotten melody suddenly demanding to become the soundtrack to our first dance? I know exactly what it means, which is precisely why I'm circling the room alone right now, letting Celeste catch up with her friends, buying myself time before I have to face what that song choice reveals about feelings I can barely acknowledge to myself.

Two hours later, my throat raw from shouting over the pulsing bass, I've glad-handed everyone from Spielberg (shorter than you'd think) to Musk (taller, somehow). I've manufactured a dozen different excuses for Celeste's absence—she has a migraine that's making her see spots, she's intimidated by the *Architectural Digest*-worthy mansion with its infinity pool overlooking the Pacific, I didn't want to subject her to the piranha tank on her first night out. The last two are probably true; the migraine is fiction. My cheeks ache from forced smiling, and I scan the crowded terrace for the bartender, desperate for some whiskey served in a glass the size of a fishbowl. Gianni's blazer flashes under the string lights near the koi pond, and I spot Ansel's perfectly coiffed hair bobbing through the crowd by the DJ booth. I should find the rest of my brothers, but my social battery is completely drained.

I step onto the terrace looking for Gianni, but every muscle in my body locks. Celeste—my Celeste—is sitting on the fountain with some stranger, his arm snaked around her shoulders, her head pressed against his chest.

Molten rage floods through me, scorching my veins. The sight of another man's hands on her skin—today of all fucking days—sends my heart hammering against my ribs like it wants to break free and attack him itself. My vision narrows, darkens at the edges. My fists clench so tight my knuckles crack. MINE. The word explodes through my skull with each violent pulse of blood. Who the fuck does he think he is touching what belongs to me?

I stride over, the world narrowing to a pinprick of red. There's only Celeste and this motherfucker with his hand around her shoulders, and my pulse hammers so hard I taste copper. Something primal claws up my throat as I imagine grabbing him by that designer collar, smashing his skull against the marble fountain edge until it cracks open like an egg, holding his twitching body under the chlorinated water until the bubbles stop. The rational part of my brain—barely a whisper now—warns that *TMZ* would have the footage before his lungs even filled with water, but I'm already flexing my fingers, already calculating the exact pressure needed to crush his windpipe.

I lunge forward, my vision tunneling to a pinpoint focused on this guy's smug face. My fist cocks back, knuckles white, blood roaring in my ears. Celeste's gasp barely registers—a distant echo drowned by the thundering of my pulse. The bastard's still laughing, oblivious that I'm about to shatter his perfect teeth across the floor. Then—pain. My arm wrenches backward, shoulder socket screaming as Gianni's iron grip locks around my wrist. "MAX, WHAT THE HELL ARE YOU DOING?" His voice slices through my rage, but my muscles still strain against his hold, desperate for release.

Lexi appears suddenly, a crimson cocktail clutched in her hand. She drapes herself over the guy's shoulders, planting a sloppy kiss near his ear. He returns the gesture, completely unaware of the confrontation I'd been about to initiate. My racing pulse begins to slow. "Got your Cosmo," she announces to the interloper, the words tumbling together. Her gaze shifts to me, eyes unfocused. "Oh hey, Max. See this? My man Shane here loves these fancy pink drinks. Whatcha make of that, huh?" Then she laughs. "Just kidding. He's not my boyfriend, but my gay boyfriend. See I have a gay husband and a gay boyfriend. My gay husband is with his actual husband tonight, so Shane it is." She's slurring her words and swaying, and Shane is still oblivious to what almost happened.

Lexi's gay bestie? My eyes dart to Celeste perched on the fountain's edge, horror etched across her face. Gianni's fingers dig into my wrist as he restrains my clenched fist behind my back. The thundering in my chest doesn't subside for what feels like forever, the rush of blood in my ears drowning everything else out. Lexi's. Gay. Bestie. Since when did I become this territorial beast? Before Celeste, I'd see exes with new guys and shrug it off without a second thought. But now? This primal surge has hijacked every rational thought. Christ. There's no running from this anymore. What I feel for her transcends mere possessiveness. It's something I can't even name—

I mumble an apology to the guy, then catch Gianni's eye with a look that says I'm under control now. He gets it immediately—nods once and releases his grip on my fist. I need to escape this scene. Can't bear to see Celeste's face— her fingers splayed across her eyes, her mouth frozen in shock. She's stunned. I'm stunned. The only one who isn't? Shane.

"Sorry for what, dude?" he slurs after me, but I'm already retreating to the bar for what will be my first drink tonight. The irony isn't lost on me—I didn't need alcohol to act like a complete jackass.

Gianni trails me into the haze of the smoking den. Men in tailored suits huddle around green felt tables, Cuban cigars dangling from their lips as they play round after round of high-stakes Blackjack and Texas Hold'em. The amber glow of wall sconces barely penetrates the cloud hanging over the room. Through archways, I glimpse the rest of the party—bodies swaying on makeshift dance floors, couples entwined in shadowy corners, empty crystal tumblers abandoned on every surface. These VIPs don't do moderation. The Macallan flows like water, and Cristal bottles stand empty like fallen soldiers. At least my near-brawl with Lexi's "gay boyfriend" happened when everyone was too far gone to remember the groom almost hospital-izing someone for the unforgivable sin of touching what's mine.

"Okay," Gianni says as we sit down to the bar. "What the fuck happened back there?"

I shake my head and snap my fingers. The bartender slides a glass of Macallan neat across the polished wood before I can even open my mouth. My usual. The only thing I ever order. A convenient lie forms in my mind—transparent to Gianni, maybe, but necessary armor against what's really happening inside me. Against what that woman is making me feel. I clear my throat. "Look, it's our damn wedding reception. Those two idiots in the fountain? That video's going viral in the next five minutes. The last thing I need is my new wife's reputation getting dragged through social media because some jackass couldn't keep his hands off her. So yeah, I lost it. Sue me."

Gianni's eyebrow inches upward, his face a billboard advertising disbelief. "Right. You exploded because the guy exercised poor judgment and created a PR nightmare. Nothing to do with jealousy. Nothing to do with the fact that seeing his arm around her made your blood boil." He pauses, watching me squirm. "It's not possessiveness—that's beneath you. It's just that you don't want anyone else touching her because..." His voice trails off, eyebrows lifting in challenge. The unfinished sentence dangles between us like bait. Because what? Because she's crawled under my skin? Because I can't stop thinking about her, and I'm... I'm...I'm...goddamn it! I shake my head. She irritates me, frustrates me, but that's all.

That has to be all.

Chapter Seventeen

CELESTE

Talk about bizarre. There I was, perched on the fountain's edge with Shane—Lexi's gay bestie who only has eyes for his fiancé Marcus. Both Lexi and Shane went overboard at the open bar, but who could blame them? The selection was ridiculous—Macallan scotch, Gran Patron tequila, Chopin Vintage Vault vodka, Appleton Estate rum—liquid luxury they'd never afford otherwise. Of course they'd over indulge.

I had my arm around Shane's waist, keeping him upright while some security guy watched us like a hawk. I figured if I stayed with him, they couldn't toss out the "bride's" friend, even if he was three sheets to the wind. I was playing babysitter to both him and my sister, who'd wandered off somewhere when Max suddenly appeared. His eyes were wild, fists balled tight, looking ready to deck poor Shane. And now I'm completely baffled—why would he act jealous when he's been treating me like I'm invisible at our own damn wedding reception?

Yeah. The moment our "first dance" ended, Max

vanished into the sea of designer-clad wealth. Suddenly I was invisible—the non-Kensington in a room of diamonds, A-Listers and old money. While my new husband worked the ballroom solo, I retreated to the wall. These people with their perfect posture and practiced laughs weren't my crowd. Mingling terrified me. One wrong comment about Cannes or wine, and I'd become tomorrow's whispered joke. Mr. Five-Languages-and-a-PhD Max belongs here. I don't have his framed credentials, but I can fix a broken screenplay in my sleep. Not that anyone with their Harvard rings would care.

When it became clear Max wasn't even pretending to want me around, I gathered my little island of reality— Tally, Mom, Lexi, Olivia, Shane and me—at a corner table with a wilting centerpiece. I talked to Joe and Ruth, of course. I have to be polite with them because if Joe is the person paying to stay married to Max. But after I talked to them, I gravitated to my tribe like a magnet.

Mom's tight smile, lipstick bleeding into the fine lines around her mouth, said everything without a word. The girls exchanged glances over half-empty champagne flutes; they knew about our arrangement, but even they seemed shocked by Max's Oscar-worthy performance of a groom who'd rather be anywhere else. The least he could do was fake some basic affection for the crowd of socialites and industry vultures. But no. Apparently even that was too much to ask from the great Max Kensington, heir to the throne. So...

But then, the absolute audacity of Max to go all green-eyed monster over Shane! Like I was batting my eyelashes and twirling my hair while giggling at Shane's jokes or something. As if I'd risk becoming tomorrow's trending hashtag—#NewBrideFlirtsWithStranger—complete with some shaky iPhone footage shot from behind a champagne fountain. Please. Max either thinks I'm three sheets to the wind (spoiler alert: stone-cold sober because someone had to make sure Tally didn't start doing the electric slide on top of the cake table again) or that I have the IQ of a decorative throw pillow.

Either option makes my blood boil. If he's assuming I'm sloshed enough to make a spectacle of myself, that's insulting enough. But if he genuinely believes I'd be stupid enough to publicly humiliate both of us at our own wedding reception? That's next-level offensive. What am I to him, some backwoods bumpkin who just fell off the turnip truck? And the hypocrisy! He spent the entire reception acting like I was invisible, which technically should have given me carte blanche to chat with whoever I wanted. It's not like he's invested in this marriage beyond the paperwork, so why the territorial caveman routine?

Then Gianni dragged Max away and I'm ready to bail. At 2 AM, only the freeloaders remain, draining the last of the top-shelf liquor while the VIPs had vanished in their Bentleys hours ago. My feet screamed in my Louboutins, throbbing with the fading bass. Sober and exhausted, I craved my Ikea mattress—one of my last nights in my bedroom before Max's beachfront mausoleum becomes home. I called a seven-seat Uber, and we all left together.

The ultimate Irish goodbye.

Chapter Eighteen

MAX

Celeste is moving in today and I'd rather be getting a root canal without anesthesia. Rosa, who's been shooting me death glares all morning, keeps muttering something about beds and lying in them. It's pissing me off, which never happens with Rosa. She's my rock, has been since I was a snot-nosed kid with abandonment issues the size of Montana.

When Dad bailed, I went nuclear—smashing vases, punching walls, the works. Granddad and Nana tapped out after a few months. Gianni and his pasta-loving clan were always jetting off to Florence or Milan. My brothers? Too busy nursing their own daddy wounds to deal with mine. But Rosa? She'd sit cross-legged on my bedroom floor for hours, piecing together thousand-piece puzzles while I sobbed, playing endless rounds of Go Fish when I couldn't sleep, making sure I didn't do something stupid like swan-dive off the Pacific Coast Highway bridge. I'd take a bullet for that woman without hesitation, and I've always treated her advice like gospel. But right now? Her "you-made-this-mess" wisdom can go straight to hell.

I shake my head. "Rosa, I can't believe you're taking her side. You know exactly why Granddad is forcing this woman into my house. This isn't my fault, so don't give me that look." My bare feet slap against the travertine as I pace the length of the infinity pool.

Rosa doesn't even look up from her needlepoint—some welcome gift for Celeste, a stranger she's decided to like without meeting.

"I'm staying at the city penthouse tonight," I say. "You can give her the grand tour. Show her which wing is hers. Teach her how to use the La Cornue Grand Palais range that she'll probably mistake for modern art. Just don't expect me to be here when she arrives."

Rosa's head shakes and that infuriating tsk-tsk sound makes my jaw clench. I hate when she's right. And she is right now. The penthouse beckons like a sanctuary, but my lungs feel compressed at the mere thought of Celeste inhabiting these walls—temporarily, I remind myself, just temporarily.

God, I need a grapefruit spoon to carve out the part of my brain that keeps picturing her here. I glance at Rosa's knowing eyes and sigh. No one reads me like she does, not even Gianni. She sees the panic rising in my chest, the futility of escape. Her favorite saying echoes in my head: "Wherever you go, there you are." I could charter a jet to Antarctica tomorrow—been there once, checked it off the bucket list, never again with those temperatures—but Celeste would still haunt me. She's lodged herself somewhere between my ribs, and distance won't dislodge her. Even with her sequestered in the east wing, she'll be everywhere. In my thoughts. Under my skin. Inescapable.

Rosa's fingers pause over her needlepoint—a humming-bird with wings of emerald and sapphire hovering above a crimson flower. The kind of delicate, handcrafted thing Celeste would probably display proudly on her wall. Rosa fixes me with that look, the one that's been stopping me in my tracks since I was seven.

"Enough pacing," she says, her voice soft but firm. "This situation? You walked right into it. Joe watches you parade those models through your house, sees the way you check your watch during family dinners, notices how you never laugh anymore." She jabs her needle toward me. "That emptiness you pretend not to feel? Joe sees it. His solution might be extreme, but it comes from love. Pure and simple." She returns to her stitching. "Give her a chance, Max. Or keep being the man who has everything and nothing at all."

And then the doorbell rings.

And my fate is about to come through the door.

God help us all.

Chapter Nineteen

CELESTE

God, today's the day. No more postponing the inevitable. Tally and Olivia are helping me pack up my life into cardboard boxes. Lexi texted that she can't make it—something about a deadline for her film project with Shane. I

believe her, I do. That short film is due Monday, and knowing Lexi, she hasn't touched the editing software yet. But there's this nagging feeling that she's avoiding me. Every time I mention my new marriage, she gets this look—like she's personally responsible for my marital sacrifice. I've told her a million times: Mom's cancer isn't her fault. If anyone's to blame, it's the universe's sick sense of humor. No tumor, no desperate need for money, no marriage to Max. Mom would still be juggling her jobs, keeping their little apartment, and Lexi would be focusing on school instead of feeling like she needs to drop out. But Lexi won't accept that. So here I am, packing with Tally and Liv while my sister silently protests the arrangement by burying herself in coursework.

I hate moving. Hate it with the burning passion of a

thousand suns. My back aches from hauling cardboard boxes down three flights of stairs, my fingers raw from the edges of packing tape. I never know just how much useless crap I've accumulated until I'm forced to wrap each item in newspaper and bubble wrap—dog-eared paperbacks with coffee stains on their pages, framed photos of people whose names I barely remember, ceramic figurines of woodland creatures with chipped ears, that hideous brass lamp I found at a yard sale in Pasadena that I swore would look "vintage-chic" somewhere, and Mom's meticulously preserved Barbie collection, in an enormous glass and wooden three-story case.

Yes, Barbie Dolls. It all started when I found out that my mother never had a Barbie Doll growing up because her family couldn't afford one. I still remember her face pressed against the glass at FAO Schwarz during our trip to New York—her breath fogging the display case that housed the Holiday Barbie in her crimson velvet gown with white fur trim. The way her fingertips hovered just above the glass, not quite touching, as if the doll might disappear if she pressed too hard.

My father was still alive then, so we conspired together, and soon it became our family tradition. Lexi and I would pore over glossy Barbie catalogs with Mom, watching her dog-ear pages and circle dolls with her red pen. Our collection grew: a Grecian Barbie with a gold laurel crown and draped chiton, a Victorian one with a bustle the size of my fist, the *Titanic* Rose with her miniature Heart of the Ocean necklace that actually sparkled under light. A fairy Barbie with gossamer wings that shimmered iridescent blue-green in the light, her miniature violin tucked under a porcelain chin. A Bob Mackie Barbie draped in a dramatic black and white sequined gown, its enormous satin collar arching behind her platinum blonde head like a peacock's tail. A Celtic Barbie with cascading copper hair that fell in perfect waves past her waist, an emerald-studded golden crown perched atop her head, her velvet dress the deep green of ancient forests. A *Gone With The Wind* Barbie with that iconic moss-colored velvet dress cinched impossibly tight at the waist, matching hat tilted coquettishly over one eye. A ballerina Barbie balanced on perpetual tiptoe, her crystalline tutu catching the light, satin ribbons criss-crossing up delicate ankles. Mom's favorite was the Bond-Girl Barbie with a tiny golden pistol strapped to her thigh in a lace garter. And about 10 different holiday Barbies. When Mom and Lexi downsized after her diagnosis, I inherited these treasures. Now they wait, each doll's limbs cushioned in tissue paper, their tiny accessories sealed in Ziploc bags, the display case swaddled in three layers of bubble wrap, ready for their journey.

Olivia leans against my doorframe, arms crossed. "You're seriously bringing your own bed?" she asks as I tug at my sheets. I wave Tally over to help me lift the mattress so I can dismantle the frame beneath it.

"Of course, why?"

Tally's eyes roll skyward. "Because Liv has this fantasy you'll be cuddling up with Mr. Hunk tonight." The nickname sticks in my ears. We've all developed our own code names for Max, as if saying his actual name might summon him like Beetlejuice. I prefer "Jack"—jackass abbreviated—while Olivia never calls him anything but "Pretty Boy." All three fit him perfectly, though I hate admitting mine hits the mark.

"That's not what I said," Olivia protests, tapping her phone screen. "I just bet Pretty Boy's got you set up with something ridiculous. One of those mattresses that costs more than my car." She turns her phone toward me, displaying a cloud-like monstrosity. "The Hästen Maranga. One hundred and fifty thousand dollars of Swedish sleep technology."

I glance at the photo and hand the phone back. "If Max has something that luxurious waiting for me, I swear to God I'll strip naked and perform the entire Nutcracker Suite. I've been sleeping on what feels like concrete wrapped in sandpaper for six years." I rake my fingers through my hair. "Liv, you're absolutely right. The man probably has guest beds worth more than my entire existence. Why the hell would we risk hernias hauling this decomposing Costco monstrosity down three goddamn flights? Worst case, I arrive to an empty room and panic order something at 2 AM." I dig my knuckles into my temples so hard I see stars. "Sure, it'll cost a fortune I don't have, but less than the spinal surgery I'd need after that death march down those stairs."

Truth is, I'm broke, so I didn't hire movers. When I saw the thousand-dollar minimum quote for professional movers, I nearly vomited. Instead, I promised Liv and Tally the most obscene steaks Ruth's Chris offers in exchange for their sweat and a U-Haul that reeks of previous tenants' desperation. They agreed—partly because they love me, partly because I've destroyed my back helping them move their shit across town approximately fifty-seven times. But let's be crystal clear: all three of us would rather perform open-heart surgery on ourselves with plastic sporks than spend another Saturday of our rapidly evaporating youth cramming my pathetic life into cardboard coffins.

Tally's eyes light up with mischief. "Listen to me," she says, leaning in close. "This marriage is a two-way street. He needed you as much as you needed him. So why not work that angle?" She points to the picture of the $150,000 mattress. "Starting with demanding this heavenly Swedish cloud as part of your marriage settlement. It could be your dowry."

A dowry's paid by the bride's family, but I get her point.

My forehead creases as a thought hits me. Wait—Max must have his own reasons for going along with this charade. What's his grandfather using as leverage? Money? The company? Some family secret? I've been so caught up in my own desperation that I never stopped to wonder why a man like Max would agree to marry a complete stranger. His grandfather's motives are clear enough, but Max's? There's something there. Something I might be able to use.

Dammit! What an idiot I've been! Whatever leverage Max's grandfather has over him could've been mine too. I could've flipped the script—told Max to handle the wedding planning himself or watch me walk. These last eight weeks might have looked like his—feet up, carefree, while someone else handled the details. But who am I kidding? He would've seen right through it. The cold reality is I couldn't afford to walk away, and Max knows that better than anyone. With his shark-like instincts, he would've called my bluff in a heartbeat. Still... I should've at least made him sweat.

I shake my head. No, I can't leverage my way out of this mess. Max knows exactly why I signed those marriage papers—Mom's medical bills, Lexi's tuition. My back's against the wall, and he's just leaning casually against his. This isn't some standoff where we're both holding loaded guns. He's got a cannon; I've got a water pistol. If I try the whole "treat me better or I walk" routine, he'll probably say "don't threaten me with a good time" and hold the door open for me on my way out. And that would be that.

I look around the apartment. "Well, I guess that's it. Let's go."

The U-Haul's door slams behind us, the sound final as a gavel. Through the smudged window, I catch a last glimpse of my third-floor condo—the one I scrimped for years to afford, the one with the mortgage paperwork I signed with trembling fingers. For three years, that place has been home: the kitchen counter where Olivia and I demolished pints of Häagen-Dazs after midnight, the bathtub where I soaked away terrible days with cheap Merlot, the couch that caught our tears when men whose faces now blur together walked away. The engine rumbles to life beneath us, and something in my chest seems to tear loose, floating untethered as we pull away from the curb.

"Bye beautiful apartment," I say, looking out the window.

Leaving this place hits me in the gut more than I ever thought it would. I'm leaving my sanctuary for a cold palace where I'll materially have everything I need, but emotionally will be bereft.

Oh, God, what the hell am I doing?

Chapter Twenty

CELESTE

I can feel my pulse in my throat as I stand before Max's imposing front door—solid mahogany with wrought iron accents that screams "I cost six figures." Thank God for Olivia and Tally flanking me like bodyguards. Their presence steadies me, even as I notice my fingertips trembling against my purse.

The door swings open to reveal a woman in her early sixties with warm brown skin, draped in a vibrant caftan that matches her head wrap. Her smile breaks across her face like sunrise, and before I can even introduce myself, she pulls me into an embrace that feels like coming home. In this massive, cold mansion, her presence radiates warmth.

"Celeste," she says, her voice musical with genuine delight—something I've never once heard from Max. Suddenly I'm sobbing against her shoulder, my body betraying me. The tears I've been swallowing for months while dreading this day come rushing out all at once. But mixed with the release of tension is something unexpected:

hope. If this woman—probably the housekeeper—will be here too, maybe I won't be completely alone after all.

Olivia puts her hand on my back. "You okay?" she asks me.

I nod, feeling the tightness in my chest finally begin to loosen. "Actually, for the first time since this whole night-mare started, I think I might be." I look at this woman, whose weathered face is creased with laugh lines, her dark eyes warm and knowing as she beams at me like California sunlight breaking through morning fog. "Um, I'm so sorry for ruining your beautiful gown like this." I gesture help-lessly at the silk fabric, now spotted with mascara and salt stains.

"It's okay, child," she says, her accent melodic and soothing as she pats my hand with fingers that are calloused but gentle. "By the way, I'm Rosa. I'm Max's housekeeper. Been with the family since he was knee-high."

I walk through the door with Rosa's arm around me and freeze. Max stands in the foyer, transformed. His black cash-mere shirt hugs his chest and shoulders, dark jeans hanging from narrow hips, bare feet against marble. His usually perfect hair falls in waves, one lock curling above his eyebrow. When he moves, his sleeve rides up, revealing a Celtic tattoo I never knew existed. My pulse hammers in my throat as I swallow, suddenly hungry in a way that has nothing to do with dinner.

That's the first thing I notice. The second thing I notice is holy God, this place! The marble foyer stretches before us like a white sea, with Grecian columns soaring to a cherub-painted dome. Crystal chandeliers cast rainbow light across twin mahogany staircases that curve to the second floor. Not a fingerprint mars the brass railings. The air smells of expensive perfume, polished wood, and fresh flowers. And this is just the foyer.

"Hello," I say stiffly to Max, who's just standing there, not saying a word. Rosa gives him some side-eye and Max shakes his head and waves his hand vaguely towards the back of the house, where I can see, way off in the distance, there is a floor to ceiling glass door that leads to the outside terrace.

Rosa rolls her eyes. "Don't mind Max," she says with a shake of her head. "Let me show you to your living quarters."

She takes my hand—her fingers cool and dry against my sweaty palm—and leads me through enormous glass doors that swing open without a sound. We pass through one room after another, each with pristine white walls that soar twenty feet high. In the first, stark black and white photographs of nude figures hang beside a de Kooning—violent slashes of crimson and ochre that seem to bleed across the canvas. The next room showcases a Monet, its water lilies floating in purples and blues so delicate they appear to shimmer in the recessed lighting. The back room stops me cold: an enormous stone fireplace dominates the far wall, rough-hewn granite blocks stacked floor to ceiling, making my heart race as if I've stumbled into some ancient temple.

I glance over my shoulder at Olivia and Tally, their jaws hanging slack, eyes wide as dinner plates. During our wedding reception, we'd only glimpsed the ballroom with its hand-painted murals, the infinity-edge terrace pool that seemed to melt into the Pacific, and the mahogany-paneled smoking room where vintage Cohibas rested in humidors worth more than my car. But this—this living space feels like stepping onto a movie set, the kind where some tragic heiress in silk and diamonds would descend those stairs with theatrical flair. I half expect Gloria Swanson to materialize at the landing, arms outstretched, declaring she's ready for her close-up while insisting she's still big, it's the pictures that got small.

We get to the back room, and go through a heavy mahogany door that leads to a hallway with gleaming marble floors and recessed lighting. The hallway stretches for what feels like fifty feet before opening into a completely different wing of the enormous mansion. It's not just an addition—it's practically another house attached to the main residence, with its own sun-drenched living room featuring floor-to-ceiling windows overlooking the Pacific and an enormous stone fireplace on one wall. There are several bedrooms with custom California king beds, bathrooms with rainfall showers and heated floors, and a chef's kitchen outfitted with a six-burner La Cornue Grand Palais range, double Sub-Zero refrigerators, and countertops of polished Carrara marble that gleam under pendant lighting.

I freeze in the doorway. "This...this is mine?" My fingers trail along cream-colored walls as I move from room to room, sinking into carpet that costs more than my yearly salary. The master bedroom steals my breath—a California king with sea foam sheets, velvet headboard, and perfect pillows. Lavender drapes puddle on herringbone floors while Diptyque candles surround watercolors of peonies. Silver frames hold photos of my family I never gave him. Everything sits precisely placed, as if measured for maximum tranquility. A crystal chandelier hangs from the vaulted ceiling. When I push open the French doors, salt air rushes in with the sound of waves. The balcony overlooks the Pacific—endless blues melting into the diamond-scattered horizon.

Somehow, Max absorbed every detail of my hastily decorated condo and transformed it into this sophisticated fantasy version that still feels unmistakably like me.

I walk into the walk-in closet and freeze. It's bigger than my entire condo. Cedar walls gleam around me, glass cabinets line the sides, and a marble island sits in the center like something from a cooking show. The soft lighting makes the designer suits and shoes glow—all probably worth more than my car.

My hands shake a little as I touch the clothes. Suits, hats, jeans, sweaters, blouses—all hanging perfectly, all exactly my size, all things I've only seen in magazines. Chanel. Dior. Armani. And the shoes below, each in its own glass case—Manolos with their curves, Pradas with their clean lines, and those red-bottomed Louboutins I once stared at through a store window. They shine like treasures, like Prince Charming collected every perfect shoe and left them here for me.

And the jewelry! Earrings in every hue of diamond imaginable—champagne pinks that catch the light like sunset on crystal waters, forest greens deep as ancient emeralds, cognac browns that warm like aged whiskey, and ice blues that shimmer with winter's breath. There are even blood-red diamonds.

They're masterfully cut into teardrop earrings that dangle like frozen tears, statement necklaces with stones the size of quail eggs, and tennis bracelets that could blind you when they catch the light, and custom platinum rings. My fingers tremble as I touch these exquisite treasures, my heart pounding. Suspicious, I slide each diamond across the compact mirror from my purse—it etches a perfect line into the glass surface, confirming what I already know: genuine diamonds. But they're lab-created. They must be. There's no way these are all natural diamonds, or any of them are, for that matter, because multi-colored diamonds costs millions apiece and Max wouldn't spend that much on me, a woman he barely knows. Still, they're gorgeous and I'm over the moon looking at them.

The mahogany jewelry chest holds treasures I never imagined touching. I lift out Prada necklaces with emeralds like quail eggs, test a pearl necklace against my teeth for that telltale sandy texture. Diamond rings in canary, ice blue, and blush wink from platinum settings. A Cartier bracelet sparkles against midnight velvet. My hands tremble, half expecting alarms. At home, my jewelry box held plastic beads and tarnished silver, save for a $50 black pearl necklace from Cozumel that had felt extravagant. All this stuff isn't just expensive—it's old money turned into fancy things that I can't believe they're letting me handle.

I spin around to find Max hovering at the closet entrance, his brow furrowed. He shifts his weight from one foot to the other and I notice he now has shoes on. "My shopper Jack picked these out. Thought you might—" He clears his throat. "Jack can take back anything you don't want. No big deal." His eyes dart to mine, then away. "So...yeah."

I stand frozen, jaw slack, unable to form a coherent thought. There's a difference between knowing your husband has billions and actually standing in the physical manifestation of that wealth. The soaring ceilings, the wall of windows framing the ocean, the imported marble —it's mine now, supposedly. Like stepping into an *Architectural Digest* spread and suddenly being told you live there. The vastness of it all tilts my sense of reality, making the floor beneath my feet feel less solid than it should.

I shake my head, fingers lingering on Dior silk while the

mingled scents of buttery leather and hothouse orchids fill my lungs. "These are..." The words catch somewhere behind my breastbone. It's a twisted fairy tale—Cinderella with the castle but without the prince's heart. Would the glass slipper have felt like enough compensation? Even with a private wing, weekly brunches with the other princesses, and maybe a royal corgi padding along marble hallways after her?

Max shrugs his broad shoulders and exits the room, the expensive leather soles of his shoes clicking against the marble floor. Then he turns around. "Uh, I hope you don't have plans tonight. I'm having my personal chef make us dinner here at the house. Olivia, Tally, you're invited too, of course."

We all nod and Max leaves us with lovely Rosa, who smiles and looks at Olivia and Tally. "I'm so sorry, I didn't formally introduce myself to the two of you."

"Yes, Rosa," Tally says, tucking a strand of her dark, rainbow-streaked hair behind one ear. "Guess you know Max pretty well, huh? By the way, I'm Tally, short for Tallulah."

"And I'm Olivia," Olivia says, extending her slender fingers toward Rosa's hand, but instead, Rosa envelopes the two of them in big hugs that smell of vanilla and fresh laundry.

"I'm a hugger," she says, her voice muffled against their shoulders. "I hope that's not a problem."

Tally and Olivia exchange glances and giggle. "Not at all," Olivia says, the tension in her shoulders melting away. After all, she comes from a warm family of huggers, a big Sicilian family where embraces last long enough to feel heartbeats.

"Well," she says. "I'll leave you ladies be." Then she snapped her fingers. "I almost forgot, Celeste. Hang on."

Then she left and came back with an exquisite needlepoint hummingbird hovering above a delicate purple hibiscus, its emerald wings caught mid-flutter, tiny glass beads forming dewdrops on the flower's velvet petals.

Tears come to my eyes as I look at the beautiful bird and flower, so lovingly stitched by caring hands. I hug Rosa's round and stout body, feeling such a strong sense of relief that there might be at least one friendly face to come home to every evening.

Chapter Twenty-One

MAX

I make myself scarce while Celeste and her friends—Olivia and Tally—haul boxes through my front door. Better to vanish than give her ideas about this arrangement being anything real. That's why I had Rosa show her around instead of doing it myself. I also stocked her closet with designer everything—clothes, shoes, jewelry, accessories. A $60K salary at Dreamscape won't buy the wardrobe she'll need to command respect, especially after our companies merge and the stakes get higher.

Of course, that's the only reason I sent Jack, my personal shopper, on a mission. He hit Neiman Marcus, Dior, Chanel, and Gucci. I gave him a list: green dresses for her eyes, leather bags, power suits in navy, gray, and red, some gold jewelry. Regular clothes too—jeans and such. And shoes. Lots of shoes. Red-soled Louboutins for parties and boots for winter. Ferragamo flats when her feet hurt. Manolos with those skinny straps. Pradas with the silver hardware. Jimmy Choos that would make her legs go on forever in summer dresses. Just practical stuff, really.

Nothing special. No, I didn't do this because I'm absolutely crazy about this woman. Not at all. It's all just business.

I had to estimate her size by memory and also called her boss, Iris, and picked her brain for hours, swearing her to secrecy.

Today is Saturday, and, for me, Saturdays are sacred. It's the only day I don't wake at 5 AM to the buzz of emails flooding my phone. The only day I'm not trapped in the office until sunset, especially now with the Dreamscape merger consuming every waking hour.

I text Ansel and Gianni at dawn: "Surf's up." Out there, with nothing but my board and the rhythm of the waves, my mind finally quiets. The ocean doesn't care who Max Kensington is. It doesn't demand quarterly projections or merger strategies.

I need that silence today before tonight's dinner with Celeste——my reluctant attempt at hospitality. I'm not naive. If I completely freeze her out, she'll vent to someone. Then suddenly *Page Six* runs a headline about our "marriage of convenience," and I'm juggling a PR nightmare on top of everything else. A decent meal and civil conversation seems a small price for her discretion.

The water's biting cold in late November, but I zip my wetsuit tight and make my way down to the private stretch of beach. Above me, clouds hang low and heavy, threatening rain, while the wind tosses my hair and stings my cheeks. Perfect. Everyone thinks Southern California weather equals endless summer, but they've never lived through our "May Grey" or "June Gloom"——those mornings when overcast clouds blanket the coast and you need a sweater until noon, only to shed layers by midday, then bundle up again as evening approaches. November feels like those months' darker cousin. The sun retreats by five now, after the time change, leaving everything in shadow. I welcome it. There's something comforting about a sky that reflects what's inside me.

I bob in the water, waiting for the guys. They paddle out in their wetsuits, boards gleaming. I raise my hand, and soon we're all stretched out on our boards, scanning the horizon. When the swells come, we catch them one by one. None of us are amateurs—Dad made sure of that. When Ansel and I were kids—barely a year apart in age—he hired Lance Williams to train us. Lance wasn't just any instructor; he'd claimed the World Surf League championship three times and represented the national team for five consecutive years.

I was four when Lance first set me on a board in the punishing Northern California surf. Dad's philosophy: master Big Sur's monster waves, and you can handle anything the ocean threw at you. Despite my initial terror, something clicked. These days, I've ridden everything from Raglan's perfect left-handers in New Zealand to Nazare's towering walls in Portugal to the legendary breaks at Jeffreys Bay, South Africa—some of the most formidable surf spots on the planet.

As I wait between swells, I catch myself picturing Celeste out here beside me. Would she surf? Or would she be like most newcomers, eyes darting below the surface, convinced every shadow is the fin from *Jaws*? I've lost count of the Great Whites I've seen glide beneath my board— sleek, prehistoric, utterly indifferent to my existence. That's the thing about sharks—they're just commuting to work like the rest of us, hunting their next meal, completely uninterested in the strange human balanced on fiberglass above them. Would Celeste be as calm about the creatures?

An image keeps sneaking into my mind: Celeste on a

surfboard beside me, her red hair piled high, tanned skin against a neon pink wetsuit. Each time I imagined this, I'd force myself to think of something else. Dangerous territory. If I let myself imagine her in my daily routines—sharing waves at dawn, across the dinner table, under my sheets—I'd be done for. She'd slip past my defenses and then vanish like my father did. That same raw, gutting emptiness from when I was seven would claw its way back into my chest, only this time it would tear me apart from the inside out. I'd clawed my way back from that abyss once and it almost did me in. There wouldn't be enough of me left to try again.

By the time we paddle back to shore, my arms feel like overcooked spaghetti. Worth it though—these hours on the water saved my sanity today. Between the chaos at Kensington Pictures and this arrangement with Celeste, I need my release valves: Gianni shouting at me to push through one more set, the satisfying thwack when Steve the mannequin takes my right hook, and days like this when it's just me, the guys, and the Pacific.

The three of us trudge back to the house, sand caked between our toes, sweat drying on our backs. "Hit the showers and stick around for dinner if you want," I tell Gianni and Ansel. Might as well have the guys over for dinner since Celeste's probably inviting Olivia and Tally - after all, I invited them myself. François, my chef, texted earlier about tonight's menu: cedar plank salmon with some kind of French glaze, roasted broccoli with garlic, and a salad that'll probably have those tiny tomatoes I can never remember the name of. Guy makes enough food to feed a football team, so we're covered.

The guys hit the showers, and I follow suit, scrubbing off the sweat and grime before throwing on a fresh henley and jeans. We congregate in the kitchen.

And I wait for Celeste in my kitchen, my fingers drumming against the marble countertop, my stomach twisting itself into knots. I check my reflection in the polished chrome of the refrigerator, smoothing down a wayward strand of hair. I haven't felt this way since I was sixteen, waiting by my locker for Melissa Donovan to walk by. Me, Max Kensington, CEO of a billion-dollar company, with sweaty palms and a racing heart.

Goddamn, I have a major crush on this girl.

What is this world coming to?

Chapter Twenty-Two

CELESTE

Once Rosa leaves, Tally, Olivia and I haul the last of my cardboard boxes into my living area—our fingertips raw from the edges, sweat beading on our foreheads—I collapse onto a plush velvet sofa the color of sea foam. I wander into my new kitchen, where afternoon sunlight streams through floor-to-ceiling windows, illuminating pristine white oak cabinets with gold hardware that gleams like jewelry. My fingers trace the cool veining in the Carrara marble countertops, brush against the professional-grade La Cornue Grand Palais range with six burners I'll get some amazing use out of since I love cooking, and pull open the massive sub-zero refrigerator door to find it meticulously stocked with color-coded containers of pre-cut fruit, imported cheeses, and a bottle of Dom Pérignon nestled between cartons of oat milk.

I get out the bottle of Dom and the cork hits the ceiling with a satisfying pop, sending a wisp of champagne mist into the air. "Woo hoo!" I squeal, watching the Dom Pérignon foam over the neck of the bottle. "Fashion show time!" I run my fingers over a silky Valentino dress, then caress the buttery leather of Prada boots. A Chanel tweed jacket feels substantial, important somehow.

I'm Vivian from *Pretty Woman*, minus the awkward blow-job-during-*I-Love-Lucy* scene, just pure wide-eyed wonder at fabrics I've only ever seen behind glass. The price tags alone would cover three months of my mortgage. I twirl, watching the clothes sway on their designer hangers, mentally calculating how to smuggle this treasure trove out when our year is up. These cashmere sweaters and hand-stitched gowns could fund my screenwriting career for another two years at least if I put them on Poshmark. Not that I would ever be able to part with them. I'd kiss, date and marry these clothes if I could.

Three bottles of Dom split between us three later, I'm wobbling in front of my beveled full-length mirror, my reflection blurred at the edges.

"Pass me that—that thing," I point, nearly toppling sideways. Olivia tosses over a mass of leather that unfolds into pants as buttery as they are black. I struggle into them, my champagne-clumsy fingers fumbling with the zipper. I pull on some Prada thigh-high boots in black with sky-high heels and a buttery Chanel cashmere sweater in burgundy and a chunky Dolce and Gabbana necklace created with different colored gemstones - rubies, emeralds, diamonds, pearls and light blue sapphires. Plus a pair of sky blue diamond tear-drop earrings. No, those don't work - something more dramatic. A pair of Paul Morellli 18K white gold earrings with aquamarine drops look amazing.

A red-soled Jimmy Choo heel dangles from Tally's finger. "Try these."

My foot slides in like Cinderella's, though my ankles immediately betray me. I grab the closet door, laughing.

"Oh!" My fingers brush feathers. I pull down a wide-brimmed hat the size of a deep-dish pizza, its stiff ivory straw woven into an intricate lattice pattern. The brim dips low, casting my face in shadow like a protective eclipse. It's one of those enormous statement pieces you see perched atop socialites at horse races like the Preakness or Kentucky Derby—a fascinator, I think it's called?

"Kentucky Derby realness," Olivia slurs, her phone camera clicking rapidly.

"Those poor horses though," I mumble, suddenly somber. "Did you know they—"

"Try this instead!" Tally interrupts, shoving a tiny purse into my hands that weighs more than it should. "Diamonds," she whispers reverently.

I reach for a cream Chanel suit, its gold-flecked bouclé wool catching the light. Pearl buttons and clean lines whisper old money. Champagne still fizzing in my veins, I add a hot pink fedora that makes Olivia snort with laughter. I throw on real pearls, then grab a Pollock-splattered Hermès Birkin. In the mirror, the conservative suit transforms beneath the riot of color. I swap the fedora for a newsboy cap, then back again. This closet isn't filled with designer labels—it's filled with versions of myself I never knew existed. For the first time, I'm not just wearing clothes. I'm developing a style. It feels electric.

"JEANS!" The word explodes from me like a confetti cannon. "Because apparently living in Chanel and Prada is like trying to breathe underwater. Though—" I strike a ridiculous Vogue pose, wobbling on one foot, "—imagine me sashaying into a writer's meeting looking like I've been marinated in money! Iris would probably choke on her kombucha. She'd be like 'Celeste! Did you rob Anna Wintour's closet? Here's a promotion!'" I pirouette and nearly crash into a lamp. Oops. Day drinking—who even am I? Not the same girl who used to iron her Target t-shirts. Not the girl whose idea of luxury was splurging on name-brand cereal. Now I'm Mrs. Billionaire with a closet bigger than my old condo. Maybe this bizarro-world Celeste will actually trick some fancy-pants agent into thinking my screenplay deserves a Palm D'Or. Stranger things have happened in this timeline, right?

I shimmy into crystal-studded Libertine pants that hug like a second skin, then swap them for flower-embroidered Valentinos. A black Prada silk top, houndstooth cap, and red diamond accessories complete the first look, with combat boots that feel like my old Docs but scream money. I spin before the mirror, grinning, before switching to a Dior tee, thigh-high Louboutins, and a chunky Prada cardigan. A pink bucket hat makes me laugh—all wrong. Black works better. I finish with my new favorite gemstone necklace and brown diamond drop earrings.

Olivia and Tally bombard me with hangers, their laughter punctuating each toss. Silks slide through my fingers, sundresses bloom with colors I'd never dare wear before, and sweater dresses promise warmth for the coming winter chill. I slip into a lavender cashmere coat—Dolce, they whisper reverently—over Prada jeans that somehow make my legs look endless. A pair of Louboutins add inches I don't need - I'm 5'10" in my bare feet - but desperately want. When I fasten the brown diamonds at my ears and sling the red Birkin over my shoulder, the mirror shows someone I barely recognize. A stranger with my face, wearing wealth like she was born to it.

The girls are already holding up more treasures: a khaki Dior trench with tortoiseshell buttons the size of silver dollars, and twin Alexander McQueen coats—one in royal red with gold military-inspired epaulets, the other in chocolate brown with intricate embroidery along the collar—identical to the ones I'd seen Princess Kate wearing during her winter tour of Scotland, her hair gleaming against the rich fabrics as she waved to adoring crowds.

I'm upteen glasses deep into the champagne, sprawled across silk sheets, surrounded by designer labels I once only glimpsed in magazines. The ocean crashes outside my window—my window—and somewhere downstairs, Rosa hums while folding laundry that costs more than my mortgage. Her presence feels like a life raft I'll need if the worst happens and my mother's chemo fails.

The bedside clock reads 4:52. Dinner's at 6. I slide open the walk-in closet door and run my fingers across fabrics that whisper against my skin. Nothing too formal, nothing desperate. I catch myself wondering if Max might notice a particular blue dress that matches my eyes, then immediately scoff at the thought. The man barely acknowledges my existence. I'm dressing for Olivia and Tally, I decide, pulling the blue dress from its hanger anyway.

I glance at my watch and turn to Tally and Olivia. "Dinner in twenty minutes. What do you think?" I hold up a greenish-blue Givenchy cable knit mini-dress with a scoop neck that dips just low enough to be interesting without being scandalous. Next to it, I've laid out a pair of coveted jeweled Manolo open toed sandals with a three-inch heel, making me over six feet tall. The mini-dress hits mid-thigh, perfect for showing off the legs I've been religiously toning since high school track, and the color brings out the stormy blue-green of my eyes in a way that even expensive makeup can't achieve.

"Love it, girl! Now get into the shower and get ready for

dinner," Tally says with a giggle. "Pretty boy won't take his eyes off your legs."

The hot water of the shower does nothing to calm my nerves. I twist my hair into a messy topknot, grateful that my wedding-day eyelash extensions means I can leave my makeup natural—just a whisper of rose-gold shimmer on my lids, a swipe of peachy blush across my cheekbones, and a dab of clear gloss that makes my lips look like I've just bitten them. My freckles are covered, but just barely.

My fingers tremble slightly as I fasten the Dolce statement necklace, its colorful gems catching the light as I add the matching bracelet and slip in the pale blue diamond earrings. I slip on the Manolos, their crystal-encrusted straps catching the light as I slide my feet into sandals. The three-inch heels transform my posture instantly, and the open toes reveal my fresh pedicure—a pale pink that matches the blush undertones of the shoes themselves.

The mirror reflects back someone I barely recognize. Maybe it's the champagne buzz, but I feel like I'm watching someone else step into a fairy tale.

Except this Cinderella's Prince Charming wishes she'd turn back into a pumpkin.

Whatever.

Chapter Twenty-Three

MAX

I'm loitering in the kitchen with the guys, pretending to savor this overpriced IPA while checking the doorway every thirty seconds for Celeste. The bottle's already half-empty, and my fingers won't stop drumming against the label. Gianni's hand suddenly cuts through my field of vision, his face a mix of amusement and concern. I force a smile, but it's no use—the guy reads me like yesterday's financial report. Always has.

"What's going on?" Gianni asks.

I shrug. "Nothing's changed." I roll my eyes. "She's under my skin. Here I am, palms sweating like some teenager meeting his girlfriend's dad for the first time. My stomach's doing somersaults. Never felt this before—like I swallowed a kaleidoscope of butterflies and they're all trying to escape at once." I shake my head. "I want her gone from this house, but I can't stand the thought of her being far away. It's like I'm being torn in two different directions."

Gianni's aware of my obsession with getting Celeste's space just right. I cornered Iris with an interrogation that would've made the CIA proud—favorite colors? Decor preferences? Clothing sizes down to the half-inch? Shoe size? European or American? Iris has that insider knowledge I need. I considered ambushing her mother and sister too, but they'd have tipped Celeste off immediately. Instead, I swore Iris to absolute secrecy with a threat that made her eyes widen—something about advocating for her firing post-merger. That's how determined I was to keep Celeste from discovering the hours I spent hunting down those perfect cashmere throws, the vintage record player, those Italian leather boots in her exact size. If she connected those dots —saw the deliberate care behind every carefully selected item—she'd read my feelings like an open book. And that terrifies me more than any business deal gone wrong.

Gianni sighs, a half-smile playing at his lips. "Ansel," he calls to my brother, who's already elbow-deep in the refrigerator despite dinner being less than an hour away. Ansel emerges victorious with an armful of ingredients, dumping them onto the marble island. Despite sharing my build—all height and lean muscle—he eats like he's storing for hibernation. I watch as he layers salami, cheese, and vegetables between two thick slabs of sourdough, creating a towering Dagwood sandwich that threatens to topple with each addition. "Maybe you can reason with him."

I arch an eyebrow at Ansel as he takes his first enormous bite. Catching my look, he swallows and shrugs. "Post-surf hunger waits for no salmon dinner," he says, then jabs a mayo-smeared finger in my direction. "And stop dodging the point. You're in love with this woman. Admit it, embrace it—who knows? Might be the best thing that ever happens to you."

I throw my hands up like I'm stopping traffic. "Hold up! Love? Where'd that come from?" My fingers rake through my hair while my throat constricts. The cashmere of my henley suddenly feels like sandpaper against my skin. Ansel watches me with that know-it-all look of his. "That's ridiculous," I tell him, my voice steadier than I feel. "Rosa and Nana are the only women I've ever—" I stop myself. They earned it. Years of staying put, of proving they wouldn't disappear like my father. Celeste? She's temporary by definition. Our arrangement has an expiration date. "Not happening," I mutter, more to myself than to Ansel. "Not with her."

Ansel takes another bite of his sandwich, mumbling "Whatever" through a mouthful of bread. His eyes meet Gianni's across the table, and something passes between them—some silent message that makes my fingers curl into fists at my sides.

I cut Ansel off mid-sentence. "Shut up. You have no idea what you're talking about."

"Really?" Ansel raises an eyebrow. "So it's totally normal for you to obsess over every detail of a woman's living space? To drop six figures on lab-created diamonds? To fill her closet with every designer label in existence?" He leans back, studying me. "For someone who claims he wants her gone, you're certainly investing a lot in making her comfortable." A knowing shrug rolls off his shoulders. "Keep lying to yourself if you want..."

I glance at Gianni. He's silent, but that smirk says everything. Damn him for siding with Ansel. If anyone can read me like a book, it's Gianni, and the fact he thinks I've fallen for her... Christ. After tonight, I need to make myself scarce. Back to fourteen-hour workdays. Back to international conference calls that stretch past midnight. If I'm never at this beach house, whatever *this* is might fade. It has to fade. My sanity depends on it.

Then she appears, and my lungs forget how to work. Her sweater dress matches her eyes exactly, clinging to her figure and cutting off mid-thigh. Those Manolos with the tiny jewels add three inches to legs that already seem to stretch forever. Her red hair is piled artfully on her head, with tendrils framing her beautiful face, and around her neck is that Dolce & Gabbana piece I'd spotted at Saks, the one with the rainbow of stones that had stopped me in my tracks. Her smile is bright, but there's a slight unfocus to her gaze that suggests she's been enjoying the premium liquor I made sure to stock—Dom included. Can't say I blame her. Her friends flank her, all three radiating the particular glow of women who've spent the last few hours day drinking, thereby turning a shitty day of moving into something a bit less stressful. Smart move. If you have to deal with cardboard boxes, might as well have champagne while you're at it.

Celeste stumbles in, cheeks flushed. "Hey, Max," she says, voice honeyed with alcohol. She acknowledges the others with a nod before making her way to me. Then she hugs me. When her arms circle my waist, the oxygen seems to vanish from my lungs. The heat of her against me sends electricity down my spine, and my hands find their way to her shoulder blades of their own accord. I'm acutely aware of every inch where our bodies connect, fighting the urge to let my fingers wander lower with everyone watching. Her lips brush my ear, sending a shiver through me. "Thank you," she breathes. "That place is... incredible. Seriously, thank you."

She pulls away, leaving a cold emptiness where her warmth had been. I jam my hands into my pockets before they can reach for her again. "Just thought I'd make the place livable," I say with a shrug I hope looks indifferent. "Since you're stuck here anyway."

I catch Ansel and Gianni watching me from across the room, their faces split with identical shit-eating grins. I narrow my eyes, willing them to knock it off. I'm not some lovesick teenager. I haven't fallen for her. But their eyebrows just climb higher, and I have to look away before I give them the satisfaction of seeing me blush.

Celeste looks around. "Rosa? Can she join?"

"She is," I say. "She usually does. She's uh, my housekeeper, but also like a…"

"Mother," Ansel says helpfully.

I nod, grateful for the word I couldn't find. Rosa's been around since I was an infant, cutting crusts off sandwiches and checking my homework long after her shift ended. The day I graduated from USC, she cried more than anyone. Her paycheck says "housekeeper," but the birthday cards she's kept for twenty-odd years tell a different story.

Celeste nods, her eyes searching mine. She has no idea about my mother. Why would she? I've never breathed a word of it, and I don't plan to start now. Something tells me that sharing that particular wound would be like handing her a key to every locked room inside me. That thought makes my chest tighten.

"Good," she finally says. "I really hoped she would be here for dinner." Then she looks around. "Where is this personal chef you speak of?"

The doorbell chimes as Ansel says, "He'll be right... here." François sweeps in wearing crisp chef whites, assistants in tow. They take over the kitchen, unpacking copper pans and knives with military precision. Soon, wild-caught salmon sizzles on my indoor grill while François whisks basil béchamel in a gleaming pot. His "simple supper" features sweet potatoes, heirloom tomatoes, and buffalo mozzarella, with broccolini awaiting hollandaise. The salmon—delivered fresh this morning by François's personal fishmonger—will surely outshine whatever frozen fillets Celeste buys at Trader Joe's.

Rosa appears for dinner, wiping her hands on a dish towel. I pour her a glass of Pinot. Though I employ a small battalion of cleaners who descend on the house twice weekly, Rosa alone stays on the property, occupying the guesthouse that rivals Celeste's quarters in luxury. "How's the cottage treating you?" I always ask, though I always know her answer. She's told me often enough she loves it there. What I don't mention is how I've grown accustomed to her company at dinner, or those rare evenings when deadlines don't loom and we settle in for whatever's new on Netflix.

A half hour later, we all sit down to dinner. Celeste takes a sip of wine, then a bite of salmon. Her eyes flutter closed. "Oh my God," she says. "This salmon is incredible. And the sauce—béchamel, right?—it's perfect with the fish."

Something in me stirs with surprise that she knew it was béchamel, then shame at my surprise. Father's voice echoes in my head: *A gentleman knows his sauces as well as his wines.* I've had years of lessons on which fork to use when, which vintage wine pairs with what dish, what sauce goes with what meat or fish. I've had summers in Provence when I was five, learning which forks to use for escargot versus fish. The "gentlemen's finishing school" occupied a limestone château with lavender fields stretching beyond its iron gates, where Madame Beaumont would rap my knuckles with a silver letter opener if I slouched or spoke out of turn during our endless formal dinners.

I assumed Celeste wouldn't know these things. What else

might I be wrong about? I study her across the table, wondering if I'll ever get the chance to find out.

I study her face. "Yeah." My eyes dart around the table. Celeste, tipsy and oblivious to my signals, continues chatting with her equally buzzed friends. Meanwhile, Ansel catches my eye and smirks. Gianni nudges Rosa, both of them watching me with knowing looks. I can feel my face betraying me, wearing my feelings like a billboard. "I'm glad you like the meal," I manage, unable to disguise the tenderness in my voice.

She laughs, that bright sound that makes my chest tighten. "Isn't it funny? This fancy béchamel sauce is basically just fancy SOS—you know, shit on a shingle. Got me through college. Made with those little packets of Buddig meat for thirty-nine cents at Aldi, white bread, and whatever gravy I could scrape together from flour, margarine, and milk. That and Top Ramen." She shakes her head, and I can't look away from the way her eyes crinkle at the corners. "Between that diet and all the cheap beer, it's a miracle I functioned. And now here I am, eating what's essentially the same thing, just with a French name and better ingredients, prepared by a fancy professional chef."

I always found it ironic that béchamel sauce—with its fancy French name that sounds like it belongs in expensive restaurants—is essentially what broke college students eat regularly. It's fundamentally just a roux with milk added. That's how Celeste recognizes it despite her modest background.

Her words continue to tumble out, the wine obviously loosening her tongue. "I was terrified of coming here," she admits, gesturing with her glass toward the sprawling house. "Walking through those doors felt like Belle stepping into the Beast's castle—all that cold marble and emptiness." She smiles, nodding towards Rosa, who's beaming at her while she sips her Pinot. "Then I met your Mrs. Potts, and suddenly..." She trails off, eyes widening as she takes in the ocean view through floor-to-ceiling windows. "And this place. It's like something from a fairy tale after all."

Her fear of moving in here should've bothered me, but it doesn't. I get it more than she realizes. She stepped from her world into mine—from Earth straight to Mars. When she compared this scenario to *Beauty and the Beast*, I couldn't help but smile. We both know how that fairy tale ends. Maybe I am her Beast, waiting for her to discover I'm not the monster she imagines. And Rosa? Pure Mrs. Potts—the maternal teapot offering comfort when everything feels strange. That cartoon played endlessly in our house when I was little. Mom loved the story, so Dad would put it on several times a year, tearing up every time, probably because it reminded him so much of her.

Rosa's laughter fills the kitchen. "Me? Like the teapot from *Beauty and the Beast*?" She gives her plump midsection a gentle pat. "I suppose we do share a certain... roundness."

Celeste's eyes go wide. "Oh! No, that's not—" She stumbles over her words. "I just meant that Mrs. Potts is just... nurturing when Belle is scared in that big castle. I wasn't thinking of anything else, no, no." She stares down at her plate, pushing a piece of salmon around with her fork. The flush creeping up her neck reaches her cheeks, and she blinks rapidly. She looks like she's about to cry about Rosa taking her comparison the wrong way.

I can't help but notice she never bothers to clarify that I'm not the Beast in her little fairy tale, even as she trips over herself apologizing to Rosa. I let it slide. The Beast was misunderstood too, wasn't he? Gruff exterior hiding something else. Somebody that made sacrifices when it mattered. She doesn't see that in me yet, but maybe someday she will.

Rosa's hand settles on Celeste's back. "I know what you meant, child. I'm sorry, I tease too much. You'll learn my ways." Rosa's smile lights up her face, and Celeste's shoulders relax as she lifts her gaze. The rim of her wineglass trembles against her lip as she takes another sip. Her knuckles are white around the stem. I can almost see the thoughts racing behind her eyes—a year of tiptoeing around me, of calculated words and careful distance. Something in my chest tightens. I want to bridge this gap between us, to tell her she won't be walking on eggshells in her own home.

I reach across the table and cover her hand with mine. The touch seems to ripple through her. Those green eyes widen, darken, before she blinks and looks away. But I caught it—that flash of heat, quickly masked. Could she feel that same current that just shot up my arm? God, I hope so. No—I hope not. This…crush…I have on her would be far less complicated if it remained one-sided. My life would certainly be simpler that way.

Celeste smiles at Rosa. "Thanks for understanding. I've never had much of a filter between my brain and my mouth. My best friend got me this coaster once—'Some things are better left unsaid, which I generally realize right after I've said them.'" She lets out a small, nervous laugh. "I keep it on my desk as a daily reminder. Though clearly, it hasn't worked yet. I suspect you and Max will have front-row seats to that particular character flaw over the next twelve months."

Ansel's eyebrows shoot up. "Character flaw? Are you serious right now?" He shakes his head, letting out a dry laugh. "God forbid a woman actually tells my brother the truth. You have no idea how many people nod along when Max declares the sky is actually green. Everyone's too busy genuflecting to correct him." He leans forward, voice softening. "That honesty you're apologizing for? It's like opening a window in a stuffy room."

When Celeste smiles and blushes, something in my chest tightens. How can I be angry at Ansel's rant about asskissers when her reaction is so damn endearing? My brother's right—people do kiss my ass. So what? They kiss his too.

It hits me that Celeste and Ansel share that same unfiltered honesty. They'd probably get along perfectly, and the thought makes my jaw clench. I'm not giving her up. Not to him, not to anyone.

I've been telling myself this marriage is just temporary, a business arrangement with an expiration date. But watching her now, I wonder if I've been lying to myself all along. The mere thought of Ansel with Celeste makes me want to put my fist through a wall—which is ridiculous. My actual brother isn't even interested in her. It's the imaginary version of him I want to throttle.

Christ, I'm losing it.

Celeste gives a nervous laugh. "So I'm an open book, huh? Not entirely. Everyone keeps parts of themselves hidden." She fidgets with her napkin. "We all have those thoughts we'd never say out loud. Those moments we'd rather forget." Her voice drops. "Those failures we replay at three in the morning." She runs a hand through her hair and winces. "God, that champagne was a mistake. Dom Pérignon and dinner parties don't mix." She shoots Tally a sideways glance and whispers, "Some friend you are. You could've cut me off."

Tally throws her head back and laughs. "Cut you off?

Please. I was right there beside you, downing champagne worth more than my first car." Her smile turns nostalgic. "That piece of junk—a 1999 Chevy Metro in the ugliest lime green you've ever seen. Paid three hundred bucks for it. Could've traded the damn thing straight up for one bottle of that Dom you were pouring. So actually, thanks for the upgrade."

Celeste lets out a laugh. "Oh please. You think that's bad? My first car was a '95 Escort that somehow wheezed its way to 2015. The thing had more rust than paint by the time I got it, and duct-taped seats to boot. When it finally died, the junkyard offered me two hundred bucks. If I would've told them I'd take one bottle of Dom Pérignon and call it even, they'd say I'd still owe them a hundred dollars."

Then both girls look at me expectantly, their eyes asking about my first car. I take a sip of my wine and study the rim of my glass. The memory of my sixteenth birthday floods back—my grandfather tossing me keys to that new Porsche Cayenne, the garage door rising to reveal gleaming silver metal worth way more than most people's yearly salary. Need to change the subject.

I clear my throat. "Have you tried the crab cakes yet?"

Celeste glances at the table and raises an eyebrow. "I don't see any crab cakes here, so that would be a no," she says, her laugh light and nervous. "But I'm definitely looking forward to a future crustacean adventure."

My cheeks burn as I replay the moment in my head. Crab cakes? There weren't even crab cakes on the table. I'm the guy who rehearses quarterly earnings statements three times before delivering them. At Kensington Pictures, my precision is legendary—a single unclear directive from me can derail a $200 million production. Yet here I am, hallucinating appetizers because Celeste looked at me. She's rewired something in my brain, short-circuited my usual operating system. I haven't felt this off-balance since... hell, maybe ever.

"Well," I say. "I meant, have you tried crab cakes in general."

Celeste catches Tally's eye, then Olivia's, the three of them sharing a silent joke before Celeste responds. "I'm familiar with crab cakes from around LA, and in Big Bear, and my grand international tour of Mexico, meaning Cozumel and Cabo." She pauses, anticipating the next question. "And no, I've never been abroad, only Mexico and Canada. Cabo was spring break one year, a trip I paid on my 35% interest rate credit card. Cozumel was a stop on a Groupon cruise where the three of us crammed into a cabin meant for two. We took turns sleeping on the floor with just a blanket and pillow between us and the metal deck."

"Yeah, but the lobster and prime rib night," Tally interjects.

Olivia nods enthusiastically. "All-you-can-eat. Our girl here devoured four lobster tails plus prime rib and dessert. Spent the rest of the night feeding the fish over the railing." She nudges Celeste affectionately. "Her exact words were 'When will I ever get unlimited lobster again?' Classic Celeste—always squeezing every last drop out of an opportunity."

Hmmm....so she does eat lobster. Interesting. I assumed she probably didn't, because...

"God, I feel like such a hypocrite about that lobster now," Celeste says, tucking her hair behind her ear. "I had no idea they—" She stops herself. "Let's just say I'm not into eating anything that screams when you cook it."

Yep. Thought so. I doubt she eats Prime Rib anymore, either.

"Factory farming is a hard no for me too." She glances out the window. "This one time I was driving to Kansas City to see extended family, and we passed what I thought was a ranch. Except it was just this horrific sea of millions of cows packed together like... I don't even know. Made me sick for days afterward."

Tally gives me a knowing look. "Having second thoughts about the marriage yet?" she jokes, nudging Celeste with her elbow. "This girl's nuts about animals and is some kind of dog whisperer. Every Thursday at that shelter, she volunteers, and I swear she wants to adopt every single animal in that place every time she goes. Olivia can tell you."

"Oh God," Olivia laughs, "you should see her phone. Hundreds of pictures. 'This one looked right into my soul, Liv!' And I'm always the bad guy reminding her about our crazy schedules and our condo's no-pet policy. She'd bring home a pit bull tomorrow if she could."

I glance at Celeste. She's gone quiet, her fork pushing the last bite of salmon around her plate. After a long sip of wine, she looks up with those eyes that always give her away. "There's this pit bull at Inland Valley, where I volunteer," she says, the words tumbling out. "I walked her yesterday and just... fell for her." Her gaze darts around the room. "But a dog would mean muddy paw prints on these floors, sand everywhere after beach walks. She'd probably howl sometimes. And I know you wouldn't want her on that ridiculously expensive bed you bought for me." She shrugs, trying to seem casual. "I couldn't bear making her sleep alone, so... forget I mentioned it."

"Max," Gianni says. "You were talking about getting a

dog too. You know Rosa would take care of it while you're gone. She already said she would."

Yeah, but Celeste wants a specific dog. And I want, more than anything, to give her the dog, but as a surprise. I could just imagine her eyes when she comes home one day to see that special dog greeting her. So, I need to ask some casual questions to see just what dog she's talking about.

I just say nothing to Gianni and turn to Celeste. "So, a female pit bull at the shelter. How old is she?"

"She's just a baby," Celeste says, her eyes lighting up. "I think she's around 2 years old. White and brown, with a pink nose and she's a lover. Gives puppy kisses to everyone she meets." Then she shows me a picture of the dog. "Her name is Piper." Then she looks at her phone and hugs it to her chest.

"Today it's Piper," Olivia says. "Last week it was a basset hound puppy named Cleo, short for Cleopatra."

"And the week before that it was some kind of a mutt, nobody knew exactly what breeds ran through that dog's blood, name was Daisy."

"And the week before that it was-"

"Yeah, I know, I obsess about a different dog every week, but Piper is the one," Celeste says and then shakes her head.

Tally smiles. "Celeste is just a big animal lover," she says. "And you know the story about Tori Spelling kicking her husband out of bed because she had to have her pigs and dogs sleep with her and her husband didn't want that? That would be Celeste. If she had a pot belly pig and you didn't want the pig to sleep with you guys, and you said 'it's me or the pig,' Celeste would be like 'sorry you gotta sleep on the couch, dude.'" Then she starts to laugh as Celeste gives her a look.

"Ixnay on the edbay alktay," she says in a low voice. "We don't sleep in the same bed, remember?"

"Oh, right," Tally says and rolls her eyes. "Like that's not gonna happen within a week."

Celeste narrows her eyes. She's apparently sobering up a bit and isn't appreciating the fact that Tally apparently isn't. "Let's just call this is a night, okay?" She throws down her napkin and pushes away from the table.

"Hey, hey, hey," Tally says. "Sorry, Celeste, I'm just teasing you like I always do. I know the score on this marriage." Then she looks at me. "I just don't think it's all gonna be platonic for long. Not with the look in Max's eyes when he thinks nobody's looking."

Busted. But Celeste didn't pay attention to that last thing Tally said. Thank God.

Celeste furrows her brows and shakes her head. "I have a headache. I don't usually day drink for a reason. It's getting to be, what is it, 11 o'clock now? The alcohol is wearing off and everything looks as bleak as it did before we started drinking, but even worse. Excuse me."

Celeste walks off, Tally and Olivia trailing behind, their arms around her shoulders. Tally looks back. "Sorry about this. She's not usually like this. Don't know what this is about, but I really should help clear the table and get the dishes in the dishwasher. Can't leave this mess to you guys."

"Don't you worry about a thing," Rosa assures her. "Don't forget, I get paid a good salary to clean up after everybody. It's my job. So, go."

Celeste and her friends leave, apparently going to Celeste's new living space, and I'm sitting at the table wondering what the hell just happened. Tally said something that triggered something in Celeste and I really need to know exactly what that thing was.

But maybe later. For now, I know how to make Celeste happy in the home. I text my personal assistant, Harry Ladue, instructing him to pick up a pit bull named Piper who's currently a resident of the Inland Valley SPCA, tomorrow at the earliest.

But I'm not getting that dog for Celeste. That would mean that I'm crazy about her and I'm just not. No. I just want her to be happy because I don't want her contacting *TMZ* with an exclusive, which she might do if she's unhappy here.

That's the only reason why I care about her happiness.

Really.

Chapter Twenty-Four

CELESTE

Tally's eyes widen when we get back to my wing of the house. "Celeste. What the hell?"

I shake my head, pressing my fingertips against my temples. The champagne buzz has faded, leaving behind the familiar throb of a day-drinking headache. Just hours ago, I'd twirled in front of the mirror in a Stella McCartney dress while Olivia and Tally whooped and clinked their Dom Pérignon flutes. The closet alone had left me breathless—racks of designer clothes I used to gawk at through boutique windows, wondering about the lives of women who wore such things.

The house itself had surprised me too. This whole place —with its ocean-facing windows and hand-knotted rugs— looks ripped from the Pinterest board I'd labeled "Someday, Maybe."

But now, as the alcohol leaves my system, reality crashes back. Soon Olivia and Tally will leave, and I'll be alone in this beautiful cage. I can't ask them to stay—that wasn't part of the deal with Max. The thought of their departure makes this mansion, despite its luxury, feel suddenly hollow. When Tally joked about me sharing a bed with Max and some future pet, something inside me just... crumbled.

I boost myself up on the kitchen counter, my legs dangling over the marble side. "I keep thinking about what happens when you both leave. I've never lived alone—not really. Home with Mom and Lexi, then with you, Olivia." My voice catches. "And now Mom's getting worse, and I just—" I stare at the floor. "Sometimes I picture myself walking down to the beach at night. Just staring at the waves like James Mason at the end of *A Star Is Born*." I don't need to finish that reference. The girls know just why James Mason goes down to the beach at the end of the Judy Garland version of *A Star is Born*. They both know he never returned from that little "swim."

"Jesus," Tally straightens. "That's not funny, Celeste. You talk like that again, I'm driving you straight to Cedars-Sinai for a psych eval."

Olivia reaches across the table, her eyes wide. "Where is this coming from?"

I force a laugh that sounds hollow even to me. "Just stupid thoughts. They come and go." I take a breath. "But I promise, if it gets bad, I'll crash at my old place."

"In your old bed," Olivia nods. "And I'll be right there like when Greg dumped you. With snacks."

"Not that garbage Häagen-Dazs," I say, grateful for the shift. "Ben & Jerry's. Minter Wonderland. And *Poldark* marathons."

Tally fans herself dramatically. "Count me in. Aidan Turner shirtless with a scythe? I'll bring the wine."

I laugh and nod. I don't know where I would be without these two.

They're both looking at me, their eyes heavy-lidded but

concerned, darting between each other in that silent communication friends perfect over years. The grandfather clock chimes midnight, and Olivia winces. She's catering a Silicon Valley brunch tomorrow—potato frittatas, gremolata egg cups and kombucha mimosas for men in Patagonia vests who'll tip exactly 18%. Plus, she has to drive back to Claremont. Tally's fingers absently trace the colorful sleeve of tattoos disappearing under her cuff; she has her own tattoo studio, with her first client expected in at 7 AM. I watch them fidget with car keys, gathering empty wine glasses, but hesitating at the threshold like they're abandoning a puppy at the shelter. My ocean drowning "joke" hangs between us like a fog that won't lift.

I raise my hands in surrender. "I promise I won't cause any trouble. But we all need to call it a night." I check my watch and groan. My 7 AM meeting with that new screenwriter—the one with the buzzed-about dystopian romance that every studio in town is salivating over— means a 5 AM wake-up call, and Claremont might as well be in another state with LA traffic. One fender-bender on the 405 and I'm screwed because the highway will turn into a giant parking lot with the cars at a complete standstill for miles. I glance at Tally and Olivia's faces, torn between wanting them to stay and knowing they need to go. "Seriously," I add, gesturing toward the door while my heart does the opposite.

We wrap our arms around each other in a three-way embrace before parting ways with promises of cocktails by Thursday. The geography of friendship just got more complicated—my new Malibu address might as well be in another solar system. Liv's still in my old Claremont condo, manageable for after-work meetups, but Tally? Between her arts district apartment and her tattoo studio three blocks away from her apartment, she's practically orbiting Saturn.

Still, we've made a pact: once a week, minimum. These women are my oxygen, my heartbeat—non-negotiable.

After they're gone, I wander through the rooms of what's supposed to be my dream house. When I fling open the French doors, the ocean's rhythm should soothe me, but the sound only hollows me out. A damp chill seeps in—forty degrees feels colder here by the water—but that's not what's freezing me from the inside. The cruel irony isn't lost on me: I'm standing in the exact home I've always fantasized about, yet somehow I've never felt more trapped.

How did my dream house become my prison?

Chapter Twenty-Five

MAX

It's been exactly twenty-one days since Celeste moved into the east wing of my Malibu beach house, with its separate entrance and the long hallway that ensures our paths rarely cross. I've timed our encounters—ninety-seven minutes total, mostly accidental collisions in my kitchen when I've forgotten something and she's having breakfast with Rosa, or brief, stilted exchanges about mail. I've mapped my morning routine to avoid her completely: shower at 4:15, coffee at 4:30, out the door by 4:45, while she doesn't emerge until 5:30. I have to maintain this careful choreography of avoidance for my sanity.

I had a plan to surprise her with Piper, that Pit Bull from Inland Valley she'd been obsessing over, according to Tally and Olivia. By the time my assistant got to the shelter to adopt Piper, some family had already claimed her. So I had to step in. I bribed the shelter administrator with $5,000 to tell me the address of the people who adopted Piper and I went there, fully intending to do whatever it took to get that dog. Nestled in a typical Encino subdivision where property values hover just below the Valley average, the single-story ranch sits three blocks from a faded strip mall anchored by a discount grocery store. White paint curled away from the siding like dead skin, and black garbage bags dotted the roof, presumably catching leaks the owners couldn't afford to properly repair.

I rang the doorbell with my checkbook ready.

The door swung open to reveal a man in his forties who squinted at me, then did a double-take. "Hold on—you're Max Kensington." He whipped around towards the interior of the house. "Babe! Max Kensington is standing on our porch!" Back to me, with an apologetic grin: "My wife follows your every move. Gail! Get out here!"

Perfect. A fan. *This might be easier than I thought.*

Moments later, Gail appeared, clutching her bathrobe closed at the neck, blonde hair sticking up on one side. Her free hand fluttered between smoothing her hair and reaching for mine. "Mr. Kensington! What an unexpected honor. Would you care to step inside?"

That's when I spotted her—Piper, the reason for my impromptu visit. The pit bull bounded up behind Gail's legs, her whole body vibrating with excitement rather than just her tail. Something in my chest softened. This shelter mutt, once abandoned and unwanted, would soon have two different parties trying to have her. I saw why Celeste wanted her.

I checked my watch and adjusted my stance. "Look, I've got a meeting soon, so I'll be direct. I want Piper. Your dog. And I'm prepared to pay whatever it takes." I ran a hand through my hair, trying to appear casual.

The man's eyebrow inched upward. "Whatever it takes?"

"Name your price." My gaze drifted past him to the

modest living room beyond. Outside in the driveway sat a weathered Corolla beside a Nissan that's seen better days. I could've written a check that would've transformed their lives—pay off the house, replace those cars, set up college funds. One signature from me, and their financial worries would vanish. It's crude, maybe, throwing money at a problem like this. But when I pictured Celeste's face lighting up when she saw Piper again... well, what else is money for, if not moments like that?

The man's eyes lit up, but Gail shook her head. "I'm sorry," she said. "Our kids are in love with this dog. We can't part with her."

"One million," I said, my checkbook ready to go.

"Are you serious?" the man asked. Then he turned to Gail. "One million, Gail. For Piper. We can go down and get another dog just like her. We can't turn this down."

Gail shook her head. "Hugh, some things don't have a price," she said pleasantly. "I'm so sorry, Mr. Kensington. But would like to come in and have a cup of tea and cookies?"

I exhaled slowly. Maybe I should've upped the ante to something truly ridiculous, though a million dollars already seemed pretty damn ridiculous. But Gail's steady gaze told me everything – this isn't about money for her. It irked me, but I can't help respecting her backbone. They clearly weren't wealthy, but she stood her ground – some bonds can't be broken with a check.

Hugh's face darkened with frustration, but then I spotted the real complication – twin girls, barely four years old, mirror images of each other. They wrapped themselves around Piper, who squirmed with delight, licking their cheeks while they dissolved into laughter. I found myself shaking my head. Of course – dogs burrow into your heart in no time, especially when little kids are involved.

"Babe," Hugh said, voice tight. "We could pay off the mortgage. Set up college funds."

Gail's expression softened toward him but remained resolute. "Hugh, I've fallen for this dog, and so have Abigail and Charlotte. You're not the one who'll deal with their heartbreak when Piper disappears. We were managing fine without a million dollars before today."

I could only nod. Her logic is unassailable, and...Hugh finally seemed to understand. His shoulders dropped as he reached out to touch mine. "We appreciate the offer, Mr. Kensington, but would you mind taking a picture with us instead?"

So I posed with them in a smiling selfie and was on my way.

I'm still working on a plan B, because I need to cheer Celeste up. Iris says Celeste barely speaks at work anymore, skips the office celebrations, hides behind her closed door. The thought of her sadness gnaws at me, but I can't be the one to comfort her. Not yet.

Not when being near her makes me forget every reason I shouldn't love her.

I can't shake her. She's like a splinter that's worked its way too deep to extract. Some mornings, I round the corner toward the breakfast nook and freeze—there she is with Rosa, laughing over coffee. I retreat before she notices me, but not before her scent hits me. That Hermés perfume from the welcome basket I had delivered—candied oranges and patchouli—mixed with the vanilla in her shampoo. Last week, I called a boutique candlemaker in Venice Beach. "I need something specific," I said, describing the exact notes.

Now my office smells like her. Johnson from Legal raised an eyebrow yesterday. "Candles, Kensington?" I just shrugged.

Ansel's words echo in my head: "You're in love with her." Ridiculous. I simply rearrange my entire schedule to avoid spending more than twenty minutes in her presence. I merely commissioned artisanal reproductions of her scent so I could breathe it in private. I unsuccessfully offered $1 million for a shelter pit bull that she fell in love with. Nothing about that suggests love.

Or does it?

Chapter Twenty-Six

CELESTE

I've lived in my new house for three weeks now, and, while the place is a Mediterranean masterpiece perched on the cliffside, it echoes with emptiness. Only Rosa, with her gentle humming and the scent of lemon polish that follows her, is keeping me sane, but I can't lean on her weathered shoulders all the time. And it's been a soul-crushing few weeks.

My mother got the results back from her last scans and the news crashed down like a wrecking ball. The cancer has spread like ivy through her lymph nodes and nearby tissues. Her tumors sit stubborn and defiant, refusing to shrink under the assault of chemicals that leave her skin sallow and her bathroom floor littered with strands of once-vibrant hair. Her doctors keep trying different cocktails of medicine with names I can barely pronounce, but they haven't yet found the key that will unlock her healing. And it's only a matter of time before the disease, hungry and relentless, spreads to a distant organ like her bones, lungs, liver or brain and becomes metastatic cancer —medical shorthand for "prepare yourself."

I've been carrying this knowledge like stones in my pockets. Every night, I lay in bed staring at the ceiling until dawn breaks. I feel like I'm living alone on the moon when I'm at the Malibu house, floating in a vacuum of silence. The nearest neighbor is hidden behind a mile of twisted cypress trees, their shadows stretching like fingers across Max's manicured lawn at sunset. I come home every evening to a dark and quiet house—my wing with its separate entrance might as well be on another continent—and sit on my balcony, where the railing is always cold against my bare feet. The Pacific stretches before me, black and bottomless, its waves hissing secrets I can't decipher while I huddle under a cashmere throw that costs more than my first car. I keep waiting for those rhythmic crashes to lull me into peace. But they don't.

And I've never in my life felt so thoroughly, completely alone.

Of course, people at work have noticed the change. I catch Elaine's concerned glances through the glass wall of my office, where I've been hiding behind my laptop screen like it's a shield. The fluorescent lights seem harsher now as I slink from my sanctuary only for mandatory meetings, my voice barely rising above a whisper when I present development notes.

The hallways echo with laughter I no longer contribute to. Bob turned 50 and the office went nuts—those stupid mylar balloons kept bumping against the ceiling all day, making that squeaky rubber sound that sets my teeth on edge. On another day, Symone wouldn't stop flashing her new three-carat princess cut, practically dislocating her wrist to make sure everyone noticed. Yesterday, Alicia's desk vanished under about fifty roses for her work anniversary, and I swear that sickly-sweet smell seeped under my door no matter how hard I tried to keep it out. The break room's basically a grave-yard of half-eaten sheet cakes, that waxy frosting that glues your mouth shut. I used to be first in line for a corner piece, clinking plastic champagne flutes like I belonged. Now? I'd rather eat glass than join their little celebration circle. It's like I woke up one day and forgot all the steps to their office dance.

I can't lose her. She's been my rock my entire life. After my father died, when I was 15 and Lexi was 10, it was just the three of us against the world. Mom somehow made sure our fridge stayed full and the electricity never got cut off, but it was more than that. She's the woman who taught me to parallel park at midnight in an empty grocery store lot, who still sends me New Yorker cartoons that make me laugh, who knows exactly how to fold fitted sheets into perfect rectangles.

There are so many memories that would vanish with her—the three of us in Vegas, Mom in that sequined vintage dress she found at Goodwill, dancing under strobe lights until our feet blistered. She'd always walk away from the blackjack tables with more chips than she started with, her eyes gleaming. The three of us skiing in Big Bear, our breath clouding in the thin mountain air, Mom having saved all year for those precious forty-eight hours. Our sun-drenched Disneyland pilgrimages, sticky with cotton candy and exhaustion. But more than those postcard moments, I'd miss our book club for two—her curled on one end of our threadbare couch, me on the other, debating character motivations over mugs of Earl Grey until midnight, even though it's been fourteen months since we last dissected someone's prose together.

I remember all those nights she'd sit with me after yet another rejection letter arrived. "Screenplay number seventeen isn't dead," she'd say, pouring more wine. "It just needs revision." Then she would remind me to keep going. "Thomas Edison tried 2,774 different filaments before he got one to work," she'd say, squeezing my shoulder. Or she'd quote Babe Ruth about how each strikeout brought him closer to his next home run. If cancer takes her, will my dreams follow her into the darkness? Or would abandoning them be the real betrayal?

I'd miss those midnight talks on the porch swing, her arm around my shoulders while I sobbed over yet another breakup. "Listen to me," she'd whisper, her voice steady even at 3 AM. "That boy doesn't deserve a single second of your time. You only get so many seconds in this life, Celeste. Don't give them to people who won't treasure them." And now, I'm seeing the truth in her words - that you only get so many seconds in your life. They're finite and will one day run out. And yet, I'm wasting precious seconds of my life with Max. Seconds that would be better spent with the people who love me.

It's only a year. I have to tell myself that. But how many seconds will I have wasted on Max if I actually do make it through the year? I Google this and the answer is 31,536,000 seconds. Or, like the famous song from *Rent,* 525,600 minutes. I blink back tears. My mother told me not to waste a single second on people who don't love me, who don't treasure me, who don't *see* me. And, goddamn it, I'll be wasting over 31,000,000 seconds on somebody who, quite frankly, doesn't deserve me.

Then, one night, I get a phone call that crystallizes everything for me. A call that puts things into such a perspective that I absolutely know it's time to do whatever it takes to get out of this deal.

"Hi, Lex," I say to my sister when she calls.

"Celeste," she shrieks, hysterical. "I'm at Cedars. It's Mom."

My heart plummets to my shoes. No. No. No. NO!!!!!

"Is she-"

"She's in critical condition, Celeste. A bladder infection that's turned septic in a hurry. They're giving her antibiotics, but-"

"On my way."

And, just like that, my mind crystallizes into a single, desperate thought. I'll race to Cedars-Sinai and kneel on those cold hospital tiles, begging whatever God might listen that Mom somehow survives. The word "sepsis" echoes in my head like a death knell—blood poisoning that could steal her from me in hours. My stomach twists into a painful knot. If she makes it through or if she—no, I can't even complete the thought without my throat closing up. Either way, I'm escaping this gilded cage with Max. I just need to plot my exodus from this Malibu prison.

I stumble toward my Prius, keys jingling in my trembling hand, when I spot Rosa standing sentinel in the driveway, her silver-streaked black hair pulled into its usual tight bun. Her weathered face creases with concern as she steps forward, blocking my path. She's always had a sixth sense for my distress, noticing what Max's cold green eyes never bother to see.

"Celeste," she says, her warm brown hand enveloping mine. Her dark eyes scan my face like she's reading a tragic novel. "Where are you off to in such a hurry, child?"

My lips quiver as I try to speak, but instead, hot tears spill down my cheeks, leaving mascara trails I can feel but don't care about. The words about Mom remain trapped behind a wall of panic. My entire body trembles like I'm standing in a blizzard rather than the seventy-degree Malibu sunshine. I yank open my car door in desperation, but Rosa firmly pushes it closed with a decisive thud.

"Celeste," she says, her Jamaican accent thickening with emotion. "You can't drive like this. You'll wrap yourself around a telephone pole because you won't see nothing through those tears. Let me drive you."

I nod weakly, surrendering my keys. "Cedars," I manage to whisper through lips numb with fear. "Please."

Chapter Twenty-Seven

MAX

When I arrive home from work, the house is quiet. No Rosa. The wall clock reads 9:17, and my stomach tightens —she always leaves a note or sends a text when she's going to be out this late. I grab my phone, thumbs already tapping out a message. The three dots appear almost immediately.

> Hey Rosa. Just got home and wondering where you are. Hope everything's okay.

> So sorry, Max. I'm at Cedars with Celeste and time got away from me. I should've texted you to tell you where we are.

Cedars-Sinai Medical Center? My throat constricts as I tug at my suddenly suffocating collar. Could her mother be...? I force the thought away with a sharp shake of my head. I won't jump to conclusions until I know the facts.

> Is everything okay with Celeste's mom?

No. Things don't look good.

ICU?

Yes

Shit. I need to get to Cedars now. My driver could take me, but the helicopter would be faster. The Bell's fueled and ready on the pad, and I've got my license. One text to Helene in hospital administration and I'll have landing clearance—just like when Granddad broke his hip last year. Whatever's happened, Rosa wouldn't have left that message unless it was serious. Minutes matter now. Maybe seconds. I'm sure Celeste has her friends there, probably her sister. And Rosa's there, too. But I need to be there if she gets the worst news that anybody can get.

My feet pound the concrete as I race toward the helicopter, thumbs flying across my phone screen to alert Helene. The rotors are already spinning when I climb in, and within moments of securing my helmet and headset, I'm airborne. The city shrinks beneath me. Minutes later, Cedars-Sinai Medical Center comes into view, its helipad a small bullseye on the rooftop. Thanks to Helene's clearance, I guide the Bell down with practiced precision. The second the skids touch down, I'm shutting systems off, tearing away my gear, and bolting for the elevator that will take me to the oncology ICU in the Pavilion wing.

Please let me not be too late. I've avoided learning anything about Celeste's mother—not even her name. All I've gathered is that they share some bond; she walked Celeste down the aisle at our sham wedding. But how would I know the depth of their relationship when I've deliberately kept Celeste at arm's length? I've constructed walls between us. Learning how she takes her morning coffee, whether she prefers scrambled or over-easy, hearing stories about her childhood dreams—these details would be my undoing. The physical pull I feel toward her is already overwhelming. Three times over. But it's just attraction, not attachment. Not yet. The moment I truly see her is the moment I'll fall.

I arrive at the Pavilion and flash my Kensington ID at the security desk. The guard's eyes widen slightly as he processes who I am, then waves me through to the ICU without question. Technically, these halls are reserved for immediate family and close friends, but money and status have their privileges. The irony isn't lost on me—I'm using my power to visit my "mother-in-law," a woman whose first name I never learned.

When I reach the waiting room, I find Rosa, Celeste and Lexi huddled together on the vinyl chairs—Rosa with her rosary beads clicking softly between practiced fingers, eyes shut in silent prayer; Celeste slumped forward, her red hair curtaining her face while Lexi leans in, murmuring something only Celeste can hear. I stand there, invisible in their bubble of worry, until Celeste finally raises her head and our eyes meet across the sterile space.

Celeste leaps to her feet just as Olivia and Tally appear in the doorway, coffee carriers in their hands. "You!" The word escapes like venom from her lips. "Out! Now!!!!! You have no right to be here." She collapses back onto the bench, trembling with fury. Olivia catches Lexi's eye, tilts her head slightly. Lexi slides over, making room. As Olivia's arm encircles her shoulders, Celeste crumbles, tears streaming down her face. Without looking up, she whispers, "Liv, please make sure he's gone when I look up."

My chin drops to my chest as Celeste's eyes flash with hurt and anger. Of course she's upset—I showed up unannounced in this sterile waiting room where her real support system already surrounds her. Her friend Olivia, whose shoulder she's leaning on. Tally, whose fierce loyalty radiates across the room. Even Rosa, who's known her for what— three weeks?—sits clutching Celeste's hand like they've been friends forever.

The question pounds in my skull: am I here to ease my own conscience after how coldly I treated her, or because I genuinely can't bear the thought of her facing bad news alone?

The truth sits heavy in my chest, but the words die on my tongue. This isn't my place.

Olivia's eyes soften toward me, but Tally stretches across her to squeeze Celeste's knee, her glare burning holes through me. When Olivia starts to rise, I wave her off.

"I get it," I murmur, then crouch beside Rosa. "Text me when you know something?"

Rosa smiles and nods and I leave.

When I get home, I toss and turn in bed. The word "cancer" pounds in my head like a hammer. I see my mother's face in the one photo I have of her holding me as a newborn, just weeks before the disease took her. I remember the smell of whiskey on my father's breath when he'd come home late, how his eyes grew more vacant until one day, when I was seven, he just... vanished. And now Celeste's mother—facing the same monster. I press my palms against my eyes.

I need to open up. I'll ask Rosa to tell Celeste everything. My fingers tighten around the edge of the blanket as my heart races. Letting Celeste see that part of me—it would be like handing someone a key I've kept buried for decades. No woman has ever gotten that close. But something in me —something I can't name—keeps whispering that with her, it might be worth the risk.

I text Rosa.

> Go ahead and tell her about Mom.

> Are you sure?

> No. But go ahead and tell her anyway.

> I will. I'm proud of you.

I stare at my phone, thumb suspended above the screen. There's no going back from this. I'm about to reveal something to Celeste that I've only ever shared with Gianni, my brothers, and Rosa.

Sleep remains impossible. I pour three fingers of scotch, no ice, and carry it out to the terrace where the rhythm of waves against shore does nothing to calm me. Whatever exists between Celeste and me will transform after tonight. I sense it like an approaching storm. All I can do now is weather whatever follows, whether it destroys or rebuilds us.

Chapter Twenty-Eight

CELESTE

Sixteen hours later, I'm still sitting in the ICU waiting room's stiff vinyl chair, my spine aching, surrounded by the antiseptic smell that clings to everything. Lexi's curled up beside me, her mascara smudged from crying, while Rosa clutches her rosary beads, murmuring prayers.

Liv and Tally reluctantly left last night after I practically shoved them out the door. Olivia has a brunch to cater for some tech bros. Her catering van is probably packed with her signature Italian cheese strata and frittatas that took her months to perfect. And Tally's prepping her tattoo station for another grueling 10-hour day. So I squeezed their hands and promised to text updates, watching their torn expressions as they finally walked away, leaving me under the harsh fluorescent lights that make everyone look half-dead.

The doctor emerges every few hours with news. His first visits brought only grave nods and those four words I've grown to dread: "We're doing our best." Each time he said it, something inside me withered. The unspoken translation hung in the air: we're trying, but prepare yourself. As night bled into morning, his updates shifted. "The antibiotics are working," he told us, though his cautious tone added the silent "but" before he mentioned she remained unconscious. Later: "She's awake now. Weak. Immediate family visitation only." And finally, as sunlight streamed through the waiting room blinds: "We'll move her to a regular room soon. Just need to observe her a while longer." Only then did my lungs remember how to fill completely.

At the doctor's words—"We're moving her to a regular room for further observation"—my shoulders slump and a sob escapes my throat. The relief hits me like a wave, washing away the tension I've been carrying. My body shakes as I finally let go, though part of me wants to leap up and shout. Just hours ago, I was preparing for the worst. Now, a sliver of possibility has opened up. Mom's still fighting cancer, still fragile, still might lose this battle. But she's cleared this hurdle, and that's not nothing. It's like feeling the first warm rays after the longest night of the year. Beside me, Lexi's face crumples as she cries too, while Rosa lifts her hands toward the ceiling, her smile radiant with gratitude.

Lexi and I make our way to Mom's room. The nurse at the station stops Rosa with an apologetic smile, explaining the "immediate family only" policy. Rosa squeezes my hand before stepping back, despite having stayed by my side all night and ignoring my repeated suggestions that she go home. "Max will understand," she had insisted earlier, her eyes tired but determined. "I need to know she's okay."

"Mom," I whisper, reaching for her hand beneath the crisp hospital sheet. Her skin feels like tissue paper against mine, cold and blue-veined, her knuckles sharp ridges beneath my fingertips. She turns toward my voice, eyelids fluttering like moth wings before settling half-open, revealing irises dulled by medication yet still that familiar hazel. The corners of her chapped lips curve upward—that same determined smile she'd wear when helping me with homework or working double shifts. "I love you. You're the strongest person I know, so I'm not surprised you're getting better."

Lexi leans in close to Mom's hospital bed, her voice cracking as she whispers, "I love you." Mom's pale lips curve into a fragile smile, and she manages a slight nod that rustles the thin pillow beneath her head. The sepsis ordeal has left her too weak to speak, her once-vibrant voice now trapped behind the oxygen tube looped under her nose. We squeeze her cool fingers and promise to return when she's stronger, maybe in a day or two, when the harsh fluorescent lights and antiseptic smell won't exhaust what little energy she has left.

And then the three of us leave the hospital, stepping through the automatic glass doors that exhale a final antiseptic breath onto our backs. Outside, the sky bleeds watercolor oranges into purples. I check my watch—4:42 PM—and realize it was also dusk when I arrived yesterday, my shadow stretching long across the parking lot just like it does now. Twenty-four hours of fluorescent lights, vinyl chairs, and the constant beeping of monitors have left me hollow.

On the way home, Rosa grips the steering wheel with her small, capable hands, the ones that brought me coffee every three hours throughout the night. She insists on driving after seeing me fumble with my keys, my fingers still trembling from everything that's happened. As we merge onto the freeway, she glances at me, her dark eyes catching the last of the sunset, and softly says, "I need to tell you about Max."

Oh, boy.

Chapter Twenty-Nine

CELESTE

I whip my head toward Rosa. "What about Max?" The words scrape out of my throat. I hadn't thought of him once while counting Mom's breaths under those hospital lights. His face in the doorway last night sparked pure rage. The audacity—after dumping the wedding planning on me, abandoning our reception, then acting betrayed over Lexi's drunk friend? After three weeks of treating me like I'm invisible in his precious Malibu mansion? He gets to be there for me after all that? Nope. My hands shake as I dig my nails into my palms. He doesn't get to be there for Mom's final moments. That space belongs to those who've shown up—Liv, Tally, Lexi, Rosa. Not him. He should've known to stay away.

Rosa's brown hand clamps down on mine, her grip fierce and steady as an anchor chain. My racing pulse slams against her fingers, then gradually surrenders. God, this woman. When she looks at me, it's like being bathed in sunlight after months of darkness—her eyes burning away the shadows that have been choking me. Without her these past few weeks, I'd have already walked straight into the Pacific, let the salt water fill my lungs, and welcomed the cold embrace pulling me down to the seafloor. She is the only lifeline I have left in Max's home.

Rosa's eyes flash. "Max is a good man." Her jaw tightens like she's ready to fight for this truth. She's known him forever—bandaged his scraped knees, listened to him cry over girls, watched him grow up. I try to argue but can't find the words. How can this "good man" be the same person who walks through rooms like I don't exist? Who's put up so many walls I can barely breathe around him? Something in Rosa's face makes me pause. Maybe I'm missing something big. Maybe something broke him so badly that pushing me away is the only way he knows how to survive.

I open my mouth to protest, but she stops me with a look so sharp I forget what I was about to say. Her eyes lock onto mine with the confidence of someone who knows something important—something about him that I don't. My heart pounds as I nod, waiting for whatever she's about to tell me about the man I can't figure out.

Her voice drops to a whisper. "Max has had a difficult life," she says, her fingers fidgeting with her beaded bracelet.

I bite the inside of my cheek to keep from laughing. *Join the club, who hasn't?* I think of my father's accident on that ski slope, how I've always felt responsible for his death. Now my mother lies in a hospital bed, her skin the color of old paper, tubes snaking from her arms. My dreams of becoming a working screenwriter are utterly destroyed. Meanwhile, Max is a billionaire with cheekbones that could cut glass, eyes the exact blue-green of the Malibu shoreline at sunset, and a smile that's graced the cover of *Forbes* three times in the past year alone. The world doesn't just fall at his feet—it prostrates itself there, begging for attention.

What am I missing?

Rosa inhales deeply, fidgeting with her gold locket. "This isn't in any tabloid. But Max..." Her eyes cloud over as she shakes her silver-streaked head. "His mother Catherine—I learned this from Michael before he vanished, and from Max's brothers after too much wine." She pauses. "Catherine was extraordinary—remembered birthdays, left wildflowers for neighbors. Michael said meeting her was like summer lightning. For ten years, they were inseparable—finishing sentences, dancing in kitchen darkness, stealing food from each other's plates, sharing private jokes. All those threads that make a marriage—they had them."

I nod, wondering where this was going.

Rosa's fingers find her necklace again, twisting the pendant in a nervous rhythm. "By thirty-five, she had those seven wild boys running circles around her. The ones you didn't meet at the wedding." She pauses, her eyes drifting somewhere past me. "Then came the diagnosis. Breast cancer—aggressive, but they caught it early. Stage 0. Her oncologist told Michael and Catherine not to worry. Even with how fast that particular type could spread, they'd found it in time. 'A double mastectomy,' he said, 'some chemo, and you'll be back chasing those boys around the yard.' That's what they promised her."

I close my eyes, a lump forming in my throat. I somehow know where this is going and it would explain a lot about Max. But I let her go on.

Rosa sighs. "According to Michael, the cancer diagnosis terrified them both, though the doctors were optimistic since they caught it early. Stage zero. Very treatable. They booked her surgery right away." Rosa's fingers twist in her lap. "Then Catherine started getting sick every morning. At first, she blamed the cancer, but her oncologist said that wasn't possible—not at that stage. So she bought a test." Rosa's voice drops to nearly a whisper. "Two pink lines appeared in that little window, and everything changed."

I nod, willing her to go on, even though I don't want to hear the rest.

"Catherine refused to end the pregnancy, despite her oncologist's warnings. The doctor had been clear: postponing chemotherapy, combined with the physical demands of carrying a child and the aggressive nature of her tumor, meant she likely wouldn't survive. Michael pleaded with her to reconsider. She remained steadfast. 'I can't be responsible for taking a life,' she told him quietly. 'This is in God's hands now.'"

Rosa shakes her head. "Catherine passed three weeks after Max was born. The disease took her so fast." She grips the wheel tighter as we come up to a light. "Michael—he'd never touched alcohol before. His grandparents were alcoholics, and he always said addiction skips generations. He knew the risk. But after losing her..." Her voice trails off. "Joe brought me in because those boys needed someone. Michael couldn't be there for them—couldn't be there for himself. Morning till night, that bottle was his only companion." She looks up, eyes distant with memory. "I remember him saying once, 'If Catherine had lived, I'd never have known what whiskey tastes like.' First drink he took, something in him just... vanished."

I swallow hard. The weight of what Max carries every day hits me like a punch to the chest. A baby born as his mother died. A father who broke from grief. A family that fell apart. Deep inside Max, a voice must whisper: *This is my fault.* I know it isn't—no baby chooses when to be born or what happens after—but how do you quiet that voice when you've heard it your whole life?

Rosa nods. "Michael did his best to hold on. He'd string together these stretches of sobriety—three months here, six months there—but you could see the strain in his eyes the whole time. During those good periods?" Her voice softens. "He was magic with those boys. Got them up at dawn for surfing lessons with this Hawaiian champion he somehow befriended. Packed the station wagon for weekend camping trips where they'd catch their own dinner. But eventually, the bottle always called him back." She pauses, her fingers twisting in her lap. "The last time anybody saw him, Max had just turned seven. Michael dropped all the boys at Joe's place with their little backpacks. That was twenty-two years ago."

I shake my head. "Poor Max." Every glossy magazine profile calls him the same thing—Hollywood royalty, the boy genius who grabbed his family's struggling studio at twenty-four and muscled it into the big leagues alongside Disney and Universal. People can't get enough of that chiseled face and million-watt grin. But I can't help wondering about the man behind the PR machine. His mother died bringing him into this world rather than end the pregnancy. His father crawled into a bottle and eventually disappeared completely. And there's Max, somehow expected to thrive while carrying all that invisible weight. What kind of castle can you really build when every cornerstone is something that's missing?

"Max blamed himself for everything. He was too smart for his own good—at five, he'd sit on my lap reading *Oliver Twist* aloud, those big eyes so serious. Nothing got past that child. When his mother died shortly after he was born, he pieced it together. He watched his father collapse in front of those home videos night after night, whiskey bottle dangling from his fingers, and draw his own conclusions.

The family photos and videos told him a story: they were happy before he arrived. In his mind, if he'd never existed, Catherine would still be alive, his father would be sober, and his brothers would have their mother. That's a crushing weight for any child to bear. No wonder he lashed out."

Reading Dickens at age 5? So he's a genius on top of everything else. Still, I wouldn't wish his situation on my worst enemy.

Rosa's shoulders drop with her exhale. "After Michael walked out, Max fell apart. Started believing it was his fault —the abandonment, his mother's passing, all of it. Reasoning with him became impossible." She looks straight ahead at the road, her knuckles gripping the steering wheel, 10 and 2. "Thank God for Joe's fortune. He could afford the best specialists for his grandson, and Max needed the help."

She looks ahead at the road, her eyes clouded with memory. "Those years... Max's knuckles always bandaged from punching walls. The dents in the drywall from his forehead. Finding him watching flames dance in his wastebasket at three in the morning." Her voice softens. "The therapy helped, but the damage was done. He built a fortress around himself—only lets in those who knew him before Michael left. Me, his grandparents, his brothers, Gianni. That's his entire world now. He once told me, 'I can't survive being left again. Not ever.'"

I close my eyes, feeling the warm afternoon sun on my face through the car window. "But what about..."

"His relationship with you?" Rosa asks, her voice gentle but knowing. I look ahead and realize that we've arrived back at Max's house, the arches and embellishments of his Mediterranean style palace gleaming against the backdrop of the Pacific. The waves crash rhythmically against the shore below, indifferent to my turmoil. "I'm hopeful that he might be willing to give it a chance."

I furrow my brows, twisting the platinum band on my finger. "Why do you think this?"

"He said I could tell you about his past." Rosa's weathered hands grip the steering wheel tighter, her knuckles whitening. "For him, that's a sign. The first crack in the wall he's built around himself."

I shake my head violently, my hands trembling. "But I'm nothing like him. Nothing. Have you seen the women he parades around? They're all six-foot glamazons with trust funds and connections. I drive a car held together with duct tape and prayer." My voice cracks. "I'm not his type."

She leans forward, eyes burning into mine. "Exactly," she whispers, gripping my wrist. "Which is why you're the only one who could ever save him."

Chapter Thirty

CELESTE

I creep into my wing of Max's home at 10 o'clock, my bare feet silent against the cool marble floors. I should find Max. The grandfather clock in the foyer chimes—still early enough that he's probably awake, but in this sprawling Malibu mansion, finding him feels like searching for a needle in a haystack of luxury. Rosa, her eyes heavy with exhaustion, retired to her quarters after we arrived, so I'm on my own.

I step into Max's territory—the main house—and wander through one massive room after another. Ten guest bedrooms? Empty, despite their crisp white sheets and windows framing the ocean. The master suite? Not a soul, just an obscenely large bed and walls of glass. No one's touched the shiny machines in the gym. The indoor pool sits still as glass, blue lights dancing across its surface. I check everywhere: the plant-filled glass room, the wine cellar that smells like cedar, even the spa with its infrared sauna, that creepy sensory deprivation tank, and the cold plunge that gives off an unsettling blue light. Nothing but emptiness.

Then I go to the theater, which is as vast and opulent as any luxury movie theater, with a forty-foot screen that dominates the far wall and approximately one hundred plush leather recliners arranged in gently sloping tiers. The air smells faintly of buttered popcorn and expensive cologne. And there he is, up front, silhouetted against the flickering blue light, his broad shoulders hunched slightly forward as he stares at the screen. He's wearing wireless Bose headphones and watching what appears to be old home movies.

I'm staring at this video of a woman with honey-blonde hair, and she's laughing with her head thrown back like she's having the time of her life. She's wearing this yellow sundress with little daisies on it. Next to her is this guy who looks exactly like Max—same jawline, same blue-green eyes that make you feel like you're drowning. Holy shit, that's his dad. The guy's chasing after what must be Max and his brothers—six dark-haired boys running around like they own the world. They're darting in and out of the shadows under this massive oak tree, looking like something out of a Ralph Lauren commercial.

Max presses a tissue against the corner of his eye. His broad shoulders—the kind that make every designer suit look custom-tailored—curl inward. From the doorway, I catch the rhythm of his breathing: tight, measured catches that never quite become sobs. I've heard men breathe like that before, fighting their own emotions like they're facing down an enemy. My foot hovers mid-step. I can't process what I'm seeing. THE Max Kensington—crying? Something clenches inside me that I refuse to name. Those hands that sign million-dollar contracts would probably shatter drywall if he caught me witnessing this moment. I retreat silently, testing each step on the antique hardwood, willing the floors not to betray my presence.

I creep back into my bedroom, my feet sinking into soft carpet that muffles my steps. The sheets feel cool as I slide under them. I stare at the bumpy ceiling, counting the little dots until they blur together. When I close my eyes, they feel scratchy and dry, but my brain won't shut off. I can't sleep. Through my window, I hear waves hitting the shore— usually they help me drift off, but tonight they just match my restlessness. Cold air sneaks in through a crack in the window, so I pull my heated blanket tighter, its quiet hum not quite covering the loud beating of my heart.

God, these 24 hours have been…consequential. Mom looking like a ghost against those hospital sheets. Then Rosa calmly spilling Max's whole tragic backstory. But nothing prepared me for seeing the guy who's been treating me like crap for weeks completely fall apart. Shoulders heaving while watching his parents on that old home movie, like he could climb inside the screen and live there instead. His dad with that arm around his mom, both of them smiling like nothing bad would ever happen. And Max just sitting there in the blue glow, trying to touch something he can't have anymore.

Around 7 in the morning, I'm still awake, staring at the moonlight casting silver rectangles across the ceiling when the door hinges give a soft whine. Max's silhouette appears in the doorway, backlit by the dim hallway sconce. He stands there for three heartbeats, his breath audible in the silence, before the door clicks shut again. He's checking if I'm home, which of course I am - my beat-up Prius is clearly visible in the circular driveway, parked like an eyesore next to his gleaming Bentley.

I call out his name. It's my day off, and Max's too—at

least I think so. Didn't he mention something about Saturdays being sacred? I start to wonder what he does with this time, then catch myself. My own Saturday stretches empty before me. Tomorrow's packed: brunch with Tally and Liv, then sneaking over to Cedars to check on Mom. She needs rest today, but by tomorrow she should be well enough for visitors, maybe even ready to come home.

He inches his way back after I call out, his footsteps barely audible on the hardwood. "Just wanted to make sure you got home from the hospital alright," he says, lowering himself into one of those oversized armchairs that somehow screams my name—the kind you sink into rather than sit on, wrapped in that soft sky-blue fabric I've always loved. How he managed to find furniture that might as well have come straight from my daydreams is beyond me, but there it is, proof he was paying attention all along.

His beauty is almost painful to look at. He's wearing a navy cotton t-shirt with matching cashmere sweats. That dark hair of his is tousled, as if he's been running his fingers through it. I search for traces of the tears I witnessed earlier, but find none. Did I imagine them? His face maintains that familiar mask, but something has shifted in his gaze. A flicker of sympathy? A hint of emotion? Whatever it is, for the first time since I've known him, he seems less like some untouchable deity and more like a man who bleeds when cut.

I nod. "I did." My fingers twist in my lap. "About seeing you at the hospital." I can't meet his eyes. "I was a mess. I shouldn't have—"

"I understand," he says, voice gentle as a hand on my shoulder. "No explanations needed." His chest rises with a deep breath. "How's your mother doing?"

"Better." I rap my knuckles twice against the wooden

headboard. "The doctors got ahead of the sepsis before it got out of hand. If Lexi hadn't rushed her to the ER at the first mention of pain when urinating—" I swallow hard. "Most people would've just grabbed cranberry juice from the store and hoped for the best. But because of Lexi, Mom was already getting treatment when things took a turn."

Max nods, smiles, and rakes his fingers through his hair, squinting against the sunlight. "Do you surf?"

I shake my head.

"Want to learn?"

The thought of being tossed around by waves while trying not to drown doesn't exactly appeal to me. But Rosa mentioned Max has been surfing since he was four—trained by some champion in the monster waves at Big Sur. He could probably teach me without much effort, assuming he doesn't lose his temper when I inevitably wipe out a dozen times. Still, it's a chance to spend time with him, to maybe crack that wall he's built.

"Sure," I say, forcing confidence into my voice. "Looks like fun."

His hands can't seem to stay still, and those ocean-colored green eyes lock onto mine. "I usually hit the waves on Saturdays. My brothers tag along most weeks—sometimes it's just Gianni, other times the whole crew shows up. Everyone's busy elsewhere today, though." He pauses, a hint of vulnerability crossing his face. "If you wanted to try surfing... this would be a good time. Just us."

My pulse quickens at the thought. A whole day with Max? I picture myself on the surfboard, still safely on the beach—he'd start with the basics, of course. He would stand so close behind me, his chest nearly touching my back as he guides my arms outward to find my center of gravity. I can almost feel his exhale against my neck, his fingers sliding between mine to adjust my grip. Just imagining it steals the air from my lungs.

I nod. "But it's late November. The water must be pretty cold."

He smiles. "That's why God made surf shops. There's a great one on the PCH. You can get a wetsuit there." He looks at his watch. "Meet in the main house in a half hour?"

I nod and smile. "Sure." My heart hammers against my ribs like it's trying to escape. Is it pounding because of fear or the thought of spending hours next to Max in the water? Probably both.

The last time I went into the ocean, I got caught in a rip tide. I still wake up sometimes gasping for air, feeling phantom seawater filling my lungs. I had to be rescued by a lifeguard, and every time I get into deep water it's like PTSD - I panic just a little. And don't even get me started on sharks. Discovery Channel's Shark Week ruined beaches for me forever.

But Max. Just the two of us. For hours. In wetsuits. God help me, I'm actually giddy about this, which is beyond pathetic. The guy's carrying around enough emotional baggage to fill a 747—dead mom, vanished dad, guilt complex the size of Montana, probably a healthy dose of survivor's guilt, too. And it's not like Rosa said he's secretly pining for me. Though he did show up at the hospital even though I ran him off, so...

Get it together, Celeste. The man probably has his breakfast cereal imported from Milan. *You're the charity case he married for his grandfather's approval.* This surf invite is just rich-person politeness. I'm not setting myself up for another emotional face-plant. This is just an adventure. A bucket list item. Nothing more.

I catch myself humming as I pull on a pair of boyfriend

jeans, a soft long-sleeve tee, and these ridiculous white Prada sneakers, all items Max's bank account paid for. I twist my hair into a messy bun, swipe on some Chapstick and call it good. Why bother with makeup when the ocean's just going to wash it off anyway?

When I check the mirror, some rich woman's reflection stares back. The clothes scream money in that quiet, expensive way I used to envy from across the studio lot. Not my money—never my money—but at least these designer threads are mine to keep. I think. God, I hope.

I deserve this. After spending 24 hours on pins and needles, wondering if Mom would see another sunrise, I need to breathe. Just one day where I'm not memorizing medication names or pretending I understand what her oncologist is saying. Tomorrow I'll be back at Cedars, nodding along to whatever new treatment protocol they've concocted, but today? It's just me, Max, a surfboard, and waves that don't give a damn about white blood cell counts. I shouldn't feel this flutter in my chest—like I'm stealing something good from a universe that's been nothing but cruel lately—but screw it, I'm practically vibrating with anticipation.

I make my way to the main house and find Max in the kitchen, waiting. Rosa sits at the breakfast nook, her face lighting up when I enter. That smile of hers—the one that makes her eyes crinkle at the corners—washes over me like a warm tide. With Rosa here, I can breathe easier; her presence alone makes this arrangement bearable. Then Max's lips curve upward too.

Max gestures toward the shoreline. "Let's get you set up at the surf shop first. Then we can come back to this stretch of beach—it's more private. Perfect for beginners. You won't find anybody to crash into here."

I raise an eyebrow. "Bold of you to assume I'll make it past the paddling stage. I'll consider it a victory if I can stand up for more than two seconds without face-planting into the water."

"I have faith in you."

"Glad somebody does."

And then we go to his garage—a huge space that could fit my entire apartment ten times over, with shiny sports cars all in a row like animals at a zoo. He takes me to a massive Rolls Royce SUV parked at the far end. I sink into soft leather seats, running my fingers over the stitching while breathing in that fresh-car smell mixed with his cologne. Outside, the sun hits the gray paint, making the car shine as we drive away.

He puts on his Ray Bans, and I can see the ocean reflected in them. "About the boards. Mine's short and made of fiberglass—that's what you get after surfing for twenty-five years. You need something longer and softer—a board that won't punish every mistake." He points to the beach. "We start on land. Learn the basics: how to paddle, how to stand up. After you've got those down, we'll try the water." His voice gets gentler. "Don't worry—nobody's perfect their first time. The ocean will wait for you to get to know her."

Max's Rolls purrs down the driveway as we head towards the Pacific Coast Highway. Our destination: some legendary surf shop where I'm supposed to find the perfect wetsuit to keep me from turning into an icicle in the frigid Pacific. Apparently, I need the perfect surfboard too, and Max insists on helping me pick one out. I already know how this will go—I'll reach for my credit card and he'll wave it away with that casual rich-guy gesture. Part of me wants to protest, to not be the charity case in this relationship, but my bank account has other ideas. Four hundred dollars for a neoprene wetsuit? Five hundred minimum for a foam board that I'll probably crash into the sand repeatedly?

What if I hate surfing? I'll try it three times before I decide, but I won't be that girlfriend who fakes loving what her crush loves. I'm not going to pretend I enjoy rock climbing when heights make me dizzy, or act like snowboarding is fun when I'd rather be inside drinking hot chocolate. If surfing's not for me, I'll tell Max straight up and we can sell the board and wetsuit to Second Chance Sports.

We pull up to Sea N Soul, a faded blue shop with a hand-painted sign swinging in the ocean breeze along PCH. Inside it smells like rubber and wax, with surfboards lined up against the walls like giant colored tiles. Two hours later, after trying on seven wetsuits—all making me feel like a stuffed sausage—Max helps me pick a black and teal board with a blue stripe down the middle and a black suit that should keep me from freezing. Now we're heading to Max's beach house where I'll spend the afternoon flopping on the board on his private beach, practicing standing up until my arms shake, before—gulp—going into the actual ocean where I'll try not to be another "city girl drowns trying to impress rich boyfriend" headline.

My knees wobble as I step onto the beach in my new suit, the sand shifting beneath my feet like my confidence. The ocean roars ahead—massive walls of water that must be ten feet high crashing down with enough force to snap a surfboard in half. This stretch of Malibu coastline isn't for beginners. I glance at Max descending toward the shoreline and force my lips into what I hope passes for a brave smile. *You've faced scarier things, Celeste.*

Like that ex who dragged me onto ATVs with those

impossible manual gears—nothing like driving a stick shift in a car. I still have the scar from when I flipped one and landed on my skull. Same guy zoomed down Double Black Diamond slopes while I stayed firmly on the blues with Mom and Lexi at Big Bear. He'd veer off-trail too, practically begging for an avalanche. When we broke up, my first thought wasn't heartbreak—it was relief that I'd never have to choose between a death-wish ski run or an hour of his disappointment.

Bad examples. I inhale slowly, searching my memory for a single instance when fear transformed into joy. My mind draws a blank. Well, there's a first for everything, right? Maybe surfing will break the pattern.

My arms flail in awkward circles as Max flashes that grin—the one that makes my stomach flip in the good way. I cling to the warmth of his smile instead of picturing myself smacking my head on fiberglass and sinking like a stone, or becoming shark breakfast, or wiping out so spectacularly that I spend six months in a full-body cast. At least the laws of physics prevent all three disasters from happening simultaneously. Maybe. Then again, I could manage the trifecta - hitting my head on the board and sinking, then becoming shark brunch. No, wait. That's only two of the three. So, it would be impossible to manage all three disasters. Small comfort.

"Okay," he says. "Let's go."

Chapter Thirty-One

MAX

Behind Celeste, I hold her surfboard with my foot while acting like I'm helping her balance. Even through our wetsuits, I can feel heat where her back presses against my chest. I've set myself up to hold both her hands in mine, our fingers locked together, all in the name of keeping her steady. When she flips her hair, I catch the smell of vanilla. I shut my eyes and breathe deep. She could easily stand on this board alone—we both know it—but I'll play along as long as she lets me stay this close to her.

I study Celeste's stance on the board. "Good balance," I tell her with a nod. "Now watch this." I drop to my chest on my own board, then spring to my feet in one fluid motion, knees bent, arms out. "Practice that move until it's second nature. The ocean won't wait for you to figure it out."

Celeste hesitates before finally laying flat on her board, attempting the pop-up I just demonstrated. Most people struggle with this move at first—that moment when you have to spring from prone to standing in one fluid motion. I've had twenty-five years of practice, hitting the waves every weekend without fail since my dad first pushed me into the whitewash on my fourth birthday. At fifteen, I had sponsors eyeing me, but couldn't commit my entire existence to chasing perfect sets around the globe. Still, I remember being exactly where Celeste is now, awkwardly positioning my feet, my muscles not yet understanding what my brain was asking them to do.

Celeste struggles to find her footing on the surfboard, her limbs working against her as she tries to push up from her chest. Sand clings to her wet skin with each tumble back to earth. I demonstrate the motion again on my board, keeping my face neutral. But again and again, she trips on her feet and falls on the sand.

After the tenth failed attempt, her shoulders slump. A tear slides down her cheek before she quickly raises her hands to shield her face—not just from embarrassment, but as if bracing for a blow. The gesture freezes me in place. She seems to think I'll start yelling at her, for some odd reason.

"Celeste," I say, my voice barely carrying over the waves. "You're doing fine."

She shakes her head without lowering her guard. "Just get it over with. The yelling, the cursing. I know it's coming."

I nod. Her wounds run as deep as mine, just in different places. "Celeste," I say, my voice softer than I thought possible. "What makes you think I'd lash out at you?" My hands find her shoulders, steadying her before I tilt her chin up with my fingertips. "Please look at me," I murmur. When she finally raises her eyes, they're clouded with something that breaks my heart. "Nobody gets this right the first time around. Or the second. Or the tenth. This isn't something

I'd ever hold against you—least of all something I'd punish you for."

She blinks back tears and nods. I clench my jaw, watching her shrink into herself like she's bracing for a blow that isn't coming. My fingers curl into fists at my sides. Who taught her to expect the worst? I catch myself and exhale slowly. I've dated supermodels and top actresses, but this girl has me ready to slay dragons I can't even see.

"You'll get impatient," she says. "This isn't for me."

I smile. "Well, okay, we gave it our all. Let's just go back to the house and grab a beer, alright?" I'm teasing her, of course. I know she's not ready to give up. She just thinks that I'll somehow blow a fuse if she can't get it right away, but I need to make her see that I'll stand out here all day if that's what it takes and will be happy to do it.

She tucks a strand of hair behind her ear, not meeting my eyes. A reluctant smile breaks across her face, followed by a soft laugh. "Fine. I haven't exactly been giving it my all." She inhales deeply. "The thing is..." Her cheeks flush. "My ex was obsessed with taking me ATVing on these insane trails. I despised every second, but there I was, weekend after weekend, because he couldn't get enough. I crashed without fail, constantly terrified I wouldn't make it back in one piece."

I nod, genuinely trying to see things through her beautiful blue eyes. I search my memory for instances where I've endured something miserable just to please a woman, but nothing surfaces. I've never felt strongly enough about anyone to put myself through that. Still, I can imagine how soul-crushing it must be—forcing enthusiasm for something you loathe, white-knuckling through fear, wondering if each outing might the time you break your neck.

She gestures wildly, recounting the ATV incident. "We rented the ATVs from some shop. Then one day I got stuck with a manual transmission one. I thought, no problem—I've driven stick-shift cars forever. But this thing..." She makes a throttling motion with her hands. "Nothing like a car. I couldn't make it budge." Her voice drops. "That's when he snapped. Right there in the parking lot, screaming so close I could feel his spit on my cheek. All these strangers just...watching." She rubs her arm, eyes distant. "At least I never had to face those people again. God, the way they must have looked at me—just taking it, frozen there like some...punching bag."

I close my eyes, my pulse hammering in my throat like a war drum. My fingers curl into fists so tight my knuckles crack. This piece of shit who hurt Celeste—my Celeste—deserves to have his face rearranged, bone by broken bone. The rage inside me is a living thing, clawing up my spine. I could find him anywhere—Mongolia, Siberia, the depths of hell itself. One call to my pilot, one flight, and I'd be there with my hands around his throat, watching his eyes bulge as he comes to understand what it means to hurt what's mine.

Celeste catches my expression and offers a half-hearted smile. "I'm keeping his name to myself," she says. "He turned out to be nothing special anyway. I just wanted you to understand why I'm terrified you'll lose patience with me fumbling around trying to stand on this board while we're still on dry land." She gestures toward the waves breaking offshore. "You could be out there riding perfect waves right now. Instead you're babysitting me on the beach."

I force the air in and out of my lungs, willing my clenched jaw to relax. Some faceless guy in her past has turned what should be a fun morning into this minefield of anxiety, and part of me wants to hunt him down. But that's not what today is for. Today is about Celeste on a surfboard, about her seeing that patience isn't something I reserve for other people. I watch her fingers fidget with the leash, and remind myself: whoever made her expect anger at every mistake is long gone. My job is to make sure his ghost is too.

I shake my head. "This isn't babysitting, Celeste." My voice stays soft, even as her shoulders tense beneath my hands. "I'm here for as long as it takes. That look in your eyes? That's determination. I recognize it." I give her shoulders a gentle squeeze, willing her to meet my gaze. "You're afraid I'll walk away if you don't get it right away. I won't." I pause, letting that sink in. "But if you want to stop, we stop. Just don't quit because you're worried about my patience. I've got plenty where you're concerned."

She gives a nod. "Okay," she whispers, then flattens herself against the board once more. Twenty-four clumsy attempts later, on try twenty-five, she nails it—chest to feet in one fluid motion. Her eyes widen, her smile breaking across her face like sunrise over the ocean. She bounces on her toes, sand flying.

"I did it! I did it! I did it!!!!! Did you see that?" Her hands clap together in rapid succession.

The childlike joy on her face fills me with something warm I couldn't name if I tried. When she flings her arms around me, we're both jumping, celebrating her victory, and then somehow my lips find hers. The surf lesson evaporates from my mind, replaced by heat coursing through me. I want nothing more than to peel away the neoprene between us and lay her down on the warm sand, to hear my name from her lips until she has no voice left. She kisses back with matching hunger, fingers tangling in my hair, breath coming in short gasps against my mouth. I couldn't stop if I tried.

The two of us crash onto the sand, me pinning her beneath me, my entire body burning with need. Her black neoprene wetsuit clings to every curve I've been fantasizing about for months—the swell of her breasts, the dip of her waist, the flare of her hips. Grains of wet sand stick to her flushed cheek as she looks up at me, pupils dilated. I'm seconds away from ripping the zipper down with my teeth, exposing inch after inch of her salt-kissed skin. My blood roars in my ears like the ocean behind us as her breath catches—I could devour her right here, right now, consequences be damned.

I tear down the zipper of her wetsuit, her groan igniting something primal in me. The neoprene peels away, revealing her salt-kissed skin, her breasts heaving with each ragged breath. My mouth claims one nipple, then the other, drawing a gasp that echoes across the empty shoreline. Her legs lock around me like a vise as I grind against her, desperate for more friction, more heat. My teeth graze her collarbone, her neck, before I devour her mouth again. The world dissolves—there's only her taste, her scent, the roar of blood in my ears drowning out even the crashing waves. On this private beach, nothing can stop us from—

Then Ansel and Gianni's voices slice through the air from the cliff above. Those fuckers. I'd kill them both with my bare hands if I could. They're chattering about surfing like it's any normal day while the most important moment of my life disintegrates. My jaw clenches so hard I taste metal as the perfect moment shatters around us.

Celeste lurches upright, fingers scrambling for the zipper at her back, yanking it closed with such force the teeth nearly break. My heart hammers against my ribs as she whips her head toward the wooden stairs where the two men descend, surfboards tucked under bronzed arms. Her ocean-blue eyes, wild with panic, dart between them and me as adrenaline floods my system. They stride past, oblivious to the electricity still crackling between the two bodies they've just interrupted—bodies that seconds ago were about to collide with the force of waves breaking against Malibu's unforgiving shore.

Ansel jogs up, surfboard tucked under his arm, salt water dripping from his hair. "Little brother! Thought that was you." His gaze shifts to Celeste. "And who's this? Another surf convert?"

Celeste's shoulders tense. "Not exactly." Her eyes flick between the newcomers and me, then down at her new wetsuit. Her board lies half-buried in sand at her feet.

"Hey Max," Ansel says, clapping my shoulder. "Gianni and I will head out to the break. You stay, work with your girl." He leans in, voice lowered. "Everyone starts somewhere, right? Remember your first wipeout?"

I watch Celeste's fingers fidget with the zipper of her wetsuit. Just minutes ago, she'd jumped up and down after nailing her first pop-up on dry land. Now that confidence has evaporated like sea spray. Damn these guys and their timing.

I nod to Ansel as he and Gianni paddle toward the horizon, then turn back to Celeste. "Ready to try the real thing? Those waves aren't getting any smaller."

Her eyes widen and she shields them with her hand, staring at the ocean. "Is it high tide?"

I check my watch. "Not for another 25 minutes." I don't mention that winter brings peak wave season to LA's coastline, or that an offshore storm has pushed the waves to eight to ten feet. The high tide will only make things worse.

I study her face, searching for clues. Is this the beginning of a new Saturday ritual she'll genuinely love, or just another performance? Like the ATV off-roading her ex apparently dragged her to—an activity she endured with a smile while apparently hating every minute.

She fidgets with the zipper of her wetsuit, eyes darting between me and the sand. The slight tremble in her lower lip gives her away.

"Listen," I say, running a hand through my salt-crusted hair. "Surfing can wait. How about the Santa Monica Pier instead? Or the Getty? Air conditioning, art, no chance of drowning."

Her gaze drifts toward the water where the guys carve through waves like they were born on boards. "But this is your thing. Your Saturday escape. I don't want to ruin that for you."

Something clicks. Rosa must have briefed her on my weekend ritual. Smart.

I jerk my chin toward the water. "Those two? No thanks. I'm up to my eyeballs in family bonding as it is. Can't take a step without Ansel breathing down my neck, and Gianni's already counting my reps three nights a week." I stop mid-sentence when the sunlight catches her profile—the slight upturn of her nose, the curve where her neck meets her shoulder. Heat crawls up my collar. I have to look away. "Anyway," I say, voice rougher than I intended, "I find plenty of inspiration wandering through galleries of marble nudes."

She narrows her eyes, studying my face for any trace of mockery. "Sure," she finally says, her voice softening. "The Getty would be perfect. I've been dying to go back—there's so much I haven't explored there yet."

"You could spend a lifetime in that place and still miss something breathtaking," I tell her, my pulse quickening as I force myself to maintain eye contact. "Let's shower and meet in the main house in an hour?"

The word "shower" lingers in the air between us, charged with unspoken meaning. I try to focus on our conversation, but my thoughts betray me—suddenly I'm picturing her in my bathroom, water coursing over her shoulders in my oversized shower. I imagine her pressed against the wall, my hands finding her waist, her breath catching as I pull her closer. The fantasy intensifies—her fingers tangling in my hair, her voice breaking as she whispers my name, the steam rising around us as we lose ourselves completely in each other.

I shake my head, my heart pounding like it's trying to escape my chest. This woman is unraveling me thread by goddamn thread, and I'm standing here letting her do it. Worse—I'm craving it.

Totally. Goddamn. Fucked.

Chapter Thirty-Two

CELESTE

Hot water cascades over my skin, washing away the salt crystals and the memory of my embarrassment when I tumbled off the surfboard for the fifth time. The Getty awaits us today—thank God, a place where I won't make a complete fool of myself. Max might rule the ocean, but those marble halls have been mine since sophomore year when I ducked into Renaissance Art 201 to fulfill a requirement and found myself transfixed. After Mom's diagnosis, I'd slip away to stand before Venus's birth or Europa's abduction, counting each brushstroke as if they were breaths, as if by understanding their perfect composition I could somehow restore order to my own chaotic world.

I've noticed the change in Max. He was so patient with me today, teaching me about his passion, surfing. And I'm surprised that he didn't brush me off today in favor of surfing with the guys. He's choosing to spend time with me instead of with them. So, he's definitely nicer to me. Perhaps we could become friends?

Maybe my mother's brush with death stirred something

in him, echoing his own loss. His mother chose to carry him to term rather than treat her cancer. Does he see some parallel I'm missing? Whatever the reason, I'm holding onto this fragile peace between us.

As for that kiss on the beach... I'm not fooling myself. The tabloids have been watching him like hawks since our "engagement" announcement. No more models, no more starlets, no more late nights at Soho House. So he's been forced to be celibate since the moment our engagement hit the tabloids and socials. For a man who used to change women like designer shirts, three months of forced celibacy must be excruciating. I was simply there—convenient, available, and technically his wife. He hasn't had sex in so long, so, yeah, he probably thinks I'm better than nothing. That's it. Nothing more than that.

Steam follows me from the bathroom as I freeze in the doorway, towel clutched to my chest. Max sits perched on the edge of my couch, his fingers hovering over my leather-bound notebook splayed open on the coffee table. My stomach drops. That's where I scribble character sketches, plot twists, and snippets of dialogue that come to me at 3 AM. The look on his face—jaw tight, eyes narrowed—tells me he's mistaken it for some kind of *Mean Girls*-style burn book with his name scrawled across every page.

I freeze, watching his eyes lock onto the screenwriting book. "Uh," I stammer, heat crawling up my neck. My fingers twitch with the urge to snatch it away, to hide this evidence of my secret ambitions. Max Kensington with his golden touch, his empire built before thirty, his life a highlight reel of achievements—and here's me, with my drawer full of rejection letters and half-finished scripts. Development executives critique other people's work; we don't fail at creating our own. I can already picture the slight softening around his eyes, that terrible moment when admiration curdles into something worse. Pity. God, anything but that —not from him, not when my heart does that ridiculous flutter every time he walks into a room. "I'm sorry. I obviously need to get dressed."

My hand shakes a little as I reach for my screenwriting book, trying to act casual. Max watches me, his eyes narrowing. I can tell what he's thinking—that it's some diary where I write down all the mean things he does, keeping a record of every time he's been a jerk.

He just nods. I slip into my bedroom and slide the screenwriting book into a drawer. Damn! What's he doing in my wing? He was supposed to meet me in his kitchen. Now he's going to assume I've been filling pages with rants about him. And you know what? Let him. Better he think I hate him than discover the truth—that I'm just another Hollywood wannabe with nothing to show for it. Another dreamer who couldn't sell a screenplay if her life depended on it.

I reach for one of the sundresses Max bought me and pair it with a blue cashmere cardigan, then hesitate. The coastal chill will creep in once the sun dips below the horizon. Better to be practical. I swap it for dark-wash Rag & Bone jeans that hug my curves just right, caramel leather Frye boots I'd never have splurged on myself, a whisper-soft Vince t-shirt in pale blush, and a chunky cream cashmere sweater with pearl buttons —all expensive things that appeared in my closet courtesy of Max's platinum card. Not that I'm trying to catch his eye. Sure, my heart still does that annoying flutter thing whenever Max walks into a room, but I've locked away any hope he might feel the same. No point dressing to impress someone who's only being civil because he has to be.

I walk out and he raises his eyebrows, his green-eyed gaze lingering on me for a heartbeat longer than necessary. There's something in his eyes—a flicker of heat that makes my stomach flutter. It almost looks like...no. I shake my head, dispelling the thought like morning mist. The man who has barely said two words for me for weeks isn't suddenly attracted to me. My imagination is running wild again. I smooth down my jeans, forcing my lips into a casual smile that hopefully masks the blush warming my cheeks. "Ready."

He nods toward my front door. "We're taking the Lucid," he says with the casual air of someone downgrading from a private jet to first class. My heart skips. The Lucid Air Sapphire—electric dream machine, 1,111 horsepower, zero-to-sixty in under 2.5 seconds. I've kept the brochure in my nightstand for three years, a glossy reminder of what I can't afford while Mom's medical bills pile up. For Max, it's merely his most modest car, slumming it below his Rolls Royces and Bugattis. Is choosing his "cheap" quarter-million-dollar vehicle consideration or condescension? I can't decide.

I click my seatbelt into place and catch myself staring at the sharp line of Max's jaw. My pulse skips, and I force myself to look away. This is dangerous territory. If he keeps being decent to me, I'm going to end up like one of those women who doodle a guy's name in the margins of important documents. Next thing you know, I'll be sitting in meetings about script revisions while mentally cataloging the exact shade of his eyes. I shake my head. No. Not happening. Romance with Max Kensington needs to stay firmly in the realm of impossible things.

At the red light, his hand drifts across the center console, fingers slightly curled. Is he reaching for my hand? Or just resting his hand there? I stare at it for a second too long, then turn to the window instead, watching a woman walk her corgi along the sidewalk. My heart thuds against my ribs. Better to focus on the dog's stubby legs than risk grabbing a hand that wasn't offered in the first place.

He finally breaks the silence. "So. Rosa told you about my mother. And my father." His voice cracks on the word "father." When he looks at me, the raw pain in his eyes hits me like a physical blow. I can't breathe. Those green eyes that always seemed so controlled, so calculated—now they're drowning in grief that's decades old but still bleeding. I want to look away—need to look away—but I'm transfixed, pinned by the naked vulnerability he apparently rarely shows. "What did you think," he whispers, "about that story?"

I inhale slowly, searching for the right words. The last thing he needs is another round of those hollow reassurances—the ones therapists and well-meaning friends have probably recited to him for years. Those empty platitudes about how he's not to blame, about how he didn't ask to be born, how he shouldn't feel guilty. I can almost see them bouncing off him, worn smooth from repetition. No, I won't add my voice to that useless chorus.

I swallow hard. "I understand the feeling that something beyond your control is somehow your fault," I say, my voice barely audible. The words are coming from somewhere deep inside me, somewhere I don't usually let anyone see. "Sometimes I catch myself thinking that my mother's cancer and my father's death are somehow... connected to me and Lexi existing in the world. Like we're the reason everything went wrong."

He furrows his brows. "I don't understand."

I narrow my eyes. "It happened on a ski trip. My father

was an expert—black diamond runs, perfect form, the whole thing. My high school was planning this big winter trip, and I'd never been on skis before." My voice catches. "Dad insisted on teaching me himself. Four days in the mountains, just the two of us. He was so patient, showing me how to position my poles, how to stop without falling. He made sure I knew every basic technique." I take a deep breath. "That's when the accident happened."

He nods. "What happened?"

"My father was so focused on me that he never saw the novice skier spiraling out of control down the slope. The collision was brutal—the kid's helmet smashed right into Dad's skull. But Dad just laughed it off. He looked at this terrified teenager and said, 'The agony of defeat!' with this ridiculous grin." I smile at the memory. "I remember laughing despite everything. The kid looked confused, and honestly, I barely caught the reference myself. It was from this old ABC sports show Dad always watched—their intro showed this poor skier wiping out spectacularly after a jump. That was my father in a nutshell—flat on his back in the snow after getting bulldozed, and still making jokes."

Max's smile breaks into a soft laugh. "God, that clip. The skier who eats it on the jump and goes flying off the ramp? 'The agony of defeat' they called it on ABC. My dad used to pull out those old Wide World of Sports tapes when I was just a little grom about to get my first board. Thought watching the surf championships would fire me up." His smile fades as he shakes his head. "Man, every time I saw that poor guy crash, I felt it right in my bones."

I flash a grin. "I know, I know. Poor guy. But ABC clearly set him up as the joke. Hope they at least cut him a decent check for turning his face-plant into America's favorite blooper. That clip ran for years and became iconic."

Max shrugs. "That skier never seemed bitter about becoming famous for wiping out. I doubt ABC paid him much for replaying his crash thousands of times." He exhales slowly, his fingers tapping against the steering wheel. "Anyway, I'm getting off topic." The car sits idle in the Getty Museum parking lot. When Max turns to face me, something in his gaze catches me off guard. Those green eyes I've always dismissed as calculating suddenly seem... different. Warmer. More human. My pulse quickens as he says, "About what happened with your father..."

"Yeah, so... when my dad crashed, they sent over some paramedics to check him out. Standard procedure on the slopes. But he just brushed snow off his jacket and told them, 'Nothing broken but my pride. You folks can head back now.'"

I shake my head. "The doctors later told us it's called 'talk and die syndrome.' Someone gets a head injury that looks minor—just a bump, maybe a little dizziness—so they brush it off. Hours later, the brain swells and..." My voice catches. I stare at my hands. "That's what took my dad."

"You blame yourself?"

"How could I not? There I was on that blue slope—so proud of myself for graduating from the bunny hill to blue in just days—and Dad standing there coaching me through every turn. 'Weight on your downhill ski, Celeste!' Those were his last words before the accident."

He nods, and something shifts in the air between us. Like a cloud passing over the sun. We're both carrying ghosts—his mother, my father—and that same stupid belief that we should have saved them somehow. My brain knows better, but my heart never got the memo. The guilt lives in my bones now. I catch the way his lips press together, mirroring exactly what happens to my face when the memories come flooding back. I can read his grief like my own handwriting, though he probably thinks his poker face is perfect.

"Your mother's cancer—you think that's your fault too?"

"That's more of a stretch than my dad guilt." I rub my temples. "After Dad died, Mom barely slept. Just worked and worked. He was only 38—one of those guys who could run for miles without breaking a sweat. Training for an Iron Man when it happened. The possibility of dying young? Never crossed his mind. Life insurance wasn't even on his radar."

"What kind of work did he do?"

"Roofing. His own business. Some months we had steak, others we had ramen. He was always chasing the next job. When he died, the bank account was as empty as our fridge."

He nods, a gesture that bridges nothing. What would Max Kensington understand about my mother hunched over coupons at 2 a.m., scissors trembling in her hand as she calculated pennies saved on toilet paper? Or her dragging herself from cashiering to waitressing to night cleaning, the smell of industrial disinfectant becoming her perfume? Or those nights I'd find her at the kitchen table, calculator in hand, eyes red-rimmed as she juggled which bill to pay and which to let slide another month? How we were always looking out for the tow truck that would come and take our car away? His childhood home probably had a name, not just an apartment number.

Still, he's trying to understand. Trying to relate. I have to give him that.

I twist my hands in my lap. "Mom was always working.

I'd wake up for school, and she'd already be gone—cleaning office buildings since 5 AM. Then she'd serve lunch at Denny's, come home just long enough to check our homework, and head to the night shift at Wal-Mart." I swallow hard. "Every penny went to keeping us fed, clothed, in school. If she didn't have us to worry about..." My voice catches. "Maybe she could've rested sometimes. Maybe her body wouldn't have..." I shrug, unable to finish.

Max's lips curl into a hesitant smile as he pokes a hole in my logic. "But how can you blame yourself for both your dad's death and your mom's cancer? I mean, if you hadn't been born..."

"I know, I know," I say, meeting his eyes briefly. "If I hadn't existed, my father wouldn't have been teaching me to ski when that teenager plowed into him. That's where logic and emotion part ways for me. My head understands the contradiction, but my heart can't let go." I reach over and rest my fingers on his hand where it grips the steering wheel. "That's why I get what you feel about your mother. Deep down. Your rational mind knows you're blameless—you didn't choose to be born or ask her to sacrifice everything. But that voice inside keeps whispering otherwise, and sometimes it's the loudest thing in the room."

"How do you live with it?" The question comes soft and urgent, like he's searching for a remedy I might possess for his own guilt about his mother's death.

"I don't live with it very well. I stare at the ceiling most nights, playing it over and over. If I'd been a better skier—good enough for the black diamond runs—he wouldn't have been with me on that blue slope. Or if I'd been worse, stuck on the green or even the bunny hill after four days of lessons, I also wouldn't have been on the blue slope. If I hadn't begged to go on that junior class trip like some entitled brat..." I shake my head, swallowing hard. "Somewhere there's a universe where my father wasn't standing on that exact patch of snow at that exact moment. A universe where he's still alive. That universe haunts me."

He inhales deeply, giving a slight nod. "No escaping the guilt, is there?" His eyes narrow against the sunlight. "We better get the tram now." This time, he extends his hand with clear intention, and after a moment's pause, I slip my fingers between his. "For appearances," he murmurs. "Someone's always watching these days. Better convince them we're madly in love."

His hand is warm and soft against mine, and I hate how I notice that. I try to convince myself I'm not feeling anything—not the electricity shooting up my arm, not the way my pulse quickens traitorously with each step. But my body betrays me, every nerve ending coming alive even as my mind screams in protest while we walk toward the museum grounds.

We shuffle forward in the snaking line for the tram, shoulder to shoulder with tourists in cargo shorts and fanny packs. Max stands beside me, his Rolex glinting in the sun, yet he makes no move to bypass the queue. He doesn't even flinch when a toddler's sticky fingers brush against his arm. No whispers to security, no flashing of his black AmEx—just patience that surprises me.

The Getty Museum comes into view as we go up, its big white stone buildings shining in the blue L.A. sky. The tram stops at the top with a hiss, and I stop walking for a second. Below us, the huge city with all its neighborhoods, roads, and pools stretches out to the ocean, which sparkles in the sun. For a moment, even the usual L.A. traffic seems still, like time has stopped up here.

The museum queue stretches even longer than the tram

257

line had. I glance at Max, wondering if his patience has limits. Most billionaire CEOs with magazine covers and Hollywood empires don't wait in lines like commoners. I brace myself for him to flash his VIP status or make a call.

Instead, he tucks his hands into his pockets and catches my eye, eyebrows lifting with a genuine smile. "I can't help it," he says softly. "This place is special to me." His Adam's apple bobs as he swallows. "After Dad vanished, Rosa would bring me, Ansel, and Roman here—we were her museum boys. For a few precious hours inside these walls, I could forget everything else and just... breathe."

I nod, shocked to discover this shared ritual between us. After Dad died, I'd ride the 720 bus here every Saturday morning for a year straight. Always alone—I couldn't bear someone rushing me through the galleries or suggesting we skip a section. I needed to lose myself completely, to stand motionless before each sculpture until I memorized every curve, to lean close to paintings until the brushstrokes became tiny universes. I'd read every word on those little placards like they were sacred texts. For those precious Saturday hours, I could step outside my grief and into a world where beauty still existed.

I sigh. The Max I thought I knew is dissolving before my eyes, revealing someone I can't armor myself against. My heart quickens at the danger. A $60,000-a-year development exec doesn't end up with the CEO of Kensington Pictures—that's not how the story goes. What happens when a mortal loves a god? Nothing good.

I clamp my eyelids together, trying to conjure up the Max who left me to plan our fake wedding by myself, the one who sliced me to ribbons with his words that first day at the restaurant. But this Max—the one standing beside me in this never-ending Getty line—won't disappear. This Max just opened up about losing his mom in a voice that cracked at the edges. This Max kissed me on the beach and left my lips tingling with salt and want. This Max held my waist on that surfboard like I was something precious. He's not dangerous because he's mean; he's dangerous because he's kind. And I'm toast.

When we finally get inside, the AC washes over us like salvation. After the furnace of outside, it feels almost illicit how good the cool air feels—like the building itself is sheltering us from everything else. November in LA is still summer anywhere else, at least during the day (night's are still really cold. Or cold-adjacent, at any rate) and today's a scorcher. I hear myself babbling about Renaissance paintings before I can stop—the gilded halos, those luminous faces that seem lit from within, the raw emotion of it all—and I don't even care that I sound like a total art nerd.

Max matches my stride for stride, then starts revealing things I'd never spot in a million years. He shows me how Titian makes red practically scream off the canvas, how Raphael arranges his saints like some heavenly chess master, and how Bellini's Madonnas somehow look both ghostly and more alive than we are. According to Max, Masaccio invented that weird trick where paintings swallow you whole, while Mantegna's figures seem ready to climb out and join our tour. With each explanation, I feel my art knowledge shrinking to postcard-size next to his—and I'm weirdly into it. We float through gallery after gallery beneath those over-the-top gold frames, and all I can think is: what masterpiece will he decode next?

I cock my head to one side and tease him. "For someone who just 'spent time here as a kid,' you sure know your way around a museum. My art history minor feels like a waste of tuition right now." My voice falters as Rosa's words float back to me—little Max at five, reading Dickens aloud like it was Dr. Seuss. No wonder he had a doctorate before most people finish undergrad. Standing in his shadow, I'm hit with a dizzying realization: I've married a mind that operates on a different frequency altogether. He's rattling off Botticelli brushstrokes in his three-thousand-dollar loafers while I'm still trying to remember if Da Vinci came before or after Michelangelo.

He lets out a soft laugh and slides his arm around my shoulders. "I know, I'm rambling. You should meet my brother Asher—he's the real art expert and our resident genius. He runs our international event planning division but his real passion is art. He knows things I can't even pronounce. Growing up, we actually banned him from our little museum trips." His eyes crinkle at the corners. "Poor kid would plant himself in front of every painting and lecture until Rosa threatened to leave him behind. Eventually, he just started coming alone. He's probably somewhere in this very building right now, torturing some innocent docent about brushstroke techniques."

A laugh escapes me when he mentions his brother being banished from family museum outings. "I'm sorry," I say, my shoulders still shaking. "It's just—I was a solo museum-goer too, but by choice. I can't stand trailing behind someone else, rushing past pieces I want to study or being dragged toward exhibits I couldn't care less about." I try picturing Asher from the wedding reception. Which one was he again? They all share that same genetic lottery win—sharp jawlines, perfect hair, eyes you could drown in—but the faces had blurred together in the champagne-soaked whirlwind of that night.

We spend hours drifting through the museum's light-filled rooms, the click of our shoes against polished stone the only sound between us. The impressionists pull me in every time—all those vibrant colors catching sunlight that somehow never faded. I can't help lingering before Degas's dancers, their fragile bodies bent like saplings in the wind, all captured in soft, dusty colors. There's one at the Getty I visit whenever I can—"Waiting," showing an exhausted young ballerina slumped beside a stern woman dressed in widow's black.

Meanwhile, Max seems drawn to Manet and Renoir. I follow him reluctantly, even though their paintings showcase the wealthy at play—all those ladies in fine dresses holding champagne flutes. Still, their technique sweeps me away until I'm practically there—feeling cool air off the water during a riverside gathering, or blushing alongside that woman in white from the Getty collection as a gentleman takes her hand on a sunlit path. As we prepare to leave, we both pause before Caillebotte's painting of a lonely man gazing out his Paris window, neither of us speaking as we absorb that perfect moment of city isolation.

We step outside into the November darkness at five o'clock. Max hasn't mentioned what's next—a restaurant somewhere? Back to his place for a movie in that ridiculous screening room? My stomach flutters at the thought. I glance at his profile against the city lights, the sharp line of his jaw softening when he catches me looking.

Why am I already planning the rest of our evening? The Getty always leaves me feeling like I've stepped into another world, but today it wasn't just the art. It was him. The way he listened when I talked about Monet. How his hand brushed mine reaching for the museum map. I'm trying to remind myself this is temporary, just business. But something's shifting between us, something terrifying and thrilling all at once. I mean, I want to think that we'll spend more time together this evening, but I just can't assume. Max is a busy guy. He probably already has plans elsewhere - maybe some big Hollywood party.

Max checks his watch. "What do you think about the Santa Monica Pier?" His voice has a hesitant quality, like he's bracing for rejection. He has no idea what's happening inside me—my pulse quickening, my cheeks warming. The Santa Monica Pier! Just the thought of it brings back memories of childhood delight: that rickety wooden roller coaster, the ferris wheel spinning against the sunset, face painters turning children into tigers and butterflies, magicians pulling quarters from behind ears. Neon signs reflecting off the waves below. But what makes my stomach flutter isn't just the promise of cotton candy and carnival games—it's the hours ahead with Max, stretching before us like the boardwalk itself.

"Well, what do you think?" I ask him. "Obviously, I love the pier." I jump up and down and clap my hands and his face lights up.

"I figured you did," he says. "So let's go."

Time flies on the Santa Monica Pier with all its bright lights and fun. I spin around to a man playing jazz on his sax, and when a magician picks me from the crowd, my face gets hot with joy I didn't see coming. The ferris wheel goes up with a squeak, and Max grabs my hand at the top. On the roller coaster, we let go of our cool, screaming bloody murder as we drop with our hands up high. At Bubba Gump's, I almost spit out my drink watching health-nut Max eat fried fish and hush puppies like he's been starved. Across from me, light hits his eyes while I drink my spicy mango drink. For a second, I think about us doing this all the time, being a real—No. No way. This is just for show. *Remember your contract, Celeste. This isn't real. It'll never be real. So stop thinking this might become something.*

A few hours into dinner, Max sets down his beer—his second—and leans forward. "So," he says. The rim of my third mango jalapeño margarita leaves a sticky ring on my fingertips. The tequila has loosened something in me, made my thoughts slippery. I catch myself staring at the curve of his mouth, imagining our children with his smile, and I have to look away. Tipsy Celeste is dangerous Celeste. I grip my glass tighter. This arrangement was never about love—he needed to appease his grandfather, I needed money for Mom and Lexi. A marriage of convenience, nothing more. No matter how much I wish otherwise. Max clears his throat. "About that book on your coffee table..."

I feel my cheeks flush hot. "Don't worry, it's not some *Mean Girls* burn book situation," I say, attempting a casual laugh that comes out more like a nervous hiccup. "Trust me, if I were keeping a list of all the ways you drive me crazy, I'd need something a lot thicker than that notebook."

He laughs. "No, I know it's not." He inhales, shoulders rising. "Can't help myself though. Put any book in front of me when I'm waiting for someone, and my fingers just start turning pages. My first-grade teacher used to catch me staring out the window instead of at the blackboard - I was always thinking of stories I'd been reading instead of what the teacher is trying to teach. Guess some part of me never outgrew that—always needing something to occupy my thoughts."

I need to steer this conversation elsewhere. "Let me guess—you were that kid staring out the window while everyone else struggled with fractions. Too smart for the classroom, right?" I flash him a knowing smile. Max shifts in his seat, and I can practically see the wheels turning behind those eyes. That's the thing about brilliant people—they never quite fit in those little desks, those rigid schedules. Did they bump him up a grade? Two grades?

He clears his throat. "Let's get back on track." He shifts closer. "You write screenplays, don't you?"

My pulse quickens, blood rushing to my face. I never mentioned screenwriting to him. Never wanted him to see the stack of rejections, the unanswered queries. "What makes you say that?"

"Those notes I glimpsed—character descriptions, bits of dialogue. I recognize the format." His hand covers mine, warm and steady, but all I feel is pity radiating from his touch. I slide my hand away. "Listen, Celeste," he continues, his voice softening. "Breaking into screenwriting is brutal. Finding representation in Los Angeles? Nearly impossible. But I might be able to—"

I shake my head. "No. Stop. I'm not good." My chest tightens, my heart fluttering like a trapped bird. He'll ask for my screenplays next, read them once, then never mention them again. I can already see his polite smile masking thoughts about my wooden dialogue and predictable plot twists. We'll pass each other in hallways, him ducking into rooms to avoid my hopeful "Did you finish reading it?" I'll catch glimpses of pity in his eyes. The silence between us will grow, filled only with my unasked questions and his unspoken criticism. This screenplay thing—it'll kill whatever's starting between us before it even has a chance. I'm certain of it.

He leans back, his gaze sharpening as he studies me. Something in those eyes tells me he sees right through my evasion. "Celeste, you need to risk it. Good screenplays? I'll assemble the team to bring them to life. It's my specialty."

"No," I counter, "it's mine." The audacity. Since when

does the CEO personally scout scripts and build production teams? That's literally my job description, not his corner office responsibility.

He arched an eyebrow. "Don't play coy. If your scripts have legs, Kensington Pictures can get them off the ground."

I shake my head, feeling the room tilt slightly. "You're missing the point. This particular plot twist is telegraphed from page one." I drain my glass and signal the bartender for another. "Want the sad truth? I've got fifteen screenplays gathering dust on my hard drive. Fifteen. Been writing since middle school. You know how Gladwell says you need 10,000 hours to master something? I've doubled that, easy. And what do I have to show for it? A collection of rejection emails from every agent with a pulse in this town."

The words tumble out faster than I can filter them. A tiny warning bell rings somewhere in my brain—the same bell that failed to sound during countless embarrassing nights before. I know the pattern: one minute I'm sharing personal truths, the next I'm confessing childhood secrets or crying about my mother's cancer. And then comes bitchy Celeste, where I start screaming at anybody in my purview. Bitchy Celeste comes out when I'm really loaded, after which passed-out Celeste makes an appearance. I must stop myself right now before I go through all the iterations of drunk Celeste.

I eye my fresh mango margarita—fourth? fifth?—and slide it firmly away from me. Whatever fragile connection we're building, I'm not about to drown it in tequila.

The room suddenly feels too small. My tequila-fuzzed brain registers something in Max's emerald gaze—that soft, tilted look reserved for stray cats and charity cases. Of course. He's the golden boy with the magic touch, while I'm just... what? Willy Loman from *Death of a Salesman*. A nobody with delusions of someday. The kind of person who thinks they're special until the world reminds them they're not. That's me in a nutshell.

I mutter something about feeling sick and push my chair back. The restaurant buzzes with conversation, bodies pressed against each other like sardines, a line still snaking out the door. My chest tightens at the thought of another sixty minutes trapped here, followed by that silent car ride home with Max's judgment hanging between us. I duck into the bathroom, pull out my phone, and order an Uber. Let him figure it out. Let him hate me again. I'm done being someone's project, someone's broken thing to mend. The Max I thought I knew wouldn't have looked at me that way —like I'm a problem with a solution, not a person with feelings.

I get my Uber and hail the ride home.

And then prepare myself for the fallout.

Chapter Thirty-Three

MAX

Monday morning. I'm at my desk, tie loose, sleeves rolled up. My office feels empty despite the view of LA spread out below. I can't stop thinking about Saturday night, but the memories come in pieces.

Things with Celeste were shifting. I caught myself watching her laugh at the Manet exhibition—the way her whole face lit up at my ridiculous art pun. At dinner, our hands touched reaching for the wine, and neither of us pulled away immediately. For the first time in years, I wasn't calculating every word, every gesture. Now I'm sitting here rolling this damn paperweight between my fingers, breathing in that Celeste candle I special-ordered after she moved in—orange and vanilla with something earthy underneath. One whiff and I'm right back to that moment she leaned across the table, her hair falling forward as she studied the menu.

But I screwed up. I get that now. I stepped right on the landmine I didn't know was there. How was I supposed to know her screenplay wasn't just some creative outlet but her actual dream? The thing she stays up writing until 3 AM, the rejection letters she hides in her desk drawer. I wouldn't understand that kind of struggle. My life's been a straight shot to the top, with my name already engraved on every door before I even reached for the handle.

My love affair with cinema began at five years old—legs crossed on the carpet, sticky fingers from smuggled Milk Duds, whispering lines before the actors could. By twenty-three, I'd turned that obsession into a PhD, my dissertation on auteur theory now leather-bound and shelved like a trophy. I started in the mailroom at sixteen, graduated to coffee-fetcher, then script reader, development coordinator —grandfather's surname stamped on my forehead, unlocking every door. Sure, I logged the hours—dawn-to-midnight shifts, birthdays spent in editing bays, girlfriends who became strangers—but I can't ignore the oil portrait watching over our lobby.

Meanwhile, Celeste battles the Hollywood machine like thousands before her. This town devours talent without connections; scripts vanish into slush piles, agents hide behind gatekeepers, and form rejections are considered courteous. History's littered with brilliant rejects: John Kennedy Toole's *Confederacy of Dunces* found glory only after his suicide; Jonathan Larson's decade of failure before *Rent*; King's wife fishing *Carrie* from the garbage; Rowling collecting dozens of "no thank you" letters. Genius works. All initially trashed.

Maybe Celeste's screenplays are brilliant but Holly-wood's closed doors won't budge for her. Or maybe—and this thought makes me uncomfortable—her writing simply isn't good enough to warrant attention, no matter who's reading it.

So. How to find out the truth about my wife?

I tap my fingers against the desk, considering the situation. She's guarding those screenplays like they're her children. And I get it. What if they're amateur hour—dialogue that makes you cringe, characters flatter than cardboard, plots with holes you could drive a truck through? I've greenlit enough projects to spot the difference between gold and pyrite from fifty paces.

If I read her work and it's garbage, I'd have to be honest. That's who I am. And then I'd become the executioner of her dreams instead of just another faceless rejection letter. She can blame the industry's overcrowding when agents don't respond, but my verdict? That would be final. That would be personal. And that would be the end of whatever's growing between us. Not a role I'm willing to play.

I need to see for myself what she's capable of. What if her writing is brilliant? What if she's that rare find everyone in this town is hunting for? I could open doors for her overnight, though probably not at Kensington. Producing your spouse's screenplay is risky business—even the best scripts can bomb for a thousand reasons beyond anyone's control, and I won't put our marriage in that crossfire. But I have other options. If her pages impress me, one call to Selena Farley would change everything. Celeste gets representation from Hollywood's top agent, never knowing I orchestrated it. She builds her career believing it was all her own talent—which it would be. That's the perfect scenario, isn't it? Her success, her confidence, no strings attached.

Roman's got this tech guy on retainer—a digital bloodhound who sniffs out hidden files during my brother's messier lawsuits. One call and he could slip into Celeste's laptop without leaving so much as a pixel out of place. I'd finally see those screenplays she's guarding like state secrets.

If they're garbage, I delete the memory from my brain. If they're brilliant, Selena gets a call. And Celeste? She'd never suspect a thing.

I dial my brother's number. "Rome," I say when he picks up. "I need to borrow Sven."

A low chuckle comes through the line. Roman and I have the rockiest relationship of all my siblings. Perpetually scowling, yet somehow always ready with a cutting joke, and reliable when it counts. Like right now. "Sven? What for?"

"Need to get into my wife's computer." I explain my plan. "Want to see if she can actually write or if she's just another Hollywood dreamer."

"Dude," he says, with a laugh, "ever consider just asking her to show you her scripts?"

I sigh into the phone. "Christ, Rome. Of course I thought of that. She doesn't think she's any good—too embarrassed to let me see anything. Maybe she's right about her talent. If so, I'd rather not humiliate her by letting on that I snooped. But if she's got something real? I can pull some strings."

"Okay," he says reluctantly. "Give him a call."

"Thanks, Rome," I say.

I reach out to Sven, who promises to deliver her screenplays to my inbox within the hour. For someone who makes his living breaking into Fortune 500 security systems, grabbing a few documents from a personal server is barely worth getting out of bed for.

Then I get back to work. My phone buzzes with seventeen new emails since lunch, three marked urgent from the legal team about rights clearances for the Spielberg project. Three scripts need notes by tomorrow, the marketing team is waiting on my approval for the winter slate poster designs, and somewhere in this chaos, I'm supposed to find time to placate a nervous investor who's threatening to pull out of our next summer blockbuster. My assistant pokes her head in to remind me about the 3PM call with the London office, and the development team has left three different script drafts on my desk with Post-its requesting feedback "ASAP."

I have plenty to fill my plate, but, somehow, this Celeste screenplay thing is paramount in my mind. I'm that anxious to find out if she has any talent.

I've got Nolan's summer slate email half-written when Sven's message pops up. My hand freezes over the mouse. I click, download, and stare at the three screenplay files now sitting on my desktop. Each one a ticking bomb that could either launch a career or waste my night. I'll know by page ten of the first script if she can write. By the end of the third, I'll know if she's worth the gamble.

Please don't let this be another disappointment.

Chapter Thirty-Four

MAX

It's been twelve hours since I cracked open the first of Celeste's screenplays and I haven't slept a wink. Six o'clock last night until now, script after script, and I feel like I've discovered buried treasure. The breadth of her work floored me. She tackles figures I'd never imagine on screen—like this nebbish Holocaust hero, Varian Fry, who smuggled Chagall and Ernst and thousands more right under Nazi noses. Then there's her take on Tamara Lempicka—Russian aristocrat turned penniless refugee who sold her last jewels after the Bolsheviks took everything, before reinventing herself as a bisexual Art Deco pioneer.

Those weren't the only ones, just the ones that grabbed me hardest. What gets me is how she makes these historical figures breathe. She finds the perfect dramatic moments without ever feeling exploitative. The rhythm of her storytelling—knowing exactly when to accelerate, when to let silence speak, when to bring everything home—it's instinctual. When her characters talk, I hear real voices. They're messy and complicated and brave all at once, never just heroes or villains.

Then there were her rom-coms—vibrant, sparkling gems that made me spill coffee down my shirt from laughing so unexpectedly. She has an uncanny mastery of that genre, weaving those perfect meet-cutes where you can feel the electricity crackling between characters from their first disastrous encounter. Her dialogue snaps with the rhythm of classic Nora Ephron, but with a modern edge that feels fresh. The genre might have gathered dust on studio shelves lately, but I've tracked the streaming numbers —viewers are hungry again for that intoxicating cocktail of humor and heart. I've been searching for months for the right rom-com to greenlight.

Next up were several quirky genre-benders: a Thanksgiving reunion where a dysfunctional family's buried secrets bubble to the surface; a redemption tale populated by eccentric locals from a forgotten town; and a road trip chronicle featuring middle-aged women in clunkers traversing America's hidden highways, confronting the paths not taken. I pictured them through different directorial lenses—Payne capturing that bittersweet heartland honesty, Anderson (Wes) framing each shot with geometric precision and candy-colored nostalgia, or Anderson (P.T.) weaving those sprawling character studies that collapse time until you emerge from the theater wondering where the afternoon went.

Celeste is a revelation. Last night, I stayed up until three reading her latest screenplay—the dialogue so sharp it cut through me, the structure as elegant as anything I've greenlit in five years. My cheeks actually ached from grinning at her third-act twist. How many studio executives have missed this? How many times has she sat across from some idiot in a corner office who couldn't recognize what I'm holding in my hands? I imagine her hunched over her laptop, rewriting until dawn, muttering lines to herself. The thought of her talent going unnoticed makes my jaw clench. This industry devours writers daily, but she deserves better. She deserves everything.

I jab Selena's number into my phone, drumming my fingers against the desk until she picks up on the fourth ring. "Selena."

"Hey, Max, what's up?"

"Three scripts landing in your inbox in five minutes. Celeste Jenkins. I need your eyes on every page by six." I pause, letting the silence stretch just long enough. "And Selena? This isn't a favor—it's your priority today."

She nods. "On it." Selena Farley doesn't say no to anyone who controls as many studio deals as I do. Even with her roster of Oscar winners and box office champions, she knows where the real power in this town lies.

"Oh, and Selena? Not a word to Celeste about who sent these to you. Not one word. This is important. And I'd like you to call her today after you read several of these scripts. I know you're busy, but this is paramount."

"Got it, Max," Selena says.

Then I hang up the phone and relish seeing Celeste tonight. Selena will call her today because I asked her to and she'll do it. Celeste's eyes will light up like I haven't seen before. And I'll secretly know that I helped her achieve her dream. That's priceless to me.

Chapter Thirty-Five

CELESTE

The memory of Saturday night makes me cringe. Who ditches someone by pretending to use the bathroom, then sneaking out to call an Uber? Especially when we were actually having a good time. A really good time. Not in a romantic way—definitely not romantic—just two friends hanging out. But for once I'd stopped overthinking every word, every gesture. I'd laughed without calculating how it would sound.

Now I skulk around the mansion like a ghost, taking ridiculous detours to avoid the main kitchen where I might bump into him. I miss my morning chats with Rosa, but what would I even say to Max if I ran into him? "Sorry I vanished without a word"?

The truth is, when he started asking about my writing, something in me just snapped. I've spent my whole life dreaming of seeing my name in credits, not expecting to be the next Phoebe Waller-Bridge or Aaron Sorkin, just wanting a chance. But after years of Hollywood crushing that hope, I've trained myself not to think about it. Max innocently pressed on that tender spot, and between that and those mango margaritas (four? five?), I panicked. I owe him an apology, but every time I rehearse one in my head, I end up hiding deeper in my wing of the house.

I'm hunched over my desk, lost in the pages spread across the glass surface. Golden afternoon light slices through the blinds, illuminating what might be the next big hit for our studio. Amber Hayes' series treatment follows two young lesbians in a coastal town, their first romance unfolding against whispers and family pressure—think "Summer I Turned Pretty" with sharper edges. Her writing cuts straight to that teenage heartache, the kind that feels eternal when you're living it. I'm reaching for my phone to tell her exactly that when Simone materializes in my doorway, all business in her signature red lips and matching nails.

"Selena Farley, line one," she says, her perfectly arched eyebrows shooting upward. "You want to take this."

I sigh. "Fine." Selena's calls are a weekly occurrence—she's got half the A-list writers in Hollywood on her roster. Whatever has Amber bouncing on her toes about this particular call is beyond me.

"Selena, hey," I say, wedging the phone between ear and shoulder. "Just email it over and I'll add it to the pile." The pile that's currently threatening to avalanche off my desk: ten screenplays with Post-its blooming from their edges, eight writer callbacks circled in red on my calendar, and a stack of fifteen scripts—fifteen!—all screaming for development notes. My eyes flick to the clock. I need to wrap this call up fast.

Selena's voice cuts through the phone. "No, not that kind of call. I've read your scripts, Celeste, and I want in. How soon can you meet? I've got contracts ready for your signature so we can start getting these in front of the right people."

My jaw drops to the floor. Selena Farley? THE Selena Farley wants to represent me? The woman who can make studio executives tremble with a single raised eyebrow? The kingmaker whose client list reads like the presenter lineup at the Academy Awards? I pinch my arm, hard. The sting confirms this isn't some wine-induced hallucination after falling asleep watching *Entertainment Tonight*. This is real. Selena Farley just said my name and the word "representation" in the same sentence.

"I, I, I…don't understand. How did you get my scripts?"

"Celeste, they've been languishing in my slush pile for months now, buried under a mountain of mediocre screenplays and half-baked treatments. God, I'm sorry." She pauses on the phone. "But when I finally cracked open your Varian Fry script this morning, I couldn't put it down. That scene where he's smuggling Ernst through the checkpoint with the forged visas? My heart was pounding so hard I had to loosen my collar. And the way you captured Chagall's haunted eyes, Arendt's fierce intellect—these aren't just historical figures anymore, they're breathing, bleeding people. This could be the next *Schindler's List*, especially with everything happening in the world right now."

I'm shaking. This isn't happening. This doesn't just happen, does it?

I squeeze my eyes shut. Max. Who else could it be? Damn him and his savior complex. I can picture him now, calling Selena Farley's office, throwing around his last name and demanding she dust off scripts I submitted three years ago. Three years. I haven't sent anything out since landing at Dreamscape—traded one Hollywood dream for another that pays the bills. And now Selena Farley just happens to call? Please.

"Selena. You don't have to do this. I can assure you that Max won't blacklist you if you don't sign me. I appreciate your offer, but-"

"Celeste. I need you to stop talking for a moment." The voice on the other end of the line softened slightly. "Your script? It's brilliant. Truly. And this has nothing to do with your connection to Max Kensington. I want to see you in my office next Monday at 9. I've already spoken with Iris about clearing your schedule. We have a lot to discuss."

The phone slips from my fingers onto the desk. Selena Farley—the Selena Farley—wants to represent me? My screenplay? Something doesn't add up.

I drum my fingers against the desk. Max will be home tonight. Those green eyes won't be able to hide whatever game he's playing. And when I find out what strings he's pulled behind my back, I'm not sure either of us will like what happens next.

Chapter Thirty-Six

CELESTE

Max's Bugatti growls into the circular driveway around 8 PM, when the sky's already gone midnight-black. I'm lounging on the veranda by the pool, wine glass dangling between my fingers. It's one of those perfect Malibu nights —crickets chirping their little hearts out, waves crashing in the distance, moonlight making the pool shimmer like something out of a movie set. I've positioned myself strategically in front of the sliding glass door.

He's not getting away with avoiding me tonight. I've memorized his routine by now—the telltale sounds of the patio door sliding open, the clink of utensils against takeout containers, the soft splash of ice in a glass. Every night like clockwork, he comes out to the pool, yanking at his tie like it's strangling him, shoveling food into his mouth at whatever ungodly hour he finally decides to come home - although it's always after 10.

He sees me and seems to be expecting me out there - he has a cardboard box in his hand, the Duke's logo stamped on its side. "Hey," he says, voice softer than usual. "Thought you might be hungry. Fish tacos and that shrimp pasta you mentioned last week."

I've been perched on the edge of this chaise lounge for forty-five minutes, rehearsing what to say. The smell of garlic and lime wafts across the space, but my stomach knots instead of growls. Max pulled strings with Selena Farley—one of the biggest agents in town—for someone whose writing he's never even seen. What did that conversation sound like? "Hey, represent my fake wife or I'll pull my company's business"? Now she's stuck representing the boss's charity case wife, resenting every minute. I need to shut this down, tell him to back off, reject his well-intentioned meddling before it makes everything worse.

I smile and nod. "Shrimp pasta sounds amazing, thanks."

He disappears into the house, returning with two plates and silverware. The shrimp pasta cascades onto my plate, releasing a cloud of garlic and herbs that makes my stomach growl.

"Max," I say, twirling pasta around my fork. "About Saturday night—I shouldn't have bolted like that. Everything was going so well until I messed it up."

His lips quirk into a half-smile. "Reminds me of our first meeting at the Centurion. Maybe I should start ordering to-go boxes the minute we sit down."

I smile in spite of him bringing up *that* particular memory that I wanted to never think about again. "Well, thanks for not getting too angry about that." The shrimp pasta is delicious - creamy sauce, fettuccine noodles, my favorite kind of comfort food.

The wine glass trembles slightly in my hand as I take a sip. My pulse quickens. I need to corner him about this, but delicately.

No. Directly.

"Max," I say, setting down my glass. "Selena Farley called today. Ring any bells for you?"

He lifts one shoulder in a half-hearted shrug. "Doesn't she call you all the time for work stuff?"

"This wasn't about Dreamscape." I twirl pasta around my fork, buying time. "She offered to represent me. Personally."

Max's eyebrows shoot up. "As in...?"

"As my agent, yes." I lean forward, studying his face for tells. "Curious timing, don't you think?"

"Selena Farley? The Selena Farley who's roster includes all the A-List screenwriters in town?" His face breaks into a grin, and he reaches over to squeeze my shoulder with unexpected enthusiasm, like I'm his favorite teammate after a game-winning play.

My God, he must think I'm an idiot if he doesn't know I know the truth. "Max, what did you do?"

"What do you mean?" His green eyes look genuinely mystified and I'm thinking that he must've taken more than one acting class along the way of getting his PhD in Cinema Studies or whatever. Must've aced those classes too.

"I mean, did you threaten her? Tell her that you won't buy any more of her clients' screenplays if she doesn't play ball? Threatened to blackball her from industry parties? What did you do?"

He rolls his eyes. "Celeste. Did you ever think for one second that she wants to represent you because you're better than you think?"

I shake my head. "Nope." I point my fork at him. "See, here's the thing. I sent my screenplays to just about everybody in town, repeatedly. But when I got my job at Dreamscape, I stopped sending them out to agents." I narrow my eyes. "In other words, I haven't sent out a screenplay to anyone in, oh, three years and some change. Yet, just out of the blue, I get a phone call from Selena Farley." I shake my head. "Hell, I don't think I even sent Selena a screenplay, come to think of it. I didn't think I had a chance with her and everyone else rejected me, so I doubt I sent her anything."

Max shifts in his chair, eyes darting to the window, then at the sky. I can practically see the gears turning as he searches for an explanation that isn't the truth.

Then his shoulders slump. Caught. The confession is coming.

He leans in, voice barely above a whisper. "Celeste. I needed to see if you had the gift."

My pulse quickens as realization dawns. "You had someone break into my laptop for my screenplays." It's not a question. The slight twitch at the corner of his mouth confirms everything.

His silence speaks volumes, those perfect features betraying no remorse.

My fingers grip the edge of my chair. I've got nothing incriminating hidden in my files—no secret correspondence, no embarrassing photos. But that's hardly the issue. What terrifies me is the casual way he's crossed this line. If he can violate my privacy without hesitation, what other boundaries might he ignore? What rules don't apply to Max Kensington?

"Oh, God," I say. "This isn't happening."

Max steps toward me. "Celeste. Listen. I never would have gone behind your back unless—"

"Unless what? You needed my amateur pages to mock? Or worse—you'd read them, then ghost me because you couldn't decide between fake praise or admitting I'm some pathetic wannabe who should stick to fetching somebody's coffee?"

"Listen," Max says, his voice softening. "I knew you'd never willingly show me. I had to find out if..." He runs a hand through his hair. "You're extraordinary, Celeste. The industry would have missed out on your voice if—"

"Just stop." I fold my arms across my chest, a bitter laugh escaping. "Wait, I see what this is. Poor Max, trapped in a fake marriage, desperate enough to seduce the only woman available to him. How convenient."

"What are you talking about?"

"I'm talking about you," I say, my voice rising. "This is some twisted seduction game, right? You want to get laid, so suddenly I'm this amazing writer? You're dropping my name to Selena Farley, probably whispering sweet nothings in her ear about signing me, all so I'll be so damn grateful I'll just spread my legs. But you don't actually want me— you just need someone. And since you're stuck in this marriage, you can't exactly hit the town without the gossip vultures circling. So here we are."

Max runs his hand through his hair, his jaw tight. "Jesus Christ, Celeste. You've got it all wrong." His eyes lock on mine, blazing. "First off, you're talented as hell, got it?" He jabs a finger toward me. "That Varian Fry script? It's brilliant. Those characters breathe. The pacing's perfect—had me on the edge of my seat the whole time. And the dialogue?" He lets out a low whistle. "You nailed every dialect, every cadence. I've read enough garbage scripts to know the real thing when I see it. And yours? Not even close to garbage."

My pulse quickens with each word. Is this happening? But still—maybe he just admires my work, not me.

"And that comedy about the women lost in the woods?"

His voice softens slightly. "I nearly ruined my copy laughing. Each character so distinct, so real. But you didn't just go for laughs—you gave it soul. That's what separates the amateurs from the pros." His expression hardens again, challenging me. "Want me to keep going?"

I stand up and he does too.

Max's fingers lock around my wrists like handcuffs. "Celeste," he says, his voice low and dangerous. "You actually believe I'm just feeding you lines to get you into bed? That I only want you because this marriage has me trapped and the tabloids would have a field day if I fucked someone else?" His breath is warm against my face, his green eyes boring into mine from mere inches away, searching for something I'm not sure I want him to find.

My breath catches in my throat, each inhale becoming shallow and quick, like I'm trying to sip air through a coffee stirrer. Heat spreads through my body like wildfire in drought-parched California hills, starting at my core and radiating outward in crimson waves until even my fingertips tingle with anticipation, the skin there hypersensitive to the cool Malibu breeze. The desire pools low in my belly, an ache so intense it makes my knees weak, as if someone has secretly replaced my leg bones with warm candle wax.

I can't say a word so I just nod.

His voice cracks. "How can you not know? I've counted every freckle across your beautiful little nose that scrunches up when you laugh. Eighteen freckles. I close my eyes and see them before I fall asleep. And speaking of your laugh….It's not one of those polite little things. It's real. Deep. Like you mean it." He grabs my wrists tighter and shakes his head. "Your scent follows me everywhere - orange blossoms and patchouli with just a hint of vanilla. And your voice." He shakes his head again as if he's mystified. "I sit with Spielberg, with Nolan, and all I hear is your voice. And that kiss on the beach - it still haunts me. Do you understand? I ran before the wedding because this—" he gestured between them, hand trembling, "—terrifies me. I've never wanted anyone the way I want you. And I couldn't face it. Couldn't face what you do to me. Is that really so impossible to see?" He shakes his head. "No, Celeste, I don't want just someone. I want you. I.want.you."

And then, his lips are on mine, crushing my bottom lip hungrily, his stubble rough against my chin. I taste mint and coffee and something uniquely him—something that makes my knees weak and my pulse race. His hands slide into my hair, fingertips pressing against my scalp, and I know now that what he's saying is the truth. The way his breath catches when I press closer, the slight tremor in his strong hands—he wants me. And, God, I want him so desperately my skin feels electric wherever we touch.

His breath is hot against my ear as he whispers, "Does this feel like I just want any warm body?" Strong hands grip my waist, lifting me onto the cool, polished marble tabletop. The stone chills my bare skin as he gently pushes my knees apart. His fingertips trace delicate patterns up my thighs before his lips follow the same path, his stubble lightly scratching the sensitive skin there. When he finds that perfect spot where my pulse throbs beneath the surface, I can't help the sound that escapes me. Heat blooms deep in my belly, radiating outward until even my fingertips tingle with wanting him.

Is this really happening? Does my fake-husband—with his chiseled jawline and those impossibly magnetic eyes that seem to drink me in—really feel this way about me? I never thought it possible. But, as his warm lips and soft fingertips make their deliberate way up my bare thighs, inch by agonizingly delicious inch, leaving goosebumps in their wake, I find that I don't care if I'm just a warm body or somebody he actually desires. Because I desire him—the sandalwood scent of his skin, the weight of his body pressing against mine. Every cell in my body is tingling like an electric wire in the rain, a current of pleasure threatening to short-circuit my thoughts completely.

Now he's kissing me again, his soft thumbs brushing my cheekbones while his fingers thread into my hair at the nape of my neck. His palms cradle my face with the reverent care of someone holding a bird with a broken wing. His lips, soft yet demanding, press against mine with an urgency that makes my knees weak. They taste of Pacific salt and something darker, richer. I breathe in his exhale, cedar and citrus cologne filling my lungs as he draws me against the solid wall of his chest, the expensive cotton of his shirt bunching between my fingers as I grip it, desperate to eliminate even the molecule of air separating us.

His fingers work at my buttons as his lips find mine, his touch whispering across my skin. The path of his mouth traces from my lips to my throat, then lower still as the fabric falls away. A sound escapes me—something primal and wanting—and I find myself holding him with my legs, anchoring him to me as though he might dissolve into the night if I let go.

Max's voice is barely above a whisper as he undresses me, his eyes never leaving mine. "Still think I only want a warm body?" The cool marble countertop presses against my back as his lips trace a path down my neck, across my collarbone, lingering at my breasts until I can barely breathe. "Would I worship you like this if I wasn't completely yours?" My skirt pools around my ankles. His hands steady me as my knees weaken, and when his mouth finds its way between my thighs, the world dissolves into sensation. Each deliberate movement of his tongue sends electricity through my body. No one has ever paid such careful attention to exactly what makes me respond. This isn't casual desire—this is devotion.

He shows me just how devoted he is to my pleasure as his nimble fingers slide inside me, his soft thumb stroking my sensitive clit while his hot, velvet tongue traces deliberate circles around the swollen clit and my throbbing, honey-slick core. The cool Carrara marble beneath my feverish skin feels almost like a blessed relief as my body blazes hotter than a January hearth.

His fingers—two, then three—pry me open further, his relentless tongue finding its way deeper inside me as I writhe helplessly, the intolerably beautiful sensation radiating like liquid lightning from my pulsing center to every trembling cell of my body as I scream out his name, the sound echoing through the cool early-December night. God, what is this overwhelming sensation? I realize that, before this earth-shattering moment, I'd never actually experienced a true orgasm, not like this all-consuming tidal wave. It feels like every one of my nerve endings is simultaneously aflame, my entire quivering body transformed into one giant, exquisite goosebump.

Max whispers my name against my lips as his fingers work the buttons of his crisp white shirt, revealing a tanned and muscular chest. He captures my mouth again in a kiss that steals my breath—his tongue tracing the seam of my lips before slipping inside, tasting of mint and desire. When his teeth graze my lower lip, I gasp. "If you could see yourself through my eyes," he murmurs, his voice a rough velvet that vibrates against my skin, "you'd never question how I feel."

His breathing comes in hot, ragged bursts against my neck. The world beyond this marble countertop—beyond his touch—dissolves into nothing. There is only the scorching heat where our bodies meet, the intoxicating scent of his cologne mingled with sweat, the masterful rhythm of his fingers exploring me, coaxing me toward the edge while his mouth devours mine hungrily. My eyelids flutter closed as my head falls back in ecstasy. I feel the whisper of fabric sliding down his legs, then the unmistakable weight and heat of his cock pressing against me—impressive, intimidating in its proportions, promising both pleasure and sweet pain as it nudges insistently at my center.

His voice breaks as he whispers my name, his hands trembling while he rolls on protection. My pulse hammers everywhere—wrists, throat, between my thighs—like my body might shatter from wanting him. I rake my nails down his back, desperate to pull him closer, to feel the weight of him crushing me. The anticipation is unbearable; I'm already arching upward, seeking him, my body a live wire. When his eyes lock with mine, something primal and possessive flashes across his face. I dig my heels into his lower back, urging him forward, silently begging. I need him to claim me, to fill the aching emptiness that's consuming me from within.

He stands before me, naked and magnificent, his erection jutting forward like a challenge. I lick my lips, my body already trembling with need. Then he goes over to a drawer and brings out a condom and slips it on.

He seizes my ass with both hands, his fingers digging into my flesh as he yanks me to the counter's edge. In one powerful motion, he impales me on his length, the sudden fullness making me cry out. My vision blurs as he drives deeper than I thought possible, each thrust sending electric shocks through my core. His grip tightens around my waist, muscles flexing as he lifts me entirely off the marble. I lock my legs around him, surrendering completely to his strength and rhythm. My head falls back, exposing my throat, which he claims with his teeth—not quite biting, but marking. He captures my face between his hands, forcing my gaze to his, and crushes his mouth against mine, his tongue invading with the same relentless intensity as his body.

No, he doesn't want just any warm body beneath him. He wants me—Celeste—with my particular scars and freckles and fears. And I've never craved anyone with this desperate, clawing hunger. His mouth claims mine with such ferocity that my lips will surely bruise by morning, his tongue exploring every corner as if memorizing the geography of my mouth. Each thrust sends shockwaves through my spine, each gentle bite on my swollen bottom lip makes me gasp. I feel his heart hammering against my ribs like it's trying to break free, his breath hot and ragged against my neck. When I finally shatter, it's like a California earthquake —a 7.8 on the Richter scale—fracturing me into a thousand glittering pieces. Heat floods every cell, electricity crackling across my skin like lightning striking the Malibu coastline during a winter storm. His name—Max—tears from my throat, raw and primal, again and again until my voice breaks.

His shoulders slump as he gasps for air, his chest heaving against mine as he pulls out. But his grip tightens—possessive, desperate—as my legs are still locked around him. When he crashes his mouth back onto mine, there's nothing gentle about it. It's all hunger and need, teeth grazing my lower lip before he lifts me back onto the cold marble, the shock of it making me arch against him. Neither of us can bear to break apart. My fingers twist into his dark hair, pulling just hard enough to make him groan against my mouth. The marble bites into my skin, but I don't care—all I feel is the delicious ache where his kisses have claimed me. "Tell me again, Celeste," he demands, voice rough and broken. "About how I don't really want you. Christ, I've never wanted anything the way I want you."

His touch maps my body, each perfectly groomed fingertip leaving trails of heat that pull sounds from my throat I barely recognize. Against my leg, I feel him ready again, insistent. He makes a sound—half command, half need—before sweeping me up against his chest and carrying me toward the cabana beside his pool, where billowing white fabric creates our sanctuary. Inside waits a world apart—deep blue velvet cushions that embrace us, candles scenting the air with amber and casting our shadows in gold, a handwoven rug from Morocco beneath us collecting our secrets. At the press of a button, music fills our hideaway, the rhythm becoming ours as we move together with an urgency that feels like both beginning and end.

Hours later, after a marathon of lovemaking that left us both breathless, we're finally sated, laying side by side on the plush crimson velvet lounge in this candlelit tent. Outside, late November winds whisper against the canvas walls, but I don't feel the coolness, only the lingering heat between us.

We're lying there, my head nestled in the crook of his arm, his fingers tracing lazy patterns through my tangled hair. He leans down, pressing his lips first to my temple where my pulse still hammers, then captures my mouth in a kiss so tender it makes my heart ache. My palm rests on his chest, feeling each heartbeat beneath warm skin and firm muscle. My body still quivers with aftershocks, every nerve ending alive and singing, saturated with a pleasure so complete I feel drunk with it.

I know that I have to get some sleep. It's now 3 in the morning, the red digits of Max's watch glowing against his tanned wrist. Six hours of lovemaking has left my thighs trembling, my lips swollen, my entire body feeling like over-cooked spaghetti sliding off a fork. The tent smells of sandalwood and sweat, our mingled scents trapped in the canvas cocoon. I dread crawling back to my empty bed with its cold sheets, but my alarm will shriek in three hours and I'll be stumbling through the office like a zombie. Max traces circles on my hip, his touch saying he doesn't want to leave either, though tomorrow he faces back-to-back meet-ings until eight tomorrow night. But when he kisses my shoulder, his stubble rough against my skin, I think: #worthit!

He takes a ragged breath. "I can't do this anymore," he says, his voice raw. "Come to bed with me tonight. I swear I'll behave, but Christ—" His hand grips mine so hard it almost hurts. "I need you there. I need to feel you breathing next to me." He shakes his head violently. "No. That's not enough. Move in with me. The main house. Now. Tonight. This separate wing bullshit is killing me when all I've wanted—all I've fucking ached for—is to have you with me. Really with me." His green eyes burn into mine, desperate and exposed, like he's offering his still-beating heart on a silver platter, terrified I might refuse it. I can't breathe.

I nod and follow him inside, my body heavy with exhaustion yet light with a happiness I'm almost afraid to trust. After grabbing a few essentials from my side of the house, I slip between his sheets. The question of whether I'll stay here permanently hangs between us—was his invitation born from the heat of the moment, or something more? I'll wait for daylight to see if the offer stands.

For now, I savor the warmth of his skin against mine, our limbs tangled together in the darkness. As sleep pulls at me, I wonder if what we've found is as delicate as morning mist, destined to evaporate in reality's harsh light, or if it might withstand the day.

Something in me hopes desperately for permanence, even as my old fears whisper that nothing this sweet ever lasts.

Chapter Thirty-Seven

MAX

I get to work at my usual 6 AM, exhausted from getting so little sleep, but feeling incredibly happy for maybe the first time in my life. It's so strange - all my life, I always thought I was happy. But maybe I really wasn't. Maybe it was just contentment, and I'm actually seeing the difference between these two emotions.

I was definitely content before. I had Gianni and my brothers, and loving grandparents who raised me like a son. I've always had a stunning woman on my arm—supermodels with legs for days and actresses with porcelain skin who looked perfect in every paparazzi shot. I had my career as the youngest CEO of a movie studio in the history of Hollywood, corner office with floor-to-ceiling windows overlooking the Los Angeles skyline, name etched in glass on the building. The A-List parties with champagne fountains and caviar stations, the red carpet walks past screaming fans, the front-row Oscars seats where legends leaned over to whisper in my ear, the glossy magazine covers where my jawline looked chiseled from marble. The billion-dollar superhero franchises with merchandise in every Target across America, the prestige biopics that critics called "transcendent," the satisfaction of having Scorsese and Spielberg on speed dial—these are all things that I thought made me happy but I now know only made me content.

But this feeling, after a night with Celeste where we made love under Egyptian cotton sheets until the early morning hours, her jasmine perfume still clinging to my skin —this must be what true happiness feels like. My face muscles ache from smiling, an unfamiliar sensation that pulls at the corners of my mouth and crinkles the skin around my eyes. Even Valentina, my usually unflappable secretary who's seen me through 18-hour days without so much as a raised eyebrow, did a double-take this morning when she walked into my office at precisely 7 a.m., her coffee-brown eyes widening at the sight of me.

Valentina breezes into my office, her dark bob swinging, iPad clutched to her chest like a shield. "Hey, Max," she says, sliding my printed agenda across the polished mahogany desk. "Lunch today with the head of Paramount, then that investors call with Tokyo today at 4—the Naka-mura Group. Sean Winter wants to discuss his Oscar follow-up at 5:30 at Nobu, you have three pitch meetings and your development team needs thirty minutes on the Netflix psychological thriller series..."

Her voice rises and falls in that familiar singsong pattern while I nod, watching steam curl from my hand-thrown ceramic mug. The rich Kona blend—flown in weekly— coats my tongue as I let her meticulous recitation wash over me. I've had today memorized since last Thursday, but her earnest brown eyes and careful note-taking deserve my patience. Valentina taps her manicured fingernail against the meeting agenda. "And you should pay special attention to the Holloway pitch at two o'clock—you know, the psychological thriller based on that best-selling novel everyone's mother has been reading in their book clubs. The one with the unreliable narrator and the twist ending. That one could be our next prestige project if we play our cards right."

She finally looks at me. "What?" she asks. "What's that smile about?"

I swivel in my leather chair, gazing at the Los Angeles skyline that stretches before me like my own personal kingdom. The thought flickers through my mind—what if I just disappeared for the day? But no. Kensington Pictures would grind to a halt without me at the helm. Still, I can't shake the image of showing up at Claremont unannounced, whisking Celeste in my Rolls, and catching the next flight to Paris or Rome—just because I can, just because I want her with me.

"Am I not entitled to smile?" I ask her. "Perhaps I'm happy today." Then I start to laugh. "Actually happy."

"Okay," she says, her eyebrows knitted and then she shakes her head. "You're acting weird."

After she's gone, I find myself thinking about sending Celeste some flowers. Cliché? Absolutely. Do I care? Not in the slightest. Paris would be better—I could fly us there Friday after work, show her the city, be back by Sunday night. Her first trip overseas. But for now, flowers will have to do. Not ordinary roses though. Celeste deserves something as unique as she is. I click on a variety I've never seen before: hybrid roses with pale pink petals rimmed in midnight purple. They remind me of her—soft but with unexpected edges. I place the order with Antoine, the florist who handles all my events, wondering if he'll notice these aren't for some corporate gathering but something far more personal.

Then, for the rest of the day, my events blur past like scenes from a fast-cut montage. I approve three pitches for theatrical releases—a gritty crime drama set in 1970s Detroit, a coming-of-age story about synchronized swimmers, and a sci-fi thriller that made even my jaded heart race.

On the 405, I belt out "Purple Rain" with the windows down, my tie flapping in the wind as I weave through traffic toward Century City to meet Brian, the silver-haired head of Paramount. Later, I lean forward in my ergonomic chair during my meeting with hot Oscar-winning director Sean Winter as we discuss his latest movie. As evening falls, I loosen my collar for the Zoom call with the Tokyo investors, their faces illuminated by distant dawn light. By this time, my thoughts have already escaped the glass tower, racing home to Celeste.

And race home I do.

The aroma hits me before I even close the front door— garlic, herbs, something rich and savory that makes my stomach growl. I follow the scent to find Celeste at the range, lost in whatever she's stirring, humming a tune I don't recognize. Her copper hair is twisted up in a messy knot, wisps escaping around her temples. The Kansas City Chiefs logo stretches across her apron, faded from too many washes. Chiefs fan? That's unexpected. Or maybe just a thrift store find. I realize how little I actually know about the woman who's now my wife—and how much I suddenly want to learn.

She whirls around, spatula in hand, her eyes widening like she's been caught stealing. A smile flickers across her face, but her fingers twist nervously around the utensil.

"Hey," she says, her voice barely audible over the sizzling pan. "I—I didn't—" She takes a breath that catches halfway. "Your kitchen. I'm in your kitchen." Her free hand flutters between us, leaving flour trails in the air. "Rosa mentioned you live on takeout, or your chef makes something, because of course you don't have time to cook, and I thought—" The spatula trembles slightly. "Maybe real food? Home-cooked?" The last words come out as a question. She bites her lower lip, watching my face for disapproval, while behind her, whatever she's cooking releases a scent that makes my stomach growl in unmistakable approval.

I step behind her, sliding my arms around her waist. Her hair smells like vanilla and salt air—enough to make me consider skipping straight to dessert, though my empty stomach protests. "Celeste," I murmur against her neck, "I want you to think of this as our home now. I meant every word earlier. That guest wing isn't where you belong anymore. Tomorrow I'll have everything moved for you." My lips brush her ear. "And if you thought that closet was impressive, wait until you see what's waiting for you in the master suite. It was built for a queen." I nip gently at her earlobe, feeling her pulse quicken against my lips. "What you making?"

She shrugs, tipping olive oil into a sizzling pan before crushing garlic cloves between her palms and tossing them in with diced onions. The kitchen fills with a fragrant cloud as she crumbles Italian sausage into the mix, adds tomatoes, and seasons with practiced flicks of her wrist. Water boils furiously in another pot, waiting for pasta. "Nothing fancy," she says, stirring the sauce. "Just a basic ragu I can make with my eyes closed. When I actually have time to plan, I promise I can do much better than this thrown-together weeknight dinner."

I inhale the rich aroma of the pasta and ragu, but the hunger gnawing at me isn't for food. "When will dinner be ready?" I ask, turning her to face me. Her lips part slightly before I capture them with mine, drawing a soft sound from her throat.

"About fifteen minutes," she murmurs against my mouth. "I just started the pasta."

"And the sauce is just simmering now?" My hands find her waist.

"Yes."

"Perfect timing," I say, lifting her onto the counter. She extends her legs as I trail kisses up her inner thighs. The pasta timer creates a deadline, but I can't wait another moment to taste her. This—her skin against my lips in our kitchen—is what occupied my thoughts all day. I pause only to send Rosa a quick message; she typically joins me for dinner when I'm home early, and some interruptions I'd rather avoid.

She's wearing a dress, and I shove it up around her waist, desperate to taste her—I've been starving for her all day. Her taste floods my senses, obliterating everything else. I devour her like a man possessed, her moans driving me wild as she clutches my hair, nails digging into my scalp. When I finally slip on protection and thrust inside her, the sensation is overwhelming—her body grips mine, hot and slick, pulling me deeper. We're not just kissing; we're consuming each other, my hips slamming against hers with a force that makes the counter shake. The timer screams just as she does, her body convulsing around mine. Breathless and trembling, she somehow steadies herself, yanking her dress down and lunging for the stove. I watch, still reeling, as she tests the pasta with shaking fingers, declaring it "perfect al dente" in a voice still raw from crying out my name. The whiplash of her composure stuns me.

She dangles a strand of spaghetti between her fingers. "Taste test?"

I open my mouth, letting her place it between my teeth. Half the strand hangs from my lips as I pull her closer by the waist. Her eyes light with recognition. She takes the other end between her lips, and we inch toward each other, nibbling our way to the middle until our mouths meet, just like the two dogs in *Lady and the Tramp*. The kiss dissolves into laughter, both of us breaking away.

"God, we're ridiculous," she says, wiping sauce from her chin. "I knew I was, but you? THE Max Kensington?"

"If only my shareholders could see me now," I say. "Though I've gotten good at disguises. Every year I sneak into Comic Con in various disguises—Doctor Doom, Guy Fawkes, The Mandalorian. Full helmet coverage is key when you're avoiding paparazzi."

She just smiles. "Oh, the things I take for granted. I go to Comic Con, too, but nobody mobs me when I dress up as Harley Quinn."

I can't help but imagine Celeste dressed as Harley Quinn—her fiery copper hair twisted into those signature pigtails, dip-dyed pink and blue at the ends. I picture her in those criminally short sequined shorts that would reveal those endless legs of hers. A ripped crop top hugging her curves, splashed with that diamond pattern in red and black. Those thigh-high boots with the three-inch heels making her almost as tall as me. The image hits me like a physical force, and I feel myself growing hard again. I force myself to take a deep breath, trying to regain control as the scent of tomatoes, garlic, and red wine reminding me there are other hungers to satisfy first.

Celeste gives the sauce a final stir. "I meant to tell you—those flowers were incredible. How'd you guess?"

I shrug, leaning against the counter. "I've got a guy who sources straight from South Africa. Finds roses in colors you've never seen." I watch her face as I speak. "When I spotted those pink ones with the purple edges, I thought of you immediately. Not conventional. Distinctive."

Her cheeks flush pink. "My entire office was green with envy." She taps the wooden spoon against the pot's edge. "Though I wasn't just smiling about the flowers all day." Her eyes meet mine. "Was smiling also about last night and this morning." The corner of her mouth lifts, and I grip the counter edge to keep myself from crossing the kitchen and pressing her against the refrigerator.

She smiles, resumes that little melody under her breath, and dishes out the pasta with a flick of her wrist that somehow makes even serving food look elegant. The mayonnaise base for the Caesar dressing she's concocted for the salad—some alchemy of egg yolks, oil, lemon, garlic, and a hint of balsamic—has me transfixed. I've always avoided making mayonnaise myself. Too many horror stories about split emulsions and wasted ingredients. Yet here's Celeste, wielding my dusty hand-blender like she's done it her whole life. The dressing slides across my tongue—bright, creamy, with just the right punch of garlic. Suddenly I can't imagine ever buying the bottled stuff again.

One bite of pasta and suddenly I'm not in my kitchen anymore—I'm in some rustic Italian countryside kitchen. Who knew Celeste could cook like this? The sauce is ridiculous—those fancy tomatoes, sweet onions, garlic that doesn't punch you in the face but somehow makes everything better. There's this perfect little kick from red pepper that hits the back of your throat, and I swear I taste wine in there too. Everything works together but you can still taste each part, if that makes any sense. And the pasta itself? Damn. It's got that perfect chew—not mushy, not hard. Just right. The woman who's only supposed to be my fake wife somehow made spaghetti that's better than what I've had at restaurants charging $75 a plate.

"How is it possible I'm only discovering you now?" I ask, twirling another bite. "Where have you been hiding this talent?"

A flush creeps up her neck. "Mom's doing. She insisted cooking was non-negotiable—said it would serve me my whole life." Her eyes cloud over. "I keep hoping for many more years of us in the kitchen together. She came over to my condo all the time, you know. Showed me how to julienne vegetables properly, corrects my sauce techniques." Her voice catches. "I can't imagine my life without her guiding me."

I put my hand on hers. "How is she?"

She lifts one shoulder. "Back home now, thank God. The sepsis scare is over." A pause. "My mom's a badass. Cancer picked the wrong woman to mess with..." Her voice trails off, her eyes dropping to her lap. "Who am I fooling? Brian Piccolo was tough too, and look what happened to him."

I tilt my head. "Brian Piccolo? So that Chiefs apron in your kitchen isn't just Taylor Swift fandom?" The corner of my mouth quirks up. "You actually follow football."

"I grew up watching *Brian's Song* with my mom—she had a thing for James Caan and Billy Dee Williams back in the day. And yeah, I bleed red and yellow. The Chiefs are my team through thick and thin. Even when they make it all the way to the Super Bowl just to crash and burn on national television, I'm still right there with them."

I eye her Chiefs apron, now hanging up on a hook. "So, when did you become a fan? Just jumping on the Mahomes bandwagon like everyone else?"

"Born and raised in KC," she says, twirling pasta around her fork. "Didn't set foot in California until Dad brought me on that Mammoth ski trip. Then again for UCLA film school." She takes a bite, chews thoughtfully. "When Lexi got accepted to the same program, we scraped together enough to move Mom out here too. Couldn't just abandon her back in Missouri." Her eyes soften. "The Chiefs were our thing—Dad's and mine. Sunday afternoons, just us two. He explained everything—first downs, touchbacks, defensive formations, the role of the secondary." She points her loaded fork at me, sauce threatening to drip. "Did you know if you fumble in your own end zone and the other team recovers, they get a safety? Two points."

I grin as I dig into my pasta some more. "Also if you're a quarterback and you get sacked in the end zone. Also a safety."

She nods. "Right." Her eyes go distant. "I never miss a Chiefs game. It's like Dad's still there beside me, you know? In his ratty old armchair with those ridiculous maracas that he would shake for every big play." She demonstrates a quick shake with her hands. "Every first down, every long run, every fourth-down conversion, every sack, every touchdown—those maracas would go wild." A smile flickers across her face, there and gone. "So that's my schedule. Sundays, Monday nights, Thursday nights. Whenever Mahomes is throwing, I'm watching."

I catch myself wishing the Chiefs make it to the Super Bowl again. The thought of Celeste's face if I surprised her with tickets makes something warm unfurl in my chest. For me, Super Bowl Sunday means the usual luxury suite my grandfather reserves without thinking—a family tradition spanning two decades. But watching her eyes light up at the roar of the stadium, at seeing her team battle for the Vince Lombardi trophy in person instead of on some tiny screen? That would be something worth remembering.

But I don't mention that. That would be a surprise for her if the Chiefs make it again, which they probably will, considering their track record of the past few years.

"So," I say. "Your mother…"

"Right." She nods and takes a sip of her wine. "I…" She blinks hard, but a tear streaks down her cheek. First one, then another. "Sorry. I can't talk about that…"

I suddenly want to just hold her in my arms, comfort her, and tell her it's all going to be OK. But, at the same time, I know that's not necessarily the truth. After all, I lost my mother to that disease. Granted, my mother's breast cancer was extremely aggressive. With any luck, Celeste's mother does not have a particularly aggressive form of the disease. And if that's the case, she has a good chance of beating it.

I take a deep breath. "Not a problem." My fork hovers over the pasta. How much do I reveal to someone I barely know? The walls I've built aren't easily dismantled.

"I understand what you're going through," I finally say, twirling spaghetti around my fork without lifting it to my mouth. "After my father disappeared, I became obsessed with learning about my mother's death. Everyone changed the subject whenever I asked." The pasta grows cold as I set down my fork. "Eventually my grandfather sat me down—I was seven, maybe eight. He told me everything. About her illness. About how my birth complicated things." My voice drops. "About how she probably would've survived if not for me. He probably figured I'd piece it together eventually. But hearing it..." I shake my head. "Let's just say I wasn't equipped to handle that truth."

Her eyes widen as she reaches for my hand, giving it a gentle squeeze. "How did you cope with that?"

"Seven-year-olds aren't supposed to know what suicide is," I tell her, my voice steady despite the weight of the words. "But I walked into my granddad's pool fully clothed, just kept walking until my head went under. Rosa spotted me from the kitchen window. Everyone kept asking how a kid who'd been swimming since three and surfing since four could suddenly drown. After that, Granddad found this child psychologist. Three sessions a week, ten years straight. Can't say if it fixed everything, but..." I shrug, attempting a smile. "I'm still breathing, so I guess something stuck."

"Oh, Max," she says, her eyes shining. "I'm so sorry."

I hold up a hand. "It's fine. Well, not fine—it's never going to be fine. Sometimes I think if I could just erase myself from the equation, maybe our family would still be together. Whole. But that's not exactly how the universe works, is it? Can't exactly pull a Superman and reverse time by flying around the Earth, so..." I trail off with a shrug.

The corners of her mouth lift, but her eyes remain heavy. "Looks like we're both members of the same club, then. The one where we'd give anything to rewrite history or slip sideways into some world where certain things never happened." But then she puts her hand on mine. She reaches for my hand across the table. "But in your fantasy, you erase yourself. I just want you to know—I wouldn't erase you for anything."

I shrug. "Well, that's something."

She nods. "And about my mom. There's a new

immunotherapy treatment. Promising results in the trials. But her insurance won't touch experimental treatments, so..."

"Fight them," I say. "Appeal their decision."

She laughs, but it's hollow. "Oh, you sweet summer child." Her eyes lock with mine, exhaustion rimming the edges but a fire still burning at their center. "I bet in your world, medical bills are just another line item between yacht maintenance and helicopter fuel. Meanwhile, my mom's on hold so long with insurance that the classical music they play becomes her personal soundtrack. Three hours last Tuesday just to get the same medication she's been taking for years. And this experimental treatment?" She waves her hand upward, like she's pointing to something impossibly distant. "They'd sooner cover her ticket to the moon."

I shake my head, suddenly aware of the invisible safety net I've always had beneath me. She's right. While her family debates whether they can afford life-saving treatment, I've never once checked a price tag on healthcare. One phone call from my family would have specialists flying in from Johns Hopkins or UCLA. Cancer for me wouldn't mean GoFundMe campaigns—it would mean a private suite at Mayo Clinic by morning. The language of insurance denials and payment plans might as well be Swahili to me.

"Let's change the subject," she says, scooping up the last streak of tomato sauce with her garlic bread before popping it into her mouth. "And Max. There's something I've been wondering."

My shoulders tense slightly. "Shoot."

"What's in this for you?" She waves a hand between us, her wedding ring catching the light. "I mean, my reasons are pretty clear. But yours?"

The question lodges itself under my skin. I stare at the empty wine glass between us, suddenly aware of the ticking clock hanging over our arrangement. Twelve months. $250,000 for her. For me, just long enough to secure the Dreamscape merger and my position as CEO—a position they can't take away without cause. Once that's done...

I look at her face, the same face I've started searching for first thing every morning, and feel the uncomfortable collision of my growing feelings and my exit strategy. When the year is up, I'll still walk away. This isn't a real marriage.

It can't be.

I take a deep breath. "My grandfather blackmailed me into marrying you," I confess, watching her face carefully. "He threatened to turn the major shareholders against me —people who control more than half the board votes—if I didn't go through with it." I then explain everything in more detail, telling her exactly how it all went down.

Celeste's expression remains neutral as she absorbs my words. No anger flashes across her features, no hurt dims her eyes. She simply nods once, then shrugs.

"Well, that explains it," she says. "Let's tackle these dishes."

Side by side at the sink, we fall into an unexpected rhythm. I load the dishwasher while she scrubs pans, humming softly to the music from her playlist filling the kitchen. Rosa won't be back until tomorrow—she's in Temecula visiting a friend, a fact I learned when I texted her earlier about giving Celeste and me some privacy. The wine glasses gleam under my careful attention with the electric brushes, and I find myself enjoying this simple shared task more than I'd ever imagined possible.

Then first notes of "God Only Knows" drift from Celeste's playlist, and my chest tightens. This song. The

Beach Boys' gentle harmonies that played in the background of every home movie my dad shot of my mom. The same melody that filled my grandfather's house that summer afternoon when my father walked out during the donor party. I can still see the French doors swinging shut behind him, the needle skipping on the record player. The last notes I heard before everything changed—before I knew what it meant to lose someone.

My chair scrapes back against the kitchen tiles as I stand, hand outstretched toward her. Those blue eyes—the ones that blindsided me from day one—lock with mine, and Celeste's lips curve upward as she realizes what I'm asking. When her fingers slide into my waiting palm, they're warm, almost fragile, and she rises with an elegance she's completely unaware of possessing. We fall into an unplanned dance, socked feet finding rhythm between the island and fridge. I spin her, and the sundress I bought her billows out, catching the glow from the pendant lights overhead. The golden light plays across her laughing face, transforming her into something so beautiful it aches—something a man like me has no right to claim.

Damn. I could get used to this.

For a full hour, we sway together, moving through Celeste's playlist as it fills the kitchen and dining room. The music she's chosen tonight wraps around us—all slow tempos and dreamy melodies, perfect for two bodies finding rhythm together. Tori Amos's haunting piano on "Winter." Taylor Swift's confessional whisper in "Slut." The Weeknd's falsetto climbing through "D.D." Then I hear the first notes of "Baby I'm Yours," the Arctic Monkeys cover that played during our first dance at that mockery of a wedding. I catch her eye, silently asking if this was coincidence or choice.

The pink that climbs her cheeks answers before she can. She remembers too.

Celeste clears her throat. "Rosa's not here at all tonight?"

She's changing the subject. I know she caught my reaction to the song, but I decide not to push it.

"Visiting a friend from way back," I tell her, checking my phone. "Got her text earlier." I lift one shoulder in a half-shrug. "Rosa makes her own schedule. She's family first, employee second."

I press my lips to hers, then sweep her into my arms and through the doorway of our bedroom. Hours pass while we slowly make love and when morning light filters through the curtains, I find myself reaching for her again. She's becoming my compass, my true north—a revelation that would have terrified me before.

Now, I welcome it.

Chapter Thirty-Eight

CELESTE

The following Monday, I'm still riding the high from my weekend with Max. Saturday found us in the ocean, my triumphant moment of actually standing on a surfboard earning his wolf-whistle from shore. Sunday, we wandered through stalls of a Farmer's Market, my arms gradually filling with heirloom tomatoes and zucchini that later became dinner for the three of us—Max, Rosa, and me. Now, with salt still seemingly embedded in my hair and the memory of Max's appreciative second helping, I head to my meeting with Selena.

Selena's voice slams against the glass walls. "Celeste!" From her corner office on the sixty-eighth floor of Horizon Tower, she commands a view of Los Angeles that stretches to the smoggy horizon. Her obsidian desk gleams like a altar, and from behind it, she directs fifty hungry agents who stalk Hollywood's elite at parties and power lunches, their Bluetooth earpieces winking blue as they hunt for tomorrow's hit screenplay. "Get over here, you."

She wraps me in a hug that smells of Giorgio Armani

En Jeu—her signature scent since forever. Selena towers at my height, 5'10", but where I'm all angles, she's solid muscle and curves. The kind of woman who could bench press you while negotiating a seven-figure deal. Her black curls cascade freely around her face, framed today by square rainbow glasses—just one pair from her legendary collection. Everything about her commands attention: her style, her stance, her smile that's both inviting and slightly terrifying. When Selena enters a room, the room adjusts to her, not the other way around.

I follow her into her office, my stomach twisting itself into knots. Ridiculous. This is just Selena—the same Selena who once spilled an entire dirty martini down her blouse at The Edison and continued her pitch meeting with the stain spreading across her chest. The same woman who texts me olive emojis whenever she's three drinks in. The same agent who overshares about her downtown loft throuple arrangement with her girlfriend and boyfriend. We've traded secrets over countless happy hours. She's seen me ugly-cry over pilot season rejections. This shouldn't feel like walking to the principal's office. But somehow, it does.

My palms leave damp prints on my skirt. This time, it's not someone else's script we're discussing over coffee—it's mine, spread across her desk with those little yellow Post-its stuck to who knows how many pages. Selena doesn't hold back. I've seen writers leave her office looking shell-shocked after she's taken her red pen to their "promising but not quite there" screenplays. Now I'm on the other side of that table, watching her flip through the pages of my heart with those manicured fingernails, probably wondering how she ended up reading such amateur work.

She slams both palms on the desk and leans in until I can smell her $500 perfume. "Listen to me," she says, her voice dropping to a near-growl. "When Max called, I almost hung up. I thought, 'Great, another CEO's pet project I have to pretend doesn't make me want to gouge my eyes out.'" Her eyes flash dangerously. "But your screenplay kept me up until four in the morning. Four. In. The. Morning." She jabs her finger with each word. "Where the hell have you been hiding? Do you have any idea what you're sitting on?"

I smile, the tension melting from my shoulders like ice cream on a hot sidewalk. She must really like the script—I assume it's the Varian Fry one, the historical drama about the American journalist who rescued artists from Nazi-occupied France, although I can't be sure. She has that script and another one I wrote—a slice-of-life comedy about three generations of Greek-American women running a failing diner in Chicago while harboring family secrets that spill out during a chaotic Thanksgiving dinner. I leaned on my mother's stories about her own Greek family for that story.

"Selena," I say. "I can't tell you how relieved I am. I really thought you might just be taking me on as a favor to Max."

She leans forward over her desk conspiratorially. "About Max," she says, eyes narrowing to slits. "I mean, we'll talk about your screenplays in a minute, but holy shit, I've been dying to ask you about him. What the hell is going on with your marriage?" She slaps her palm on the table. "One minute you're a nobody development exec deleting Tinder and complaining about the jackasses who ghosted you, the next you're Mrs. Fucking Kensington." Her lips curl into something between a smile and a snarl. "Not that I blame you—the man's walking sex—but everyone knows he's the kind of manwhore who'd rather die than wear a ring. What kind of black magic did you use on him?"

I flash Selena my most dazzling smile. "Well, it's actually quite the story." My rehearsed lines flow effortlessly after weeks of practice. "Picture this: pouring rain, me frantically checking my phone for my Uber, then diving into what I thought was my ride." I roll my eyes dramatically, remembering how Max insisted on this ridiculous tale despite my protests about his Rolls Royce Cullinan SUV being the least convincing Uber vehicle in existence. He liked the story because it makes him look spontaneous and charming, while making me look like an idiot, but whatever. "Instead of kicking me out, this gorgeous stranger offered to drive me all the way to Claremont. Two hours of gridlock later, we'd shared our entire life stories. Three days after that?" I wiggle my ring finger. "Sometimes when you know, you just know."

Selena's coffee sprays across the table when I finish telling her, she's laughing so hard. "No way," she says, dabbing at her blouse with a napkin. "That sounds like the pitch for some ridiculous rom com. You know, the kind where some ordinary girl somehow lands a billionaire after they meet cute?" She leans forward, eyes narrowed. "Come on. What actually happened?"

I smile. Well. This is a scenario that I somehow didn't see coming. But no way can I tell her the truth. She's not known to be the most discreet when it comes to really juicy Hollywood gossip. She knows the truth, then the whole town knows the truth, which would be embarrassing to both Max and me. But I should've known that she would be too smart to fall for the bullshit story Max and I came up with.

I meet her gaze, my voice flat. "Just your classic Tinseltown romance. There I was, working on the corner of Hollywood and Vine, rocking stilettos and a platinum wig, barely covered by this white dress, when he rolled up in his fancy silver Lotus. Rich boy couldn't work a stick shift or find his hotel, so guess who played tour guide?" It's straight from *Pretty Woman*—a reference any woman breathing would catch, because seriously, who hasn't seen that movie at least once? My smile is all teeth, no warmth. She opens her mouth, then thinks better of it, reading the warning in my eyes. Point made.

She nods. "About these scripts of yours." Her eyes widen as she shakes her head. "Celeste, how are you not already writing for a living? Reading these felt like stumbling across buried treasure on an ordinary beach. They're all extraordinary, but especially—" She taps the cover page of my Thanksgiving family drama. "This one stands out above the rest." In my greatest fantasies, I've always pictured Alexander Payne directing it—his signature touch with family dysfunction would be perfect. Sometimes I fall asleep imagining him bringing my words to life, the way he did with *The Holdovers*, that David Hemingson masterpiece that wrecked me when I saw it last year.

I nod. "I like that one, myself," I say. "Is that the one you want to sell?"

Her eyes gleam as she leans forward. "Bidding war with this script and the Varian Fry screenplay." She taps the script with her manicured nail. "This one's gold. The way you wove Fry's rescue of Chagall with their personal journeys..." She presses a hand to her chest. "I actually cried. Three times. It's criminal no one's put Fry on screen before, but that's about to change." She gives me a knowing look. "When Academy voters see this? They'll be reaching for their ballots."

I can't believe this is happening. Selena Farley—the Selena Farley—is sitting across from me discussing a potential bidding war over my screenplays. My screenplays!

"This all sounds incredible," I manage to say, fidgeting with my coffee cup. "But I have to ask—you're not just doing this as a favor to Max, are you?"

She gives me a look that could wither concrete. "Seriously? Listen, when these scripts landed on my desk, I couldn't figure out why you weren't already being fought over by every major agency in town. CAA, William Morris, UTA—where have you been hiding? Did you stop submitting or what's the story here?"

I lean forward, my voice dropping. "Trust me, Selena, I tried. Every agency in this town has a copy of my work somewhere in their slush pile. After rejection number one hundred—and yes, I counted—I just... broke. Couldn't face another 'thanks but no thanks' email. So I buried myself in development at Dreamscape, filed my scripts away on some forgotten hard drive, and pretended I'd never written them. At least until recently."

She shakes her head. "Classic Hollywood gatekeeping. No agent gives you the time of day without credits, but how do you get credits without representation?" Her manicured nail taps my Thanksgiving script. "Their loss. This is gold. Thank God Max pulled some strings." She leans forward, voice dropping to a conspiratorial whisper. "Between us? We're looking at six figures before Christmas. High six figures."

I can't close my mouth. Six figures—high six figures—for my script? A lifeboat materializes before me, bobbing on uncertain waters. When Max and I... No. I blink hard. Our arrangement was always temporary. He gets his merger with Dreamscape, his CEO title, and then we part ways. I was counting down to that one-year mark, but now everything's shifted. Joseph's money? I don't need it anymore. If I break the contract to stay married to Max early, would he sue?

Doubtful. He'd just withhold payment—which suddenly doesn't matter. Not when Selena's looking at my portfolio like it's gold and diamonds. The way her eyes gleam tells me everything: my other screenplays will sell too.

I could walk away from Max the minute the merger with Dreamscape finalizes. I wouldn't do it earlier - Max doesn't deserve that, because if I walked away before the merger, he gets shafted. But, yeah, once he's installed as CEO of the merged company, I can walk away. I don't have to wait my year.

My chest tightens at the thought, a physical pain I wasn't expecting. I press my hand against my sternum, willing the sensation away. This is business—was always business. Two people with separate agendas sharing the same roof, the same last name. When those agendas are fulfilled, the contract dissolves. Simple as that.

My fingers find the pendant hanging from my neck— one of many in the collection Max has given me. Nothing special, just beautiful. I slide it back and forth along the chain while Selena's brows furrow in confusion. She must be wondering why I'm not jumping for joy at her "six figure bidding war" prediction.

The answer is simple but impossible to explain. This money from my scripts means I'll have no excuse to remain Mrs. Kensington after the merger completes in March. The timeline is set for that merger, the deal proceeding without complications. And the thought of our marriage ending on schedule hollows me out completely.

Her voice cuts through my daze. "Celeste? Earth to Celeste." She leans forward, tapping manicured nails against my scripts. "Trust me, I've been at this long enough to recognize gold when I see it. The Fry piece, the Thanksgiving one—we're talking serious bidding war territory.

Seven figures, maybe." She stops, studying my face. "But from your expression, I might as well have told you your car's being towed."

I force my lips into a weak smile. "Oh, Selena, this is amazing news. I'm just... processing it all. It doesn't feel real yet." I bob my head mechanically while stretching my mouth wider, hoping enthusiasm might follow the gesture. "Should we discuss contract details?" I place my fire-engine red Hermés Birkin—Max's gift that costs more than I make in a year—on her spotless solid marble desk and dig through it for my phone so I can see what time it is. The walls of her minimalist office are predictably clockless, and I'm already anxious about my afternoon meetings at Dreamscape. Time to wrap this up.

She eyes my hand hovering over my purse. "Oh, don't bother hunting for a pen—though that is a gorgeous bag. Hermès?" She slides a Mont Blanc across the desk along with a stack of papers. "Standard contracts. Nothing you haven't reviewed before, but have your attorney look them over if you'd like. I'm eager to get these to marketing, but take whatever time you need."

I nod and scan the contract. She's right—standard stuff. Still, I read line by line, paranoid about hidden clauses. Not that Selena would screw me over, but Hollywood's taught me to trust no one.

An hour later, I've scrutinized every paragraph and signature line. I scrawl my name and slide the papers across her desk. "Well," I say, forcing a smile, "guess we're officially in business." We shake hands, but Selena's eyes narrow.

"Everything cool?" She sips her coffee, studying me. "You seem weird."

I shake my head. How could I possibly tell her the truth? *Sorry, just realizing I've lost my last excuse to stay married to*

Max after March. Can't exactly admit our "marriage" is basically a business transaction with an expiration date. Everyone probably suspects our bullshit story anyway—the whole lightning-struck-us-on-the-drive-to-Claremont fairy tale, our instant connection, the perfect Hollywood romance. Thank God Max's publicist is a miracle worker, or *TMZ* would've exposed us months ago.

"I'm fine," I lie, pressing my palm to my forehead. "Just feeling kinda crappy today."

She raises her mug. "Feel better, rockstar. Talk soon."

I fake another smile and escape to the street, gulping fresh air. Things with Max are good lately, surprisingly good, but I can't let myself believe it. The man collects and discards women like trading cards. Why would I be any different?

Chapter Thirty-Nine

MAX

The one thing that would truly make Celeste happy would be fixing her mother's situation. I'd considered a spontaneous Paris getaway last weekend—still on my to-do list—but instead, we stayed local. Watching her catch her first wave after a morning of tumbles made me want her joining our Saturday surf crew permanently. Later we wandered the Farmer's Market stalls, then she transformed winter vegetables into this incredible pasta primavera—zucchini, broccoli, and kohlrabi swimming in cream sauce. Having a wife who cooks is something I never knew I needed. My personal chef François might have his Cordon Bleu credentials and Food Network fame, but there's something about Celeste's cooking that feels like home.

Paris can wait. What Celeste needs most is her mother's health. I tracked down Patricia's oncologist—a Dr. West at UCLA—and made an appointment. When I arrive at his office, the receptionist reminds me about patient confidentiality laws. I nod politely, then lean in.

"I understand HIPAA," I say, sliding my business card

across the counter. "But perhaps you could mention to Dr. West that Joe Kensington's grandson would like five minutes of his time. The same Joe Kensington whose name is on the oncology wing."

Twenty minutes later, Dr. West ushers me into his office with a knowing smile.

"Mr. Kensington," he says, gesturing to a chair. "How can I help you?"

I hate leveraging my family name, but for Patricia—for Celeste—I make an exception. What matters is getting Patricia the treatment she needs, anonymously. No strings, no gratitude required.

I clear my throat. "Patricia Jenkins is under your care. My wife—her daughter—mentioned an immunotherapy treatment that could help her. But the insurance company..." I let my voice trail off, my fingers drumming once against the polished desk. "They've denied coverage."

He nods and summons his medical assistant to bring him Patricia's file. She leaves to find the file and is back with the file in a matter of minutes. "Thanks," he says, looking over the file. "And yes, Mr. Kensington..." He studies me. "I'm struggling with how much to tell you. HIPAA laws dictate that I can't tell you anything without a waiver, but..."

I raise an eyebrow and sit back in my chair.

Dr. West leans back in his chair. "Your grandfather has been quite generous to our research department." He taps a folder on his desk. "There's a promising immunotherapy, Keytruda. It helps the immune system recognize and attack cancer cells. It's specifically used for Patricia's type of cancer " His eyes brighten as he explains further how it works. He slides several journal articles across his desk.

I scan the abstracts, pulse quickening. "And Patricia's

been on the standard protocol until now? Chemo, radiation, surgery?"

"Yes," he confirms with a tight nod.

"Without significant improvement."

His pen taps against the desk three times before stopping. "I've already said more than I should." The unspoken hangs between us. His eyes dart to the family photo on his desk, then back to me—the universal language of physicians who've exhausted conventional options.

I swallow hard. "What's the price tag?"

"Each treatment runs about $24,000, administered every six weeks. Annually, we're looking at $200,000 plus."

My finger lands on one of the studies. "Cut to the chase —could this save Patricia's life?"

"The studies and real-world results are encouraging." He removes his glasses, rubbing the bridge of his nose. "I've been battling with her insurance provider, but they keep denying coverage." A weary sigh escapes him. "These companies see patients as numbers on a spreadsheet. It's maddening."

I take a deep breath. "Let's do it. If this treatment is our best shot, I want her to have it." My fingers tremble slightly as I pull the Black Amex Centurion from my wallet. "This should cover everything. And doctor? I'd appreciate if you'd keep my involvement between us. Tell Patricia it came from an anonymous donor. She doesn't need to know."

"That's very generous," he says, nodding. "I'll call her today and we can begin the treatment."

I thank him, drumming my fingers against the polished mahogany. When Dr. West tells Patricia she's been approved for treatment, she and Celeste will immediately think of me. But I've got plausible deniability on my side. Since our wedding, the tabloids have been obsessed with Celeste, digging into every corner of her life. Patricia's cancer battle is public knowledge now. I can always claim some anonymous philanthropist stumbled across her story online and decided to help.

That's what I'll tell Celeste when she inevitably confronts me about it.

Chapter Forty

CELESTE

December's early darkness had already fallen when my mother calls. It's barely 5 PM, but outside the world is pitch black. Still, I couldn't resist the pull of the ocean sounds and cool air, so I take my usual spot by the infinity pool, huddled under the heat lamp with my cashmere blanket draped around my shoulders.

"Celeste," she says, her voice carrying a spark I haven't heard in months. "I've been approved for that immunotherapy!"

I press my back against the chaise lounge and close my eyes, my free hand involuntarily covering my mouth. For weeks I'd been bracing myself for that dreaded conversation with her oncologist—the one where words like "palliative care" would replace "treatment plan" and "remission." I'd memorized the survival statistics, could recite them in my sleep: months, not years. But this—this was the treatment I'd highlighted in all those medical journals, the one that showed promise in cases exactly like hers. The one her insurance had flat-out refused to cover, no matter how many appeals we filed.

"Mom," I whisper, my voice breaking. "How?"

Mom's voice rises excitedly. "Someone anonymous paid for the entire treatment."

My heart skips. Max. Has to be. He'd shake his head if I asked, look away with that half-smile he thinks hides everything. He's the kind of man who'd write a check for six figures then bury the evidence. Who else could afford experimental immunotherapy like it was takeout sushi?

I can't get the words out. "Mom, that's..." My voice catches as something swells in my throat. Hope? Terror? Both? "What if we celebrate your birthday properly this year?"

Her birthday's next Saturday, and I've been racking my brain for ways to make it special without endangering her. With her immune system shot from the treatments, even a restaurant dinner could be a death sentence. But now, with this new treatment...

Mom's laugh is gentle. "Let's not count our chickens, Celeste. We'll celebrate next year, I promise."

Next year. The words hang between us. No one gets promises like that—not really. People walk out their front doors on ordinary Tuesdays and get hit by trucks or have aneurysms or—I press my fingertips against my temples. This spiral of morbid thoughts won't help anyone, least of all Mom.

I whirl at the sound of someone clearing their throat. It's Max, propped against a poolside statue with his arms folded across his chest. One side of his mouth quirks up, sending an unexpected flutter through me. The terrace lights catch his green eyes, softening them at the edges—nothing like the cold stare from our first weeks together. I almost reach out, wanting to touch his jawline just to confirm he's flesh and blood, not some phantom created by my own longing. If you'd told me months ago I'd ever look at Max Kensington this way, I would have doubled over laughing.

I cut my mother off mid-sentence. "Mom, I need to call you back. Max just walked in and it's—" I glance at my watch, blinking twice. "Six o'clock?" I don't think he's ever been home before eight. "I'll call you back in a few minutes," I whisper, ending the call. When I look up, our eyes meet, and my lips curl into an involuntary smile. The word still catches in my throat sometimes. Husband.

He settles beside me on the outdoor couch, his fingers finding mine. The quiet stretches between us like a cat in sunlight—languid, warm, requiring nothing. I watch his profile, the steady rise and fall of his chest, and realize I've never felt this peaceful with anyone else. Mom's voice echoes in my memory: "When you can sit with someone and the silence feels like home, that's when you know." Looking at our intertwined hands, I think she might have been right.

Max settles back into the cushions and draws me against him, tucking me into the hollow beneath his shoulder. "Hungry?" he asks, his fingers wandering between mine, a lazy dance of touch and release.

"Rosa and I were planning to start dinner soon— curried goat from her homeland. I didn't expect you until later, so we haven't begun prepping yet. She's teaching me the recipe. Says nothing reminds her more of home."

He presses his fingertips to his lips in a chef's kiss. "Rosa's curried goat is divine. Most people think it sounds strange, but honestly, it's not far off from lamb. Though I wouldn't have pegged you for someone who'd eat it. You have that petting zoo energy about you."

"Can't deny that," I say with a laugh. "I'm the one holding up the line at every petting zoo, buying those little ice cream cones of feed pellets. There's something so satisfying about tiny hooves stepping on your shoes while they eat from your palm." I pause, my smile fading slightly. "I compartmentalize when it comes to food. One mental box for the adorable animals I coo over, another for what's on my plate. Otherwise, I'd never make it through a meal."

Max runs his hand through his hair. "Let me check with Rosa about changing the menu. I'm sure she won't mind. Actually, there's something I wanted to discuss with you anyway."

I nod, watching him disappear into the kitchen. When he returns a few minutes later, his expression has softened. "Rosa's making something else. Guess she wants to show you how to make her favorite dish, so she wants you in the kitchen with her when she makes it. So don't worry—no goats were harmed in the making of tonight's dinner." The corner of his mouth lifts in a half-smile. "I'm not teasing you. It's... nice to meet someone who still cares that much. Rare in Hollywood."

"Oh, that's too bad. I was kind of looking forward to curried goat. What's she making instead?"

He sniffs the air. "Curried paneer with sweet potatoes," he says, nodding with approval. "Smells like she's making her special blend again—the one with that red chili oil that hits you in the back of the throat. Not restaurant-hot, but damn good. You can actually taste the food instead of just surviving it. And she does something with cardamom that I've never figured out."

Saliva pools under my tongue at the thought of dinner. Living here has made me soft—in all the right ways. Max and I have decided to only go out to eat once a week, mainly because it's a pain in the ass dodging the paparazzi, so I've decided to cook three nights a week and Rosa cook the other three nights a week. And God, Rosa's cooking. The way she transforms ordinary ingredients into treasures from Jamaica—spicy jerk chicken that makes my lips tingle, plantains caramelized to sticky-sweet perfection, dumplings that somehow taste like clouds, and saltfish that's briny and complex. Before moving here, I couldn't have pointed to Jamaica on a map of Caribbean cuisine. Now I dream about it.

"So," Max says. "Your mother's birthday…"

I smile. "You heard me talking to her." I take a deep breath. "We can't do much this year, I'm afraid. She's still immunocompromised, so we'll have to wait until next year to do the zoo."

"The zoo?"

I nod. Oh, Mom loves the zoo. The wrinkled gray elephants with their gentle, swaying trunks. The silverback gorillas, so human-like in their movements, watching us with deep, knowing eyes. The hippos, deceptively graceful as they glide through murky water despite their massive bulk. The playful sea lions, sleek and agile, barking and clapping as they perform. They fascinate her. Like me, she's drawn to creatures with souls in their eyes. So, we've gone to the zoo every year on her birthday for the past 20 years.

"Hmmmm…." Max says.

"What?"

"Well. I think I have an idea. Maybe, maybe not. I'll let you know tomorrow."

"What do you have up your sleeve?"

Max just shrugs. "Not saying anything."

But the next day, I find out what Max has in mind.

Max's eyes sparkle with excitement. "I've arranged a private tour of the zoo for your mother's birthday. The whole family—you, me, Patricia. And of course Tally and Olivia can join us, plus anyone else your mother would like."

"Max, that's incredibly thoughtful, but she can't be in crowds while she's immunocompromised."

"Already considered," he says, squeezing my hand. "We'll go at 5:30, after closing. The head of private events owes me a favor—we went to prep school together."

I bite my lip, thinking of the expense. "This must be costing—"

"Not another word about that," he says softly. "If the zoo makes your mother happy, then that's what she deserves on her birthday."

Something hot and sharp pricks behind my eyelids. Mom's birthday wish—watching the elephants spray each other at the new habitat—might actually come true.

Max's arms encircle me, and I exhale deeply. "Thank you," is all I can manage.

His lips brush against my hair, and I melt into the shelter of his embrace.

"By the way, you're home early," I murmur, pulling back to look at him. "Everything okay?"

"Just rearranged some things," he says with a half-smile. "Figured dinner with you and Rosa shouldn't be something I miss every night. Real dinner, not just reheating plates at ten o'clock." He tucks a strand of hair behind my ear. "I'll still need to tackle some emails later, but first..." His voice drops to a whisper, eyes darkening with promise. The heat in his gaze makes my cheeks flush, and I can't help but mirror his smile.

I give him a playful smile. "Let's save that for after dinner." But his lips find mine, and the kiss is so tender and thorough that suddenly dessert seems too far away. My phone buzzes in my pocket, reminding me. "I should call Mom back first, though. Tell her about our zoo adventure and—" I pause, watching his face carefully. "The good news about her treatment. Apparently some mystery benefactor is covering the immunotherapy her insurance wouldn't touch." I tilt my head. "Any ideas who that might be?"

His face breaks into that sunshine grin I've come to love. "The treatment was approved? That's incredible news." He takes my hand, squeezing it gently. "I looked into that Keytruda regimen. The success rates are really promising for her type of cancer."

I nod. "Yes, I agree. It does seem..." I shake my head. No. I can't do this again. I've watched her hair fall out in clumps on her pillow. I've held the pink plastic basin while she retched after treatments. I've seen the radiation burns bloom across her chest like some terrible flower. Each time the doctors switched protocols, their voices lifted with that cautious optimism I've grown to hate. "This combination shows promise," they'd say, while Mom just grew thinner, grayer. Sometimes I want to scream at them all. What's the point of poisoning her if it doesn't work? Even this new drug—Keytruda—I can't bear to hope. What if we're just stealing her good days? What if instead of sitting in infusion chairs, she could have been watching sunsets, or tasting wine, or just sleeping in her own bed without pain?

Max's gaze holds mine, waiting. I try to speak but can't. Instead, I see Mom's nightstand—the amber bottles lined up like tiny soldiers, her calendar with its battlefield of red X's. When I part my lips, only a trembling exhale emerges.

There's a shadow I refuse to acknowledge hovering at

the edges of my thoughts. A future without her Sunday pancake ritual, without her snorting when she laughs too hard, without her terrible puns that somehow always land perfectly. Without her late-night phone calls where she quotes obscure movies until I guess them. Without her leaving me voice messages just to tell me terrible jokes. Without her knowing exactly when to push and when to just listen.

I shake my head. "Nothing." The aroma of Rosa's signature curried paneer wafts from the kitchen, mingling with the sweet earthiness of roasted sweet potatoes. My stomach growls in response. "Dinner smells ready." Right on cue, the delicate sound of Rosa's dinner chime echoes through the house. Max offers his arm, and I take it, our steps falling into rhythm as we make our way to the kitchen.

Just for now, I'll savor each bite of this perfectly seasoned curried paneer and sweet potatoes. Just for now, I'll push away the image of Mom's thinning hair against the hospital pillow, the way hope and dread have become tangled like IV lines. Just for now, I'll picture only her smile when she sees the giraffes at the zoo on Friday—her favorites since I was little.

Just for now, I'll silence the voice whispering that I should be planning not just a birthday but a goodbye.

Chapter Forty-One

CELESTE

The Los Angeles Zoo at 5:30 PM belongs entirely to us—a birthday gift for Mom. She's brought along Zoey and Grace, her closest confidantes, while I've got Tally and Olivia flanking me. Lexi shows up with Shane in tow—yes, the same Shane who draped himself all over me at my wedding reception, drunk enough to make Max see red.

I'd always wondered why Max went all caveman on Shane during our reception. Last night, as we lay in our bed after making love, he finally told me: even then, standing at that altar with our fake vows, something primal in him had already claimed me. What???? The man I thought was glaring daggers at me that day had actually been staking his territory—marking what he already considered his.

Mom stands beneath the entrance arch, her colorful silk scarf catching the evening light. She'd chosen it over the wig that never sits right against her scalp. The emerald wrap blouse brings out something in her eyes I haven't seen in months. "My son-in-law rented an entire zoo," she whispers to her friends, who exchange looks of delighted disbelief.

Max's eyes sparkle mischievously. "Before anything else —dinner awaits." He extends his arm to my mother, who accepts it with a blush and a giggle, shooting me a look of excitement I haven't witnessed since before her diagnosis. I trail behind them as our little procession moves toward an elegant table set beneath the night sky. White linen drapes the surface, flickering candles cast golden light across polished silverware, and a formal waiter stands nearby, napkin draped precisely over one forearm, crystal water pitcher poised in his hand.

When Max had asked what Mom craves most, I didn't hesitate. "Pizza," I told him, "but not the greasy meat-lover's kind." I described how she'd close her eyes in bliss over a pie loaded with mushrooms, artichoke hearts and sun-dried tomatoes. "She used to pair it with red wine," I added, my voice catching slightly, "before everything changed." I found myself smiling as I detailed her perfect side dish: a Greek salad with black olives nestled among tomatoes, more of those artichoke hearts she can never get enough of, crumbled feta, peperoncini for kick, homemade croutons, all dressed in that particular vinaigrette that walks the line between zesty and overwhelming.

We settle in at the table as servers present our meal—pizza, the dish Mom loves most. I take a bite and immediately know this isn't some cardboard delivery box creation. The cheese stretches in silky strands, melting perfectly—definitely not the rubbery stuff from the corner pizzeria. There's complexity here: something nutty underneath, something sharp at the edges. The tomatoes taste concentrated, intense. Even the mushrooms aren't ordinary; they're rich and woodsy, varieties I've only seen in fancy markets. I spot artichoke hearts that someone clearly prepared by hand. The whole thing glistens with good olive oil, smells of real garlic, and wears fresh basil like jewelry.

I bite into the pizza and close my eyes. "Oh my God." The word 'pizza' feels inadequate—like calling the Sistine Chapel a 'ceiling.' My taste buds are still dancing when the server sets down our Greek salad. The feta crumbles like it was made this morning, nestled among plump Kalamata olives and crisp pepperoncinis. Every cucumber slice snaps with freshness. The tomatoes burst with summer, and the croutons shatter perfectly between my teeth. I drag a piece through the dressing—tangy, spiced, with just enough oil to coat my tongue without drowning the ingredients.

My mother seems as transported as I am by the food. Her eyes flutter closed with each bite, and her smile—a real one, not the brave face she's been wearing for months—lights up her whole face. "One perk of this chemo break," she says, dabbing her lips with a napkin, "is that I can actually taste things again. No more metallic aftertaste, like I've been licking dirty pennies." She has a week's reprieve before starting the new Keytruda treatment her doctor prescribed. She takes another bite of pizza, then presses her fingertips to her lips in that classic chef's kiss. Raising her sparkling grape juice, she simply shakes her head. "Heaven. Absolute heaven."

I can tell from Max's smile that this isn't some chain delivery. The crust shatters perfectly between my teeth, the cheese stretches in silky strands, and the basil perfumes each bite. I savor it while taking in the zoo at night—empty pathways bathed in moonlight and twinkling string lights. Beyond the fence, the giraffes and lions are sleeping, unaware of our little celebration. Mom laughs at something Max says, and my chest constricts. No, this won't be her last birthday pizza at the zoo. The immunotherapy has to work.

By this time next year, she'll be tossing carrots to the elephants again, her hair grown back, her smile full.

I take another bite of the pizza, the flavors still dancing on my tongue. "Max," I say, setting my fork down. "Did you fly in some celebrity chef for this?" The crust is so perfectly crisp, the sauce so rich—I half expect him to casually mention Bobby Flay or Giada De Laurentiis is hiding in the kitchen.

Max shrugs, sips his wine, and slides his arm around my shoulders. "Giorgio Bartolin prepared this dinner," he says with practiced nonchalance, as if everyone has celebrity chefs cooking their meals. I nearly choke on my bite. Giorgio's show *Mangia* on The Food Network has me glued to the screen every Thursday night, my kitchen counter littered with scribbled notes and ingredients I can barely pronounce. Six months ago I burned three attempts at his famous risotto before giving up and ordering takeout.

Mom lets out a delighted giggle at the revelation of our chef's identity. Beside me, Olivia's jaw drops, her eyes widening to saucers. I can practically see the culinary worship radiating from her—the same reverence I feel. After all, Giorgio Bartolin's techniques have shaped the signature dishes she's becoming known for in her catering business: that creamy seafood risotto, those miniature pizzas topped with peppery arugula, the shrimp scampi with just the right kick of heat, each inspired by Giorgio. And now, somehow, the maestro himself has prepared our dinner. Pinch me.

Mom reaches for another slice of pizza and adds a generous helping of salad to her plate. "No wonder this dinner is incredible," she says with a wink, then raises her glass toward Zoey and Grace. The three women clink their glasses together in a toast. "Ladies, I promised you something special tonight, didn't I? Just look at that sky—crystal clear, with that perfect chill in the air and a full moon hanging over us. If there was ever a night for something magical to happen," she pauses, her eyes twinkling, "this is definitely it."

We've just demolished three pizzas and a mountain of salad when Giorgio emerges from the kitchen. I grip the edge of the table to steady myself. Beside me, Olivia's practically vibrating, her eyes wide as saucers. Meeting her culinary hero on tonight of all nights—the universe has perfect timing. "So pleased to meet you," he says, each word precise and musical with his Italian lilt. In person, he's devastating—those dark curls falling across his forehead, eyes like espresso, and that mouth that curves like a perfect bow. No wonder the camera never quite captures him right. "I hope the meal is to your liking."

My mother jumps to her feet and embraces Giorgio, her eyes wide with delight. "This is the best birthday surprise ever!" she gushes. "Celeste never misses an episode of your show, and Olivia here—" she gestures toward my friend, "—she's your biggest fan. Just last week she was raving about recreating your risotto recipe. Her kitchen shelves are practically a shrine to your cookbooks."

Giorgio clasps his hands together as he studies my mother. "Another Sagittarius! I knew it the moment I saw you—that spark of adventure, that generosity of spirit." His fingers fan outward dramatically, tracing invisible constellations. I can't help but smile. Before the diagnosis, Mom was the woman who'd leap from thirty-foot cliffs into the Ozark lakes while I watched from shore, who'd gun an ATV through mud trails while I clung white-knuckled behind her, laughing into the wind. The cancer may have temporarily dimmed her light, but Giorgio—meeting her just minutes ago—somehow sees past the hospital pallor to the shooting star beneath. Some people just recognize their own kind instantly.

Mom's laughter bubbles up like champagne as Giorgio bends over her hand, his lips brushing her skin before he extends an invitation to dance beneath the night sky. The familiar croon of Sinatra fills the air, and she takes his hand. We fall silent, watching Giorgio guide her through expert twirls and dramatic dips. Mom follows his lead effortlessly, her body remembering steps I could never master. If I tried those moves, I'd be a disaster of tangled limbs, stepped-on toes and apologies, but she glides across the floor with feline precision, making it look easy.

After the dance, Giorgio and Mom are both laughing hysterically and Mom's shaking her head. "Oh, I feel like a girl of 20 tonight," she says. "Thank you for the dance, and for the best meal I've ever had," she says to Giorgio. "Would you like to join our entourage as we walk through the rest of the zoo?"

"I'd love to," he says modestly. "My husband is here with me tonight, too. Would you mind if both of us came along?"

Mom laughs uproariously. "The more the merrier! Bring him along, too. His name is Marcello, right? I remember seeing him on the show."

"Right, Marcello," Giorgio says. "We will catch up to your group in a few minutes." Then he turns to Max. "Just text me, Max, where you are in five minutes and we'll meet you there."

Max's fingers intertwine with mine as he guides us through the nighttime zoo. Mom's eyes light up at the gorilla exhibit despite the massive creatures being curled up in slumber. Later, we pause at the koalas, their bodies somehow defying gravity as they cling to branches in deep sleep.

"There's something magical about the zoo after dark," Mom whispers, her face illuminated by the soft exhibit lighting. "Even with half the animals sleeping."

"But just think," I point out, "all your favorites are putting on a show—the hippos are splashing in their pool, the sea lions darting through water, the tigers are prowling. Even the giraffes are stretching their necks beneath the stars."

We wander over to the hippos. Beneath the water's surface, their massive bodies perform an unexpected dance of weightlessness. I think of *Fantasia*—Walt Disney knew what he was doing when he put tutus on these creatures and imagined them as graceful ballerinas. Max and I settle onto a bench, mesmerized. Time slips away as Rosie and her calf Mara twirl and glide in their watery stage, defying every expectation their bulky frames suggest.

Mom's eyes never leave the hippos. "Everyone thinks lions or crocodiles are Africa's deadliest," she murmurs, "but it's these guys. Something about those mothers—they'd do anything for their babies. And the bulls?" She clicks her tongue. "Pure territorial rage. That's what makes them so dangerous. One second they're floating there like peaceful river potatoes, the next—" She snaps her fingers. "They're charging through the water at sixty miles an hour with jaws that can snap a canoe in half."

I nod. "It's strange, isn't it? They look so adorable from a distance—all fuzzy and innocent. But up close..." I trail off, thinking of Max. He's just the opposite from the hippos who look cute and cuddly but are actually aggressive killers. When we first met, his eyes were winter, his words ice. The whispers around the office painted him as the executive who reduced Harvard MBAs to stammering apologies. Yet somehow, beneath that frost-bitten exterior beats a heart I never expected to find. He arranged all this for my mother—a woman whose name he's barely had time to learn. And I'd bet my career he pulled strings for her Keytruda treatments when insurance denied her only real chance against the cancer. And those nights when his hands trace my body with such tenderness that I forget to breathe....there are no words.

At the lion exhibit, we find the pride scattered across the enclosure. The male perches in a tree, tail flicking back and forth, his amber eyes tracking our movements. Females groom their cubs while others bound through the night air, tumbling over one another. "This is rare," Max whispers, his breath warm against my ear. "Lions aren't strictly day or night creatures—they adjust their schedules based on their surroundings. We got lucky tonight."

I nod and smile. "It's like they're performing just for us."

For another two hours, we wander the zoo, lingering at exhibits where the animals are awake and doing their thing. At the marine mammal pool, Rocky and Buddy, the two male sea lions, bark and splash at each other, their voices echoing across the concrete. Something about them tugs at me—these bachelors confined together when in the wild they'd be competing for females. Buddy, with his clouded eyes, at least has a reason to be here. Rocky's story remains a mystery. They glide through the water alongside several Harbor seals, who watch their antics with what looks like dignified indifference, their whiskers twitching.

Mom squints at her phone. "Says here Rocky was found with a bullet lodged in his skull. Only has vision in one eye now." She taps the screen, scrolling further. "Poachers, probably." She'd been wondering the same thing I was—why he wasn't swimming free somewhere. She looks up at the solitary figure gliding through the water. "Shame they don't have any lady sea lions. These bachelors could use some company."

She turns around to find Giorgio and Marcello beside her, their eyes also fixed on the sea lions. Giorgio drapes his arm across Marcello's shoulders with a playful smile. "Maybe those two bachelors out there have the right idea—no ladies, no problems." A chuckle escapes him as he gives Marcello a gentle elbow to the ribs. Marcello returns the gesture, his eyes crinkling at the corners.

Our group moves through the nocturnal animal exhibits, pausing at each enclosure. I'm surprised to find giraffes among them. "They're not actually nocturnal," Max whispers, his breath warm against my ear. "They just don't need much sleep—always watching for predators." I glance up at their towering forms, some dozing on their feet while others stretch their long necks toward leafy branches. "What could possibly hunt something that tall?" I whisper back. Max's eyes gleam in the dim lighting. "Lions. They hunt in prides."

We move on to where leopards pace behind glass, their spotted coats gleaming under moonlight. In a different enclosure, maned wolves trot with their distinctive fox-on-stilts gait, while nearby, an aardvark burrows its snout into artificial soil. An ocelot watches us with jewel-like eyes, and at the Australian exhibit, a kangaroo joey peeks from its mother's pouch, then ducks back into safety.

Of these animals, the kangaroos fascinate me the most. Their powerful hind legs propel them in graceful bounds across the yellowing grass, their alert eyes tracking our every movement from beneath furrowed brows. Two males suddenly rear up on their tails, balancing perfectly as they swat at each other with their paws. Max's laughter mingles with mine as we watch this primal dance of dominance unfold mere yards away.

The zoo closes at ten, and as we make our final loop past the flamingos, Max turns to Mom. "Patricia, what do you think about heading back for something sweet?"

Mom's eyes light up. "I've been saving room," she says, patting her stomach. "Giorgio mentioned tiramisu earlier, and I haven't stopped thinking about it since."

Max's lips curve into a smile. Earlier, he'd quietly asked me what dessert Mom loves most. "Tiramisu," I'd answered without hesitation. Now we're making our way back to our table beneath the canopy of stars, still savoring the memory of Giorgio's pizza—hands down the most incredible any of us had ever tasted. I catch Mom's eye and see my own anticipation mirrored there; we're all wondering what magic Giorgio might work with ladyfingers and mascarpone.

Giorgio emerges from the kitchen carrying a tiramisu the size of a small suitcase, a single flickering candle standing tall in its center. Our voices blend together in the familiar birthday melody as Mom leans forward, closes her eyes for a wish, and extinguishes the flame with a gentle puff. Applause ripples around the table. Giorgio's knife glides through the layers of mascarpone and coffee-soaked ladyfingers, and when my first bite dissolves on my tongue, I can't help but close my eyes and let out a small, involuntary moan. Heaven has a taste after all. The mascarpone cream melts into a silken cloud against my palate, each delicate layer of espresso-drenched ladyfingers yielding beneath my fork with the gentlest pressure. The bitter cocoa dusting mingles with the sweet marsala undertones, creating a perfect harmony that makes my shoulders drop in surrender. This isn't just dessert—it's Giorgio's masterpiece.

Mom's face lights up as she takes another bite of the tiramisu, her eyes closing briefly in that way they always do when she's savoring something delicious. The dessert's cocoa dusting leaves a faint brown smudge on her upper lip that she doesn't notice. I'm scraping the last creamy remnants from my own plate when she suddenly pushes back her chair. The legs scrape against the hardwood floor as she rises, reaching for her crystal wine glass. The delicate ping of her spoon against the glass silences the dinner conversation, and all eyes turn to her as she fixes her gaze on Max.

Patricia raises her glass. "To Max," she says, her voice carrying across the room. "When Celeste first told me about you, I thought she'd gone completely crazy." She gives a small laugh, shaking her head. "A man she barely mentioned, suddenly her husband? I hadn't even met you! But now—" her eyes soften as she looks between them, "—I see you're the perfect match for my daughter's particular brand of insanity."

I plaster on a smile and sneak a glance at Max, who's practically glowing as he talks to Mom. Something twists in my chest. Mom's looking at him like he hangs the moon— and why wouldn't she? The man's making her mountain of medical bills disappear like some financial magician. Great for her. For me? I keep seeing that merger date circled on the calendar. Once my scripts actually pay the bills, what's left? Our little Malibu playhouse gets packed up. This whole fantasy comes with a timer that's ticking down, even if no one else can hear it. I've been stealing moments with Max like they're samples at Costco, knowing damn well I can't afford the full-size version. When our time's up, Mom's heart will crack in two right along with mine. Better she doesn't get too attached to my temporary husband.

Later, we fall into bed, both of us buzzing from the day's emotional rollercoaster. After sex, Max conks out immediately, his face all peaceful, those stress lines vanished. I prop myself up, memorizing him—the stubborn jaw, those ridiculous eyelashes—like I'm cramming for a test I'll have to take alone.

"Max," I whisper, my voice barely disturbing the darkness between us. "What you did for Mom today..." My throat tightens. The treatment might fail—I know this—but he gave her something insurance statements and medical jargon couldn't: hope. "You didn't just give her a birthday. You might have given her more birthdays."

His lips curve slightly upward, and I wonder if somewhere in his dreams, he hears me.

Chapter Forty-Two

CELESTE

Time blurs with Max in my life. Three months ago, I nearly dropped my phone when Selena called asking to represent me. Now I'm frozen at my kitchen table, staring at a check that makes my previous salary look like pocket change. Six hundred and seventy-five thousand dollars. For words I wrote. My signature wobbles across the endorsement line, and after taxes and Selena's commission, I know exactly where the money's going. I put a substantial down payment on a condo for Mom, over her objections, and the greatest thing is, she's strong enough to move now.

So, a week later, I watch Lexi toss her backpack onto the cream-colored sofa in Mom's new Westwood place, UCLA's iconic bell tower framed perfectly in the window behind her. Just weeks ago, Mom's hands shook too much to hold her tea. This morning, she planted herself in the doorway, spine straight, finger pointing as she commanded the moving crew. "Oh, for chrissakes, that's a Tiffany lamp, not a base-ball!" she barks to the movers who are still bringing her stuff into the new place. The hollows in her cheeks have filled in, her jeans fit again, and though Max denies it every time I ask, I know exactly who paid for the treatment that's bringing her back to us.

Max. Soon-to-be my ex-husband. The expiration date on our marriage ticks away silently between us, neither of us acknowledging the countdown. I catch myself watching him sometimes across the breakfast table, wondering how I'll feel when this is over. But there's Mom—her color returning, her appetite back, her laugh no longer forced. "No evidence of disease," the oncologist said last week, his voice betraying surprise at how quickly she'd responded to the treatment. May is circled in red on our calendar now— merger completion, divorce papers, as the merger has been postponed from March until May now, so there's some reprieve but not a lot. I've practiced saying the words "irreconcilable differences" in my bathroom mirror. Yet every time Mom calls, bubbling with energy she hasn't had in years, I know whose signature is on those medical bills she never sees.

While Max jet-sets to Tokyo for some gaming company deal—something about expanding Kensington's "intellectual property portfolio," as he calls it—I'm here with cardboard boxes and packing tape, helping Mom and Lexi move. Things between Max and me have been like something from a movie these past months, but I find myself stepping back. Creating distance. When he texts from Japan, I wait hours before responding. Our nightly Face-Time ritual? I've let it slide completely. I tell myself he's swamped with meetings anyway, that I'm doing him a favor by not interrupting. But really, I'm protecting myself. Because fairy tales end, and I can't bear the thought of building my whole world around someone who might disappear.

Mom staggers through the doorway, her arms wrapped around a cardboard box labeled "Kitchen—Fragile" in my hurried Sharpie scrawl. Her cheeks are flushed pink against her newly cropped blonde hair, evidence of its post-chemo regrowth. "Oh, Celeste," she groans, setting the box down on the hardwood floor with a muffled clink of dishes. "Why did I let you talk me into this?" Then her weathered face breaks into that familiar crinkle-eyed smile. "Ah, but look at this!" She rolls up the sleeve of her faded blue t-shirt and flexes her bicep with theatrical flair. "Just started Pilates. Can you believe it?" The muscle is small but defined—a victory flag raised against everything her body has endured.

I grin. "You know why I helped you buy this condo, Mom. It's super close for Lexi, it's gorgeous and it's yours, not a rental. And I know you need this sunroom." I sweep my arms towards the sunroom where afternoon light streams through floor-to-ceiling windows, casting honey-gold rectangles across the polished maple floors. I love everything about this place, and Mom does too - from the rich amber hardwood that gleams under our feet, to the intricate crown molding that frames each room like artwork, to the soaring 10' ceilings that make even this modest space feel palatial. The terrace outside, barely larger than a postage stamp but perfectly positioned to catch the morning sun, already holds Mom's collection of jewel-toned glass hummingbird feeders and three terracotta pots where tiny green tomato seedlings reach skyward - a world away from the water-stained ceilings and peeling linoleum of her dingy old apartment.

Tally and Liv push through the door with cardboard boxes stacked to their chins. Tally blows a strand of hair from her face and sets her load down with a thud. "Tell me we're done after this round, Celeste." She turns to Mom with an apologetic grimace. "Patricia, you know I'd do anything for you, but my back is killing me. Thank God it's cool today."

I bite my tongue to keep from mentioning my upcoming move from Max's place—Mom doesn't need to hear that right now. She and Max have developed this unexpected connection since Christmas, when she stayed with us. I still can't get over the sight of Mom hunched over a poker table with Max, Gianni, and the rest of the Kensington brothers —Ansel, Roman, Kalen, Asher, Cameron, Silas and Connor—all of them locked in their family's traditional Christmas Eve tournament. Turns out they do it every year instead of singing Christmas carols and opening gifts, and I was there for it. Mom's face when she raked in that final pot! The next day, on Christmas Day, the wind whipped through our hair as Max steered his sailboat towards Catalina Island. I watched them from the bow, and then watched their heads bent close together over a museum exhibit, then later splashing each other like kids during our kayak adventure.

Mom's laugh—that full-throated one I hadn't heard in years—echoed every time Max launched into another outlandish tale, such as the one about him about stealing his grandfather's yacht at thirteen and accidentally docking at a nudist beach, his hands painting elaborate pictures in the air, voice dropping to a conspiratorial whisper at the punch-lines that made Mom double over, clutching her sides. Or about the time he accidentally set his prep school headmaster's toupee on fire during a chemistry experiment gone wrong. Mom got a kick out of these stories and by the time she went home after staying with us a week, she told me how much she adored my husband.

Mom grimaces and jabs a thumb in my direction.

"Don't look at me. This genius right here is responsible."
She rolls her eyes so hard I'm surprised they don't get stuck.
"You should move, she said. You'll love it, she said. Meanwhile, I'm seriously contemplating whether they'd let me
plead temporary insanity if I strangled her. Lucky for her I
love her too much. And I guess she was trying to help. So
there's that."

I can't help but laugh. "Well, the silver lining is I can
actually pay for movers now." I catch Tally staring at one of
the movers—the one with arms like tree trunks and a
jawline that belongs on a movie poster. I nudge her with my
elbow. Earlier, I overheard him mentioning his husband
while arranging boxes. Mom nearly spilled her coffee when
I whispered it to her. Classic Tally—somehow always gravi-
tating toward men who couldn't possibly be interested.

We spend the next few hours lugging boxes while the
moving guys handle the furniture for Lexi's new condo.
Once everything's inside, Lexi—who orchestrated this entire
move like a general—collapses onto the bare living room
floor. She fans her arms and legs across the hardwood,
making invisible snow angels and dissolving into laughter. I
join her, our limbs sweeping in unison. The gesture trans-
ports me back to Kansas City winters, when we'd fall backward into real snowdrifts, our breath clouding above us. Los
Angeles hasn't seen actual snow since '62. Sometimes I miss
the Midwest's clear-cut seasons, though I conveniently
forget how much I cursed those icy mornings while scraping
my windshield, my nostalgia selective as always.

"What are you two nuts doing?" Mom asks, laughing.

Lexi's eyes sparkle as she surveys the new place. "This is
heaven compared to the rat colony we were living in before.
Though I was always partial to sweet Willard."

I groan at the memory. Only my sister would name a

disease-carrying rodent after a horror movie. The whole nightmare started when her neighbor Bill's "pet" Suzy turned out to be pregnant. Instead of dealing with the babies responsibly, Bill released them into the wild—the wild being their apartment complex. Six months later, management was setting traps while Lexi conducted her one-woman rescue operation, relocating captured rats to "the countryside" where they're probably staging a takeover of some poor farmer's barn. She even kept one as a pet until her class schedule made rat-parenting too demanding. I still remember her tearful goodbye when she surrendered Willard to the animal shelter, gender still undetermined.

Three and a half months into marriage with Max, and I still catch myself wondering if this is real. I wake up in our bed, his scent lingering on my skin, and have to pinch myself.

Last month, he casually mentioned tickets to the Super Bowl—as if everyone just happens to have access to a private suite at SoFi Stadium. When we found out the Chiefs were playing, his eyes lit up with that look I've come to recognize: the one that says he's about to make me deliriously happy. Mom, Lexi and I all got to share his family's suite at this past Super Bowl. Mom and Lexi couldn't stop gaping at the champagne fountains and celebrities, while I couldn't stop watching Max watching me celebrate as Kansas City demolished Detroit. I screamed every obscenity known to man during that game - couldn't help myself, it was a nail-biter for the first three quarters before the Chiefs broke it wide open in the fourth quarter, scoring 21 unanswered points. So, yeah, that was yet another fantasy brought to life by Max.

Another fantasy brought to life? The *Vanity Fair* Oscar Party, where the champagne flowed like liquid gold in crystal flutes and the air sparkled with diamonds catching the light from every direction. My jaw literally ached from hanging open as Emma Stone glided past in emerald silk that whispered against the carpet, while Ryan Gosling's cologne lingered in the air long after he'd moved on with a casual nod in my direction. The Hemsworth brothers towered nearby, their Australian accents cutting through the elegant hum of conversation. Brad Pitt's laugh echoed from across the room, his hand resting on Leonardo DiCaprio's shoulder as they shared some private joke. Colman Domingo's purple velvet suit made him impossible to miss, while Margot Robbie's platinum hair caught the light like a halo. Zendaya floated by in architectural couture that defied gravity, Spielberg gesticulated animatedly to a circle of rapt listeners, and Nicole Kidman's porcelain skin seemed to glow from within.

For Max, this was merely another networking party, a chessboard where he moved pieces with practiced ease—his hand at the small of backs, his smile calculated to charm, his whispers making investors lean in closer. But for me? My borrowed Louboutins pinched my toes as I floated through this dreamscape, terrified I'd wake up.

A month later, Max transformed our marble-floored living room into a similar scene, though more intimate. Famous faces lounged on our Italian leather sofas, ice clinked in crystal tumblers, and the scent of catered truffle hors d'oeuvres hung in the air. Despite my trembling hands as I greeted Oscar nominees whose posters had once adorned my bedroom walls, by midnight I found myself stifling yawns behind a napkin, watching Max work the room with mechanical precision, and longing for the cool silence of our bedroom upstairs.

But, yeah, to say that I feel like Cinderella after the ball

—glass slipper found, tiara firmly in place—would be the understatement of the century. I mean, how did I, a development exec who used to share a cramped office with three other people and eat sad microwave lunches, suddenly find myself pouring champagne for Scarlett Johansson in a marble kitchen bigger than my old apartment? Robert Downey Jr. used our guest bathroom. Meryl Streep complimented the view from our—well, Max's—balcony overlooking the twinkling Los Angeles skyline. Yes, the reality is that this is Max's scene, this is Max's house, and those movie stars are coming for him, not for me. But for now, the ridiculous palace with its infinity pool and temperature-controlled wine cellar is technically my home too, and these stars are technically coming to a home that I share.

It's past midnight when I finally make it home after helping Lexi and Mom settle into their new place. The house is empty—Max won't be back from Tokyo until tomorrow—and I stand for a moment in the dark stillness, listening to the distant rhythm of waves against the shore. My fingers trace the outline of my phone, still warm from Mom's call thanking me again. Two screenplay deadlines sit in my inbox. And somewhere over the Pacific, a man I never expected to love is flying back to me.

I can't help but smile at the ceiling, even as a tiny voice whispers: surely the universe won't let me keep all this.

Chapter Forty-Three

CELESTE

The bathroom scale doesn't lie: five pounds. I stare at the number, remembering how Olivia and I used to pound the pavement together, training for 10Ks around Los Angeles. These days, my running shoes gather dust in the corner of Max's closet. Last weekend, we watched runners stream past during the LA marathon, their faces etched with determination. Something twisted in my chest as they crossed the finish line—something like longing. That night, I find myself circling November's first Sunday on the calendar. The NYC marathon. My finger traces the date again and again until the ink smudges. Ambitious? Absolutely. But as I tape the calendar to the refrigerator, I feel something I haven't in months: a hunger that has nothing to do with food or sex.

The alarm buzzes at 5 AM, and I slip out of bed, careful not to wake Max. My running shoes wait by the door like old friends I'd neglected too long. I stretch in the dim hallway light, muscles protesting the early hour, then ease the front door closed behind me.

The rhythm of my feet hitting pavement had always been my therapy—no earbuds, no playlists, just the sound of my breathing and the space to untangle my thoughts. I needed that clarity again. One hour each morning to pound the Malibu roads while the world slept, letting my mind wander through the maze I'd created of my life.

This morning, as my feet sinks into the cool sand with each step, my mind drifts between thoughts of my mother's recovery and the screenplays that would soon bear my name. The beach stretches before me, empty and peaceful in the pre-dawn quiet. I breathe in the salt air and smile. Our stretch of Malibu faces east rather than west—a geographical quirk that means the sun would soon emerge from the ocean horizon rather than sink into it. While the hills behind us capture magnificent sunsets, there was something magical about watching light break across water, painting the waves in gold as they rush towards shore.

My breath comes in ragged bursts as I pound down the beach toward the stairs that lead up to Pacific Coast Highway. The coffee shop is miles away, but the thought of a latte pulls me forward like a lifeline. I take the wooden steps two at a time, sand flying from my sneakers. At the top, I barely register a blue Corolla pulled onto the shoulder, hazard lights blinking lazily. Just another broken-down car on the PCH. I've got exactly forty-three minutes to reach the café, down my caffeine, run back, shower, dress, and get into my car for my hour-long commute to the office, so I can arrive at 8 AM, which is my new start time and has been since I moved in with Max.

The coffee shop barista slides my latte across the counter. I gulp it down, burning my tongue, and dash back outside. There it is again—that blue Corolla with the tinted windows. I hesitate, wondering if I should check on the driver, but my watch says I'm already fifteen minutes behind schedule.

Days blur together. My morning route never changes, but that car appears like a ghost in different spots. Monday, it's pulled onto the gravel shoulder near the bend. Tuesday, it's lurking in the Malibu Farm parking lot. Wednesday, it claims the spot directly in front of my regular coffee shop, the Malibu Farm Pier Cafe. Thursday, it's stationed outside that boarded-up Italian place that went under last year.

The feeling reminds me of that *Twilight Zone* episode where a hitchhiker keeps appearing to a woman driving cross-country. She sees him in Pennsylvania, then Ohio, then Nebraska—the same haunting face at every turn. Only in the final moments does she learn the truth: she died in an accident back in New York, and he's been Death all along, patiently waiting for her to realize that she's dead. That's how I feel about this car—like it's following me with some terrible message.

Then one Saturday morning, I finally discover who's behind the wheel. I'm lingering at the Blue Bottle Café, nursing a latte and picking at a blueberry scone, with nowhere particular to be. Max is buried in merger paperwork at the office, as he has been every weekend lately, leaving me to fill these empty hours however I can.

A man appears beside my table and pulls out the chair across from me without asking. My spine stiffens. The café suddenly feels too warm, too close. His weathered jeans have a tear just above one knee, his red-and-navy plaid flannel shirt is rolled to the elbows revealing tanned forearms, and his brown leather work boots are scuffed at the toes as if he's kicked something hard, repeatedly. He's about 55, with salt-and-pepper hair that curls slightly at his collar, crow's feet around eyes that are a startling shade of green, the same color as Max's. Those eyes lock onto mine with unsettling intensity.

"Hello, I don't want to scare you. But you're Celeste Jenkins, am I right?" His voice is deep, gravelly, with the faintest hint of a British accent. But it's not quite British... it's more American with just a hint of Brit. I shake my head. His voice, although slightly accented, sounds familiar. Like Max...

I nod, breaking off a piece of my scone with trembling fingers. Crumbs scatter across the white tablecloth. "Yes. Who's asking?"

"My name is Michael Kensington. I believe you're married to my son, Max."

Chapter Forty-Four

CELESTE

My ears ring. The man's face blurs in front of me as I try to process his words. Max's father. Here. Now.

"Um—" My mouth opens and closes. I grip the edge of the bench until my knuckles turn white. "I—" The words stick in my throat like sand. "Does Max—"

He shakes his head, eyes darting to the sidewalk. "No." His weathered hands twist together in his lap, dirt crusted under his fingernails. "I sleep in that blue Corolla." He points to a car parked across the street. "Been parking it near his beach house for months now." His voice cracks. "Just hoping to catch a glimpse of him someday. Haven't yet, but I've watched you jog past every morning at five."

"How do you know who I am?"

He flashes a smile that doesn't quite reach his eyes. "Your wedding made headlines everywhere—couldn't escape it even tucked away on my little farm in the English countryside. Read about it after a hard day of milking cows." His gaze drops to the floor, fingers fidgeting with his cuff. "That's... well, that's another conversation entirely."

My eyes widen. "The English countryside?" I lean forward, coffee forgotten. The son of a California billionaire somehow ended up milking cows in rural England? There's a story there. But before I can stop myself, I'm picturing the Highclere Castle—that magnificent structure from *Downton Abbey*, a show I've watched religiously since college. Every episode, every Christmas special, memorized like scripture. I catch myself mid-fantasy, imagining this man—this stranger—somehow introducing me to the Earl of Grantham. Maybe his farm is near Highclere, England, where the Highclere Castle is located?

I press my lips together, embarrassed. Sitting across from me is Michael Kensington, the man who abandoned Max two decades ago, and here I am daydreaming about using him as my personal tour guide to fictional aristocracy. Classic Celeste, getting lost in fantasy when reality is sitting right across the table.

Now that I'm studying him, I realize that Michael Kensington's face is how Max will look 30 years from now—if Max traded his Armani for a wrinkled department store clearance shirt and his protein shakes for bourbon. The resemblance is there in the jawline, the slight arch of the eyebrow, and the eyes, but Michael's face has collapsed into something softer, sadder. His salt-and-pepper hair sticks up in tufts like he's been running his hands through it all night, and when he exhales, I catch the layered scent of fresh whiskey over stale. His shirt is buttoned wrong.

I should hate this man for what he did to Max, but my fingers itch to straighten his collar instead. I've seen this before—people who pour drinks to quiet their demons, only to wake up with louder ones. He's not the villain in Max's story. He's just another casualty.

"So you've been hanging around Max's home, living in

your car. How come you're just hanging around Max's place, not your other sons?"

He exhales slowly, his shoulders dropping. "Max is the only one of my boys who's married. When I heard the news, I did a little digging—found out you work at Dreamscape, climbing the ladder there. Impressive." His eyes, weathered but sharp, study me. "I figured you might be my best shot at reconnecting. All I really want is to know they're okay, that they've found some happiness in their lives."

I meet his gaze. "So I'm your only way in?"

"Right," he says. "So can you tell me about Max?"

"What do you want to know?" I ask.

Michael's eyes drift to the floor. "I've read about him in the trades. CEO of Kensington Entertainment. Tabloids always showing him with some new starlet or supermodel." His voice catches. "Then suddenly, he's married to you." He looks up, pain etched across his face. "I did that to him, didn't I? Made him unable to trust anyone."

I twist my wedding ring, choosing my words carefully. "He was... guarded when we met. But he's different now." I study Michael's expression, wondering how much he can handle hearing. The truth hovers between us—I can't erase the memory of finding Max alone in the dark, tears streaming down his face as home movies flickered on the screen, ghosts of a family that no longer exists. Or how his fingers still trace the edges of that faded photograph— father and son balanced on surfboards, sun-kissed and laughing—before he tucks it away with a heaviness that fills the room. But telling Michael everything feels cruel, even if he deserves to know what his absence created.

His eyes search mine. "Is he happy?"

"He's..." I fidget with my sleeve. "Happy-adjacent?

Happier than before, at any rate. I think - I've only heard stories about how he used to be."

He nods slowly. "Good. That's all I want for my boys."

Words bubble up inside me, but I press my lips together. Something must show on my face, though.

"Whatever it is, just say it," he says, leaning forward.

I inhale, steadying myself. "Max puts on a good front, but there's this... emptiness. He stares at fathers with their sons in restaurants. Keeps a baseball glove in his closet that's never been used. He doesn't talk about it, but your absence is like this wound that never closed. And I don't think it will, not until you're actually there."

He nods, his shoulders slumping. "I know. I know. But I couldn't be the father they deserved while I was drowning in the bottle. That's why I walked away. Every time I looked at those boys, I saw eight futures I was destroying day by day." His voice cracks. "I begged my parents to take them. They refused—said it was my responsibility, not theirs. So I made the only choice I had left."

The pieces suddenly click into place. Michael hadn't abandoned his sons—he'd orchestrated their rescue. By disappearing, he'd forced Joseph and Ruth's hand. They couldn't let their grandsons end up in foster care, so they stepped in. And looking at Max now—successful, driven, accomplished—wasn't that proof his plan had worked? The boys had thrived under their grandparents' stable roof in ways they never could have with a father who probably couldn't stay sober enough to make breakfast. Michael hadn't run from responsibility; he'd embraced it in the only way he knew how—by removing himself from the equation.

"Tell me about the last time you saw Max," I say, leaning forward in the plush leather chair.

His weathered face crumples, eyes glistening with

unshed tears that catch the afternoon light streaming through the coffee shop windows. "It was my parents' fortieth anniversary party at the lake house. Crystal champagne flutes everywhere. I stayed stone-cold sober for three days beforehand—not even a drop of mouthwash. I needed a clear head when I asked them to take my sons." His voice breaks. "I told them I couldn't handle it anymore. Some mornings, I'd stare at my toothbrush for twenty minutes, unable to lift my arm. The weight of everything... it was crushing me, like drowning in quicksand."

"Didn't you have help with the boys?" I ask, watching him twist his gold wedding band—still there after all these years.

He nods, running a trembling hand through his silver-streaked hair. "Rosa was there, bless her. But eight wild boys with their muddy cleats and science projects? The woman already worked sixteen-hour days. And they needed more than that—someone to teach them to bait a hook at dawn, to navigate the black diamond slopes, to become men worth becoming." His shoulders slump. "Instead, they got me—passed out by dinner, reeking of whiskey. I was on my knees begging Mom and Dad to rescue them."

"Your father's response?" I prompt gently.

He shakes his head, a bitter smile playing on his lips. "Dad put his hand on my shoulder—that firm grip he always had. His eyes were kind but unyielding, like polished granite. 'Use them as motivation to get off the sauce,' he said. 'They'll be your way off the bottle.' Classic Silent Generation talk. He believed willpower could overcome anything—just decide to stop drinking, like turning off a faucet. He couldn't see the invisible chains, how they tightened every time I tried to break free."

My chest tightens as I watch him. The hollows beneath

his cheekbones seem to deepen with each word, like someone's scooping him out from the inside.

"It was a disease," he says, voice cracking. "Dad couldn't see that. He thought I could just...stop. For the boys." His fingers drum against his thigh in an anxious rhythm. "But there were mornings when I'd open my eyes and the only reason—the only reason—I could force myself upright was knowing there was a bottle waiting. Without that..." He swallows hard. "I'd have put a bullet in my head before noon."

His hands shake so badly he has to press them flat against the table. "I knew what was happening. I knew my sons deserved better than a father who chose the bottle over them every single day. But I couldn't stop. So when I realized my father might refuse to take them..." He stares at some invisible point beyond me. "England seemed far enough away."

I study his face. "Joseph knew your whereabouts the whole time, didn't he?"

He nods, his eyes fixed on a spot beyond my shoulder. "Dad's been begging me for years to come home, be a father to my boys." His fingers tighten around his coffee mug. "I always gave him the same answer—couldn't do it, not while the bottle had me. So yeah, we stayed in touch. Mom too. But they've kept me a ghost to my own sons. No questions, no explanations. Buried the subject. Suited me fine."

"Why England of all places?" I ask.

"My Uncle Thomas lives there. Took me in without question."

"And Joseph was okay with that arrangement?"

His mouth twists. "My father and his brother Thomas started with nothing—Scottish orphans. Dad came to

America chasing dollars. Thomas stayed in the UK, moving from Scotland to England. While my father built empires, Thomas built fences. Tended his land. Lives in a stone cottage that hasn't changed in a century." He traces a circle on the table with his finger. "Thomas thought Dad sold his soul for mansions and sports cars. Dad thought Thomas wasted his life milking cows and watching seasons change. Thirty years without a phone call between them." He looks up, eyes hollow. "Yet when I showed up drunk on Thomas's doorstep, he just handed me a blanket and never mentioned the whiskey on my breath."

I smile. "So Thomas is the black sheep of the family? Like Ewan Roy on *Succession*?" I love *Succession*, and on that show, Logan Roy is the media titan and billionaire. His brother Ewan is anti-wealth and an environmentalist and doesn't get along with Logan because the two men are fundamentally opposed to how the other lives.

He returns my smile. "You could say that. Uncle Thomas rejected everything about Dad's world. He's content with his dairy farm in the English countryside, knows all the locals by name. Thinks billionaires are just glorified thieves who never pay their fair share. Dad won't even mention his name anymore—can't stand knowing there's someone out there who sees through all the mansions and private jets to what he really is."

I nod. "If Thomas thought Joseph was morally bankrupt from chasing wealth, how did he feel about your sons being raised by him?" I ask.

He shrugs. "Thomas hated it, but what choice did we have? I couldn't raise them." His eyes drift toward the window. "He just prayed Dad's values wouldn't rub off on the boys." He turns back to me. "You don't think they did, do you?"

"From what I've seen, no," I say. "I'm not close with them, but they seem grounded, despite all they've achieved."

He nods. "One's got an Oscar on his mantle, another saves lives in the OR, five run companies, and another fills stadiums." A wistful smile crosses his face. "More success than any father deserves, really."

"They've certainly made their mark professionally," I say.

"But how are they doing emotionally?" he asks. "I haven't spoken to Dad since I came to California, so I don't really know what's been happening with them these past few months."

I shrug. "I only know Max well. Truthfully, he's devastated by your absence. I can't say how the others feel—I only hear so much—but Max has always told me how much he wants you back in his life."

He lowers his head. "I know. Guilt's been my shadow all these years."

"So why return now?" I press. "You've been gone this whole time. What changed?"

He exhales. "I'm tired of running. I want to meet my sons, but I can't quit drinking."

I reach out and touch his hand. "Do you need help? Can I help you stop? More importantly, are you ready?"

He nods. "If I wasn't ready, I wouldn't be here. But I don't know where to start. I know I should go to Alcoholics Anonymous meetings—I've even looked up some locally—but something's holding me back."

"Would it help if someone went with you?" I suggest. "Maybe Max and I—"

He shakes his head emphatically. "No. Not Max, or any of my sons. I don't want them to see me until I'm sober and whole. And if you tell Max you've seen me, I'll just go back to England and stay with Uncle Thomas."

I nod, resolve settling in. Max helped me by financing Mom's experimental treatment. Now I'll step in to help Max reconnect with his father. It seems Michael's willing to attend meetings if he has support—and I'll be there with him. I'll go to those meetings, pray he recovers, and hope he can reunite with Max and his brothers.

I lean forward. "I could go with you. To the meetings."

His eyes light up. "Really? I know we barely know each other, but there's something about you—" He pauses, searching for words. "Something trustworthy. Would you do that? Help me stay on track? I want my sons back in my life. I'm ready this time." His voice cracks on the last word.

I reach across and place my hand over his weathered one. "I'll help you."

"But Max can't know," he says quickly. "Not yet."

"He'll wonder where I'm disappearing to every evening."

Michael's face falls. "I'm putting you in a terrible position."

I bite my lip, weighing the options. Telling Max means risking Michael fleeing back to England. Lying to Max means betraying his trust. The scale tips easily—Max deserves a chance to reconnect with his father, even if I have to manufacture late nights at the office for a while.

I glance at my watch. "When do the meetings start and end?"

"Seven to nine," Michael says.

"That means I won't be home until almost ten each night."

"Just for the first few weeks," he says, leaning forward. "Until I get my footing in recovery. Then I can scale back to two or three meetings a week." His eyes search mine. "Is that going to be an issue?"

"Not at all," I say, the lie sticking in my throat. "I'll tell Max I'm working late."

Michael's weathered hand covers mine. "You're somebody special, you know that? Helping a stranger like this."

I shake my head. "I'm not just doing it for you. I'm doing it for your sons—for Max and his brothers. For your parents too." I meet his gaze. "They deserve to see you sober. They deserve to have you present in their lives again."

As I jog home, a knot forms in my stomach. Max isn't stupid. How long before my nightly "work sessions" raise suspicions? This could explode in my face.

I take a deep breath and push the thought away.

Chapter Forty-Five

CELESTE

That Monday, I accompany Michael Kensington to his first AA meeting. I phone Max with a fabricated story about an urgent project with Elaine keeping me at the office until ten. I cushion the news that this late schedule will continue for two weeks. Michael's decades-long relationship with the bottle means he'll need fourteen consecutive nights of meetings before we can scale back to a few sessions weekly.

Is that realistic? I'm not sure, but it's my hope. I'll repeat the work excuse to Max, day after day, explaining my delayed homecomings. At least right now, he accepts the excuse without complaint—naturally. His own schedule often stretches well beyond mine. Still, these AA meetings with Michael will disrupt the rhythm Max and I have established. I've grown fond of arriving home by seven, preparing dinner together. Now we'll each be on our own.

Just temporary, I reassure myself. This won't damage what Max and I have built.

The church basement in Topanga Canyon is already filling with people when I arrive at 7 o'clock. I spot Michael immediately—hunched on a hard plastic chair, head hanging down, coffee cup trembling between his palms. The violent shaking in his hands makes my chest tighten, though I recognize it as progress. Withdrawal, not intoxication.

I slide into the empty seat beside him, reaching into my bag for the provisions I'd packed: a Lara bar dense with dates and cherries, and a small jar of macadamia nuts. While the donuts and coffee being offered might temporarily comfort him, what his recovering body needed was real nutrition—healthy fats to stabilize his crashing blood sugar.

"Here," I whisper, pressing them into his quivering hands. "Eat something."

His eyes meet mine, relief washing over his face. "You came," he says softly. "I convinced myself you wouldn't."

I squeeze his arm gently. "I said I would, didn't I?"

The room fills quickly with people from all walks of life. Once everyone is seated, Miguel, the meeting leader, calls the group to order. We all rise, join hands, and recite the serenity prayer in unison. The words hang in the air like a promise.

"Welcome, everyone," Miguel says warmly. "Any first-timers tonight?"

Michael raises his hand tentatively alongside a few others. Miguel acknowledges them with a nod. "As is our tradition, we'll hear from our newcomers first, if you're comfortable sharing."

After two others speak, Michael's turn arrives. Miguel's voice softens. "No pressure to share, but we're here to listen if you'd like to."

Michael inhales deeply, his chest expanding with the effort. "My name is Michael," he begins, voice barely above a whisper, "and I'm an alcoholic. Twenty-four hours sober."

"Hello, Michael," the room responds, their voices a gentle chorus of understanding.

Encouraged by their warm reception, he continues. "I never touched a drop until my wife passed. Not one. My mother's parents both died of liver failure before I was born. I'd read somewhere that addiction often skips generations, so I always suspected I might be... susceptible. That one drink might be all it would take for me."

Heads bob around the circle. Miguel leans forward. "Science is catching up to what many of us have always felt. That predisposition you sensed in yourself? Researchers are finding genetic markers for it now."

Michael's shoulders curl inward as he nods assent to what Miguel just pointed out. "I avoided it for years. Just... knew somehow." His voice drops to a rasp. "After my wife died, everything collapsed. There I was—thirty years old with eight boys looking to me—and all I could think about was ending it." His knuckles whiten around his coffee cup. "The bottle became my only barrier between living and... not. Sober, I'd find myself staring at my shotgun. Drunk, I could at least push that thought away for a few hours."

A chill runs through me. I'd known about his dark thoughts, but hearing him speak so plainly about the shotgun, about how close he'd come—it hollows me out.

Michael's voice grows steadier as he continues, detailing his abandonment of his sons, the crushing weight of that choice, and his recent decision that redemption required facing them again. For thirty minutes, he lays himself bare. When he finally falls silent, the room responds—voices rising one after another with gentle affirmations. "You're exactly where you need to be," murmurs a gray-haired woman. "The first step is the hardest," adds a man with weathered hands.

Others share next—some newcomers with raw confessions, but mostly regulars offering updates on jobs regained, relationships mended, temptations resisted. The meeting closes with everyone standing, forming an unbroken circle of clasped hands for the serenity prayer. As the formal structure dissolves into casual conversation, Michael hangs back, watching the others talking to one another with a mixture of longing and hesitation.

Relief floods through me as several people approach Michael to tell him how good it was for him to join them. Then a man with salt-and-pepper hair, a worn Dodgers' cap and steady hands extends his palm.

"Greg. Ten years dry," he says, his voice carrying the weight of someone who's walked through fire. "Everyone needs a lifeline when the cravings hit. I could be yours."

Michael's shoulders drop an inch as they exchange contacts. Greg presses a business card into Michael's palm with a firm grip.

"Call before you pour," Greg says. "Someone did it for me back when I couldn't see past the next hour. Changed everything."

Michael nods and puts his hand on Greg's shoulder. "Thank you," he says quietly. "I'll definitely take you up on it."

Outside, the night air hits our faces as we leave the church. Streetlights catch the sheen of sweat still on Michael's forehead.

"That took courage," I tell him, my voice soft. "Twenty-four hours is huge. Tomorrow I'll bring proper food—protein, something substantial."

Michael's eyes, clearer than I've seen them, meet mine. "You being here was enough."

"Maybe," I say, watching his hands still trembling slightly. "But your body needs fuel to rebuild."

I'm prepared when I meet him the next night. His protests can't hide the truth—a man living in his car isn't eating properly. Despite getting home at eleven after lingering at Michael's first meeting, I still stayed up chopping vegetables and browning meat.

During the break, I hand him the ceramic crock, still warm through the dish towel I've wrapped around it. Steam escapes when he lifts the lid—a rich aroma of grass-fed beef swimming alongside carrots, sweet potatoes, and tomatoes. I've added broccoli florets and asparagus tips too—unconventional additions, but the extra greens will do him good. The bag of apples comes next, shiny and firm.

He thinks me profusely, then doesn't speak as he takes the first spoonful, then another, then another. The hollow places in his cheeks seem to fill as I watch. My chest tightens. Soon we'll need to talk about proper shelter, but for now, this is enough.

After weighing my options, I've decided the most practical solution is securing him an extended-stay accommodation. I've already reserved a Marriott suite for the next month—my screenwriting career has made it possible for me to pay for this room, which has a small dining table where he can enjoy the meals I'll prepare.

I wait until after the meeting to mention it. His reaction is exactly what I anticipated.

"This is too much," he insists, shaking his head. "Your time alone is a gift. And this meal..." He gestures at his empty plate. "I can't accept anything more."

I meet his gaze directly. "This isn't negotiable, Michael. Recovery requires stability—a safe environment, proper nutrition, consistent support. I'm providing those things."

My motivation isn't entirely selfless. Behind my closed eyelids, I envision Max embracing his father, the Kensington family whole again. That reconciliation would heal so many wounds.

Michael can only focus on surviving each sober day. But I'm looking further ahead, picturing the reunion he can't yet imagine for himself. That vision has become everything to me.

Michael transforms with each passing week. The grey pallor fades from his cheeks, replaced by a healthy flush. His freshly cut hair frames a face that's begun to look familiar—Max's eyes, Ansel's jawline. The threadbare clothes are gone, replaced with simple but clean button-downs from Goodwill that he wears with a quiet dignity.

At 2 AM, while Max sleeps, I slip from our bed to the kitchen. My bare feet pad silently across the cool tile as I prepare containers of homemade chicken stew, kale salad with cranberries, and apple tarts with cinnamon-laced crusts. I leave no evidence behind—wiping down counters, washing every dish—this secret mission of nourishment that I can't yet share with my husband.

Last night, Michael mentioned Max's childhood baseball trophy. "I wasn't there when he won it," he said, his voice steady but his fingers trembling around his coffee mug. The way he spoke his son's name—tentative, reverent—told me everything. Soon, I'll witness them in the same room, these two men with the same eyes, same hands, same laugh. And when that day comes, I'll need tissues. Lots of them.

Some stories deserve their happy endings. This one will have its.

Chapter Forty-Six

CELESTE

Six weeks into our AA journey together, Michael calls me. "Let me take you to dinner," he says. "My treat. I've got some things I want to discuss."

I hesitate. "Michael, you don't have to spend money on me."

"Actually, I can now." His voice brightens. "Thanks to you, I landed a job at Whole Foods in Malibu. Minimum wage, but that's nearly seventeen bucks an hour. First paycheck just came through, and I want to celebrate. Plus..." He pauses. "I'm thinking it might be time to reconnect with my sons."

My pulse quickens. Could this be the breakthrough we've been waiting for? I try to keep my voice steady. "That sounds wonderful. But let's keep it reasonable—you should be saving."

We settle on Kristy's Malibu—casual enough for his budget but with those gorgeous ocean views I adore. I've already decided on one of their flatbreads—under twenty-five dollars and absolutely worth every penny, unlike that fifty-seven-dollar lobster linguini they're famous for.

So I meet him at Kristy's Malibu that Friday night. The restaurant perches on a craggy bluff overlooking Zuma Beach, its weathered cedar shingles and white trim reminiscent of a Nantucket boathouse. We're seated at a corner table on the intimate deck where strings of Edison bulbs sway gently in the salt-tinged breeze. It's late May, and the evening air carries that perfect California crispness—not quite summer warmth, but far from chilly. The hostess mentions the sun will set at 7:30, and I can't help but smile. We make it by 7, and I manage to get my hands on a frosty glass of Sauvignon Blanc just as the sun starts its descent into the Pacific, painting the horizon in shades of liquid pink, purple and gold.

When I arrive, Michael wraps me in a bear hug that nearly lifts me off my feet. The transformation stuns me. Gone is the gaunt, disheveled man I first met. His once-hollow cheeks now have a healthy fullness, his shoulders broader beneath a crisp button-down that he later tells me came from Goodwill. "Got these jeans there too," he says with a hint of pride, smoothing his hands over denim that fits him perfectly.

I smile, remembering my own pre-Max days of hunting treasures at Plato's Closet and various thrift shops. His green eyes—Max's eyes—meet mine, clear and alert where they once were bloodshot and vacant. When he laughs at something I say, I catch myself staring. The years seem to have fallen away from him; he could easily be mistaken for Max's older brother rather than his father. But what strikes me most is what's missing: that sour cloud of whiskey that once surrounded him like a second skin.

We take a table on the patio, settling into wrought iron chairs. The server appears, pen poised.

"Sparkling water with lime, please," I say, my usual order when I'm out. Plain water feels too frugal, alcohol isn't what I want, and I've sworn off sodas entirely.

Michael echoes my order, then hesitates. "Unless you'd prefer wine?" He gestures toward me with an open palm. "I should practice being around temptation anyway. That's what my sponsor calls it—the dragon in the room."

I shake my head. Michael insists I can order wine, but his sobriety ribbon is barely frayed at the edges. Why dangle temptation? "Just Evian with lime for me," I say, squeezing his hand, then brushing my fingers against his smooth cheek. I just can't stop looking at him. The change is just unbelievable.

Then the unmistakable click of a phone camera freezes me mid-caress. I don't need to look to know who it is.

Elody Martin. My stomach drops. There she is, the woman who graced Max's table months ago when we first met—the woman I barely registered then beyond a starstruck moment. With her cascade of honey-blonde hair catching the light and that trademark emerald gaze sweeping the room, she embodies everything Hollywood worships. Three Oscars on her mantel. Her face plastered across Chanel billboards worldwide.

Any other night, I'd be fumbling for my phone to sneak a discreet photo. Not tonight. Not with what I now know about her and Max. They dated for about six months three years ago, and the gossip blogs have documented her continued obsession with Max since their break-up—the lingering touches at premieres, the "accidental" vacation overlaps, the thinly veiled quotes in *Vanity Fair* about "the one who got away."

She wants him back and would do anything to accomplish this, which would mean that she would do anything to break up my "marriage" to Max. And that photo of Michael and me—my hand tenderly against his cheek, my eyes soft with affection—would be the perfect weapon. One strategic leak and suddenly I'm the cheating wife. One more day of digging and they'll discover Michael isn't just any man but Max's estranged father. The tabloid perfect storm that would follow would destroy everything.

By midnight, my innocent gesture will be the headline on *TMZ*. I can already see it—the photo of my hand resting on his, my fingers grazing his stubbled cheek. The tabloids won't care that I'm just being me, the same woman who hugs baristas and touches friends' arms mid-conversation. They'll only see Max Kensington's "wife" with another man. Three seconds of normal human connection, and tomorrow I'll be branded as the billionaire's unfaithful bride. *Stupid, stupid, stupid.* I should know better by now - every innocent gesture will be misconstrued.

She flashes those bleached teeth at me—that same smile I've seen in all her movies, now in front of me, and I'd do anything to get them out of my sight. The woman didn't win three Teen Choice Awards for nothing; that flawless face can manufacture sincerity faster than a Chinese knockoff factory.

I flatten my palms against the table and flash her my most practiced Hollywood smile. *Game on, bitch.* "Elody," I say, then glance at Michael, my stomach knotting. If his connection to Max gets out, he'll be trending by dinner. That meat grinder would be brutal to him - the comments, the memes, the vicious speculation - I can see it all now. Michael's only six weeks sober. He wouldn't survive it.

"Well," she coos, her voice like honey, yet extremely insincere. "Look at you!" Her violet eyes—colored contacts, I'd bet my next royalty check on it—dart between Michael and me and then back again. "Celeste, aren't you going to introduce me?"

Shit. "Elody," I say, catching Michael's eye. Recognition flickers there; of course he knows who she is. The world's biggest actress and entertainment's most notorious gossip vulture. "Why don't you and I step outside for a minute?" I arch one eyebrow to Michael, trying to telegraph my desperation. I need five minutes alone with her to negotiate, bribe, whatever it takes. One viral photo, and Michael's name would be everywhere by nightfall. The tabloids would have his backstory before breakfast, and he'd be reaching for a bottle before the first comment calling him "deadbeat dad" hit the internet.

And Elody's Instagram following is practically its own country—half a billion people who hang on her every post. One tap of her perfectly manicured finger, and that photo goes live. Five minutes later, Michael and I might as well be trending on every gossip site from here to Tokyo. The photo wouldn't have the proper context, of course. This bitch would supply the context, and it'll be whatever she makes up in her head.

She tilts her head like a predator who's just spotted a limping gazelle. My thoughts scatter in panic. *Shit. Shit. Shit.* Michael deserves to reunite with his sons on his terms, not because some viral photo forced his hand. I squeeze my eyes shut and imagine tomorrow's headlines if Elody releases that picture—me holding Michael's weathered hand, my fingers gentle against his cheek, my expression so tender anyone would assume we're lovers. The truth is simpler and more complicated: I've watched this broken man fight for sobriety day by day, victory by painful victory. I've become his cheerleader, yes, but not for my own ego. This is the one gift I can offer Max after everything he's done for me—the experimental treatment that saved my mother, the connections that launched my writing career. Why must I justify this one act of gratitude to Elody and her vulture audience?

I catch Michael's eye and tilt my head slightly. "Would you mind if Elody and I had a moment?"

Michael reads my expression and nods with an understanding smile.

"Elody, shall we take a walk down to the shore?"

She glances at her feet, where four-inch Prada heels gleam in the patio lights. "These cost more than your car, I'm sure," she says with a grimace. "The parking lot works just fine. My car's parked out there."

I nod silently and trail behind her to the parking lot. She stops beside a gleaming silver Aston Martin Vantage convertible, the price tag of which probably exceeds 10 years of my annual salary at Dreamscape. When she swings the passenger door open, her "Get in" sounds less like an invitation and more like a command from the mob princess character she played in Scorsese's latest film. As I slide into the buttery leather seat, I can't help but wonder if this ride ends with me wearing concrete footwear at the bottom of the Pacific. *Better keep that thought to yourself.*

I meet her gaze. "Is there any possibility you might keep that photo to yourself instead of blasting it across every tabloid website and to your Insta followers?"

Her eyes narrow to slits. "None whatsoever," she says. "Max Kensington and I had six perfect months together. Six months that changed everything for me." She leans closer, voice dropping. "I still see myself as his endgame. And now you have evidence that you're cheating on him?" A laugh escapes her, sharp as broken glass. "And you thought I'd keep your little secret? You really have no idea who you're dealing with."

My voice drops to a whisper. "Name your price. What would it take to keep that photo private?"

She examines her French manicure, tilting her hand to catch the light. "I've uncovered your little secret." Her eyes flick up to mine. "Do you have any idea how many nights I spent trying to understand? Max—brilliant, gorgeous Max, the man I'm absolutely in love with—choosing someone like you?" She gestures at me with a dismissive flick of her wrist, her lip curling. "Then I discovered the truth. Your marriage is nothing but theater. Old Joe blackmailed his own grandson with his livelihood. One word from Granddad to those ancient board members he plays golf with every Sunday, and Max loses everything. Just—" She snaps her fingers inches from my face. "Like that."

My stomach drops like an elevator with cut cables. Of course Elody wouldn't let this go—she's like a terrier with a bone. Plus, someone talked. Max swore the board members all knew but signed those ironclad NDAs—breach one and kiss a few million goodbye. Still, money talks, but secrets walk. I rack my brain for who else might have spilled. Whoever it was, I've got to admit—Elody nailed us dead to rights.

I decide honesty is my only option. "Fine," I say, crossing my arms. "You clearly know something. What's your price for keeping that photo off social media?"

"That man," she says, leaning forward. "He's practically Max's twin, just older." Her eyes narrow to slits. "Are you sleeping with your husband's father behind his back?"

Shit. This woman misses nothing. "Max hasn't seen or

spoken to his father in over twenty years." Technically true. The complete story? Hardly. But I haven't actually lied to her face.

She taps her foot impatiently. "I'm well-versed in the saga of Max and his runaway dad. But that man? He's Max in three decades. The resemblance is... striking."

My throat constricts. I picture Michael being thrust into a reunion he never planned for, or fleeing back to his uncle's farm to escape the tabloid frenzy. Michael wouldn't stand a chance. The careful reunion I've been orchestrating between him and his sons dissolves before my eyes. Elody's no fool. Without the truth from me, she'll unearth it herself and plaster it across every headline. Michael's newfound sobriety hangs by a thread too delicate for this kind of exposure.

What demons lurk in Michael's past across the pond? Two decades drowning in whiskey doesn't leave clean hands. I imagine hotel rooms he can't remember leaving, names forgotten by morning, maybe visits to sex workers, perhaps nights in holding cells—all waiting to become tomorrow's headlines. I'm not privy to his specific sins, but we all have chapters we'd rather keep unread. Michael likely has volumes, and Elody won't stop until she's devoured every word. Her network stretches into corners I didn't know existed. He's never whispered his worst moments to me between sobriety chips. Of course he hasn't. We all build walls around our darkest selves. But if those walls come crashing down...

I exhale slowly. "Name your price."

She leans forward. "You know the Dreamscape-Kensington merger is almost finalized, right?" Her eyes narrow to slits. "Ever wonder why I haven't leaked your little arrangement to *Page Six*?"

The thought hadn't crossed my mind until now. But now that she mentions it - why would someone like her—who clearly despises me—sit on Hollywood's juiciest scandal of the year?

"No," I say quietly. "Why?"

"Max." Her voice softens for the first time. "If this got out—the real reason behind your marriage—those share-holders would pull support faster than you can say 'unfit for leadership.' They'd never let someone so..." she pauses, searching for the word, "...impulsive take the helm of a billion-dollar company. He'd lose everything." She taps her designer purse. "So I've kept your dirty little secret. For him."

"Thank you," I say, bowing my head.

She leans in close, her voice dropping to a venomous whisper. "Trust me, I've lost sleep thinking about exposing your little charade. You know those gossip sites that publish anonymous celebrity dirt, blind items they call them? *Crazy Days and Nights* would have eaten this up. One email from me, and your precious arrangement would've been the biggest blind item of all time and trust me, the sleuths on that site would've figured it out in no time. But I restrained myself. Aren't you lucky?"

I lean forward, my knuckles white against the edge of the table. "Let's not waste time here. Name your price."

She taps her phone screen with a crimson fingernail, the photo of Michael and me glowing between us. Her lips curl into something that isn't quite a smile.

"I want to see moving trucks at that Malibu house the day after the merger closes." She examines her manicure, tilting her hand to catch the light. "*TMZ* will need those divorce papers by the following Monday." The phone disappears into her Hermès bag. "Nothing messy until after Max gets that CEO title, of course. The board hates... instability."

She looks away from me. Maybe she secretly feels bad about what she's doing. Probably not. But I use her moment to look away as a chance to snatch her wallet from her purse. I need her address for future reference. Don't ask me why I want her address, but it's just something I think I might need. So I nervously look at her driver's license and commit the address to memory before slipping the wallet back in her purse. Then I take out my phone and I hurriedly put her address into my contacts.

She finally looks back at me, not suspecting what I did, and I swallow hard. "And if I don't divorce Max?"

Her eyes narrow to slits. "Cross me at your own risk." She gives a dismissive head shake. "That man with you? Max's father—no question about it. Same eyes. Same smile that pulls you in. Same posture that makes it look like he owns the room." She leans closer. "His sudden reappearance? That's headline material. And you're *desperate* to protect that man. Makes me wonder why." Her gaze sharpens, calculating. "Whatever it is, I'll uncover it. By next week, his face will be splashed across every gossip site from here to New York." She taps a manicured nail against her temple. "Screenwriting isn't just about dialogue—it's about spotting the story nobody else sees. Finding the soft underbelly." Her lips curl into something between a smile and a sneer. "I'm exceptionally good at that part."

I shake my head. She's a screenwriter on top of everything else? No wonder she pieced together Michael's identity so quickly. It takes a certain kind of person to notice the small details that make characters feel real—the slight tremor in someone's hand, the way they avoid eye contact when lying. She has that gift. Too bad she's using it like a weapon. I can see it in the calculated stillness of her expression—she'll tear Michael apart piece by piece if I don't give her exactly what she wants.

Her eyes narrow as she leans in. "And Celeste? That man's secrets won't stay buried for long. I'll dig them up, or if I come up empty..." She taps a manicured nail against the table. "Well, I've always had quite the imagination." The corner of her mouth lifts in a self-satisfied smirk.

My eyes burn as I blink back tears. God, Michael doesn't deserve this. Michael's sobriety hangs by a thread, his gentle spirit already so damaged. I remember Michael's trembling voice at the AA meeting, how he admitted that without the numbing fog of whiskey, the thoughts of ending it all became too clear, too possible. The gun in his nightstand drawer had called to him every sober night. One public humiliation could shatter the fragile peace he's built, brick by painful brick.

I nod. "Okay. I'll divorce Max after the merger." Outside the window of her Aston Martin, the parking lot teems with happy people heading into the restaurant. Happy couples, like Max and me. I sigh.

Then again, a divorce was always the plan, wasn't it? This was always a business arrangement with an expiration date. I should view it as a contract fulfilled, not a heart broken. Yet somewhere between our first horrible dinner and last night's shared laughter, I'd started collecting moments like seashells—tiny treasures of possibility. I'd catch myself wondering if Max might want to extend our arrangement...indefinitely. I thought maybe the merger deadline might pass without either of us mentioning divorce. Now I know better. The fantasy ends here, and I'll be the one filing the papers.

Her smile makes my fingers curl into fists. Those beautiful and magnetic eyes, the ones on every magazine cover—I could claw them out. I could text *TMZ* right now with the truth about America's Sweetheart. The articles nauseate me: how she spends weekends at homeless shelters (photo ops, nothing more), how even the lowest crew members adore her (probably paid off to give her good reports to the sites). The stories about her unfailing politeness, her perfect memory for fan names. Whoever manages her public image deserves a Nobel Prize in fiction. They've transformed this viper into a saint, and not one person sees through it but me.

Well, Max probably sees through it, too. Which is why they broke up.

I tilt my head. "Planning to boil any rabbits soon?" Her eyes flash with something unhinged—pure Glenn Close as Alex Forrest in the movie *Fatal Attraction*, turning a lamp on and off while staring into space. I can picture her apartment now: Max's photo with pins jabbed through his eyes, candles burning while she sobs to her publicist on speakerphone between consultations with her psychic. Poor thing doesn't realize the truth yet. He'll never be hers. When I'm gone, she'll still be standing outside in the rain, watching his windows go dark. The thought curls my lips upward. Neither of us gets the prize, but at least we'll be equally miserable. Small victories.

She lets out a cold laugh, her eyes flashing. "Call me obsessed if you want. Maybe I am." She leans in, voice dropping. "But with you gone, I can resume my real project." Her perfectly manicured fingers form air quotes. "Operation Marry Max." Her lips curl into a smile that doesn't reach her eyes. "Just picture the headlines—Academy Award winner, hottest actress in the world and the face of Chanel paired with Hollywood's most eligible billionaire studio head. We'd rule this town." She straightens, tossing her hair. "No one would even remember your name."

No lie detected there. "Okay. You'll get your wish. Now, can I please go? My friend will be wondering where I am."

She flicks her wrist dismissively. "Get out. But listen carefully, Celeste. When the merger closes, I want those divorce papers filed within a week. Otherwise..." She waves her phone at me, screen displaying the photo. "One tap, and this cozy moment with Max's estranged father goes viral. *TMZ, Perez Hilton, Page Six*—they'll all have it before dinner. And my Instagram?" Her perfectly manicured finger hovered over the share button. "Five hundred million people hanging on my every word, Celeste. I can craft whatever narrative I want around this little family reunion."

She raises her palm when I open my mouth to lie that Michael is not Max's father. "Save it. The resemblance is obvious. I'm guessing there's some pathetic reason he abandoned his family. One whiff of scandal—real or invented—might just push him back into whatever hole he crawled out of. And I'm perfectly willing to test that theory."

I nod. Defeated. God, what I wouldn't give for some Sopranos-style justice right now—Elody in designer cement shoes at the bottom of the Pacific. But that's not how this works. She's Hollywood royalty with the power to crush anyone who crosses her, and right now she's gunning for Michael. Sweet, gentle, fragile Michael who's hanging onto his sobriety by a gossamer thread. She's not wrong—I *am* protecting him. I've watched him fight for every sober day, seen how badly he wants to make things right with Max. So here I am, about to do the hardest thing I've ever done. It's going to break me into a million pieces, but at least it's for something that matters, right? That has to count for something. Because I'm choosing to give up the man I love—and God, do I love Max—to save his father. The father he's been missing since he was seven years old. The reunion he's needed his entire life.

Even if it means I can't be part of it.

Chapter Forty-Seven

MAX

The ink is dry. At last. Twelve months of boardroom battles, legal wrangling, and terms that ping-ponged between parties like a tennis match. Dreamscape balked, then Kensington wavered, then back again. The merger nearly collapsed a dozen times when someone would toss in an eleventh-hour demand. But we survived the tightrope walk. Kensington emerged the victor in the fine print, but the real win is what we've created: Dreamscape's indie credibility that dominates Sundance and Cannes now stands alongside Kensington's Academy Award and box office blockbuster pedigree. We've built a juggernaut. And, most important, the board members have voted me CEO of the merged company. Time to exhale. Time to steal away with Celeste to Paris, where I'll open French doors to a terrace view of the Eiffel Tower, order champagne with our croissants, lose ourselves in each other, and ask her the question that's been burning in my pocket—to be my wife not just on paper, but in truth.

Christ, I've fallen for her completely. The old man knew

what he was doing all along. Should've trusted him from the start. The attraction hit me like lightning that first moment I saw her, but loving her? That came later, in all the small moments. In watching her fight like hell for her family. In reading pages of her screenplay that left me breathless. In tasting that pasta she makes with three kinds of exotic mushrooms. In the way her nose crinkles right before she breaks into that laugh—the same laugh that erupts when we both catch the same stupid joke no one else gets. In how she sobbed through that children's book about the stupid giving tree, clutching it to her chest when I'd asked for a bedtime story as a joke. How she tears up watching sentimental commercials and sobs in her approximately 150th rewatching of the movie *Beaches* - she cries every damn time she watches that movie, which amazes me, because she has the dialogue memorized so of course she knows how it'll end. In her refusing to give up after falling off the surfboard for the twentieth time. In her fierce debates about wealth gaps and ocean acidification that would make my grandfather disown her if he heard. And yes, even in those ridiculous Tarot cards she shuffles when she thinks I'm not looking. All of it. She's going to be my wife—my real wife this time.

Valentina bursts into my office, champagne bottle in one hand, two flutes dangling from the fingers of the other. "The votes are in, Mr. CEO," she announces, her glossy red lips spreading into a grin. The cork pops with a satisfying thunk against the ceiling. "I told everyone you were a lock." She fills the glasses, pushing one toward me across the desk. "Iris can handle things for a week. When's the last time you saw a beach that wasn't through your office window? You've earned some time off." Iris Dimas, CEO of Dreamscape, is the deputy CEO of the new company, which I knew she would be.

Damn right I earned this. After all those endless days hunched over contracts, the tension headaches, waking up in cold sweats thinking the whole deal was imploding. Just thinking about escaping with Celeste makes my shoulders unknot. Even if we only have three days, they'll be three perfect days away from everything.

I can't help but smile mysteriously. "Let's just say I have something special planned," I tell her, thinking about Celeste's reaction to my Paris property. I can already picture her face when I present her with that ornate brass key. Wait until she sees it—the entire top floor of that classic building with its stone railings and intricate ironwork. The way the morning light hits the herbs on the wraparound terrace. Those perfect wooden floors inside catching the sparkle from the chandeliers overhead. And that view—the Eiffel Tower framed in every window, glowing amber as the day ends, close enough to feel like our own private light show.

Then me, kneeling before her, holding a ring I know was made for her. The stone catches light like nothing else—a rare pink diamond nestled in a vintage setting that reminds me of her grandmother's jewelry she once described. I've given her diamonds before—blues, yellows, even other pinks—all beautiful, all created in labs. But this one came from earth, from time and pressure, and is extremely rare in its perfection. When the auctioneer at Christie's brought down the gavel at $2.5 million, I didn't flinch. Three perfect carats that make my pulse quicken every time I imagine sliding it onto her finger.

Hours later, I'm humming in my car, picturing the look on her face when I reveal the private jet waiting to take us to Paris. Maybe I'll even blindfold her for the big reveal. It's cheesy, I know, but Celeste thrives on cheese. This is the woman who marathons those Hallmark Christmas movies and still manages to sob at the predictable endings. I've watched her wipe away tears a hundred times when the small-town baker finally kisses the big-city executive who's rediscovered the "true meaning of Christmas." Pure formula, but she falls for it every.single.time. My sweet, soft-hearted Celeste deserves her own movie moment.

I push open the front door to find Celeste in the living room, surrounded by stacked cardboard boxes. Her eyes are red-rimmed, mascara smudged at the corners. When she looks up at me, her shoulders slump forward like she's carrying something too heavy. "So," she whispers, voice cracking slightly, "congratulations on the CEO position. Heard about the merger going through today." She forces a smile that doesn't reach her eyes. "Guess that means our arrangement is complete."

I blink, stunned. "Wait—you think this is over now that the board voted me in?" The weight in my chest drops straight to the floor. I search her face, desperate for some sign I've misunderstood. But of course she'd think that. Our arrangement had a clear endpoint: merger complete, CEO position secured. I'd never once told her I wanted more. We'd never discussed what comes after. But did we need to discuss it? All these months of morning coffee, dancing in our kitchen and late-night script readings, of her falling asleep against my shoulder—I'd just assumed she felt what I felt. That she knew I couldn't imagine my life without her now.

She shakes her head, eyes cast downward. "Max. We're kidding ourselves here. People like you don't end up with people like me. Not in real life."

"Stop." I place my hands on her shoulders. "Don't you

dare finish that thought. I won't let you stand there telling me what I deserve, when what I want—what I need—is standing right in front of me."

Celeste's eyes drops to her hands. "Max, I'm begging you. Don't drag this out." Her voice catches. "These months with you... I never expected..." She swallows hard. "But we're kidding ourselves. Out there—" she gestures towards the window, towards the world beyond my house, "—out there, someone is waiting for you. Someone who makes sense." Her lips curve into a smile that doesn't reach her eyes. "You'll forget all about this by Christmas." Then she looks down at the floor. "I can't stay married to you, Max. I don't love you and you don't love me. We both deserve something real."

I squeeze my eyes shut. Her words—*I don't love you and you don't love me. We both deserve something real*—cuts through me like shrapnel. The old nightmare returns, the one I've dreaded since this began. Just a business arrangement after all. A marriage as counterfeit as a Rolex being sold out of a back-alley van in Tijuana.

She's leaving, just like my father did, tearing open wounds I'd convinced myself had scarred over. I thought she was different. *What a fool.*

My ribs seem to cave in on themselves as I'm dragged back to that seven-year-old boy, nose pressed to the window-pane, breath clouding glass, waiting for someone who never returned. I clawed my way out of that abyss once. I can't do it again. Ice spreads through my veins, hardening around what's left of my heart. Thicker armor this time. Impenetrable. *Let her go.* I won't become the shadow chasing her car down the driveway. I refuse to mirror my grandparents, pleading on their knees for someone whose mind is already made up.

I snap my eyes open, my vision tunneling to pinpoints. "Get. The. FUCK. Out." My voice is a razor. "Take those boxes if you want, but touch one goddamn thing I bought you and I'll destroy you. I'm going through every inch of that closet—every thread, every heel, every diamond—and if anything's missing, I swear to God I will bury you in legal fees until you're living in your car. Everything in those pathetic little boxes better be only the things you dragged into this nightmare of a marriage, or you'll see exactly what I'm capable of."

"Max, I-"

"OUT!" My voice shatters against the walls. Blood rushes to my face as I slam my fist into the doorframe, splintering the wood. "I can't stand the fucking sight of you." My chest heaves, lungs burning with each breath. I step toward her, trembling with restraint. "Take your goddamn boxes and get out before I throw them into the ocean myself. Tomorrow I'll have movers collect whatever shit you've left behind. But so help me God, if I ever see your face again —" I choke on the words, knuckles white, jaw clenched so tight I taste metal.

Her tears fall faster now, and I have to look away. Each sob feels like a knife between my ribs. I can almost hear the wet thud of my heart hitting the floor, can almost see her heel grinding what's left into dust. I built walls. I kept my distance. What was the point when she scaled them anyway? The man I was before her is gone. *Granddad, you bastard.* You pushed me into this marriage knowing exactly what would happen. You knew she'd break me open, and Christ, she has.

Celeste's eyes flicker toward the door. "Goodbye, Max."

The doorbell rings. Tally and Olivia stand on the threshold, avoiding my gaze. My stomach drops. How long has she been orchestrating this exit? The silent parade begins—box after box is carried past me to the U-Haul parked in my driveway. Celeste remains outside, a shadow I glimpse through the window with each trip her friends make. When the last cardboard corner disappears from my house, Tally returns alone. Her hand extends toward mine, cool and formal.

"I'm sorry, Max," she says, her voice soft. "She loves you, you know. She's grateful for everything. She just doesn't believe you two fit together anymore."

By now, I'm numb, like I've taken a right hook to the jaw and the adrenaline's worn off. The anger that kept me standing has drained away, leaving me hollow as a spent shotgun shell.

Chapter Forty-Eight

MAX

From my office window, I survey the sprawling city below—a kingdom at my feet, every skyscraper and street corner subject to my authority. Yet inside me: hollow space. Not grief. Not joy. Just absence. This emptiness has been my constant companion since I was 7 years old, I realize, except for that brief interlude with Celeste. Now the void has returned with sharper edges.

Granddad thought he was doing me a favor by orchestrating my arrangement with Celeste. He couldn't have predicted how quickly it would unravel, leaving my world more colorless than before. I'm not angry with him, though - how could I be? I can barely access emotion at all right now.

The numbness isn't exactly suffering. It's like watching life through an old black-and-white television set. Remember how *The Wizard of Oz* begins? That sepia-toned Kansas farmhouse before the tornado hits? I'd sit there as a kid, impatient, wondering when the promised Technicolor would arrive. With Celeste, I finally saw those vibrant hues.

But black and white is serviceable enough. Really. Everything's perfectly fine.

Valentina, my assistant, peeks her head in. "Max! Great news!"

I swivel in my chair, leaning forward.

"Nolan just signed the contract. Kensington gets his next six films." She sets a small bottle of champagne on my desk—our little ritual whenever something huge goes down. This is the Oscar-winning director, the man behind *Oppenheimer* and a string of blockbusters and awards-season triumphs, pledging himself exclusively to my studio. I've spent years schmoozing, sweetening every deal, and now it's finally sealed—and I feel nothing.

I force a smile. Can't let Valentina think I'm unmoved by this coup. "That's fantastic," I say, trying to sound enthusiastic. I glance at the champagne. "I'll join you later for a toast." Without another word, I turn away, hoping she'll take the hint, and she does. A few seconds later, I hear the door click softly behind her.

A week passes before Gianni stops by. I've been ghosting his texts and skipping our gym sessions—unlike me. Lately I've been chained to the office until midnight, rather than grabbing dinner at the Centurion, hitting the weights with him, then finishing work at home. I hate how fractured my days feel now.

I avoid home because every corner is haunted by Celeste. I see her at the grand piano, plunking out Chopsticks—her only tune—while I followed with Debussy's "Clair de Lune" just because she said it was her favorite. I picture her in the kitchen, chopping vegetables while singing to every song she knows. Her voice was always off-key, but goddamn, she didn't care and that's one of the reasons why I...nope. Not thinking that particular l word.

I see her in the waves on that enormous surfboard, her wetsuit clinging to her curves like the wetsuit was bespoke. I remember hunting down the biggest board I could find, knowing how new she was to the sport. Those first few sessions, she'd hesitate at every wave, eyes wide with a fear she'd never admit to. But that day she finally caught one clean—the look on her face—pure joy. After that, Saturdays became our thing: me, my brothers, Gianni, and her, paddling out as the morning fog burned away.

I see her in my empire-size bed, copper hair fanned across my pillow, the tiny heart-shaped birthmark on her shoulder, the eighteen freckles dancing across her nose. I see her in the screening room, a bowl of popcorn on her lap, snuggled under a blanket against me as we'd watch a movie together. She's everywhere in that house—so I hardly go there.

Gianni calls my name, and I realize I never told him what happened between Celeste and me. "What's going on?"

I shake my head. "Just busy," I say, picking up a pencil and studying the teeth marks on its shaft. I don't usually chew pencils. Somebody else? No, probably me—just not paying attention anymore. "Sorry." That's all I can manage. No apology for ghosting him, no real explanation. If I start talking, the dam will break, so I inhale and hold it in.

"Busy?" He tilts his head. "Seriously—what's up?" Then he sighs. "Come on, Max. It's all over *TMZ*. Has been for a week."

"Celeste filed, then," I reply, shrugging. "Fucking *TMZ*. Can't leave well enough alone."

"It's their business model," Gianni says. "But that's not the point." His dark eyes are worried—concern, not pity, which is good, because pity and I aren't on speaking terms. "Why?"

I shrug again. "Our partnership ended. Contractual obligations discharged. I got my CEO title and got Granddad off my back, so I was done. She was done, too. She didn't make it a year, so no payout—but I doubt that matters anymore." I tap the pencil. "You ever chew your pencils? I never did—now I can't stop."

"Max," he says softly. "We've known each other since you were five. Don't bullshit me. It wasn't just business."

I glance at the clock. "Look at the time. Shit's piling up, as always. Anything else?"

He nods, getting the point. "Alright. I'll be at the gym around eight. Hope you swing by."

"You won't see me," I say. "Too much work. Thanks, though."

Later that night, I do go out—dinner with Elody Martin. She called; I thought, why not? I need someone I don't give a damn about, and I need her spark. We'll be Hollywood's golden couple again—Maxody, the dumb portmanteau social media came up with the last time we dated. I won't feel a thing, just like before, which is the point: Elody never expects emotion, and she'll never care.

So that's exactly what happens. And for the next few weeks we once again become the hottest couple in Tinseltown: billionaire studio boss with the face of Chanel who happens to be the hottest actress in the world. Parties, paparazzi, breaking the internet—I knew it would. After all, this is our "reunion", the "reunion" that apparently lots of her fans have been waiting for with bated breath.

Everything's perfect.

Except I can't enjoy any of it.

Chapter Forty-Nine

CELESTE - SIX WEEKS AFTER BREAKUP

Olivia nudges my shoulder. "Celeste." She's been sleeping beside me for three weeks now, a debt repaid from last winter when I spent fourteen days wrapped in blankets with her after the Jake fiasco. I'd held tissues while she sobbed through reality shows and devoured paperback romances with shirtless cowboys on the covers. "The outside world still exists, you know."

Forty-two days since I walked away from Max, and I'm still a human shipwreck. The heartbreak alone would be manageable, but there's something else—a deeper fracture I never saw coming. My bed has become an island of wadded tissues and salt-stained pillowcases, the TV my only window to the outside world.

On the TV, a woman in diamonds throws champagne at another woman in diamonds - I've mainlined every season of Real Housewives—from Orange County to Dubai—memorizing their champagne-soaked feuds and designer-draped meltdowns. I can recite reunion episodes verbatim now. Their voices fill my empty house with meaningless chatter that drowns out the thoughts I can't face in silence.

It's been six weeks since Max and I broke up. I wasn't bed-ridden right away—that came later. At first, I just worked. I'd sit at my desk until my fingers cramped from highlighting scripts, scribble notes until three a.m., and schedule so many meetings with writers that their faces started to blur. Work was easier than feeling the hollow ache in my chest. Easier than admitting I was falling apart.

In other words, for three weeks after our breakup, I functioned like a robot with its emotions switched off. Which was fine. I was productive as hell. But then the head-lines hit. Max and Elody. Dating. Again. Reunited as the Hollywood power couple they once were.

I scrolled past those tabloid rumors, refusing to let them register. When Elody blasted their "relationship status" to her half-billion followers, I rolled my eyes and kept scrolling. But the day when they became Instagram official broke me - there they were, silhouetted against a perfect sunset, his arm around her shoulders, her perfect teeth gleaming. *US Magazine* called it "Maxody Reunited!"

At that point, something inside me just... collapsed. Before I could fully disintegrate, I went numb instead. Apparently, my version of emotional numbness involves memorizing every Real Housewives episode from Beverly Hills to Dubai.

I cashed in three years' worth of unused sick days and vacation time from Dreamscape - two full months I'd hoarded because who gets sick when they can't afford to, and where would I vacation on my salary? Dreamscape approved my sudden leave request with surprising speed. I went home, pulled on the pajamas I save for period cramps and flu, and I've barely left my bed since then. My daily routine has narrowed to the bare essentials: a reluctant shower (because even heartbreak doesn't justify that level of funk), a fresh pair of equally depressing pajamas, and the occasional trudge to the bathroom. That's the full extent of my accomplishments lately.

Not that there haven't been bright spots. Selena emailed me with the news that three scripts sold. Netflix snatched up my Varian Fry script about the American who smuggled artists from Nazi-occupied France and will be producing it as a limited series next spring. The Thanksgiving family drama caught Jeffrey Huxley's eye—he's the indie darling making waves with those quiet, emotional family pieces. And Hallmark? They're not just taking one of my rom-coms; the exec practically begged me to pen three Christmas specials. Perfect timing. I could churn out mistletoe meet-cutes without the emotional drain of my historical work.

So now I'm on Day Twenty-Three of my bed prison. This mattress has become my island and Reality TV my only companion. *The Real Housewives* franchise has consumed me. Three weeks ago, I couldn't have named a single cast member. Now I can recite their divorce settlements and predict their alliance shifts like some reality TV fortune teller.

"Just let me finish this episode," I mumble, clutching the remote. "Tamra and Heather's New Orleans blowout is about to resolve, and she's clearly setting Gretchen up for the next ambush. Classic Tamra dick move."

The mattress dips as Olivia slides in beside me, her fingers gently prying the remote from my death grip. "Orange County's drama queens will survive without you. Real life won't wait forever. Your mom misses you—she was glowing at the Susan G. Komen event I catered yesterday.

They want her to speak at their Spring fundraiser, and you didn't even ask about it. That's when I knew this"—she gestures at my nest of blankets and snack wrappers—"needs to end."

I shoot Olivia a death glare as she clutches my remote. Mine. Not hers. My look says it all: touch that power button and die. *The Real Housewives of Orange County* is reaching its boiling point—Gretchen's homophobic social media scandal is about to explode, and Tamra's going for blood. The producers have been building to this moment all season, manipulating footage and stirring drama like master puppeteers. I'm here for it. All of it.

"Fine, finish this episode," Olivia concedes with a dramatic sigh. "But then we're getting you outside. Fresh air, bike ride, beach trip—maybe even boogie boarding. You used to love that."

"Boogie boarding is off-limits," I mutter, already reaching for my Kleenex. "Bad memories." Boogie boarding reminds me that I learned to surf and I should be surfing with Max today. If it's Saturday. But I can't remember if it's Saturday or not. Is it Monday? Tuesday? Three weeks of this and I'm already losing track of days. They all feel the same now. What month is it even? I don't know even that.

The tears come right on schedule. They always do when his name materializes, even in my own thoughts.

The thoughts of Max, which come whenever something comes up that reminds me of him, is why I've barricaded myself behind 247 episodes of Real Housewives franchises for three weeks straight. Those wealthy, wine-throwing women from Orange County to Dubai don't trigger memories of Max. Unlike the latest gossip site headline on *TMZ* —"Max Kensington and Elody Spotted Canoodling in

Palos Verdes"—which sent my laptop sailing out the window last week. And that stupid nickname - Maxody. Idiotic. Wish that portmanteau trend would die a merciful death, but nope.

And just when did she become "Elody"? As if she's earned single-name status like Beyoncé, Cher, Adele, Madonna or Rihanna? Thinking about that headline again makes me want to hurl my television through the window, but I'd regret it when I can't watch *Real Housewives* anymore. I need those catfights and champagne-soaked meltdowns more than I care to admit. My life revolves around other people's drama now—the only thing keeping me from completely losing it.

Olivia shakes her head. "Once this episode ends, we're getting out of here. Beach time. I already texted Tally to meet us at Redondo. The sea lion pups are waiting."

Before Max entered my life, I'd spend whole afternoons at Redondo Beach just watching the sea lion colonies. Something about their barking, their piling on top of each other, the way they'd nudge rivals off the dock – it was better than therapy. This season, with all the newborns nursing from their mothers, would normally have me grabbing my keys without hesitation, but...

I bury my face in the pillow and yank the comforter up until only a tuft of my hair remains visible. "Can't do it," I mumble through the cotton. "Possibly ever."

Olivia sighs. "Fine, but reinforcements are on the way."

"Please tell me you didn't call—" I already know the answer, but I'm praying I'm wrong. Tally's the last person I need right now, with her take-no-prisoners approach to my problems. Not like Olivia, who at least lets me wallow for five minutes before pulling me up.

"Just wait and see," Olivia says, a hint of mischief in her voice.

About a half hour later, Tally bursts through the door and snatches the remote from my hand, then yanks my comforter to the floor in one swift motion.

"That's enough," she announces. "Pity party's over."

I groan and reach for the blanket, but Tally's already marching toward my bathroom.

The shower hisses to life as she calls over her shoulder, "Shower. Clothes. Then we're watching baby sea lions at Redondo and eating fish tacos at Old Tony's." She reappears in the doorway, hands on hips. "And if your ass isn't out of that bed in thirty seconds, I'm dragging you out myself and burning the whole damn bed to the ground."

I let out a groan but surrender to her demands. After my shower, I emerge to find Tally and Liv perched on the edge of the bed like intervention specialists.

"Human again?" Olivia asks with that hopeful tone she reserves for my lowest moments.

"I wasn't feral," I mutter. "I've been showering this whole time. Just because I've been horizontal doesn't mean I've abandoned hygiene."

"Three weeks of pajamas says otherwise," Tally counters, gesturing toward an outfit laid out on the bed. "Real clothes today. Non-negotiable." The ensemble includes stain-washed jeans, Mickey Mouse socks, my rainbow combat boots, a purple tie-dyed bucket hat, and a sarcastic graphic tee with "I'm currently unsupervised... I know, it freaks me out too... but the possibilities are endless!" splashed across the front.

The boots make my stomach clench. Those damn rainbow boots—the ones I wore when I first met Max. Will I ever be able to lace them up without thinking of him?

My hands shake as I get dressed and pull my boot laces tight. I twist my too-long hair up, wishing I had scissors and better face cream, then put on lip gloss like it might help. I get up and look in a full-length mirror, which shows the truth. My clothes are too big at the waist, sleeves too long for my hands. For three weeks, Olivia brought me fancy food to eat in bed—mushroom risotto, glazed salmon, chocolate mousse—and I threw it all away. I'd smile until she left, then dump the food in a bucket under my bed, and empty it after she went to work. She thinks I'm eating while I'm getting thinner, a stick figure in Kohl's clothes.

I sigh, staring at my reflection. My clothes hang off me like I'm a wire hanger. Turns out heartbreak is the ultimate weight loss program—who needs juice fasts, Keto diets and Ozempic when you can just have your soul crushed by Max Kensington? From the looks of it, I've lost about fifteen pounds in three weeks. Maybe I should pitch it to those bougie weight loss spas in Ojai. "The Devastation Diet: Guaranteed Results or Your Dignity Back."

Tally's eyes widen. "You're basically Skeletor at this point. We need to get some calories in you ASAP."

Liv's face falls. "But Celeste, I've been dropping off food three times a day. How did you get so—"

I squeeze her shoulder. "I know, and I love you for it. But I just...I haven't managed more than a few bites in three weeks. Haven't really slept either."

Her eyes glisten, and guilt twists in my chest.

"Today's different," I promise, forcing a smile. "Once I break the fast, I'll demolish all those gourmet leftovers you've been bringing." The words sound hollow even to me. My stomach still feels like a closed fist, and I can already envision myself at Old Tony's, pushing fettuccine around my plate while Tally stares daggers at me and Liv exchanges a worried glance with Tally.

We cram ourselves into Tally's Jeep and tear off toward Redondo Beach, sixty excruciating minutes from the condo. Tally and Olivia babble about anything—the weather, some Netflix show, their horoscopes—desperate to avoid the bleeding wound between us: Max and that silicone-injected parasite Elody are now splashed across every entertainment site as Hollywood's reunited power couple. My jaw aches from grinding my teeth. I'd rip out my own heart with my bare hands if it meant watching her Aston Martin burst into flames with her inside it. I swear to God, I would.

Tally giggles as she speeds down the highway. "You'll never believe who walked into my shop."

"Mother Teresa," I deadpan, rolling my eyes in the backseat. The last thing I need is another round of Tally's celebrity worship.

"Chris. Fucking. Hemsworth." Each word punctuated like a gunshot. "I swear to God, Celeste, I nearly passed out. Six-foot-four of pure Australian divinity. When he rolled up his sleeve for the tattoo, I saw veins I would happily let drain me dry. He's filming downtown and—" she presses a hand to her chest, "—I had to excuse myself to hyperventilate in the bathroom."

"Ah. Chris Hemsworth," I say. "He's got those hands—mechanic's hands—perfect for wiring a car bomb under Elody's driver's seat. I've thought about it. The exact placement. The trigger mechanism. The blast radius." A savage smile. "Those eyes of his—there's something feral there, something that understands revenge. Next time you're alone with him, ask him how much C-4 it takes to turn an Aston Martin into confetti."

Tally rolls her eyes. "Annnnnddddd somehow Celeste

manages to steer yet another conversation towards blowing up Elody's car."

"I'm just saying—"

"I get it. I'd want to turn her Aston Martin into a fireball too. But what if Max is riding shotgun when you—"

"Don't threaten me with a good time," I mutter, turning to stare out the window. My pulse quickens at the thought of Max beside Elody, his arm draped over her leather seat. For a split second, I imagine the satisfaction of them both going up in flames. I catch myself. What kind of monster am I becoming? Despite everything, I still love him with an intensity that hurts. He doesn't know I ended things to protect Michael. From his perspective, *I'm* probably the villain deserving fiery vengeance.

I need to stop this explosive train of thought. Tonight, the only detonation I'm allowing myself involves dropping whiskey and Bailey's into a pint of Guinness.

I fall silent as Liv and Tally chatter away in the front seat. Their laughter stabs at me. Eight months ago, before Max, I'd have joined right in. Even with Mom's treatments draining me emotionally, I always woke up excited for work, hunting for that perfect script, that hidden gem I could champion. I met friends for brunch. I lit candles in my tiny condo just because.

Now? I'm the woman who has worn nothing but different pajamas for weeks, who knows every *Real Housewives* plotline by heart, who can't remember when she last ate a real meal. All because of Max. Max with his hands that knew exactly where to touch me. Max who looked at me—really looked—when no one else did. Max who paid for Mom's treatment and reserved an entire zoo just for her. Max who got my screenplay in front of a real agent, an agent who's put rocket fuel into my dream career. I never deluded myself that someone like him would stay with someone like me forever. But for four perfect months, I lived inside a fantasy. Now I'm back in reality, and I can barely breathe without him.

We arrive at the beach where sea lions have claimed a dock as their territory. A cacophony of loud barks cuts through the air—all from one massive bull, his sleek body twice the size of the females surrounding him. Hundreds of the females crowd the wooden planks, nursing pups tucked between their bodies, while the bull's persistent calls echo across the water. According to the Sierra Club volunteer standing nearby with a spotting scope, this bull has earned his position as colony patriarch, fathering most of the pups and guarding his family - amusingly called a harem - during their rest stop on their migration route.

Usually, I'd be transfixed by their blubbery soap opera, giving them all backstories and accents. The alpha male—this enormous blob with a bump on his head like nature's crown—I always voice as an exhausted Southern gentleman. "Lawdy mercy," I'd drawl, flopping an imaginary flipper, "managin' this many wives is givin' me the vapors." Then I'd switch to a breathy Marilyn Monroe for his favorite female sea lion: "But sugar-blubber, that teenage hoodlum is eyeing your spot again." And sure enough, some adolescent male would inch onto the dock, and I'd narrate the alpha's thunderous barks: "Scram, punk! This here dock is invitation-only, and your name ain't on the clipboard!" Then I'd make little splashing noises as the youngster retreats, complete with tiny sea lion tears.

But today, I just watch them silently.

Tally pokes me with her elbow. "Come on, Celeste. What's that big male sea lion's deal? Is he all, 'Bernice, if I catch you with Larry one more time, I swear I'm changing the Netflix password,' or more like, 'Hey ladies, check out these whiskers—I condition them twice daily with kelp extract'?" She wiggles her eyebrows at me in what I assume is her impression of a seductive bull sea lion. I just smile and shake my head. My sea lion impression is gone for now. Just one more quirk that Max has managed to steal from me.

Olivia's arm loops around my shoulders like a safety harness. "You'll get back to you, Celeste. Eventually. But this is a good step, coming out here with us."

I manage a weak nod. "Let's be real—I'm only here because Tally threatened to drag me out of bed by my hair," I say. "Otherwise I'd still be in my pajamas watching Gretchen rip Tamra's fake eyelashes off one by one. Which, honestly? The woman deserves for what she pulled last episode."

We head down to the beach where I spot something nestled in the sand—a piece of sea glass! Pink, smooth, and glossy. I've scoured countless beaches my whole life without finding a single piece of sea glass. Any other day, I'd be ecstatic. I'd craft some elaborate backstory about its journey, explaining how ordinary glass transforms into these treasures after decades in the churning ocean.

I can picture exactly how it would've gone with Tally and Liv. "This? Oh, definitely from a French Can-Can dancer's perfume bottle, circa 1870. She hurled it at her cheating lover, missed, a shard ended up in the toilet, where it ended up flushed out to sea." Tally would immediately poke holes in my geography: "A French bottle on the West Coast?" I'd double down with some nonsense about it drifting around South America via the Cape of Good Hope, and she'd counter with facts about how currents along Los Angeles come from the north, not south. And then I'd just grin and tell her to shut up and stop ruining my fantasy.

I stare at the piece of sea glass, my lips curving upward. An actual smile. First one in twenty-three days. Tally slides her arm around my shoulders, her eyes on the frosted pink shard in my palm. "There she is," she says. "My Celeste, mesmerized by sea glass. You're finding your way back."

I nod slightly. Perhaps. This sea glass has sparked something in me that isn't the hollow ache I've been carrying. It's not much, but it's not nothing.

We make our way to Old Tony's on the pier, the three of us. A steaming plate of seafood Alfredo waits in my future. Maybe I'll taste it—really taste it—and for those few bites, remember what pleasure feels like. These small moments might be all I get now: a weathered piece of glass, a forkful of pasta, brief respites in an otherwise barren landscape.

But real joy? The kind I once had? It feels like trying to return to a hometown that's been demolished, with nothing but old photographs to prove it existed. I'm picking up the fragments of what's left, trying to map out some livable space in the wreckage of what I thought my future would be.

Chapter Fifty

MAX - SIX WEEKS AFTER THE BREAKUP

Elody fusses with my bow tie, her red lacquered nails clicking against each other. The tennis bracelet on her wrist —three carats minimum—throws prisms across my shirt collar. "No one compares to you, darling," she says with that rehearsed tone she uses for both compliments and complaints. Tonight makes three Hollywood bashes in as many weeks. Brockton Wilder's throwing this one—the producer with the golden touch and six Oscars on his mantle—which means the guest list reads like a who's who of industry royalty.

I force my lips into what I hope passes for appreciation. It's been 43 days, 8 hours, 23 minutes and counting since Celeste left and the hole remains unfilled. I still command boardrooms and close eight-figure deals with Korean streaming giants. I still work fourteen-hour days and but no longer feel that familiar rush when large contracts are signed. I no longer feel satisfaction out of all the other things that go into a typical day—the early morning calls with London investors, the tense budget meetings where careers hang in the balance, the endless script revisions with nervous writers clutching coffee cups, the lunches where I pretend to eat while negotiating sequel rights, and the late-night screenings where I force enthusiasm for mediocre films that will nevertheless make us millions. And at night, when Elody chatters about which Kardashian is dating which celebrity, I realize I've traded Celeste's warmth for expensive emptiness in Louboutins.

Elody is a bulletproof vest. That's why I'm with her this time. Why I was with her the last time. When she touches me, I feel nothing—no spark, no warmth, no danger. After Celeste carved out my heart with surgical precision, I needed someone who couldn't hurt me. Celeste's parting words—"I don't love you and you don't love me. We both deserve something real"—left a wound that hasn't closed. So here we stand in my living room, Elody fussing with my bow tie, me manufacturing a smile while mentally reviewing talking points for tonight's party. As with any big Hollywood party, I see this one as strictly a networking opportunity, so I always rehearse my pitch before going.

Before Celeste, I'd wake up with random songs playing in my head—some Pixies track I hadn't heard since college, or maybe a Morrisey deep cut, or even one of those Billy Joel songs nobody remembers. Those morning melodies were as reliable as sunrise. Now my alarm clock is Celeste's voice on repeat: *I don't love you and you don't love me.* The same brutal chorus, day after day, with no skip button in sight.

The latest *Us Weekly* sits on my coffee table, our faces splashed across the cover with the headline "HOLLY-WOOD'S HOTTEST REUNITED POWER COUPLE." I trace my finger over the glossy photo—her hand on my chest, my practiced smile never reaching my eyes. Last night at Nobu, she leaned across the table, her perfume overwhelming as she brushed her lips near my ear, paparazzi everywhere ready to snap because of course Elody tipped them off as to where we'd be that night. Always does. "Let's give them something to talk about," she whispered, leaning in for a kiss. I turned my head and ordered another scotch. At this morning's meeting, I nodded at appropriate intervals while scrolling through box office projections. The numbers climb. Contracts pile up. My assistant brings coffee I don't taste. When everyone leaves, I stand at the window, thirty floors up, pressing my forehead against cold glass, unable to feel even that.

We get to the party. At some point, I sip my third glass of champagne, nodding mechanically as Senator What's-His-Name drones on about tax incentives. I catch the eye of Netflix's new acquisition VP, and the two of us chat for awhile. Across the room, *Variety's* publisher catches my eye, raises his glass. Two studio heads suddenly find reason to drift toward us. Beside me, Elody laughs—that practiced, musical laugh that's made her the face of Chanel —and every photographer in the room swivels our way, flashbulbs erupting like a miniature lightning storm. I press my hand on the small of Elody's back and give the cameras my practiced smile that never reaches my eyes anymore.

Once the last guest leaves, I yank my bow tie loose and fish out my phone. My inbox glows with messages—ten Spanish investors, all ending with variations of "eager to continue our investment discussion." The knot in my shoulders finally unwinds. Tonight wasn't just champagne and small talk; I walked away with fifteen solid investor commitments. In my world, that's what victory looks like.

Outside Elody's Brentwood condo, she slides her hand up my thigh, her red nails catching the streetlight. "Just one drink," she whispers, leaning in so I can smell her Chanel

No. 5. I remove her hand, gentle but firm. Her lips—the ones that smiled perfectly in every photo tonight—twist into that familiar pout. I check my watch. "It's late." Her eyes flash, but I'm already shifting into drive, mentally reviewing Monday's meetings while her silhouette shrinks in my rearview mirror.

After I drop Elody off, I notice a black Tesla gliding down the street, catching my eye. Despite Elody's $20 million mansion sitting on three acres behind gates, the neighborhood isn't exactly deserted, so maybe it's not unusual for a Tesla to be driving through Elody's neighborhood at 2 AM. But it puts me on my guard nonetheless.

The car stops, and I freeze—Celeste emerges, wine bottle dangling from her fingers. From my position in the shadows, tucked inside my new Rolls Cullinan that she wouldn't recognize anyway, I watch her wobble toward the Uber driver's window. "Don't leave, 'kay? I'll be just a minute," she slurs, pinching her index finger and thumb together in the universal symbol for small. "Just a second. Don't leave!" She pounds on the roof of the car with her open hand and then stumbles away.

Of course the driver pulls away immediately, while Celeste lurches toward Elody's gate and begins screaming at the top of her lungs. I almost laugh. In her state, she clearly doesn't understand the difference between a waiting taxi and a rideshare that's already hunting for its next fare. Not that she seems to care.

My hands shake as I watch her stumble down the sidewalk. I grip the steering wheel until my knuckles turn white, my breath fogging the window in quick, shallow bursts. Forty-three days since she walked out. Forty-three days of sleepless nights and tasteless food. Forty-three days of numbness. I hate how my throat tightens at the sight of her, how I can't swallow past it.

Christ, my body ignites at the sight of her—my skin burning, my blood surging, my lungs forgetting how to function. I'm drowning in oxygen. Alive. After forty-three days of sleepwalking through a fog so thick I'd forgotten what color looked like, what hunger felt like. What wanting something—someone—so badly it physically hurts could do to a man.

She's stumbling around, looking like she might fall to the ground, that loose curl falling across her forehead the way it did when she told me we were done. I start to open the car door, then freeze. Even with my Rolls gleaming under the streetlight, she'd look right through me, her glassy eyes already fixed on something—someone—else.

She's yanking at Elody's gate, her knuckles white with fury.

"YOU BACKSTABBING BITCH!" Her scream tears through the night. "I'LL DESTROY YOU! EVERYONE WILL KNOW WHAT A MANIPULATIVE, SOUL-SUCKING PARASITE YOU REALLY ARE!" She's bellowing into the gate keypad, her fingers randomly punching numbers as if she thought she might eventually guess the 6-digit code, spittle flying. "I HATE YOU! I FUCKING HATE YOU! I SWEAR TO GOD I'D BLOW YOUR GODDAMN CAR TO PIECES IF I COULD!"

Jesus Christ. Death threats. My stomach drops. Any second now someone could hear her—some neighbor walking their prissy dog or some fitness freak on a 2 AM jog. One call to the police and she's done. I lunge from the shadows toward her. "CELESTE!" I grab her arm. She needs to get out of here now, but her Uber's long gone. "What the hell are you doing?"

She blinks at me, her pupils blown so wide her eyes look black, like twin abysses. "Max." My name slithers from her mouth like venom. "Of course you'd be here. At Elody's goddamn MANSION." She practically screams the last word, spittle flying. "Maxody, I mean. The two-headed publicity BEAST." She violently jerks her head side to side, her hair whipping across her face as she sings with manic intensity: "MAX AND ELODY, SITTING IN A TREE. K-I-S-S-I-N-G!" Her face contorts into something feral. "Power. Couple." Each word punctuated like a knife thrust. "HOW COULD YOU?!" Then her gaze snaps to the empty curb, panic flooding her features. "My ride... where'd he—" She stumbles forward, nearly collapsing. "I told him to wait." The words slur together, drowning in whatever she drank.

"Celeste, rideshare drivers don't wait. They take the next fare and move on." It's basic knowledge she'd understand sober, but alcohol has clearly short-circuited that part of her brain.

"Right." She sways slightly before lowering herself to the curb in front of Elody's imposing gate. "Guess I'm stranded. Can't even...my fingers won't...app's too complicated now. Everything's too complicated." Then she lays down on the ground in front of Elody's gate, hugging her wine bottle to her chest like a stuffed animal.

I scoop Celeste off the curb and hoist her over my shoulder like a fireman. "Let's get you home."

Her only response is a soft snore that makes me smile despite everything. Classic Celeste.

The roads are nearly empty at 2 AM, and I make good time to her place. When we arrive, I carry her limp form up to the door and lean on the doorbell. After what feels like an eternity of ringing, Olivia appears, hair mussed and eyes squinting against the porch light.

"What's going on?" Her gaze lands on Celeste draped over my shoulder. "I had no idea she went out. Where'd you find her?"

"At Elody's. Don't ask me how she knew her address."

Olivia rubs her forehead. "God knows. Can you take her up to bed?"

I navigate the stairs and ease Celeste onto her mattress, but something stops me from leaving. What if she gets sick in her sleep? People choke that way. At least that's the excuse I give myself as I slide in beside her, drawing her against me. With her warm weight in my arms, I sink into the first real sleep I've had since everything fell apart over six weeks ago.

Chapter Fifty-One

CELESTE

A hatchet's cleaved my skull in two. Every beam of sunlight through the window feels like a personal attack. Even my damn hair hurts. After whiskey number six at Old Joe's, everything gets fuzzy. Did I seriously Uber to Elody's? I've got this vague memory of her ranting about destroying Michael while I slipped her wallet from her purse, memorizing the address on her ID while she stared out the window. Been holding onto that little nugget for when I might need it. Guess my drunk self decided last night was showtime.

I freeze. There's someone beside me. Male. All I can see is dark hair against the pillow and bare shoulders tapering to a muscled back. The sheet barely covers his—I peek under—black boxer-briefs. For one impossible second, he reminds me of Max. But that's ridiculous. I must still be dreaming.

He turns to me with that lazy smile I've memorized, and for a moment I'm convinced I'm dreaming. He can't actually be here.

"Hey," he says, his voice barely above a whisper. "How are you feeling?"

Nope. Not dreaming. I shake my head, unable to form words as my chest constricts. The math is simple and brutal: if Max comes back to me, Elody releases that photo of Michael, and everything implodes.

"Um, good," I manage, pulse thundering so loudly I'm sure he can hear it. The familiar green of his eyes pulls at something deep inside me.

Michael. God, I've ghosted him too. And Mom. Three plus weeks of barely answering texts, screening calls. If Max and Michael have connected somehow... does that change things? No, Elody wouldn't hesitate to burn everything down—Max included—just to hurt me.

Unless... she actually cares about Max's feelings? She did keep our arrangement secret to protect him from humiliation. Maybe Max is her blind spot, the one and only person she cares about besides herself?

I catch myself. This desperate search for loopholes is pathetic. His fingers brush my hair from my face—that tender gesture that always undid me—and those green eyes hold mine. Everything in me wants to beg him to stay forever, but I can't. The equation remains unsolvable: Max plus me equals Michael's destruction.

I can't. If Max leaves Elody for me, she'll destroy his father. The price is too high. It just is.

He smiles as his fingers thread through my hair, his thumb grazing my cheekbone with an electricity that makes my skin burn. His eyes bore into mine with such naked longing I have to tear my gaze away before I drown in them. My chest constricts—sending him away again will shatter me into a thousand pieces, but I have no choice.

His eyes darken. "You sure you're good?" His voice drops to a concerned whisper. "Because you look—"

"Rode hard and put away wet?" My smile wobbles dangerously.

"Your words." His laugh hits me like an electric shock. "Jesus Christ, last night was insane. You literally tumbled out of that Uber, shrieking like a banshee. You were attacking Elody's gate keypad like it personally offended you, screaming that you'd destroy her career if it was the last thing you ever did." He shakes his head, eyes blazing with amusement. "I swear to God, you were convinced you'd crack her gate code through sheer rage alone, hammering random numbers until your fingers bled." Heat floods my face—I was completely out of control if I did half of what he's describing. "Then you just stood there in the middle of the street, swaying like a storm-tossed ship, looking absolutely devastated when the Uber abandoned you." He seizes my chin, roughly tilting my face up until I can't look away. "My wild, beautiful disaster."

I shake my head. The love of my life is in bed with me right now, and I should be ecstatic, but instead my skull is splitting open with panic about Michael while my stomach churns acid because of last night's bender. I'd give anything to surrender to this moment. Max's fingers trace fire across my scalp, down my cheek, and his eyes—Christ, those eyes —burn into me with such raw devotion I have to look away before I combust.

"Um," I choke out. "What do you mean, upset when the Uber left? That's ridiculous. Ubers leave. That's literally their job—they drop you off and disappear. You can't just —" I'm babbling, desperate to fill the space between us with anything, words, noise, static, before he—

Too late. His mouth crashes against mine and everything explodes. The hunger in his kiss devours me whole. My body betrays me instantly, every nerve ending screaming his name as electricity arcs between us. Six weeks of wanting him has built to this nuclear reaction. My fingers dig into his shoulders, drawing blood. I can't breathe. Don't want to. God, I love him until it hurts. Until it tears me apart. And what would be so wrong if I just let him...

His hands claim me, possessing every inch they touch. I'm down to just a tank top and underwear—my jeans, t-shirt, and Mickey Mouse socks from last night vanished sometime while I was drunk and passed out, I know not how. The heat between us is unbearable, scorching through the thin cotton separating our bodies. Max lays next to me in nothing but boxer briefs, the outline of his arousal impossible to ignore. My body aches for him with a desperation that makes me dizzy. I need him inside me, stretching me, filling the emptiness that's consuming me from within. When his fingers slide beneath the elastic and find my clit, I arch violently off the bed. My vision blurs as he works against my flesh, each stroke sending electric shocks up my spine until I'm gasping, clawing at his shoulders, drowning in sensation.

My body ignites under his touch—electric, relentless. His mouth claims my breasts before descending, a scorching trail down my stomach. When his tongue finds my clit, I fracture instantly, his name torn from my throat as pleasure detonates through every nerve. I'm still convulsing when he devours me with savage hunger, like a man rescued from starvation who's discovered a feast he might never taste again. The pleasure builds impossibly higher, crashing through me in violent waves that leave me gasping, begging.

His fingers stretch me open, reaching places that make my vision blur. I scream so violently I feel something primal break loose inside me, the sound reverberating through the house like thunder.

His tongue sears a path up my stomach, each touch like wildfire against my skin. When his mouth captures my breasts again, I arch violently against him, a desperate animal sound escaping my throat. My hands tremble so badly I nearly knock everything off my nightstand before finding protection. He takes it, our eyes locked in silent challenge as my lungs fight for air. My mind screams warnings —stop this madness now—but my body has declared mutiny. I want him with a ferocity that terrifies me.

When he finally drives into me, the force tears a scream from somewhere primal inside me. His kiss consumes me, devours my very soul as he establishes a punishing rhythm that makes coherent thought impossible. Each savage thrust pushes me closer to oblivion until reality shatters completely —my entire universe imploding into a supernova of sensation that leaves me convulsing, drowning in pleasure so acute it borders on agony.

God, I never want this to end. My entire body is electrified, dissolving at his touch, as he drives into me with a force that steals the air from my lungs. I'm drowning in him. Our mouths crash together, desperate and hungry, as my spine bows against the sheets, fingernails digging half-moons into his shoulders. The world narrows to this bed, this moment, this man.

Then his voice, raw and broken with need, scrapes against my ear: "Celeste, I love you. I'm in love with you." The words brand themselves onto my soul. The words are an incision—irrevocable, stunning in their vulnerability. I feel them cut through me, burning away every layer of disbelief and defense.

For one terrifying, beautiful moment, I cannot breathe.

Then I whisper the three words I never thought I'd say to him. "I love you too."

Chapter Fifty-Two

CELESTE

I'm trembling in Max's arms, our bodies still slick with sweat, my heart hammering against my ribs like it might break free. The afternoon light catches the flush on his skin. We've been making love all afternoon, desperate and ravenous, our bodies slick with sweat, the sheets twisted beyond recognition beneath us, neither of us willing to come up for air.

Max loves me. The words exploded from him at the height of our passion, and even now, hours later, they echo in my ears, drowning out every rational thought. This morning and afternoon wasn't just sex—this was a revelation, a seismic shift that's left me raw and exposed. I've never felt so utterly consumed by someone, like he's invaded every cell of my body. I've been fighting it since that first meeting when fury and attraction collided like lightning striking water. I've been drowning in him ever since, pretending I could still breathe on my own.

It was always this—this devastating, terrifying love that's been growing like wildfire inside me.

But it changes nothing. He has to leave—now—before I weaken again. If Michael's life implodes because of us, I'll never forgive myself. I've already betrayed Michael by letting Max through my defenses. I shouldn't have surrendered, not even for this.

My fingers tremble against the dark hair on Max's chest. "This afternoon was a mistake," I whisper, my voice catching. "We can't—"

Max grabs my wrist, his eyes blazing as he presses his finger against my lips. "NO." The word comes out like thunder. "We're done running. We're going to rip this wound open right now." His jaw clenches. "Something drove you away that night, and it wasn't lack of love. I see it in your eyes every time you look at me." He pulls me closer, his breath hot against my face. "And now you know I'm drowning in you. Every. Single. Day. I love you until it physically hurts. Never thought I'd be the man begging, but here I am." His voice breaks. "Tell me what's really happening, because I swear to God, I will burn down the world before I let you walk away from us again."

My pulse pounds in my ears as I pace the floor. Father or son? Loyalty to one means betrayal of the other. Max finally let me in after a lifetime of keeping everyone at arm's length. If he learns I've been helping Michael—the man who abandoned him—and kept Michael's return a secret for weeks, the hurt in his eyes will destroy me. But he might forgive and we might get past this. Yet Michael's fragile sobriety, his trembling hands when he speaks of facing his son... he's not ready. I keep Max, and Michael is destroyed. Or I choose Michael, and my heart will shatter again because I'll have to once again walk away from the man that I now know loves me.

I'm caught in an impossible vise: betray the broken man

I helped rebuild, or keep lying to the man I love so desperately I can barely breathe when he looks at me. My hands shake as I realize there's only one way forward. The truth will shatter everything we've built, but I can't live another day with this poison inside me. I'll confess everything and pray that what we have is strong enough to survive the wreckage.

I blink and shake my head. Oh, God, this will be impossible. But I have to get through it.

"Max," I say as gently as I can. Then I take a deep breath. "Your..." I shake my head. "Let me start from the beginning. No. Wait. I.."

Max puts his hand on my shoulder to steady me and then looks me in the eye. "Go on. Whatever it is, we'll handle it."

I nod. God, I'm so nervous. "Your father..."

"My father..." His face looks completely confused. "How does he figure into this?"

That answers my question about Michael reaching out to Max. Clearly he hasn't. I fumble for my phone, swiping through unanswered texts and emails. God, I've left Michael hanging for weeks. My stomach twists with guilt. Is he thinking I've abandoned him too? I picture him alone in his motel room, or worse—back in a bar, ordering that first drink. And for what? Because I couldn't drag myself out of bed, couldn't see past the fog of my own misery long enough to respond to a simple message. But, yes, now that I look on my phone, I see that he has sent me message after message. I can't look at them right now. They'll break my heart.

I try again. "Your father, he's..." The words dissolve in my mouth. Michael trusted me with his secret, made me promise to let him approach Max in his own time. My phone buzzes in my pocket—probably him again. For weeks I've ignored his texts while I've taken to my bed, mindlessly binging *Real Housewives* marathons. Just the other night, I binged 10 episodes of *Real Housewives of Beverly Hills*, watching Lisa Vanderpump's perfectly orchestrated take-downs, then switched to Atlanta just to see NeNe read someone to filth. I've watched women flip tables in New Jersey, throw wine in Beverly Hills, and scream across dinner parties from Miami to Dubai, all while Michael's messages pile up, each one probably more concerned than the last.

"He's...."

"He's in town." There, I said it. "He's in town, Max. He's..."

Max's expression shifts from confusion to disbelief. His eyebrows knit together, then rise toward his hairline as my words sink in. He stares at me like I've spoken in tongues, like the mention of his father materializing in town after a twenty-two year absence must be some kind of hallucination. The muscles in his jaw tighten. His eyes search mine, silently demanding how I could possibly know something about Michael that he doesn't. "I..." He shakes his head. "I mean..."

I put my hand up. "Please, Max, please ask no questions until I explain everything."

He just nods, stunned. Shocked into silence. But clearly wanting to know more.

So, for the next hour or so, I tell him everything. How Michael sought me out, desperate to quit drinking and determined not to contact his sons until he was sober. How I helped him behind Max's back—attending AA meetings, cooking meals, securing him a hotel room. How Michael improved steadily. How he found work, maintained sobriety, and we celebrated at a restaurant. How Elody's camera caught us: my hand holding his, my other hand against his cheek, my expression one of pride that could easily be misread as desire. How she threatened to destroy Michael unless I left. So I filed for divorce, terrified Michael would suffer public humiliation that might've sent him back to the bottle and to the English farm where he lived for over two decades.

I tell him all of this, and Max just listens.

I clear my throat. "Penny for your thoughts?" My voice comes out higher than I intended, and I twist my wedding ring around my finger, watching Max's face for any hint of the rage I'm sure is building. After all, I kept his father's existence from him. For weeks.

The clock on the wall ticks so loudly I swear it's mocking me. I might as well start queuing up those *Real Housewives* episodes I've been saving, because I sense another binge-watch in my near future. At least I'll finally see if Gretchen and Tamra ever resolve their mess—something I apparently know how to create, not fix.

Max's jaw tightens. "God, Celeste." His voice breaks. "You risked everything for him—my father—a stranger." He grabs my face between his hands, his eyes burning into mine. "That's why I can't breathe without you." The kiss crashes against me like a wave, desperate and consuming, stealing every thought from my mind. When he finally pulls away, his fingers dig into my shoulders. "Tell me where he is. Now."

My pulse quickens. Is Michael truly prepared for this? I need to check his messages. "Max, I'm not certain..."

"Celeste. Tell me his location. Now."

"Hold on," I say. "I need to... excuse myself for a moment." I dash to the bathroom, phone clutched in my hand, and frantically open the thread of texts Michael has sent throughout these past weeks.

Scanning through them brings immediate relief. Though disappointed by my silence, he's found temporary shelter in his sponsor Greg's garage apartment while awaiting my response. His most recent message practically begs for a meeting—he's finally ready to face his sons! Sixty-plus texts over forty-three days tell the story of a man who's maintained his sobriety and stability. My lips curve upward. Greg's address is still in my contacts from when he first agreed to sponsor Michael.

I come out of the bathroom. "I know where he is. I'll take you there, but shouldn't we get the entire family involved."

Max runs a hand through his hair. "I need to meet him first. Then I'll gather the family." He taps his fingers on the counter. "Though my brothers are all over the map. Ansel's in Berlin signing some techno DJ." His jaw tightens. "Roman's here, but..." He winces. "Christ. Roman and Dad in the same room? Recipe for disaster." A wry smile crosses his face. "Rome's our family powder keg. Pure Sonny Corleone energy—loyal to a fault, but he'll tear Dad to shreds. Connor would be better—he's in town and has that diplomat gene." Max's eyes drift toward the window, calculating. "And Ash? Probably hovering around some LAMA auction, hunting down obscure art pieces." He lets out a short laugh. "Half the time I couldn't tell you where any of them are. Still, I can probably wrangle two or three of them. It's a start."

She started to say, "What about—"

"Cameron's back in the ER at Cedars, so he can meet our father and he'll definitely welcome Dad home with open arms. He's such a good guy." He shrugs. "Kalen's in

Australia, playing out stadiums. Silas is…in England? Maybe?" Max grabs me, his kiss fierce and desperate, his eyes blazing with a wild, feverish light. "Oh my God," he whispers, his voice cracking. "I'm about to see my father. Twenty-two years—twenty-two fucking years—and now he's right there. Because of you." His fingers dig into my shoulders, trembling. "And Celeste? If Elody thinks she can ruin this—"

"But Max, she threatened to—"

He cuts me off, his jaw clenched so tight I can see the muscle pulsing. "I run one of the largest movie studios in the world. She's nothing but a replaceable face on a screen. If she comes for my father, I'll destroy her so completely they'll need dental records to identify what's left of her career." His eyes lock onto mine, burning. "Now let's go meet my dad."

Max keeping Elody from making trouble.

Why didn't I think of that?

Chapter Fifty-Three

MAX

The Rolls purrs beneath us as Celeste and I speed towards Woodland Hills. My father—a man I haven't seen since I was seven—is staying in some sponsor's garage apartment in the Valley. He's working at Whole Foods now. Whole Foods. The man who once ran international operations for Kensington Pictures is bagging organic produce.

My knuckles whiten against the leather steering wheel. My heart hammers so hard I can barely breathe. After twenty-two years, I'm finally going to see him. The man whose absence carved out everything inside me. According to Celeste, he moved to England to live with my Uncle Thomas. An uncle I've never even met.

What surprises me most is how little anger I feel. Just this desperate, childlike need to see his face again.

We pull up to the house—a single-story ranch that makes our old ten-bedroom estate look like Versailles—and I'm still processing the transformation. My father, who once commanded boardrooms and private jets, now lives in a converted garage and scans organic produce for a living. At

Kensington, his signature authorized million-dollar marketing campaigns across six continents. His strategies determined which films thrived internationally and which died quiet deaths. Now he wears a green apron and asks if people found everything they were looking for today. The strangest part? According to Celeste, he seems content. I doubt Celeste has any idea she befriended a fallen titan of the industry. He wouldn't have mentioned it.

Well, as long as he's happy...

My pulse races as Celeste and I approach Greg's front door. When it swings open, the man standing there—Greg, I assume—brightens at the sight of Celeste. "There you are!" He pulls her into an embrace. "You've got to come in. Michael's been beside himself. He's been searching accident reports online, calling hospitals—the works. Couldn't figure out why you went radio silent on him."

Celeste hangs her head, obviously ashamed. "It's...a long story."

That's when I truly see her—her collarbone rises from her skin like the ridge of a mountain, her wrists so thin my fingers could circle them completely with room to spare. How the hell did I miss this? Six times we made love today and I never noticed how her hipbones press against me like stones? I've been lost in the high of having her in my arms again, seeing nothing else.

While we were broken up, she stopped eating. Fading away in my absence. Dad's calls went unanswered because she was already half-gone. Meanwhile, I've been my own kind of phantom—functioning but empty, every feeling scorched away just to endure the white-hot agony of her absence. These past six weeks, I've been nothing but ash wearing the shape of a man.

Greg leads us through his living room and into the

converted garage. Hardwood floors, framed photos, and a shelf of succulents give the space a polished feel. There's a gray sectional with The Serenity Prayer stitched on it, and pendant lights hanging over a made bed. Sunlight comes in through French doors at the back. The whole place is neat as a pin. Dad's not there yet - must be in the bathroom.

A man emerges from the bathroom, and I watch his green eyes—the same shade as mine—widen in shock. His gaze darts between Celeste and me, his jaw slackening. "Celeste," he breathes, crossing to her and pulling her into an embrace that seems almost paternal. "I was so worried." Then his attention shifts to me.

Twenty-two years since he left, but I'd know him anywhere. His dark hair's going silver at the temples, and there are a few more lines around his eyes. Otherwise, he looks just like I remember. I catch myself smiling. Well, at least I'll age well too.

He stares at me, eyes widening. "Max?" The word comes out like he's afraid to say it. His gaze drops to the floor, shoulders hunching. I want to reach for him, but I hold back. But even though I don't reach out right away, I don't get angry - that would just send him back to drinking. He's sober now. That's what matters. The past is done. I take a breath and make my choice: I won't be the one who breaks him this time.

I whisper "Dad," and open my arms. He collapses against me, shaking with sobs. His grip is tight, and I fight back tears. Twenty-two years gone in an instant. The man who left all those years ago, leaving a hole in my heart that had never healed, never even close—he's actually here. Real. His fingers dig into my shoulders. Something shifts inside me. Not trust, not forgiveness. But maybe a beginning. A crack in a door I thought I'd sealed forever.

Dad and I finally break apart, and he holds me at arm's length, his weathered hands gripping my shoulders. "My God," he whispers, reaching up to muss my hair the way he did when I was eight. "A man now. And tall. So tall." His eyes crinkle at the corners. "Not that I haven't kept tabs. Got scrapbooks for you boys—every magazine spread, every newspaper mention." He squeezes my shoulders, then drops his hands. "Pictures never quite capture it though, do they?" A smile spreads across his face before he glances away. "Listen to me go on. Somebody shut me up, Celeste."

He must have recognized me instantly. Somehow he'd been keeping tabs on us all these years. When he left, I thought that was it—out of sight, out of mind. Turns out he was watching from afar the whole time. We had no idea, but he knew exactly who we'd become.

Celeste, still teary-eyed, slips her arm around Dad. Her head rests on his shoulder, and he grins. Something twists in my chest as I watch them together—she looking up at him adoringly, him already treating her like a daughter. I can't help wondering if she's replacing the father she lost.

"Michael," she says, her voice soft but certain. "Remember your promise not to filter yourself? What was that saying from group—keep your feelings bottled up and the bottle starts looking good?"

It's not a phrase I've heard before, but truth rings in it. Dad's generation of men were taught to swallow their emotions, to equate vulnerability with weakness. No wonder so many of them drowned themselves trying to stay afloat.

Dad nods once. "Right." His eyes find mine, weighted with something unsaid. "Son, I love you. All of you. I need you to know I didn't leave because I didn't care." His chin dips toward his chest. "I left because I thought you deserved better than the mess I'd become."

Celeste bumps his arm gently with hers. "Not a mess," she corrects. "Someone with a genetic predisposition to addiction facing unbearable grief. Look around you now—this beautiful home, your new position. You clawed your way back. That takes extraordinary strength."

Watching them together, my heart swells. She's become essential to both of us, a bridge I never knew we needed.

He gestures to the modest space, his eyes fixed on the floor. "It's just a garage apartment." I exhale slowly. Sure, we once lived in that sprawling Bel-Air mansion—ten bedrooms, that ridiculous pool that flowed from outside to in. But that was before the drinking swallowed him whole, before he lost it all. Now he's standing here, three months sober, with a roof over his head and a steady job. How do I tell him that this garage apartment means more than that mansion ever did without making him feel like I'm patting him on the head?

My voice cracks. "Dad." I grip his forearm, my fingers digging in. "I'm not just proud—I'm in awe of you. You could have disappeared forever into that bottle, hidden away on that farm until the day you died. But you clawed your way back from hell. You got sober. You're facing everyone you hurt." Tears burn my eyes. "Most men would rather die than do what you're doing right now. Do you understand that? Not one ounce of shame belongs to you. Not. One. Ounce."

Dad just nods and tears form in his eyes again. Something ruptures inside me. My chest heaves, and suddenly I'm drowning, gasping for air as twenty-two years of locked-away grief floods my lungs. When Celeste left, I'd turned to stone. Now I'm shattering—breaking apart in violent, jagged pieces.

I pull him to me, fingers clutching his shirt, bunching

the fabric between my knuckles. And I break open in sobs that wrack through me like a thunderclap. The hurt splits me open—sharp and alive—Mom's face frozen on paused VHS tapes blurring with cake candles I blew out alone, with phone that never rang. Yet somehow, this breaking feels like healing. Better than the time I bloodied my fists on Steve's jaw. Better than pushing through that last impossible rep. Better than catching that perfect wave at dawn.

But better than Celeste? Nope. Nothing—nothing—compares to her. She's oxygen after decades of suffocation.

The tears dry on my cheeks when my father's face cracks into that familiar smile. "What do you think about me returning to Kensington? Head of international operations again?"

Our eyes meet, and somehow we both know what the other is thinking. "Maybe not," we chorus, the words tumbling out in perfect unison. His laugh joins mine, filling the space between us, and in that moment, I feel the weight lifting from my shoulders.

I know that everything will be okay. More than okay. We're going to be great.

Chapter Fifty-Four

MAX

After seeing my father, I sent an emergency text to my brothers and Granddad. Within hours, they all converged on Los Angeles. Ansel abandoned his recording studio in Berlin, landing his Gulfstream at LAX. Cameron left his ER shift early. Roman simply drove up from his Verde Resort in Palos Verdes, while Asher stepped away from the LAMA auction where he'd been bidding on a Basquiat. Kalen flew in from Australia, his private jet touching down just after midnight. Connor merely walked off his Burbank set. Silas flew in from France, where he's been engrossed in multiple acquisitions of rare royal jewels. Not one of them hesitated when they heard our father wanted to see us after all these years.

Granddad's house feels different tonight with Celeste at my side. Earlier, she'd hesitated at the door.

"Max, I don't belong at a family reunion," she whispered.

I placed my hand on the small of her back. "You're my wife, remember?" Technically true, despite the divorce

434

papers Elody forced her to file—papers I intend to have dismissed immediately. What Celeste doesn't know is that I'm planning a proper wedding this winter. One where we're both smiling instead of looking like hostages.

As we settle around the table, I catch her eye. "Different from our last dinner here, isn't it?"

She winces. "God, when I started rambling about healing crystals, I was certain your grandfather would show me the door." Her eyes narrow playfully. "Then you swooped in to save me. Curious timing."

I laugh, surprised she'd read me so well even then. She knew I'd planned to sabotage her that night but changed course mid-dinner. I'm still not entirely sure why I changed course. All I know is that if I'd continued making her look bad to Granddad, and Granddad changed his mind about forcing us to marry, I'd never have fallen in love with her—and my father might never have found his way back to us.

My dad occupies the center seat at the table while my brothers enter the dining room one by one. A tense silence hangs in the air as each brother greets him in his own distinct way—no two reactions alike.

Roman stands back from the reunion, arms crossed, glaring daggers at Dad while the rest of my brothers crowd around. The family hothead—our own Sonny Corleone minus the Lawman revolver but with enough exes to form a firing squad. Cameron goes in for the hug first, all heart as usual, embracing Dad with tears streaming. Kalen offers a stiff embrace, face unreadable, while his identical twin Connor follows with the same hug but adds a warm smile. Ansel and Asher mirror Connor's approach exactly— embrace, smile, step back. I mentally tick off the scorecard: seven brothers welcoming Dad home, one holding out. Roman, of course. Figures.

My father's face drains of color. I want to reach for his hand, but I'm not sure he'd welcome the gesture.

Granddad rises at the head of the table, his six-foot frame casting a shadow across the polished mahogany. He locks eyes with Dad. "Well," he announces, voice cutting through the clink of silverware. "The prodigal son returns. Michael, perhaps you'd care to enlighten us all about your extended absence."

I wince. Nothing like a public execution before dessert.

Celeste catches Dad's eye and offers a reassuring smile, which he returns weakly. Wine glasses glint at every place setting—an unspoken Kensington ritual. I watch Dad eyeing the Cabernet being poured around him, his knuckles white against the tablecloth. The collision of all his estranged sons plus alcohol could send him spiraling back to his old ways by midnight, and honestly, who could blame him?

Dad's Adam's Apple bobs before he speaks. "Well." He fidgets with his water glass. "I suppose I should be thankful nobody's slipped arsenic in my drink or tried defenestrating me yet." I force out a laugh—not because it's funny, but because I can't bear the silence that would follow if nobody laughed. Nothing is worse than trying to make a joke and have nobody laugh. On cue, my brothers join in with half-hearted chuckles. All except Roman, who sits like a statue, jaw clenched, arms folded across his chest.

Dad lowers himself into the chair. "I should mention I've been attending AA religiously. My sponsor Greg will get a call after dinner, though he'd know if I slipped up—I rent his converted garage." His eyes drift to the tablecloth. "Quite the fall, isn't it? From closing eight-figure international deals to stocking organic produce and sleeping twenty feet from someone else's laundry room." He smooths a wrinkle from his napkin. "But there's a strange peace in simplicity I never found back then. Nothing compared to life with Catherine, though. She anchored me. When cancer took her..." His voice catches. The clink of silverware stops, leaving only the sound of breathing around the table.

Cameron's voice cracks. "Dad." His knuckles whiten against the edge of the table. "You don't have to beat yourself up for us. I can't speak for everyone, but Christ— twenty-two years and I still remember how you carried me on your shoulders at the pier. How you were before Mom's casket went into the ground. I see it in your eyes—you think you're some kind of coward. You're not." His breath catches. "I've spent 22 years of my life praying you'd come back. And now you're here."

Roman slams his palm against the table. Wine glasses rattle. "Bullshit." The word hangs in the air like gunsmoke. "Cameron, you're handing him absolution he never earned. He abandoned us. All of us. No note. No calls. Nothing." His eyes bore into Dad, voice dropping to a venomous whisper. "I don't speak for everyone, but look around this goddamn table. They're choking on words they're too afraid to say. What you did destroyed us."

Dad lowers his head for a moment, then gestures toward my other brothers. "Thank you for speaking up, Roman," he says, his voice steadier than I expected. "I'd like to hear from the rest of you too. My sponsor keeps telling me that buried feelings only fester." He spreads his hands, palms up. "So let me have it. All of it." His gaze settles on Cameron, whose jaw is still clenched tight. "You were right about one thing, Cameron. I'm through running away. I love you boys more than you'll ever know. I haven't earned back your trust yet—" his voice catches, "—especially yours, Roman. But I'm here to try."

Connor clears his throat before speaking. Despite his Oscar and the confident characters he portrays on screen, at family gatherings he's just Connor—the shy, introverted brother who'd rather lose himself in novels than ride waves. Back in middle school, he'd stutter through conversations, eyes fixed on his shoes. It wasn't until Granddad nudged him toward that school production of *Our Town* that something shifted. "Acting gave me permission to exist in the world," he once confided over beers. "I could pretend to be someone who knew how to talk to people until eventually, I could actually talk to them."

"Dad," he says now, voice steady. "I'm somewhere between Roman and Cameron on this. It's good to see your face again, but I need to understand why we stopped seeing it for so long."

Dad nods. "Right, right." Then he takes a deep breath as he launches into the when and why of his disappearance. His voice cracks when he mentions Mom's name the first time. By minute fifteen, his hands tremble slightly around his coffee mug. At thirty minutes, he's pulled his AA sobriety coin from his pocket and is turning it over and over between his fingers. Roman sits with arms crossed, jaw tight, gaze fixed somewhere above Dad's left shoulder. But when I glance at Connor, he's leaning forward, elbows on knees. The same posture he had in Glenn Kelly's room at Ocean-side Recovery last month, when he'd driven three hours just to sit there every Saturday. Kalen's eyes have that same hollow look they carried at Jason's funeral last year—his casket lowered as Kalen clutched the tambourine Jason always played. Connor catches my eye and gives a small nod. Kalen's hand finds my shoulder. They don't say a word.

Connor rises and moves beside Dad's chair, crouching

down and resting his hands on the armrests. "Dad, I forgive you. I know about addiction—my best friend is in rehab. I won't dwell on what led him there, but it was dark, full of demons. I wouldn't wish that on anyone. I wish you'd made different choices for us, but I understand why you made them. You didn't want our role model to be someone struggling with addiction. And Granddad stepped up for all of us. So I'm with Cameron—you have nothing to be ashamed of. But if you feel yourself slipping, you have my support, and Cameron's, and Max's." He glances around the table; Kalen nods.

"Mine as well," Kalen says, swirling his wine. "Connor's friend is in rehab; mine died of an overdose. I know how it goes. Count me in for any support you need, Dad."

At this point, Dad has support from Connor, Kalen, Cameron—and from me, too. I assume Ansel will come around, but he's still hesitant. He was only eight when Dad left, just a year older than me, so he abandoned us when we were quite young. Kalen and Connor were nine then—old enough to remember and to have seen addiction up close, which probably explains their empathy. Roman was ten; Asher and Silas were twelve; Cameron was fourteen.

Ansel, across from me, toys with his napkin and sips his wine, visibly torn. Finally, he speaks: "Dad, I forgive you—but can I trust you? Can any of us? What if something else goes wrong—God forbid one of us is in crisis? Will you disappear on us again, vanish once we open up? I can't speak for everyone, but I don't know if I could recover a second time."

Dad's shoulders slump. "I can't promise I'll never leave again. All I can say is that with my sons behind me, I stand a better chance. My AA meetings give me strength I never had before. And I love you boys more than anything..."

"Ansel," I say, leaning forward. "Think about it. We were just kids when he left—vulnerable, needing everything from him. The weight of that responsibility..." I gesture between us. "Look at us now. Grown men with our own lives, our own successes. Dad doesn't have to be perfect anymore. He just has to be present."

Ansel's expression softens. "I hadn't thought of it that way."

Ansel will come around. But what about Asher and Silas? Of all my brothers, Asher is the one I understand the least. I was labeled gifted—reading Dickens at five, earning my PhD at twenty-two—but Asher has always been on another plane. Celeste jokes that I'm "Good Max Hunting," riffing on the genius in that Gus Van Sant film. I'm nowhere near that level; Asher is. He can absorb a thousand-page nuclear physics text in thirty minutes and grasp every concept. Physics may not be his passion—art is—but his encyclopedic knowledge of every work in art history astonishes me. Both he and Ansel are prodigious musicians—Ansel a near-maestro on piano, Asher a cellist rivaling Yo-Yo Ma. Asher also speaks six languages fluently, accents down perfectly—like Oppenheimer mastering Dutch in six weeks. He's also an accomplished artist in his own right. It's always been a struggle for me to relate to Asher; his mind simply processes faster than anyone I know.

All eyes turn to Asher. He's the only one who hasn't spoken or rendered a verdict on whether or not he's willing to forgive Dad and reestablish a relationship with him.

Asher clears his throat when he notices our stares. "I don't think Dad will abandon us again. Max is right—we're grown now. Things will be different." He shifts in his chair, turning toward Dad with the same expression he wears when examining a new painting. "I'm curious about your internal evolution. What changed between then and now? You say you felt ready, but ready how? Why this particular moment?"

That's Asher for you. Always dissecting emotions like specimens. Back in high school, I'd find him in his room with art books spread open beside psychology textbooks, cross-referencing them with sticky notes. "The brain processes beauty mathematically," he once told me while we stood before a Rothko, his eyes tracking invisible patterns while mine just felt the weight of all that red. Even now, when we visit galleries, he carries a small notebook, jotting observations about viewer reactions rather than his own feelings. "Art isn't about what you feel," he insists. "It's about what you know."

Dad chuckles. "My Asher," he says. "Always digging for the root cause." He nods. "I was standing on a cliff overlooking the Celtic Sea near Uncle Thomas's farm outside Cornwall. I'd escape there whenever I needed space. Something shifted that day—like a fog lifting. I couldn't keep running. My life had become this endless sprint away from everything that mattered." His voice drops. "But the drinking... that demon stayed with me until Celeste dragged me to my first AA meeting. That woman saved me in ways I can never repay."

Asher's face remains carefully neutral. I recognize that expression—he's processing, searching for the logical progression my father's story lacks. Asher needs methodical transformation, documented steps of psychological evolution. A single moment of clarity on a windswept cliff? Too mystical, too convenient for his analytical mind to embrace without skepticism.

He exhales heavily. "I'm struggling to understand.

Didn't you seek professional help during your time in England?"

Dad's gaze drops to his hands. "The farm was my therapy. Waking before dawn to milk the cows. Watching calves take their first steps. The quiet mornings with only birdsong breaking the silence. Evenings at the pub where Mrs. Wilcox would save my usual seat by the fire." His voice softens. "In a village of just 200 souls, you're never truly alone. You have close friends and neighbors everywhere you look. When I wanted to be alone, I retreated to my home on Uncle Thomas' farm. When I wanted company, I showed up at places - the pub, the square, various private celebrations that everybody in the village was invited to." He glances up. "Though I suppose a proper therapist might have been wise. I'll concede that point."

Asher's brow furrows, his eyes meeting mine in silent understanding. Dad found his peace among England's rolling hills and quiet village pubs serving where he probably went and talked and sang with lots of friends. Los Angeles offers no such sanctuary—just bumper-to-bumper traffic and strangers brushing past without a glance. The village where everyone knew his name is five thousand miles away. I can't help wondering: if the gentle rhythm of country life couldn't keep the bottle from his hand, what hope does he have surrounded by billboards advertising premium tequila and old haunts on every corner?

Ash finally just nods. "Okay. I guess…"

I place my hand on Ash's shoulder. "I get it. You won't slam the door in Dad's face, but you're not exactly rolling out the welcome mat either. Same with Ansel. Just… take it slow. One step at a time. The more we rally around him, the better his chances of staying sober."

Silas swirls his wine, eyes fixed on the crimson whirlpool

in his glass. His expression gives nothing away—never has. He possesses Asher's intellect but with both feet planted firmly in reality where his twin brother's head remains in the clouds. His jaw tightens before he exhales. "Okay," he announces, scanning the faces around the table—all of us who've tentatively sided with Dad against Roman. I can already tell he's choosing Roman's island of exile over our mainland of forgiveness. "I'm with Roman. I'm not ready to forgive yet." We collectively groan while someone mutters "et tu, Silas," but he just shrugs, corner of his mouth lifting. "I'm not from Missouri, Dad, but you still need to show me."

Classic Silas—thirty-something going on fifty with his dad humor. Dad meets his gaze and nods. "I understand," he says quietly. "And I hope to earn your trust."

My eyes drift to Roman, who's leaning against the wall with arms crossed. When our gazes meet, he rolls his eyes dramatically. Progress, I suppose—at least he's not glaring at Dad anymore like he's plotting his murder. I mentally count where everyone stands: Cameron, Kalen, Connor and myself firmly backing Dad; Ash and Ansel cautiously neutral; and Roman... well, Roman's still a hard no. But even concrete cracks eventually. Silas, too, is a no, but not a hard one like Roman. He's willing to see where things lead.

Could've gone worse.

Later that night, I'm back at Celeste's place—her territory, not mine, at least until she wears my ring for real—and our bodies are still trembling from three sessions of sex that left us breathless, speechless, and clinging to each other like survivors of some beautiful disaster. Her eyes lock onto mine, blazing with something I've never seen before. "The way you took control today," she whispers, her fingers digging into my shoulder, "your brothers all looked to you—

their baby brother—and you didn't flinch. You're going to save Michael when no one else could."

I press my lips against her forehead, tasting salt. "You saved him first," I say, my voice breaking. "What you did for my father—" I crush my mouth against hers, desperate, drowning. I can't stop touching her, can't bear a millimeter of space between us after nearly losing her forever. "My brothers will worship you for it. I already do. I love you, Celeste. God, I love you."

"I love you," she gasps against my lips. Then we make love again, clinging to each other like we're falling from a great height. When we finally collapse, her heartbeat thunders against mine, and I know with absolute certainty—this is what I was born for.

Chapter Fifty-Five

MAX

I need to handle the Elody situation. When Celeste revealed what Elody had done, I was so enraged that I wanted to treat Elody like I treat Steve- but wouldn't, because she's a woman, but that's the only thing saving her - and, like Celeste, imagined her precious Aston Martin erupting in flames. Not that I'd ever act on such thoughts—the board might overlook many things, but cold-blooded murder isn't one of them. Still, I have other weapons at my disposal. One phone call from me, and her acting career, not to mention her Chanel N°5 campaign, become nothing but a distant memory.

I need this breakup to be a spectacle—something that'll dominate tomorrow's headlines. I call Bill O'Brien at *Variety*, offering him an exclusive. "I'll be at the Centurion tonight at six," I tell him. "Front row seat to the end of Hollywood's most boring power couple." Better *Variety* gets it right than let the tabloids twist everything.

I arrive early, choosing the Centurion partly for its visibility, partly for the bitter symmetry—this is where I first met Celeste. The maître d' leads me through the room where Hollywood's elite hold court. Lauren McCall catches my eye from her corner table; her performance in *Midnight Crossing* has made her an Oscar frontrunner. Her husband Eldridge nods coolly—still hasn't forgiven me for passing on his sci-fi project last year. Saige Fuentes, whose adaptation of *The Glass Hour* is in production at my studio, is deep in conversation with Woody Bruce, the rock star she somehow snagged last month at Coachella. Even Liberty Landry is here with Elisha Tapia—the supermodel and the indie director whose surprise romance broke Instagram last summer. I take my seat, order a scotch, and wait for Elody to walk into my trap.

Elody sweeps in like she owns the place, her crimson crocodile Birkin bag emitting high-pitched yips. A tiny white Maltese with kohl-rimmed eyes and a diamond-studded collar, Charlie, pokes his fluffy head out, pink tongue lolling between pearly teeth. No gilt-framed "Dogs Prohibited" sign in Los Angeles applies to Elody Martin. She just got Charlie and he accompanies her everywhere—Michelin-starred restaurants, red-carpet premieres, probably even the marble-tiled bathroom of her Bel Air mansion. She's wearing butter-soft leather thigh-high Louboutins and a skintight Hervé Léger fire-engine red bandage dress that clings to every curve of her impossibly toned body, her caramel-highlighted hair bouncing with each deliberate step as she drinks in the slack-jawed and appreciative stares from the other male diners.

"Max," she purrs, sliding into her seat without waiting for the maître d'. "So nice to see you. I'll have my usual." She puts her purse with the dog in it on top of the table, violating God knows how many health codes. "Now, about my thirtieth next month—I'm thinking my place near

Cannes. Twenty rooms right on La Guérite beach, perfect for the party of the decade." Her fingers brush my forearm, lingering. "Perhaps we'll have something special to announce by then?"

I don't bother hiding my eye roll. For years she's been dropping marriage hints like breadcrumbs, convinced we're heading toward some fairy-tale ending.

"Elody," I say, catching Bill's eye at the next table. His notepad is out, pen poised. I give him a subtle nod. "There's something you should know."

She snaps her fingers at a passing waiter who practically sprints to her side. If he'd been slower, she'd have eviscerated him publicly, then slipped him a hundred to keep quiet —her standard operating procedure.

"Dirty martini. Double. Extra dirty." She exhales a slow, rehearsed sigh and swivels to face me, every inch the poised predator. "I suspect I'll need it."

"No doubt," I reply, voice cold and smooth like obsidian. "I'll hang tight. Wouldn't want to waste a perfect martini if you decide to fling it in my face."

Her brow lifts, sharp as a blade. "And why on earth would I do that?"

I let my shoulders slump, muscles coiling beneath my shirt. "I'll wait," I repeat. Minutes later, a frosty glass of olive-studded sludge clinks onto the table. She studies me with guarded eyes as she lifts it.

"Well?" she prompts. "Still waiting for your answer."

"Because," I say, leaning in until my breath fans her lips, "I know exactly what you did to Celeste and my father." My chest clenches remembering her threat—to drag my newly sober, fragile dad through the social-media muck if Celeste didn't back off. My gentle father, so proud of his recovery. And Elody would've torched him to get at Celeste, which is the only reason why Celeste broke up with me. Love doesn't come sharper than that kind of loyalty, and Celeste has it in spades.

She flicks her hair, amusement dancing in her eyes. "Please. What did I do? I've never met your father. I've only seen Celeste that one time—here, of all places—when she gave me a ketchup-stained napkin to autograph." She chuckles softly. "I've signed stranger things, but that napkin... that's a new low."

I shake my head. "Cut the fucking gaslighting. You know exactly what you threatened. Celeste told me herself—"

"Celeste? Your ex-wife—ex-fake-wife, really." She leans back, smug. "Why on earth would I have anything to do with her—or your dad? I have no idea what's going on."

Rage thunders through me, but I swallow it down and draw a steady breath. She can play the innocent Oscar darling all she wants, but I'm not here to be toyed with.

"Elody," I say, each word a promise of violence. "Hand over your phone. I want that photo of Celeste and my father deleted. And hear me loud and clear: if you ever, and I mean ever mention my father, Celeste, or anyone in my family—ever—I will bury you. One call from me to any studio head, and your so-called A-list career is ashes. You'll be lucky to get cast in an off-off-off Broadway reading."

I release her with a cool stare. She can keep up the act, but she knows the truth: cross me or mine, and she won't just lose a drink—she'll lose everything.

She leans in, her voice razor-sharp. "You can't fucking touch me in this town. My last three movies combined? Over a billion dollars box office receipts. No superheroes. No sequels. Just me. People don't stream my films—they line up around the goddamn block. I open movies when nobody else can. Nobody buries me, Max. I'm the one who does the burying."

"Watch me," I snarl, blood pounding in my ears. "You're not that fucking special."

But Christ, she is. The air crackles between us. She's box office lightning in human form, dragging audiences away from their precious streaming services through sheer magnetic force. Critics worship her like she's cinema incarnate.

But I'm Max fucking Kensington. I don't just run this town—I own it. Her publicist might be good, but mine is Ezrah Braun, Hollywood's personal grim reaper. One call from me, and he'll blast every skeleton from her closet across every headline in America. Another five calls to studio heads who owe me favors, and she'll never work again. She'll be radioactive.

She knows it too. I can see it in her eyes—the fear beneath the fury. She's holding a pair of twos and betting like she has a royal flush.

Elody narrows her eyes to slits, her hands violently trembling as she thrusts the photo at my face. My blood freezes. There's Celeste with my father—her fingers intertwined with his, her other hand pressed against his weathered cheek, her eyes locked on his with such raw intimacy it punches the air from my lungs. Anyone seeing this would believe they were lovers—there's no other possible interpretation. The truth behind it doesn't matter; the image screams betrayal. If Elody had unleashed this on Instagram, it would have been a wildfire I couldn't control.

Christ, no wonder Celeste surrendered to blackmail. But my stomach twists with the realization that she didn't trust me enough to fight this together. I could have destroyed Elody with a single phone call. Instead, we both suffered while Celeste protected my father until he found the courage I've been waiting my entire life for him to discover. Goddamn her beautiful, misguided heart—always making the wrong choices for all the right reasons. Foolish, reckless, beautiful Celeste—breaking herself to spare others, flawed in ways that make me love her more fiercely than ever.

She deletes it, thrusting the phone at me. "There. Satisfied?"

"Not even close." My arms lock across my chest, fingers digging into my biceps. "But I will be when you understand this: my father, Celeste, me, my brothers, my grandparents, Gianni, Rosa—anyone I give a damn about—their names don't exist to you anymore. Because if I ever hear any of their names coming out of your mouth…" I lean in until I can see my reflection in her pupils. "Test me. I fucking dare you. The hell I'll rain down will make you wish you'd never learned to speak."

She exhales, a tremor in her voice. "Jesus, Max. I really thought we'd end up married."

"Then you're not just delusional," I spit, "you're certifiably fucking insane."

I catch Bill's eye and give him the signal. My pulse quickens. I need Elody to throw that fucking drink in my face. But she's holding back. For now.

She uncrosses her legs, then recrosses them deliberately —a calculated move that sends every man in the room adjusting their collars. Those legs could cut glass. She's sculpted herself into a weapon, and I respect the discipline. You don't get a body like that without bleeding for it. She leans forward, her cleavage practically daring me to look away. I don't.

"Fine, Max," she hisses through perfect teeth. "You win. Not a single word about Celeste, your father, Gianni, your brothers, Rosa, your grandparents—nobody. I'm not about to commit career suicide."

"Smart girl." I lock my arms across my chest and flick my eyes toward the dirty martini. Her smile turns predatory. She glances at Bill, then grabs her glass and hurls the contents at me—vodka burning my eyes, olive brine soaking my $3,000 shirt. She's on her feet in an instant, chair scraping back with a screech. Charlie erupts in a frenzy of high-pitched barking as she storms toward the exit, leaving a wake of shocked faces.

Perfect. Inevitable. Elody would rather die than exit without scorching the earth. But something's off—her rage felt too precise, too controlled. Maybe that's the real performance—acting like she's fine when she's plotting my murder. With Elody, you're never safe.

But one thing's certain: Elody is neutralized. Not for now. For fucking ever.

Chapter Fifty-Six

CELESTE

Six months flew by like a montage in one of my screenplays. Mom's oncologist actually high-fived her at her last appointment—"No evidence of disease" still scrawled in his messy doctor handwriting across her chart. She still needs those quarterly check-ups, but I caught her throwing away her head scarves last week. She's slinging plates at Mastro's Ocean Club now, where Lexi hosts. You should see them in their matching black outfits, Mom winking at Lexi as she glides past with trays of seafood towers. Between the $17 hourly and the tips from tech bros trying to impress their dates, she's covering the mortgage on that Westwood condo I helped her buy.

And then there's her thing with Michael Kensington. Max orchestrated the whole setup—dinner for five, just us, Michael, Mom and Rosa. I knew something was up when Max kept refilling Mom's wine glass. Mom and Michael started finishing each other's sentences by dessert, Mom laughing at Michael's stories like they shared some private joke. Five minutes in, they were debating the best Elvis era;

by coffee, they were planning a Vegas weekend. Mom came back from that trip with a craps table story and $1,000 in winnings. Michael didn't gamble—"one addiction was enough for this lifetime"—but he said he followed her around the casino floor like a lovesick teenager, saying he could feel the universe's energy there.

I sat in the back row during his last AA meeting, watching Michael accept his 9-month sobriety chip with trembling hands. Later, over coffee, he squeezed my arm and whispered, "Your mother saved me." Mom texts me daily updates about their conversations—how he finally talked about the night Catherine died, how she showed him her mastectomy scars. How he recited an entire Frost poem from memory and how he knows the plots of every single Shakespeare play ever written. Yesterday, I caught them in Mom's garden, Michael's weathered hand resting on hers as she laughed at something he said. "He makes me feel young again," she told me later, her cheeks flushed pink. When I mentioned this to Max, he smiled and said his father hadn't looked this alive in years.

Then Max froze mid-sentence. "Wait—if they got married, you'd technically be my stepsister." We both burst out laughing at the absurdity of it all.

As for Max and me...well, he finally proposed—properly this time. Down on one knee, he presented a ring that stole my breath: a rare pink Argyle diamond, natural and flawless, nestled in platinum filigree that mirrored my grandmother's wedding band—the same intricate vine pattern with tiny diamond-dusted leaves that had adorned her finger for sixty-two years of marriage. I'd once lingered over her photo while flipping through dusty albums with Max, never imagining he was committing every delicate curve of that antique setting to memory. Three carats of pink perfection—the kind of stone that makes insurance agents nervous—now catching light on my finger. And we're going to get married in jolly old England.

Why England? It all started when Max discovered my not-so-secret obsession with *Downton Abbey*. I'd never told him, but everyone else in my life has endured my endless rewatches, my passionate defenses of Lady Mary's misunderstood character, and my encyclopedic knowledge of the estate's floor plan.

One night over dinner, I mentioned offhandedly that visiting Highclere Castle—the real-life Downton—topped my bucket list. Two weeks later, Max casually mentioned he'd looked into it, and apparently, you can rent part of the castle for weddings. With his connections, we could have hosted a hundred guests under a marquee on those iconic grounds. We opted for something smaller, but still—Highclere Castle. My Downton-loving heart nearly stopped.

As Max explained it: "We keep it to thirty. Family only —my brothers, their plus-ones, Dad, grandparents, Rosa, Gianni. Your mom, Lexi, Tally, Olivia, and any plus ones they might bring. That's our list." He ran a hand through his hair. "It's not that I don't want to invite industry people, but it's all or none with that crowd. Start with one producer, director or actor, then I have to invite them all and suddenly we're at three hundred guests minimum. Lady Carnarvon would throw us out if we turned her estate into some Hollywood circus."

Good enough. But soon we'll be flying over the country and then flying over the Atlantic in my very first overseas trip! Max teases me about my lack of worldly experience, but it's just friendly ribbing. He doesn't actually judge me about this. But yeah. I've never been over an ocean, ever. Max, who's been to all seven continents, including Antarctica, couldn't quite believe this although I'm sure I told him this fact earlier in a dinner we had. He must've just forgotten this.

While I've never been overseas, I have been out of the country, technically. Once on that disaster cruise to Mexico with Liv and Tally, crammed into a cabin the size of a walk-in closet designed for two people, where we each traded off sleeping on the floor. We docked in Cozumel and I tried SNUBA—that weird hybrid where they strap a twenty-pound yellow helmet over your head connected to oxygen by a flimsy-looking tube. Twenty feet underwater, my chest tightened as I imagined air bubbles clogging the line, my lungs burning as fish circled, watching me suffocate. In my panic, I barely noticed the rainbow parrotfish darting between coral fans. My clearest memory: tequila shots at Señor Frogs, and dancing on the tables, the sticky wooden table wobbling under my bare feet while Liv screamed the lyrics to "Livin' La Vida Loca." Canada was my other "international experience"—Toronto with its gleaming glass towers and sidewalks so pristine you could eat off them, then Montreal with its crumbling stone facades and narrow cobblestone alleys that smelled like fresh bread and cigarettes.

I still laugh about that time in Montreal when I grabbed what I thought was "raisin" soda from a convenience store cooler. My stomach turned just picturing the flavor, the grossest thing imaginable, raisin pop. Tally spun the bottle around to show me it was just grape soda – "raisin" being French for grape. Max would probably chuckle at this—the man speaks four languages, French, Italian, Spanish and Mandarin flawlessly, as any proper international CEO should. But I'll keep my linguistic humiliation to myself, thank you very much.

Because I've never been overseas before, my stomach flutters with anticipation as I board Max's Gulfstream. Just us—no other passengers, no flight attendants, nobody else but the pilots. The wedding party will follow on his company's Boeing, but Max insisted we take his personal jet. I run my fingers along the buttery leather of the heated massage seats, marvel at the mahogany tables that fold out from hidden compartments with the punch of a gold button, peek into the marble-tiled bathroom with its rainfall shower, and blush when Max gives me a private tour of the sumptuous bedroom, with its king-sized bed draped in cream silk sheets, polished mahogany paneling that gleam under recessed lighting, and a ceiling painted with subtle gold accents that catch the sunlight streaming through the oval windows.

"Eleven hours to London," he whispers against my ear, his hand sliding around my waist. "I've been thinking about all the ways we could pass the time." The look in his eyes makes my cheeks burn hotter than the engine turbines.

I gasp as Max pulls me into the private bedroom, his voice a rough growl against my ear: "This is why I demanded an empty plane. No one to hear what I'm about to do to you." My knees nearly buckle as he claims my mouth, not gentle now but hungry, desperate. He tears at my blouse, buttons scattering across the floor. His fingers find my nipples, pinching hard enough to make me cry out, the sweet pain shooting straight between my legs. I arch against him as his mouth replaces his hands, teeth grazing sensitive flesh. He shoves me onto the bed, yanking my jeans down with such force I hear the fabric tear. His eyes are dark, possessive as he spreads my legs. When his mouth finds me, I don't just scream—I shatter, his fingers merciless as they drive me beyond coherent thought.

His voice drops to a growl. "You're mine," he says, gripping my wrists so tightly I can feel my pulse throbbing against his fingers. "You've always been mine. And tomorrow, about this time, you'll be mine forever." The possessiveness in his words floods my body with heat, making it hard to breathe. I've never craved belonging to someone the way I ache to be claimed by him—completely, irrevocably, with nothing held back.

He devours my breasts, his mouth claiming each peak with hungry desperation that tears a gasp from my throat. His teeth graze my nipples—gentle then sharp—sending electric currents straight to my core. I arch against him, begging without words. He blazes a scorching trail down my stomach, each kiss branding me, marking me as his. The scent of his cologne—sandalwood and sea salt—floods my senses until I'm drowning in him. His hands suddenly pin mine above my head, fingers crushing together as our bodies crash into each other with the violent force of a storm surge against Malibu cliffs, both of us breaking and reforming with each devastating wave of pleasure.

He drives into me with a force that steals my breath, each thrust deeper than the last, his teeth grazing my neck as his fingers dig possessively into my hips. The silk sheets twist beneath us, drenched with sweat, as the private jet cuts through storm clouds at 40,000 feet. Lightning flashes through the window, illuminating the raw hunger in his eyes for half-seconds of electric clarity. The plane drops suddenly —violent turbulence—and I cry out as the sensation merges with the building pressure inside me. "Mine," he growls against my ear, the word burning into my skin. I rake my nails down his back, leaving crimson trails across bronze muscle, desperate to mark him as thoroughly as he's marking me. The luxury around us blurs as we crash together, the jet's engines roaring in harmony with our release. Later, I lie sprawl across his heaving chest, both of us gasping for air. His heartbeat thunders against my cheek as I trace the welts I've left on his skin, watching his eyes flash dangerously when I whisper, "Again."

Later still, we lie in the bed of his private jet's bedroom, our bodies cooling. I trace lazy circles through the dark hair on Max's chest, feeling it rise and fall with each breath. A smile tugs at my lips that I couldn't suppress even if I wanted to. This happiness feels almost dangerous—like tempting fate. A gorgeous man who looks at me like I'm his world, my mother's health restored, and my name on scripts that actually matter. How did I get here? Tomorrow we exchange vows that will mean something this time—not the hollow performance we put on before, but a promise I'm finally ready to make.

Chapter Fifty-Seven

MAX

I keep picturing Celeste's face when she sees Europe with me. After Highclere Castle—where we'll have our second ceremony—I want to show her everything - Rome's fountains, the Eiffel Tower, the Tower Bridge of London, the Swiss Alps, the streets of Spain, the spires of Prague. For our wedding, Lady Carnarvon has helped arrange it all: the state rooms, the Saloon, that oak staircase. Even in December's cold, we'll be fine. The first wedding was just business. This one's real. No contracts, no obligations. Just us.

I had a bachelor party, but not the kind people expected from me. No strippers or shots. No hangover disasters. For once, I wasn't hunting for the next model to take home. Instead, I flew to Lake Como with Gianni and my brothers. We stayed at his family's old villa, skied black diamonds during the day, and relaxed in hot springs at night with good wine. A month ago, I would've called this boring. Now it felt right.

Not that Celeste would've given me grief over a typical

bachelor party - she has faith in me, and rightfully so. Damn right, rightfully so! Before her, I never earned a woman's trust, always keeping an escape route ready. The harder they tried to hold on, the faster I bolted. But with Celeste? There's this... stillness. I don't look for exits anymore because she's everything I didn't know I was searching for.

Never in a million years did I imagine needing someone like her - this brilliant, fearless woman with creativity pouring out of her veins. She doesn't put up with my bull-shit, which is refreshing because so many others do. She cracks up at the same ridiculous jokes I do, even the ones that make everyone else stare at us like we're insane. We've built this private universe of inside jokes and references that only make sense to us, which is exactly how it should be. She sees through me. I understand her. And that's nothing short of magic.

Now I'm in my hotel room at the Vineyard Hotel, a 5-star resort nestled among rolling vineyards with views that stretch to the horizon. The castle's medieval spires are just visible in the distance, a ten-minute drive away. We've been given the Grand Suite—a sprawling space where my heels sink into plush ivory carpeting as I wander from the separate lounge with its crystal chandelier to the bathroom where veined marble gleams under soft lighting. The wedding party is in the split-level Atrium Suites downstairs, where I imagine them unpacking their garment bags while I run my fingers along the cool granite of the wet bar.

Celeste enters our suite, drops her bags, and I can't help but watch her face. After months of living together—and soon to be married—she still hasn't grown jaded to the luxury surrounding us. She circles the room with those ocean-blue eyes widened in wonder, radiating joy like a spotlight. That's what hooked me—how she finds magic in what I've always dismissed as ordinary. I needed someone who could make me see my world as the miracle it actually is. Without her, I'd sleepwalk through this privileged life, blind to its gifts. She keeps me grounded too, challenging me when needed—hence the $10 million check I wrote to the animal shelter last month.

Speaking of which, I've secured the ultimate wedding surprise that will mean more to her than our marriage itself: Piper! Hugh and Gail are divorcing, and their kids lost interest in the poor dog. I honored my million-dollar promise, splitting it evenly between them. Piper's currently at our Malibu house with a professional sitter (Rosa's here in England for the wedding). I can picture Celeste's face already when that dog's whole body starts wiggling with excitement. Her other wedding gift, the red diamond necklace from Christie's—one of fifty natural specimens on earth—cost me ten times the amount I "paid" for Piper, but I know which gift will truly capture her heart. That's precisely why I love this woman.

Celeste's lips part as she steps through the suite. "Max, this is..." Her voice trails off as she wanders from room to room, fingertips grazing the velvet upholstery, pausing at the fireplace. In the bathroom, she gasps at the marble tub big enough for two. "I keep waiting for someone to realize I don't belong here and kick me out," she says with a self-conscious laugh. "At least I can ask for extra towels without having to use Google Translate. Small victories for the girl who's never owned a passport before now."

I laugh and wrap my arms around her waist, feeling the delicate curve beneath my fingertips. "Yes, you know the language here, but we're going on our grand tour of Europe after this. So you'll have to stick with me, otherwise you'll be lost, lost, lost, Ms. Raisin Pop girl."

The memory flashes between us—Celeste's animated retelling of her horrified expression in that fluorescent-lit Canadian convenience store, her nose wrinkling at the purple can labeled "Raisin" in French. I can picture it perfectly: the way she dramatically recoiled, declaring it the most disgusting flavor concept she'd ever heard, until Tally explained, through tears of laughter, that "raisin" meant "grape" in French.

"Stop," she says, her giggle bubbling up like champagne. Her cheeks flush that perfect shade of pink that always makes my chest tighten. "I'm sure I'm not the only tourist who's been traumatized by Canadian bilingual labeling. But yes, with your linguistic superpowers, I'll need you as my personal translator through the cobblestone streets of Paris and the wintry plazas of Barcelona." She taps my chest with one manicured finger. "But when we reach Prague, with all those impossible consonants stacked together, I think we'll both be delightfully lost. I can't wait to see the great Max Kensington struggling to order coffee."

"Well," I counter, pulling her closer until I can smell the jasmine in her hair, "lucky for us, most Czechs speak English. But we'll be lost together under those Gothic spires, so there's that."

Prague wasn't my idea. It was the way Celeste's eyes had lit up when she showed me those photos—medieval bridges dusted with snow, Christmas markets glowing amber against twilight, baroque facades catching the golden hour. "Magic," she'd whispered, and I'd immediately called my travel coordinator. We'll see it first, wrapped in its winter splendor, before continuing to France, Italy, Spain, and Portugal—six luxurious weeks of honeymoon that we've carved out from our careers. Iris can handle Kensington Pictures; she's been practically running it anyway while I've been distracted by falling in love. This time, it's a real honeymoon for my real wife—not like our first "wedding," that sterile business arrangement that somehow transformed into everything I never knew I needed.

Chapter Fifty-Eight

CELESTE

My heart races as Highclere Castle comes into view through the window of our rented 1922 Rolls Royce. The vintage car was my touch—I wanted our Downton Abbey wedding to feel authentic down to the last detail. I've dreamed of walking these grounds since falling headfirst into the Crawley family saga, though I came to it backwards. While everyone else was obsessing over the series during its original run, I kept seeing headlines in my daily *Washington Post* scrolls about shocking plot twists and character deaths. I filed it away as another British phenomenon I'd eventually check out. Then the first theatrical film released, and on a whim, I let a friend drag me to see it. I liked the movie so much that I decided to try out the series on Amazon Prime. One week and six seasons of binge-watching later, I was completely transformed. That first episode—when Lord Grantham showed more concern for third-class passengers on the Titanic than the aristocrats—had me hooked.

Now, after watching each episode at least half a dozen times, I'm actually here. My heels click against the polished

464

marble as I wander through Highclere Castle's grand corridors, trailing my fingertips along cool stone walls that have witnessed centuries of history. Our wedding will take place in the saloon—that breathtaking central hall where ornate oak paneling climbs toward a vaulted ceiling, and stained glass windows cast kaleidoscope patterns across the floor. I pause at the entrance, tilting my head back to admire the balconies of the upper floors that encircle the space like a Victorian theater, imagining guests leaning over the intricately carved railings to witness our vows.

My hands aren't shaking. My heart isn't racing. This wedding feels right—a celebration Max and I crafted together, not some spectacle thrust upon me. The guest list reads like a family album rather than *Variety's* power rankings. The castle's in-house caterers will serve our meal, no celebrity chef required. Each face I'll see today belongs to someone who matters deeply to one or both of us. We're exchanging vows because we can't imagine life without each other, not because a contract demands it. The absence of Hollywood royalty (except Max's brother Connor) feels like a blessing rather than a compromise.

I wander through the castle's grand rooms, tracing the fictional footsteps of the Crawleys. In the saloon, the library, the breakfast room where aristocratic dogs once lounged beneath the table. I pause in the spot where Lord Grantham received news of the Titanic disaster. Standing in the formal dining room, I'm surrounded by ghosts of dramatic dinner conversations. I close my eyes, smile, and let the castle work its magic. The iconic theme music practically echoes off the ancient stones.

This time around, I picked my own dress - a simple white column with a halter neckline that flatters my swimmer's shoulders. Instead of a cathedral veil, tiny crystal flowers crown my hair like stars. No Episcopal bishop in gold-trimmed robes today; just a smiling magistrate in a simple suit.

When we say "I do," the small crowd erupts. Later, under a white tent on the castle grounds, Max takes my hand for our first dance. The familiar notes of Arctic Monkeys' "Baby, I'm Yours" fill the air - the same song from our first wedding.

"I picked this song the first time because it was already true," Max whispers against my ear. "I just couldn't admit it then."

I pull back to search his face, my heart stuttering. All those months of tension, of fighting feelings behind cold shoulders and closed doors - he'd been falling too. That first night at the dinner when he glared across the table, when I thought he despised me... we were already orbiting each other, caught in a gravity neither of us understood.

Two people, secretly in love while pretending otherwise. What are the chances?

Chapter Fifty-Nine

CELESTE

The six-week honeymoon melted away like gelato in the Roman sun. In Rome, we zipped through narrow cobblestone streets on a mint-green Vespa, my arms wrapped around Max's waist, the cool air tousling my hair as we chased the golden light to the Trevi Fountain. His body tensed against mine with each turn, a preview of how he'd move above me later that night.

In London, we huddled under a shared umbrella on the top deck of a crimson double-decker, his lips finding the sensitive spot behind my ear that made me forget about the tourists around us.

Paris greeted us with buttery croissant flakes on our laps at a wrought-iron café table, my foot tracing up his calf beneath the table, his eyes darkening with promise. Max's surprise—a Parisian penthouse with herringbone floors and floor-to-ceiling windows—became our sanctuary where love-making filled our nights and my back arched against cool marble countertops in the afternoons while my screams of pleasure filled the walls.

Barcelona's Sagrada Família casted rainbow shadows across my naked skin as we christened the hotel balcony at dawn, while Prague's Christmas Market warmed us after hours spent learning each other's bodies in ways that made even December evenings feel like midsummer.

Max guides me through our front door with his hands over my eyes. "This tops even the pink diamond," he whispers, his breath warm against my ear.

When he lifts his hands, I freeze. There, tail whipping so hard her entire body sways, stands Piper. My Piper. The same pink-nosed pit bull I'd cried over for weeks after a family adopted her from Inland Valley.

"Piper!" I drop to my knees as she bounds toward me, her paws skidding on the hardwood. Fifty pounds of muscle and slobber collide with my chest. I bury my face in her brown and white fur, breathing in that familiar dog smell as she covers my cheeks with frantic kisses.

"How?" I manage to ask, looking up at Max through tears.

He kneels beside us, one hand on Piper's head, the other finding mine. "Let's just say I made the previous owners an offer they couldn't refuse."

Piper wedges herself between us, tail still going wild, as Max pulls me closer. "Welcome to your forever home, sweet girl," he says to Piper, then turns to me with eyes that hold everything I never knew I needed. "Both of you."

As his lips find mine, I think about my mother's recovery and new love with Michael, my inbox filled with three major studios offering commissions to me to write screenplays, and now this—this man who tracked down the dog I thought I'd lost forever. The man I was forced to marry, the man I once despised—now the absolute center of my universe.

The impossible has become my everyday life.

vinci-books.com/TheMalibuDestiny

Some fates can't be ignored... or controlled.

Roman Kensington controls everything—except Lilith Sydney, a stubborn tarot reader who sees the truths he's spent a lifetime hiding. Their clash ignites desire, secrets, and a pull neither can resist

Turn the page for a free preview…

The Malibu Destiny: Chapter One

ROMAN

I prowl through my exclusive oceanfront resort in Palos Verdes, each step of my custom Ferragamos echoing off Italian marble like a warning shot. Imperfections assault me from every angle—the Rothko that maintenance can't seem to level in the east wing feels like sandpaper against my nerves, some brat's sticky handprint desecrating my twenty-foot glass walls has my teeth grinding until my skull throbs, and Christ, those peonies—edges already curling brown barely a day after I ordered fresh ones. This isn't merely a resort; it's meant to be my bulwark against the world's endless tide of mediocrity, my testament to the standards everyone else has abandoned.

All the rooms and bungalows in this resort start at $1,000 a night and go up to $100,000 for the luxury packages connected to the top suites with hand-carved Balinese furniture and Italian marble soaking tubs that could fit a family of four. My guests expect Egyptian cotton sheets with thread counts higher than most people's credit scores and champagne that costs more than a month's rent in most cities. This is not some fucking Marriott where you can get away with wilted orchids drooping in dusty corners and mass-produced watercolors hanging at a three-degree tilt.

I storm across the marble lobby, my voice bouncing off the twenty-foot ceilings. "Marcus!" The concierge's shoulders hunch as if bracing for impact. Charlie should be here taking this heat, but the maintenance manager conveniently vanished the moment I spotted the disaster. "That Rothko is crooked enough to fall off the damn wall, and those peonies look like they died last week." I jab my finger toward the smudged window. "Find Charlie. I want him here with cleaning supplies in five minutes. Call Nicolle's for fresh arrangements—I don't care if you have to drive there yourself." My fingers snap toward the massive canvas that would require a construction crew to adjust. "And get that painting straightened. Everything fixed by the time I circle back. Understand?"

Marcus lowers his head. "Yes, sir." He's barely old enough to drink—some USC hospitality program kid with big dreams of running his own hotel someday. His shoulders slump under my criticism. Too bad. The real world won't coddle him like his professors do. If anything, I'm preparing him for the shitstorm that is hotel management. His eyes might be all wounded right now, but he'll thank me later when some entitled guest is screaming about thread counts at 3 AM.

I glance at my Patek Philippe and curse. Three minutes behind schedule for the marketing meeting. Unacceptable. I stride faster through the lobby, my jaw clenching at the sight of a crumpled brochure on an otherwise immaculate marble side table. Someone's getting written up. When I push through the conference room doors, eight faces snap to attention. Good. They're all here. They should be. Anyone walking in after me wouldn't just be late—they'd be unemployed. Not that I'm looking to fire anyone today, but rules are rules. The Verde Resort didn't become what it is by tolerating mediocrity.

Two hours later, the marketing meeting wraps up, but my day's marathon has barely hit mile one. My schedule knows no mercy—Dubai's on the line at dawn, Tokyo keeps me up past midnight. Between reviewing the Milan property blueprints, analyzing quarterly projections, and playing referee between our temperamental executive chef and some Saudi prince demanding white truffles in August, there's no pause button in the luxury hospitality game.

By noon, I've personally escorted the Crown Prince of Abu Dhabi and his twenty-person entourage to their presidential suite and prepped the staff for tomorrow's Danish royal arrival when my phone buzzes. Miranda, my luxury services director, has apparently green-lit a new "exclusive experience" without my approval—a tarot reader.

A what? I nearly choke on my espresso. A tarot fucking reader? I can already see it: some crystal-clutching charlatan in flowing scarves charging our billionaire guests two grand to light "cleansing candles" and babble about mercury retrograde.

Absolutely not. This five-star property isn't transforming into some incense-soaked retreat center on my watch. We cater to people who run countries and corporations, not consciousness workshops. Next thing you know, we'll have barefoot "spiritual guides" wandering the marble lobby, offering chakra alignments between spa treatments.

I sprint down to Miranda's office, skidding to a halt at the sight of her visitor. The woman perched on the edge of the chair can't be a day over thirty—all tumbling dark hair and honey-gold eyes that catch the light like expensive whiskey. But what is she wearing? Some Eileen Fisher knockoff draped over premium denim, paired with scuffed Pradas that have seen better days. I feel my lip curl. This is the Verde, for Christ's sake. We have sheiks dropping fifty grand on champagne towers and A-listers booking entire wings. Our helicopter pad has a waiting list. Our yachts don't even dock—they hover. And this woman thinks she can waltz in here dressed for a Target run and land a job?

She smiles at me and Miranda stands up. "Mr. Kensington, this is-"

I lock eyes with this woman and keep them there as I address my resort manager. "Ms. Baudelaire. A word." My glare at this woman could turn the Caribbean to ice as Miranda glides to my side and follows me out of her bungalow office.

Once outside, I hiss, "Who exactly is that woman?" I can't believe this. Miranda has been my right hand since I leveraged Grandfather's $40 million loan into what's now a $50 billion luxury empire. Through every punishing 18-hour day that built this place, she's been there. Yet here I am, contemplating her termination because she's interviewing... what? A fortune teller?

"Roman," she responds, her British accent precise as a surgeon's knife. Miranda embodies everything this resort stands for—aristocratic pedigree (her father's an Earl), Oxford polish, and a willowy six-foot frame crowned with that immaculate blonde bob. Her makeup never smudges, her diplomacy never wavers. She's the perfect concierge to the elite, solving their problems before they know they have them. "I anticipated you might resist adding tarot readings to our luxury experiences."

"Damn right I'm fighting this. What is she, some kind of fortune teller?" My fingers rake through my hair, pulling it tight against my scalp. "If she's so good at predicting the future, she should've seen security escorting her off the property. Which is happening in about five seconds."

Miranda folds her arms across her chest, her eyebrows arching in that way that silently calls me out for being a complete jerk. Which—fair enough.

"Finished with your tantrum?" she asks, voice clipped.

I exhale slowly. "The floor is yours."

"Right. So I was at the Kimpton Fitzroy last month—"

"That old Victorian palace where royalty stays when they're slumming it in London?" I interrupt, unable to help myself.

She ignores my commentary. "They've added tarot readings to their amenities. I tried it on a whim, and it was... illuminating. Turns out, it's becoming quite the trend. I've looked into it—luxury hotels worldwide are adding metaphysical services to their concierge offerings. The demand is significant."

I raise an eyebrow. "Tarot readings? At The Verde? Since when?"

"Since the data supported it," Miranda says, not missing a beat. She ticks off points on her manicured fingers. "Client surveys, focus groups, the works. Turns out our VIPs are desperate for someone to tell their fortune between spa treatments." She shrugs. "Ms. Sydney comes highly recommended. Has her own shop on Venice Beach. They say she's the real deal."

"I'll be the judge of that," I mutter. "And if she starts waving crystals around or communing with dead relatives, you're fired."

Miranda just smiles that knowing smile of hers. We both know my threats are empty. I've been "firing" her for years.

But good help—especially help that calls me on my crap—is harder to find than an honest psychic.

I slam the door behind me as I re-enter Miranda's office and drop into the chair across from Ms. Sydney. Her resumé crinkles in my grip. "So. Why Verde?"

She tilts her head. "I'm sorry, you are...?"

"Kensington," I snap.

"Ah. As in Roman Kensington, who owns this resort."

No shit, Sherlock. I resist the urge to slow-clap.

She straightens her spine. "Mr. Kensington, I sense you weren't expecting me and have doubts about what I bring to the table."

"Impressive deduction. What's next—you'll guess my zodiac sign?" The sarcasm drips from my voice before I can stop it. But Jon Bevin, the five-star chef at our flagship restaurant, just handed in his resignation for some Food Network gig, and my patience was thin to begin with. Though if I'm honest, my default setting isn't exactly sunshine and rainbows anyway.

She smiles knowingly. "Oh, I already know your zodiac sign. You're an Aries."

I lean back, arms crossed. "A what?"

"An Aries. Born late March to late April. Stubborn, ambitious, fiery, natural leader." She ticks each trait off on her fingers. "Basically, you."

I narrow my eyes. April 15 is my birthday—she nailed it. But there's my Wikipedia page, my *Forbes* profile, the *Wall Street Journal* piece last quarter. Any halfway competent person would've researched me before walking in here and would discover my birthday. This little parlor trick doesn't prove anything except she can use Google.

She mirrors my stance, arms crossed tight against her chest. "Look, Mr. Kensington," she says, voice steady despite the flush creeping up her neck. "I battled the 405 all the way from Venice Beach because your recruiter called about a tarot position for your VIPs. That's an hour of my life I won't get back. So if you don't mind, I'd like to finish what I started with Ms. Baudeliere." Her eyebrow arches like a challenge. "It's not my problem if you're out of the loop on your own company's hiring practices." Something dangerous flashes in her eyes, and I return it with a glare cold enough to make hell freeze over.

I lean forward, my jaw tight. "Let me make this crystal clear. Your employment at this resort is my decision, not Ms. Baudeliere's. I sign the checks around here. You want in? You go through me."

"Fine," she says, her eyes darting to Miranda like a life-line. I catch the glance—she's hoping I'll walk away so she can work her mumbo-jumbo on my more susceptible employee. Fat chance.

I check my watch. The Blackstone meeting starts in fifteen minutes. Any sane CEO would delegate this tarot card situation and move on. But I'm not going to. If I leave now, Miranda might turn my five-star establishment into some New Age retreat center with incense and wind chimes. No thanks. This tarot reader either impresses me right now with something substantial, or security shows her the door.

"So," I say, leaning forward. "Why should I let you stay five more minutes on these resort grounds?"

Without a word, she reaches into her worn canvas bag and pulls out a deck of tarot cards. The cards make a soft shuffling sound as she divides them into two neat stacks on my desk. Her gaze meets mine directly—steady, unblinking.

"Mr. Kensington," she says, gesturing toward the twin piles. "Choose one."

I fold my arms across my chest, jaw tightening. The last

thing I need is some fortune-telling nonsense. But Miranda's insistence echoes in my head—something about high-profile clients requesting this service. I exhale slowly. Perhaps my skepticism is limiting me. If the ultra-wealthy are paying for this, there must be some value I'm missing. The only way to know is to let her demonstrate.

She fans the cards across the table, studies them with narrowed eyes. "This is a 17 card Celtic Cross. Much more involved than the typical 10 card spread." Her mouth twitches as she studies them. "I see a child with deep scars," she murmurs. "Alcoholic father who vanished early. Mother has died. You've navigated life feeling abandoned, and now even within your own family, you stand alone."

My gaze snaps to Miranda. That's it—Miranda's fired for real. If she fed this fraud my personal history, crossed that line to get her friend hired...And she must have. How else would this Lilith Sydney know about my father's drinking, his disappearing act, my mother's death when I was barely two? How else would she know my brothers have ostracized me because I refuse to welcome our father back with open arms?

But "child with deep scars"? I'm the fucking CEO of a $50 billion international resort. I'm thirty-three years old. Not a fucking "child with deep scars."

I lean forward. "What in those cards tell you all that?"

She nods. "The reversed King of Cups at the center shows someone trapped by trauma, unable to move forward, emotionally unstable, unreliable, making poor decisions. That's your father. The Devil crossing signifies an addiction or entanglement—clearly not yours but your father's."

"Okay," I say, narrowing my eyes. "Go on." In spite of myself, I'm becoming intrigued.

She nods and points to some more cards. "Your foundation card—the Five of Cups—speaks of loss and disappointment. The Tower in the past confirms a sudden upheaval: his abandonment."

I sit back in my seat and nod for her to continue.

She points to the future card: "Four of Wands—a joyful reunion waits. But your present mindset is the Five of Swords: resentment, unwilling to forgive."

My fingers drum the polished wood. Cool blue light from the window frames her profile. I glance at Miranda. "If I find you breached my privacy—fired. Understood?"

Miranda simply nods. "On my honor."

Lilith returns to the spread. "Eight of Cups—abandonment, walking away—surrounds the situation. Position nine: Six of Cups—longing for reunion but fearing repeated loss. Yet The Sun as the outcome promises lasting joy. So…"

"Sounds like you might have the happy reunion with your father after all," Miranda says, clearly amused.

I lean in closer. "That thing you mentioned—about me feeling isolated in my own family. How can you tell?"

"See this?" She taps the upside-down card. "Reversed Ten of Cups in your house position. It represents your current situation—family discord, tension, fighting. And considering this entire spread revolves around your father walking out and those unresolved wounds, I'd say you're in conflict with your family over your father suddenly showing up again."

"Hold on. How could you possibly know about him coming back?"

"That your father returned to your life?"

"Exactly."

"Simple," Lilith says. "All these abandonment cards appear in your past. But here—" she points, "the Six of

Cups, symbolizing reunion, sits in your present. And these cards here that suggest you and your father will eventually reconcile, they're all in future positions."

"What about my mother's death?" I ask. "How did you figure that out?"

Lilith tilts her head. "Queen of Cups beside the Three of Swords, both in past positions. Deep grief connected to a maternal figure—significant enough to appear prominently in your reading."

I drum my fingers against the custom mahogany desk that cost more than most people's cars. Miranda's eyes are fixed on Lilith, her expression almost reverent. If Miranda had leaked information about my family's darkest secrets, she wouldn't look this genuinely awestruck now. The abandonment by my father. My mother's passing. The ongoing cold war with my siblings since Dad suddenly decided to reappear in our lives and I told Dad to fuck off while the rest of those pussies rolled out the red carpet. The cracks in my foundation that I've spent years concealing. The deep psychic wound that this woman somehow sees.

How could Lilith possibly know? The Kensington name appears in headlines weekly—my four brothers running their corporate empires, Connor collecting his Oscars, Kalen's face on billboards for sold-out concerts—but certain topics remain untouchable. Any journalist who's ever profiled us knows: mention the family trauma, and your access vanishes permanently. Red line. So, none of the 100s of profiles on us have ever mentioned our family's history.

Yet somehow Lilith spoke directly to wounds I've never displayed publicly.

Maybe there's something to her abilities after all.

I exhale sharply. "You're hired." I snap my fingers at Miranda. "Contract. Now."

My Patek screams five minutes late. Fuck. The investors are waiting. I despise tardiness—it reeks of weakness— but something made me stay rooted to this damn tarot reading until the bitter end.

I sprint down the corridor, my Italian leather shoes hammering the marble. Doubt claws at my throat.

What the hell was I thinking? Bringing in someone who just gutted me with her eyes, who peeled back my skin without permission and read the entrails of my ambition?

Too late to turn back now.

The beast is already in the house.

The Malibu Destiny: Chapter Two

LILITH

I can't stop grinning as I drive home from Verde resort, my cheeks actually aching. The job is mine! God knows I need the money with how Mystic Tides has been performing lately. Summer brings the sunburned tourists flooding into my little psychic shop on Venice Beach, wallets open after a day riding waves or baking on towels. But winter? The boardwalk empties out, and so does my bank account. This Verde gig couldn't have come at a better time.

Just imagine—me, reading tarot for actual royalty and A-listers! That's who stays at Verde, after all. The elite. The one-percenters who'll pay triple what my regular clients shell out for a glimpse of their gilded futures.

The Verde will only see me twice a week, with all my tarot readings crammed into those days, but oh my God—the space they've given me there! Picture this: a private luxury beach cabana with cream-colored canvas walls that billow like sails in the ocean breeze, teak floors polished to a honey-gold sheen, and a ceiling fan spinning lazily above a white linen chaise lounge. Floor-to-ceiling windows facing the ocean, a mini fridge stocked with San Pellegrino, and an actual assistant who brings fresh fruit every hour.

The only problem? Roman Kensington, the owner of this resort. Every time he looked at me, his eyes narrowed like he's spotted a counterfeit bill. I could practically hear his thoughts: "Fraud. Con artist." And sure, I've seen the type—psychics who charge $1500 for "blessed" candles that supposedly break spiritual chains, or sell $1000 crystals with promises of instant wealth. The ones who whisper "You're cursed" just to charge thousands more to lift that imaginary hex.

But my shop? The price tags match what you'd find at any retail store. My readings cost forty bucks for half an hour—peanuts in this industry. When Mrs. Abernathy came in last week convinced she needed some kind of super-expensive "ultimate spiritual package," I sent her home with a $15 journal and told her to write down her dreams instead. I've built my business on helping people find clarity, not emptying their wallets. In a world where everyone seems to be chasing the next dollar, my little corner operates differently. If only Roman could see that.

I get to my shop, the little bell clinking as I walk in and see Jack, my roommate, my partner in crime (and in this shop) ringing up a sunburned blonde who looks like she needs aloe much more than she needs crystals, poor thing. Jack sees me and his eyes light up. "Lil! Spill the tea, girly. How did it go?"

"I'm in!" I grab a chunk of rose quartz from the display, rubbing my thumb over its smooth surface. Rose quartz is the stone of gratitude, and I always try to be grateful for all the abundance that comes my way, like this new gig. "Can you believe it? Me, reading cards at Verde! A-Listers, billionaires, royalty - those are the only people who could afford to stay at Verde, so those will be my clients there."

Jack finishes with the sunburned girl before turning to me. "Slow your roll, psychic woman. You're acting like the Harry and Meghan will be on your client list."

"Why not?" I toss my hair. "Meghan would totally get a reading."

"Girl, please." Jack rolls his eyes dramatically. "Next you'll be telling me you're besties with Oprah."

"You laugh, but Angie Banicki reads for Gwyneth Paltrow and Emma Roberts. Not to mention Usher. That could be me someday!" I frame an imaginary marquee with my hands. "Lilith Sydney: Tarot Reader to the Stars!"

Jack leans across the counter. "Forget celebrities. Tell me about those gorgeous men serving drinks poolside."

Typical Jack—I'm living my dream and he's thinking about eye candy. "Oh, I'm sure the cabana boys will be just as polished as everything else at that place. It's where the beautiful people play, after all."

Speaking of beautiful people...Roman Kensington is walking perfection. The resort is like a living *Vogue* magazine, but that makes sense when the owner himself belongs on *GQ*'s cover. He probably has a "gorgeous people only" hiring policy. Shame he seems to despise me...

Jack narrows his eyes at me. "Lil," he says, catching me mid-daydream. "I know that face. Which ridiculously hot resort person has you all flustered?"

I can't help but sigh. Roman's dark waves that he tries—and fails—to tame with expensive product. Those obsidian eyes that see right through you. The way his Tom Ford suit stretches across shoulders that could carry the weight of the world. Beneath that polished - and heartbreakingly beautiful - exterior lurks something untamed. I saw it in his eyes, and the cards confirmed it. Turbulence swirls beneath his surface, and God help me, that only makes him more attractive. I've always had this self-destructive thing for complicated men, and Roman is a beautiful, tangled knot of complications.

Not that it matters. He exists in a stratosphere I'll never reach. I can't seriously consider him—but that won't stop me from dreaming. Who could blame me?

"Why do you say that I'm daydreaming?"

"Oh, puleeze," Jack says, slapping his hand on the counter hard enough to make the crystals jump. "When you said 'beautiful people,' your eyes practically rolled back in your head. Now spill it before I die of suspense."

"It's nothing," I say, my cheeks burning as I imagine Roman's razor-sharp jawline, those piercing dark eyes that could melt steel. God, I'm pathetic—like some teenager fantasizing about a celebrity she'll never meet. "It's just—"

"It's just WHAT?" Jack leans in so close I can smell his cinnamon gum.

I take a deep breath. "Well, the owner of this place, Roman Kensington," I begin.

"Roman Kensington? The Roman Kensington? Holy mother of—"Jack clutches his chest and collapses against the booth. "That man is walking sex. I literally had to fan myself through that twelve-page *Vanity Fair* spread where he was wearing that charcoal Armani suit with no tie. Annie Leibovitz should've been arrested for what she did with that camera."

"I forgot about your *Vanity Fair* obsession," I mutter, suddenly desperate to see these photos.

"Well, right. He's been in that magazine twice. Once was a profile of him and his brothers, and once a profile of just him. And oh my God..." He grabs my wrist. "You're going to be working for an absolute adonis, Lilith. I would kill—KILL—to be in your second-hand Pradas now!"

Oh great - now I'm really intimidated. *Vanity Fair.* Twice. Once just him—all chiseled jawline and brooding stare, no doubt—and once with the whole Kensington dynasty. I flip through the mental images: Roman in Tom Ford, lounging on some mid-century furniture worth more than my car, while Annie Leibovitz adjusts the lighting. Of course the glossy magazine crowd can't get enough of guys like him. Rich, gorgeous, powerful—he's like catnip sprinkled with cocaine for that set. And his brothers...

"Why did *Vanity Fair* feature his brothers too?"

Jack's eyes widen as he slams his palm on the counter again. "Are you kidding me right now? You don't know about the fabulous Kensingtons? Jesus Christ, what planet have you been living on?"

My face burns. "Sorry, I—"

"Listen," Jack leans in, voice dropping to an urgent whisper. "Roman is just the tip of the iceberg. That family is like some genetic experiment gone perfectly right. Eight brothers—all of them walking gods with bank accounts that could bail out small countries. Connor's got three Oscars on his mantel and makes grown men weep with his performances. Kalen sells out Madison Square Garden in four minutes flat."

"Wait. Connor and Kalen Kensington are his brothers?" My stomach drops as the realization hits me like a freight train. "Holy shit."

"And that's not all." Jack's fingers grip my wrist. "Max runs Kensington Pictures with an iron fist. Ansel dominates the music industry. Silas has half the celebrities in Hollywood dripping in his jewels. Asher throws parties that make the Met Gala look like a backyard barbecue. And then there's Cameron—" Jack laughs bitterly, "—poor Cameron only saves lives as an ER doc at Cedars."

I feel dizzy. But then again, I saw in those tarot cards the truth about Roman and his family. In those cards, I saw the absolute tragedy that befell that family - the alcoholic father who left when they were young, the mother who died when they were even younger. The turbulent relationship Roman has with his brothers. Those beautiful, powerful men were forged in the same hellfire that created Roman—abandoned by their broken father, never really knowing their mother. The glittering Kensington empire was built on a foundation of absolute devastation. Talk about a beautiful house built on a foundation of sand…

I clear my throat, desperate to change the subject. "Well. Looks like I'll be gone two days a week at Verde. Think you can survive without me?"

Jack's eyes flash playfully. "Oh, I'll survive just fine," he says, voice dropping lower. "Picture it—me trapped here with the unwashed masses pawing through crystals while you're down there with the gods and goddesses of Verde." He leans in, close enough I can smell his cologne. "And Roman Kensington, who makes mere mortals weep with his perfection. Maybe light a black candle for me while I'm rotting away in your absence."

"I'll do that."

Then I exhale slowly. This position could be everything I've wanted.

If only Roman Kensington didn't look at me like I was something stuck to the bottom of his Italian leather shoe.

Grab your copy…
vinci-books.com/TheMalibuDestiny

About the Author

Bella Christina lives with her hubby and two fur-babies in Southern California. When she's not binge-watching *Grace and Frankie, Succession* and *Downton Abbey*, she's reading historical and women's fiction and scouring the beach for sea glass and sand dollars.